CHASING KELVIN

A HUNTINGTON ADVENTURE

Thom Reese

SPEAKING VOLUMES, LLC

NAPLES, FLORIDA

2012

CHASING KELVIN

ISBN 978-1-61232-026-7

For Kathy

Acknowledgments

Another book complete. Another journey at its end. Writing a novel is a journey. There are false starts and detours, plenty of u-turns, and even a few rest stops, though these are few and unevenly spaced. But like every journey, it's not the road, but the people sharing that road that make the difference. Thank you to those who have shared this road with me as I've labored over this manuscript. A special thanks to Kathy, my critic, my strength, my love, my life. Words will never be enough where you're concerned. Trista, your encouragement and love are appreciated far more than you could know. Amy, I miss you deeply and am so happy for you. Brittany, you're developing into such a wonderful young woman. You three stir my soul and provide me with a smile to wear. As always, a special thanks to Jeff Granstrom, my constant reader and friend, for his insights and encouragement, to Kurt Mueller at Speaking Volumes for his faith in my writing, and to the talented actors that brought the Marc Huntington audio dramas to life: Jeff Granstrom, Tanja Montez, Ken Chapman, Phil Smith, Rick Ginn, TJ Hampton, Troy Nelson, Allistair Baylardo, and Shannon Macintyre.

Chapter 1

The cramped confines of the cell made it difficult to maneuver. The smaller man, Kocak, was quick, undisciplined, but feisty. Jonathan Thorpe had seen him fight before and the man had a propensity to use his teeth as a weapon, usually with savage glee and ferocity.

Thorpe ducked a punch from the larger man, a lumbering Buddha named Ganis, and jabbed him beneath the jaw, sending him into the concrete wall. Kocak was on him before he'd completed his follow through. Thorpe shuffled sideways only partially deflecting the thrust. Ganis swung wildly, connecting with Thorpe at the right shoulder blade and causing a shot of pain to shoot up into the base of his skull. Kocak kneed him in the groin and Thorpe fell to the cold concrete floor. A quick kidney kick from Ganis and Thorpe felt his internal organs shift to the north. Now, Kocak bared his teeth. Thorpe knew what was coming. The little man's trademark was to bite a man in the Adams apple.

Despite his intense pain, Thorpe head butted Kocak, and then, grabbing him at the base of the skull, slammed him face first into the iron bars of the cell, making sure it was his mouth that encountered the metal.

Again.

Again.

Even amidst the wavering falsetto screams, Thorpe heard teeth shattering with each strike.

Ganis grabbed Thorpe by the shoulders, flinging him across the room. Thorpe's head connected with the filthy toilet situated at the back wall. Brilliant shapes pulsating before his eyes, Thorpe made to move, but received a kick to the gut and then another at his right hip. He tumbled backward, even then forcing the panic from his brain. This wasn't merely a beating. These men meant to kill him. They wouldn't stop until he was a bloodied heap staining the filthy concrete floor. Fatalism crowded courage into a forgotten corner of his brain. It was too late. The blow to the head had disoriented him. He couldn't bring the room into focus. His limbs were loose and ineffectual. He was at the mercy of the lumbering ox.

Ganis stepped forward, grabbing Thorpe by the front of his shirt and hoisting the quivering form to a standing position. A fist to the right cheek, another strike just above the jaw, Thorpe thought he might have just felt his brain slosh from side to side. The brute was going to beat him to death and Thorpe had no idea what he'd done to cause their ire.

Thorpe blinked.

The images before him were fractured, incomplete.

He shifted, attempting to pull free of the aggressor.

Just as Ganis lifted his fist for another blow, a prison guard barked a command. *"Dur. Onu asagrya koy!"* The order must have been to drop Thorpe, because Ganis immediately released him, allowing the bloodied Brit to stumble to the concrete floor with a feeble grunt.

Thank God!

There were two guards. Neither tended to the whimpering—and near-toothless-Kocak. Nor did they chastise either of Thorpe's assailants. In truth, it was likely these guards had admitted them to his cell—perhaps even ordering the attack themselves. Thorpe had been sleeping at the onset of aggression and had not seen the brutes enter. By the time he'd come fully awake, he'd already taken several harsh blows.

Thorpe was pulled roughly to his feet, handcuffed, and led out of the cellblock and down the long gray hallway. Blinking repeatedly, he brought his vision into focus. His body screamed from seven different hells, his limbs had the consistency of thrice-boiled potatoes, but with each step he realized all the more that he had survived the encounter. He was bloodied and bruised, but he didn't believe there had been any permanent damage: no broken bones, no ruptured organs. Bloody well amazing!

He'd been imprisoned for nearly two months and this was his first trip beyond the block. Thorpe wasn't entirely certain that he was comfortable with the change. He'd seen other prisoners escorted away never to return. Some inmates concluded that they had been released, others that they'd been released from life itself. He wondered which awaited him beyond the cold metal doors.

The guard on the right, a large square of a man, broad-chested and thick limbed, pressed a button on a metal box to the right of the double door. A speaker squawked. The guards on either side of the obstruction exchanged words, and then the doors rumbled open.

Thorpe was led down yet another corridor, around a corner to the right, and then around one to the left, where eventually they came to a narrow room populated by two other prisoners and three additional guards. The upper half of one wall was wired glass. The lower portion featured a long metal table with several telephone receivers with adjacent chairs.

Thorpe blinked, his vision finally returning to something approaching normal.

He blinked again.

She was seated on the other side of the glass. Was that…? Yes.

Tina Collins.

The last time he'd seen her had been Brazil, what was it, three months ago, perhaps four? It seemed a year or better, but prison time has its own unique pace that has little to do with that experienced in the outer world.

She smiled at him as the cuffs were removed and he was allowed to approach the divide. It was a wide luscious smile enhanced by perfect white teeth which contrasted sharply with her smooth chocolate skin. She was thin, too thin for Thorpe's tastes, but athletic, fit. With her large clear amber eyes and high cheek bones she was a very attractive young woman.

Thorpe didn't trust her for a second.

"Tina dear, you look magnificent," said Thorpe as he picked up the phone receiver and nearly collapsed onto a metal folding chair. "The silk blouse is so much more appealing than that GI Joe getup you wore in the rainforest."

Collins maintained her grin, despite Thorpe's rather dire appearance. "Well darlin', you look like a junkyard dog's favorite chew toy," she said in her southern belle drawl.

Thorpe shrugged and then winced. Even this minimal movement caused severe pain.

"Looks like you're not playing well with others, Johnny."

Thorpe forced a smile, determined to present himself as capable and in control. He didn't yet know the purpose of her visit. "Yes, well, when one is forced to cohabitate with simians, there is only so much to be done."

The two stared at one another for a long moment. This was not a social call. Thorpe and Collins were not friends. They'd been forced together when tracking a fossil known as the Amazon skull, but aside from that they'd had no other dealings.[1] "The last time I saw you," said Thorpe, "you carried CIA credentials. I severely doubt you're in any way connected to the intelligence community."

"Johnny darlin', do you actually expect me to confirm or deny such a thing?"

"I was simply making an observation," replied Thorpe, now making direct eye contact. "But, I will also speculate that you have a specific purpose in coming here."

"That would be a given."

"Care to elaborate?"

Collins feigned mock indignation. "What? No small talk? You don't want to know how I've been all this time? I'd thought we'd bonded, what with me helping you escape the Brazilian authorities and all."

"That's charming, dear, but we both know you did only what was necessary to get the skull to the client without his being implicated in the theft of a cherished artifact. Am I to assume that it's at his behest you've come?"

Tina cocked her head, offering a wry grin. She was rather stunning. "You are a perceptive one."

"That, my dear, is a talent of mine. Now, will you please make your proposition so that I might be done with this hell hole?"

"You do like getting to the point, don't you?"

Thorpe offered a fleeting smile. "I've a reservation at the Four Seasons. I wouldn't want to be late."

Collins chuckled at this. "What makes you think I can get you out of here?"

---

[1] For details, read DEAD MAN'S FIRE

"Because that's why you've come, of course. But, first you'll make a request of me. Some spectacular theft for the client. What was his name again? It seems to have slipped my mind."

"You never knew his name. You never will. And trust me, darlin', it's better that way. You're a thief. Nothing more. Quite skilled, I'll admit. But your uses to the man are limited."

"Well, you really are just an astounding boost to my ego." He paused for a moment, wiping blood from his right cheek. "Now, what is this grand assignment that will gain me my freedom?"

Collins shook her head, leaning forward on her elbows. "Aw, Johnny darlin'. You've got to know better than to think I'd discuss details here. The walls have ears."

"And so I'm expected to agree to this bleeding assignment with no knowledge whatsoever?"

"Oh, you have all the knowledge you need to make an informed decision."

"Really? And what knowledge might that be?"

"That if you don't agree to the assignment, Kocak and Ganis will be waiting in your cell when you return."

Thorpe nodded and grinned. "Ah. You know their names. Well, that does explain a thing or two. I suppose you—or the client—were responsible for my imprisonment to begin with?"

"You were caught stealing the famous Tortoise Trainer by Osman Hamdi Bey. How could I have had anything to do with that?"

"Yes, well, that's all well and good, but the man who paid me to steal the bleeding painting had never before shown the slightest interest in Turkish art. I thought his request peculiar at the time. Now, I find it rather enlightening."

"Darlin', you can believe what you want, but I've got a plane to catch. The only question is whether you'll be sitting beside me."

Thorpe glared into her stunning, near ethereal eyes, and then offered his trademark grin. "I would be delighted to travel with you, my dear. How could you have thought otherwise?"

Already, Thorpe felt deep trepidation. He had done work for this client before, always delighted in the sums the man would pay for stolen artifacts. That he was now being so obviously coerced could only mean that whatever it was that he was meant to steal was something so horrible that he never would have agreed to it otherwise. Thorpe almost wished he could simply return to his cell and rot.

Almost.

Chapter 2

The man Jonathan Thorpe knew only as "The Client" sat in a private dining room across a narrow table from an attractive woman of about forty years in age. Ah Kum was her name, a high government official of some value. Though this was one of the finest restaurants in the city, he did not share a meal with the woman. Ethnic fare, as he called it, left him ill and poorly tempered. He sipped buttermilk from a small bowl-shaped cup, the beverage, he'd supplied for himself, the cup, he'd graciously accepted from the restaurant manager.

He rarely slept well. The previous night had been worse than most. It was often better that he remain busy, not allowing his mind to go to those places it so frequently visited in the long midnight hours. Linus would say that the previous night's issue had been the result of his involvement in the seedier side of their endeavors, that someone of the blood should not lower himself to such matters.

Linus was wrong.

It was because he was of the blood that he must show his willingness to do what he so often asked of others. The commitment of those who were merely followers was so much greater when they knew that those above them, those truly superior in both mind and body, fully understood and had experienced those things they demanded of adherents.

Not so Linus. He lived for the shadows, a wraith flitting beyond society's curtain, nudging, pulling, manipulating. He was not entirely wrong in this approach; quite often this was as it should be. It was just incomplete.

The irony was that, of the two, Linus was far more suited for these endeavors. It was his temperament. He enjoyed the thrill and the intrigue, the risk, the deadly conclusion. The brothers were so entirely different for two persons so entirely alike. Yet Linus was not here, and though a subordinate could have tended to the issue, the man did not feel this to be the best option. He did not enjoy the act as Linus did, but neither did he shy from it. Duty. It was his duty.

And duty was not something to be shirked or handed off to others simply because it was unpleasant.

The woman, Ah Kum, said something. Her voice did not waver; her tone was firm and filled with strength. Admirable. In truth, she was a fine woman, worthy of her position and his respect. He met her gaze and, despite herself, she averted her eyes; only briefly, less than a second, but noticeable none-the-less. She found it peculiar, his heterochromia, his eyes being of two different colors, one blue, one green. In truth, his entire bearing was peculiar. It was something he embraced rather than concealed. It was part of his strength, a tool to be utilized. "P...lease speak in... English," he said. "I have no... use for the... lesser tongues."

In truth, he was fluent in several languages, but it was important for others to recognize his stature, his preeminence in every situation. Every word, every implication was a piece of the whole. Forcing her to speak in another tongue put her at a disadvantage. It would distract her, cause her to pause, possibly to simplify her statements, making them less effective.

Ah Kum hesitated for only a moment, and then spoke in lightly accented English. "I said that I am unable to do as you have asked."

He smiled and raised his glass as if in salute. "Oh, I understood... you p...erfectly." Another sip. He would wait for her to speak again. His was the upper hand. There was no rush.

It took less than ten seconds before she spoke. Certainly, to her, it seemed an hour of deathly silence. "What you have asked of me, it would undermine my government and my people. I cannot betray that trust."

He took a moment to respond, appearing to study her, to appraise her strength and fortitude. In truth, the pause was meant merely to unnerve her all the more. But it was never unpleasant to study such a fine specimen. Smooth unlined skin. Bright intelligent eyes. A noble posture, confident and assured. "You do, I'm sure, und...erstand... the consequences of... this decision."

She squared herself, directing her gaze at him, no hesitation, no apparent fear. In fact, she leaned forward, assuming an offensive posture. "Sir, I do not know you by name. I have found no information concerning you or your organization. But you have provided adequate evidence of your atrocities. I believe you can do as you have claimed. You may threaten me; you may succeed in an attack against me, but I will not succumb to your pressure."

He grinned and nodded. A fine woman. Why was it the noble must die while the scoundrel flourished? This woman was a person of principle. She was brave, tenacious, and held to what she believed to be right. And yet she would perish this day while another far less noble, far less deserving, assumed her position.

"Have you h...heard of An...ntonio Exili?" he asked after a pause.

She did not reply.

"No? How... about Catherine de Medici? Maybe Christopher Glaser? Cesare Borgia? All heroes of... mine. E...ach skilled in the art... of poisoning."

Here, she looked down at her half eaten meal, a delicacy named *Bak Kut Teh* which featured cow's lung. He had ordered the dish for her and she had shown him her strength by eating it despite obvious reason for trepidation. But now the darkness of the tiny room, the deep red wallpaper, nearly black wooden screen and trim, suddenly seemed to steal the light from her clear brown eyes.

"No," he smiled. "Not... your fine meal. That, I had learned was a... favorite of yours, and requested in order to s...show my admiration. I... have more subtlety than to behave as you may have suspected. Though, Borgia was known to eliminate many rivals th...through simple dinner engagements, that is... not my way."

"No? You do not poison? Then why bring it up? What is the game?"

Curious. Why had he broached the topic? It was an interest of his, true. But, the statement had been meant to induce fear. Simply that. He could be cruel, he supposed. With the merest hint of a grin, he reached across the thin ribbon of a table, touching her right hand with his left. "I... admire the p...poisoners, their craft and craftiness. I find the... variety of poisons astounding: ipecac, Croton oil, betel nut s...seed, henbane, various venoms and ph...pharmaceuticals. I marvel at the s...skill, but feel that... if a man means to slay an... opponent, especially one of such obvious character, that the intended victim has a right to meet the... executioner's gaze face... to f...face." He shrugged. "Sometimes this is not possible, but... when it is, then it is... my way."

"And what else is your way; to manipulate foreign governments for your own gain?"

Squeezing her hand so very slightly he said, "There are sometimes... things greater than a... man. There are events and destinies, th...there are dreams so bold as to be tangible. That is my way. Surely one... such as you can understand this."

Their eyes locked, neither speaking for several moments. Finally, pulling her hand free of his, she cut a small piece of meat, inserted it between her lips, and when she had finished chewing, said, "We have spoken before. Always we are at odds. Though you have revealed nothing, you have revealed much. You feel there is a grand destiny, a predetermined plan. Perhaps you would call it a dream. But consider this." Here, she paused, again leaning closer for emphasis. "What does one do when he comes to the culmination of a dream and finds that dream wanting?"

He smiled. Clever. The woman was clever, even now attempting to seed doubt. "Your successor has... been chosen. A man. Not of... your abilities, but adequate to the task and to... our needs. He will assume the position next Tuesday after... an appropriate time has p...passed."

"You seem quite sure of your plans. I will see that you do not succeed."

Curious. She seemed not to understand her situation. That was logical, he supposed. No one would voluntarily become a sacrifice. Surely, she mistakenly believed that her guards were still stationed just beyond the flimsy screen. Surely she believed that it was he, not she that would be crushed. "You... have a daughter," he said. "Chunhua, meaning, Spring Flower."

Ah Kum stilled. It seemed ice encased her features.

"Again... you misunderstand me. I mean your Spring Flower no... harm. On... the contrary. I... simply wanted you to die knowing th...that she will be well c...ared for. Her education funded. Her needs met. Th...ere is no... need for her to suffer unduly for choices made by her... mother."

His meaning slipped through her brain less than a second before, from under the narrow table, the needle-like stiletto slid beneath her breastbone and into her heart.

Chapter 3

The train was designed to be something special. The American Cry, it was called. Each car offered a different decor, each of these depicting a different era or event in American history. The dining car was made to resemble a 1950's era diner with an art deco vibe, vinyl booths, and even a juke box belting out Elvis Presley and Buddy Holly classics. The lounge resembled a prohibition era speakeasy. There was a Wild West themed car, a Hollywood car, even a NASA car. The recently-completed train traveled coast-to-coast from Los Angeles to Washington DC and back with stops in major cities such as Phoenix, Denver, Chicago, Cincinnati, and New York. The American Cry had only been in operation for three months and still had that quintessential new smell about it. But, Marc Huntington wasn't here as a tourist. He wasn't sightseeing or off on some romantic getaway. This trip was about business.

"I did not," he whispered as he made his way up the narrow aisle of one of the passenger cars, this one designed to resemble Tara from the film Gone with the Wind.

"Hunt, you did too," retorted his wife and partner, Dana. "And will you please put that yo-yo away!"

"It calms me."

"Hunt!"

"Okay, okay. Yo-yo away," said Hunt as he rolled the string and shoved the purple Duncan into his right front pocket. "But, don't forget, this yo-yo helped us break out of jail in Brazil."

Dana rolled her blue-violet eyes and shook her head. "How could I ever forget? You remind me every day."

"Only when you gripe about my yo-yo."

Dana sighed in mock exasperation. "Did you take your meds today?"

Hunt hesitated, not responding.

Dana offered him a very sharp and very familiar look. "Take them. We can't have you getting one of your migraines in the middle of this operation."

The truth was, he had taken his meds and had been taking quite a bit more than his prescription dictated. He now had three separate doctors prescribing the stuff, but Dana knew none of this. Better that she didn't. He'd wean himself off—eventually. The headaches had simply become too great. He needed to function.

"Hunt!" pressed Dana. "Your meds."

"I took them earlier. I need a clear head for this."

"Just like you did when you dropped the infra-red."

Now it was Hunt's turn to roll his eyes. Did she really need to bring this up again? "I was distracted."

"Distracted! Hunt, when aren't you distracted?"

"Well, there was that time in Malta when…"

"Hunt!"

"Well, at the time I was trying to come up with something better than 'Bop him on the noggin.' Seven years with MI6 and the best you come up with is 'Bop 'im on the noggin.'" For the last sentence, Hunt imitated Dana's often colorful east London accent.

Dana couldn't help but grin. "It's effective," she said in a half-hearted defense. She was so cute when they squabbled.

"It might be effective, but it's not exactly subtle."

They came to the end of the car and Hunt slid the door open so they could continue forward to the next. Upon entering, they stopped at the threshold and scanned the dining car. Bill Haley and The Comets belted from the juke box. There were black and white four-seat booths on either side of the aisle; nearly all were occupied by passengers: families, business persons, tourists. In the sixth booth on the right, with his back to them was Kelvin Donnelly, a tall man of about fifty with deep brown hair and a salt and pepper beard. He was sipping a glass of orange juice and reading from a Kindle eBook reader. Even so, his eyes darted from side-to-side and he frequently whisked his finger across the base of his nose. At a glance, he appeared twitchy and nervous. As expected, He wore his navy pin stripe blazer. Dana had pointed out that it was Prada. A Midwestern guy with nearly adolescent sensibilities, Hunt couldn't have distinguished it from a Wally World special—this despite the fact that his recent ventures had catapulted him to a net worth in the lower seven digits.

The Stonemeier diamond would be in Donnelly's left breast pocket. As recovery experts, Hunt and Dana made a living recovering stolen or lost items of rare value and collecting the reward money offered. They had located and returned rare artifacts and paintings, hijacked yachts, and even kidnapped persons. Dana was a former British intelligence officer and Hunt a former Delta Force operative. Both were highly skilled in their respective specialties and could boast a string of successes and only a handful of notable failures.

Kelvin Donnelly was a jewel thief of marginal skill who operated primarily in the United States, but had been seen recently in both Germany and the UK. Though they'd never encountered Donnelly before, Dana had compiled a dossier on the man. They knew he would likely leave the train two stations prior to the one stated on his ticket—Denver. There would be a car waiting, rented under an alias. The diamond would never leave his possession. Likely, within twenty-four hours, it would be sold on the black market. Or, if the particular piece was too conspicuous, it would be parted out into two or three smaller diamonds, diminishing the value, but still gaining Donnelly a handsome sum due to the lack of imperfections, the clarity, and the color of the stone.

Despite their research, Hunt was leery of the man. There were some glaring gaps in his background information. If the operation had been more complicated in nature, and if they had expected any continued contact with Donnelly, they would have researched him more thoroughly, but time constraints prohibited the type of in-depth background checks that both Hunt and Dana preferred. Still, this was a simple recovery. Donnelley was nothing more than a second rate thug taking a stab at the big time. They'd probably already learned far more than needed.

The plan was for Dana to approach Donnelly, strike up a conversation, and generally distract the man. She was an intelligent, witty woman, and with her striking Euro-Asian features, guaranteed to turn most any man's head. Donnelly, a known womanizer, would surely take the bait. Hunt, wearing a steward's uniform, would then serve the jewel thief a second juice complete with a sedative. They'd considered having Dana drug the man herself, but both agreed that—out of the sheer paranoia inherent to being a criminal—he would likely be suspicious of her. Much better that the tranquilizer be administered by someone garbed as an employee. Dana could then slip the diamond from his pocket, and then complain to the wait staff that she'd just met the man who must have had too much to drink the night before because he'd became belligerent before passing out. With that cover story, the staff would not expect her to remain involved as they tended to the unconscious thief. If all went well, Hunt and Dana would exit the train some five minutes later at the next stop, and Donnelley would have only the vaguest recollection of what had occurred.

In truth, it all came down to timing. Dana needed to engage Donnelly between three and six minutes before Hunt's arrival as a steward. If Hunt arrived too soon, Donnelly might not be ready for a refill or yet inclined to offer Dana a drink. If Hunt delayed too long, an authentic steward might have already taken the order, or even worse, they'd miss their stop and be forced to stay on board as Donnelley regained consciousness. The couple had memorized the crew's routine and knew their window of opportunity. Now it was simply a matter of execution.

"Alright," said Hunt. "We've confirmed his locale. Give me five minutes to change into the uniform and then approach Donnelly. Remember, he's a fan of the Miami Dolphins, James Patterson novels, and 70's era muscle cars."

"None of which interest me in the least."

"Ah, but, you've done your homework."

"Of course," smiled Dana holding up the Patterson novel, Cross Fire. "I've read the first seven chapters as well as the synopsis of each of the previous novels in the Alex Cross series."

"Very good," said Hunt who knew she would have much preferred spending her reading time on ancient history, or listening to a college course on MP3. Dana was a consummate student. "I'll see you back here in just about eleven minutes."

"Be careful, dear."

"Always, gorgeous. You too. Don't let that creep get too fresh. That skirt you're wearing could make a dead man drool."

"I can take care of myself."

Hunt smiled. "I know. That's what frightens me. I don't want to come back and find him laid out on the floor with a broken collar bone."

Dana chuckled. "Who? Me? Never."

"Need I remind you of that Boston marina this past May?"

"Ah. Well. The man had it coming."

"My point exactly."

*****

Hunt chose to change clothes in a baggage car. It was a stainless steel cube piled high with luggage and crates and, at this point in the journey, would likely be unoccupied. He first heard voices as he prepared to slip into the neatly pressed pants. The conversation originated at the far end of the compartment, and Hunt was obscured from the men by a towering Samsonite jungle.

"He's late," said one voice. American, male, youngish.

"Probably doing his usual," said another, older, man, raspy, the voice of a lifelong smoker, accented with a tough Jersey attitude.

The younger man was insistent, his voice tinged with nervous excitement. "No. Not at a time like this. Something must have happened to him."

"Nick, relax. You know the guy. He's off relieving his nervous energy—by one means or another."

"Yeah, well, he'd better be here soon." There was a pause, some pacing. Hunt heard what sounded like the clink of metal, the shuffle of plastic and/or metal items being lifted from a box and placed on the floor. "I don't know. I mean, he's a smart guy. He's got this whole thing figured out. But, I don't know."

"Just calm down," said the older man. "You do your part. I do mine. We all do what we're supposed to do; it all works out—no matter what the boss is into. Got that?"

"Yeah." A pause. "How's the mechanism coming?"

The *snip, snip* of wire clippers and then the sound of one metallic piece sliding into another. "I should have everything assembled and fully operational well before we reach Denver."

More pacing. Another shuffle and clank. "I wish the boss was here."

"Kid. Lighten up. Our message will be heard loud and clear in the mile high city. Those that live won't even know what hit 'em."

"Really? You just said that? You sound like some cheesy villain out of one of those action adventure novels."

"Yeah? Your point?"

"Nothin'. Just saying."

Chapter 4

Winchester England

Jonathan Thorpe stroked the woman's auburn hair, caressing her scalp, eliciting a satisfied purr from his date. Her name was Liza. They'd met the night before. He gazed down at her as she snuggled against his breast, her naked form warm against his. Beautiful. Charming. Very adventurous. He didn't know why he did it—seduce women. Well, he knew why, he supposed. He was a single man, still in his prime, he had his needs. With his winning smile, trim physique, and creamy milk chocolate eyes, woman found him quite attractive, and he'd never had difficulty finding companionship. But, it wasn't women he desired. It was a woman, one specific woman. Dana Bell. Well, Dana Bell Huntington now. Of course, he'd first known her as Martha Booth—and then Martha Thorpe. His wife for a time. But, Martha had been an alias. She'd been a MI6 spy ordered to get close to him, to use him to gain access to some of his most controversial contacts. Who could have imagined they'd actually fall in love?

Liza stirred a bit. He pulled her closer and gave her a peck on the top of the head. She was lovely. At some level he felt bad laying here thinking of another woman. But not too bad. There was no expectation of a long term relationship. This was just sex.

And companionship.

That was it, he supposed. The sex was part of it. But, if he was to be true to himself, he'd admit that it was more about acceptance. Most women believed men sought sexual adventure out of a need to dominate, to conquer. Perhaps that was true for some men, but for Thorpe it was a need for true intimacy and perhaps endearment. Thorpe led a largely solitary life. He was a thief, specializing in fine art. It was difficult to get close to someone in that line of work. And at his core, Thorpe was a social creature. A peculiar trait to be sure. He was intellectually superior to most, and found much of day-to-day conversation boring and tedious, but still he adored socializing, mingling, schmoozing. The curse of the baser aspects of his nature, he supposed. Still, at his core, he longed for a more intimate relationship. Someone with whom he could share his life. Someone of his own mind. Someone to challenge him to grow and to excel.

He'd thought he'd found that person in Dana—Martha—whatever. But she had betrayed him at a most profound level. That she had been spying on him, that the person he had loved so deeply had been a fiction, a legend created by British intelligence, devastated him. But that she had walked so casually from his life had shattered him at a level he hadn't known to exist. Had she stayed with him, he could have forgiven her the other. He had started out as an assignment, this he understood, but both knew the relationship had become much more. They could have worked it through, come to know one another anew.

But now she'd remarried.

As much as he wanted to hate the bloke, he just couldn't bring himself to it. Marc Huntington was rather rough about the edges, not as refined as Thorpe, and due to an explosion in Iraq, rather unsightly to behold, but at his core the man was solid. Under other circumstances, they might have been friends.

It was getting well on into the day—nearly three pm—and Thorpe was rather annoyed that Liza remained asleep. Though, he had to admit, he'd kept her up till nearly dawn with a brief interlude just past noon. His fault, he supposed. Still, he was ready for her to leave. Rarely did he entertain women at one of his own domiciles. It was simply too risky. But he'd fallen under this girl's spell, and, well, here they were. Now, he only wanted her away.

Slipping gently from the silk sheets, Thorpe pulled on a pair of sweat pants and made his way to his laptop computer situated on an antique desk in the corner of the room. He'd been doing quite a bit of research since his return from Turkey and the subsequent assignment he'd taken on as payment for his freedom. Thorpe didn't like being manipulated, and even worse, this man, this anonymous client, now had something on him that could put Thorpe away for the rest of his life, perhaps even get him executed.

Well, that was bollocks. It was time for countermeasures.

Thorpe typed in a security code and then another. Then came three questions which only he could answer. There was a pool of twenty-five questions, three of which would appear at random with each log-in, after which a coded series of transfers would redirect the IP address to a computer located in southern France. It would be very difficult for someone to hack into this computer.

Thorpe opened a recently added file and began scanning through the numerous photographs within. He was getting close. He could feel it. Where six months ago, he'd only had one image of the client, now he had seven, all from different sources. And though he'd not yet managed to put a name to the man, he could now place him on three separate continents, meeting with world leaders from six different countries. Whoever the man was, he traveled in political circles, usually meeting behind closed doors and away from prying eyes and ears. He met with some of the most powerful people on earth, and as such, would soon be known to Thorpe. This, because powerful people had large staffs. And as with any work environment, someone is always disgruntled, someone will always leak information. It makes them feel powerful. Thorpe's task was to identify and exploit these weak links. Someone had seen this man. Someone knew his name. And once Thorpe had that name, he would gain more knowledge, which would grant him leverage and even power.

Thorpe moved to another site and then typed in a code. He clicked enter.

Nothing happened.

He clicked again.

The same.

The computer seemed to be frozen. Absurd. The capacity was much greater than that needed for these simple maneuvers.

A minute went by, and then another.

Thorpe hit the escape button.

Nothing.

The screen flickered.

It flickered again.

Suddenly, images flashed across the screen—*flash, flash, flash*—so quickly that Thorpe couldn't identify more than one in ten of the pages. He'd been breached. And without a doubt, he knew who had done it.

He stabbed the on/off button, but the computer did not respond. It was no longer his to control. Quickly, he lifted the thing and threw it against the nearest wall, breaking it into two large segments, the screen and the base. Thorpe snatched the base slamming it again and again against the floor until it was nothing but useless wires and plastic. There was no way of knowing how much of his hard drive had been offloaded before he'd interrupted the transfer, how much incriminating information had been stolen.

Liza was awake now, screaming at him to stop smashing the computer.

"Quickly," he said. "I've no time to explain, but you must leave. It's no longer safe here."

"Matthew, what are you talking about?"

Rarely using his true name for his escapades, he'd told the girl that he was a stock broker named Matthew Greene.

"I'm so sorry, dear, but, well, you see, my security has been breached and we could be attacked. These people, I fear, might be quite efficient. Do hurry. Put your clothes on as we go."

Thorpe marched across the room to a closet, pulled down a pair of trousers and a shirt, and dressed quickly while mentally cataloguing the condominium's contents. This was not his primary residence. Beyond the computer files, there was very little that could implicate him. He was dressed and ready to run in less than a minute. The girl, though, was still fumbling with her flimsy panties as she shook free the last remnants of sleep.

"Liza, truly, we must be gone."

He helped her to slip her slinky club dress over her head, and then grabbed her six-inch stiletto shoes from the floor, shoving them into her hands. "You can put these on later. We must leave." He grabbed her by the arm and pulled her toward the door.

Thorpe's condominium was on the third floor. It was an older building with plaster walls and thick oak wood doors. A central hallway between units and a stairwell at each end, the corridor was dimly lit with frosted globe lamps, vaguely yellow in hue. It reminded Thorpe of the Overlook Hotel from the movie, The Shining.

Two men, both wearing black, both armed, were moving quickly toward Thorpe from the left as he exited his unit. Bloody hell! He'd thought the client would locate him, but Thorpe was surprised that even this man could mobilize men so quickly. Perhaps he'd narrowed his search prior to the final computer breach, or maybe the breach had initiated well before his logging on. In any event, this was not the time to contemplate the how of the thing.

Thorpe had a pistol, a Walther P22, which he'd shoved into his right front pocket. He was loathe to use the thing, especially in confined spaces such as this. There were simply too many opportunities for things to go terribly wrong.

A gunshot rang out, shattering one of the glowing yellow globes in a splay of frosted glass.

Liza screamed as shards of glass sprinkled her auburn hair.

My God! Thorpe had no idea they'd leap immediately to lethal force.

Another shot, this one furrowing into a wall.

They were at the stairwell now. Thorpe took the stairs two at a time, but he was still holding Liza's hand. She couldn't quite keep up, and the resistance caused him to lose his footing. He tumbled perhaps three steps, slamming against the wall on the first landing, the Walther discharging a round into the bottom step in the process. He'd felt a twinge in his right ankle, but had no time to tend to it.

Liza ran past him, continuing down the steps, as Thorpe scrambled to his feet.

The first man was now at the top step. Thorpe fired, hitting the assailant in the right shoulder, before launching himself down the stairs. He could hear footfall from the second man behind him.

He was at the level two landing now, rounding the corner toward the first floor. Liza was below him. The first floor door swung open, a shot was fired.

Liza tumbled backward, a bullet hole just below her left eye, her lips twitching in a silent scream as she stared sightless toward the ceiling.

"Damn!"

Having pursuers coming from both above and below, Thorpe had no time to check on the girl. Likely she was dead. If not, he could only hope that one of the residents or perhaps security would find her and tend to her needs. Quickly, he turned, racing onto the second floor. There was a window at this end of the hallway adjacent the stairwell. A large potted plant sat against the wall. Flicking the Walther's safety and shoving it into his pocket, Thorpe lifted the planter and hurled it through the window. He had only seconds.

There was a row of sculptured shrubbery below, a small grassy lawn, and then a narrow avenue. Thorpe leapt for the grass, trying to land with the bulk of his weight on the uninjured left leg. Barely clearing the shrubs, he hit, rolled, and then scrambled to his feet, racing across the street to then disappear between buildings.

Chapter 5

Southern Colorado

Kelvin Donnelley whisked his index finger across his nostrils, made to sip his orange juice, thought better of it, and offered Dana a transient smile. "Yeah, the Alex Cross novels. Patterson's best known. The Maximum Ride series, a better escape—heh?" His words were quick, clipped. His face twitched as he sipped his juice. "Besides, the Cross character—what?—too morally rigid. I mean, who's like that?"

Dana cocked her head and grinned, intentionally saucy. "I've only read the Cross series, but a bit of escapism could prove interesting."

Donnelley studied her for a moment, his deep-set Kelly green eyes bloodshot but clear. Again his finger slid across his aquiline nose. "A beautiful woman. You have plenty of offers. For escapism." His smallish mouth and modest overbite gave him a quirky but endearing quality.

Here it comes, thought Dana, the seduction. She was hoping to avoid this. But Donnelley's conversation had been peppered with innuendo, his gaze shifting between her eyes and bosom. It was only a matter of time. The man had seemed a bit bedraggled, and quite preoccupied, continually glancing at his watch, and then up and down the narrow aisle; he seemed to be looking for someone, but still he'd managed to leer.

She glanced up, met Donnelley's gaze. He was older than her by nearly two decades, fifty-one, to be precise, but he was still, at some level, an attractive man. His face was long and gaunt, offering a hint of mysterious character. His complexion was ruddy: pocked and tough, his beard salt and pepper. But, his thick wavy hair was still full and brown. The shoulders rolled subtly, his belly had the beginnings of a bulge, but only just.

Physically, he was rather appealing, but as a person he was twitchy, perhaps moody, and prone to prolonged silence amidst near manic conversation. A peculiar man to be sure. A run-of-the-mill thief trying to hit a significant score. He'd been imprisoned on three separate occasions. Surely at his age he sought to avoid another sentence. Perhaps this was his way of finishing off. One big hit and out. One last risk.

"You're thinking too hard," he said, observing Dana's scrutiny. "We both know the game. I pursue you. You allow yourself to be caught. Let's forget that nonsense. Come to my cabin." He slid a finger across his nostrils, glanced right then left. "I've got a business meeting. Shortly. Then I depart. If we like each other's company, we exchange numbers. If not, we still had a good time."

"Hmmm, how very... direct."

He shrugged. "We're adults. Why pretend? We both know what this is."

"What it is, is over," came a voice from behind Dana and to her left.

Donnelley looked up to see Hunt standing beside their booth. But, where was his porter's uniform? Something wasn't quite right.

"Excuse me," said Donnelley. "I was speaking. With the woman."

"Yeah, we've been introduced. Dana's my wife."

What was Hunt doing? He'd just blown the entire plan. This was not like him.

Hunt slipped into the booth beside Dana and leaned toward Donnelley, elbows on the red Formica tabletop. "Listen, Donnelley. Let me get right to the point. My name's Marc Huntington. Dana and I tracked you here. We're in the business of recovering stolen items and returning them to their rightful owners. We know you have the recently-stolen Stonemeier diamond."

Donnelley stiffened. "Really? What is it, Huntington? I..."

"Hunt. You can call me Hunt. Anyway, you have the diamond. It's not yours. Naughty, naughty. We're here to retrieve it."

Donnelley leaned back in his seat, attempting to affect a casual air. "Are you police? Even rent-a-cops—heh? You can't do anything. Can't prove anything. So, leave. Your little missus. Has some real interest in me." Here, he winked, offering Dana a knowing leer. "Maybe she was tired of closing her eyes. In the bedroom—heh? Keep from looking at your hideous face."

Dana winced internally at the jab. A suicide bomber in Iraq had severely damaged the entire left side of Hunt's face. He'd had several surgeries, and looked much better than he had even a year before, but the injury was still obvious and Hunt was quite self-conscious of it. To his credit, he didn't take the

24

bait, though, despite the neatly trimmed beard which hid much of the damage, Dana noticed his skin redden and his jaw clench.

"That's classy, Donnelley. I can tell you're a man of superior breeding. Listen—can I call you Kelvin? Here's the deal, Kelvin. You give me the diamond. It's in your left breast pocket, by the way. You turn it over and we let you walk away, no harm no foul. We're not after you, we're after the rock."

"Yeah, you have no authority."

Hunt shrugged. "Define authority. Besides, Dana and I have photographs of you with the diamond."

At this, Donnelley whisked his nose, repressing a subtle tremor. "How?"

"In your hotel room," offered Dana. Hunt had gone completely off-grid; she might as well jump in and go along for the ride. Maybe they could still salvage something of the operation. Either way, she and Hunt would have words after this.

"Infra-red," added Hunt. "Great resolution, really. You have very skinny legs. And those pink boxers…"

"Hunt!"

"Right. Anyway, if you don't surrender the diamond, we'll, A: inform security here on the train, and, B: transmit the photo of you, your boxers, the diamond, along with the train's I.D. number and itinerary to every law enforcement agency along the route. You won't be able to disembark with the diamond for fear of immediate arrest."

Dana's stomach took a dive at this. If Donnelley called Hunt's bluff and the authorities were brought in, they'd have no opportunity to secure the diamond and would therefore forfeit the reward money.

Donnelley clucked his tongue. "Sounds desperate, Huntington. Any other threats, heh?"

"Well, if you continue on this train and don't disembark before Denver—boom!"

Donnelley nearly laughed. "Boom?"

Hunt leaned forward, resting his weight on his elbows and forearms. "There's a bomb on board, Kelvin, along with a rather brutish group of men intent on detonating it in Denver. Kinda antisocial, don't you think?"

Donnelley rose, a smug look on his ruddy face. "Heh! Huntington, you are pathetic." He paused and then added, "Young lady. You and me. We'll have a romp." With that, the thief turned and walked away, the diamond still secure on his person.

"Hunt, have you gone entirely daft?" hissed Dana. Donnelley now knew them by sight. The diamond was lost to them. "The buffoon was purring like a kitten until you showed up. And what's this poppycock about a bomb?"

Hunt shifted slightly in his seat so that he could better face her. "There's a terrorist cell on board. I overheard them in the baggage car. They plan to detonate in Denver."

Dana went cold. Hunt was serious. "Al Quida?"

"Don't think so. Looks to be homegrown."

"Lovely, another Timothy McVeigh. Have you notified security?"

Hunt nodded. "Yeah. They were skeptical, but I persuaded them to call the authorities."

"Is onboard security investigating the matter?"

"So they say, but I'm not convinced they're equipped to handle a legitimate terrorist cell."

It was then that they felt the first lurch and heard the metal on metal sound of the train's emergency breaks. Dana leaned to her right, glancing through the window in an attempt to see forward of her position. "Looks to be a roadblock ahead," she said. "Plenty of flashing lights. Police activity."

Before Hunt could respond, the front door to the dining car was thrust open and a young man carrying an automatic weapon marched into the car and opened fire.

Chapter 6

Chaos.

A young mother cradled her two year-old son to her breast.

An Asian man, suddenly pale and breathless, cautiously pulled his hands from his laptop computer where he'd been looking at Russian brides.

A middle-aged man babbled, "Oh my God, oh my God."

Hunt smelled urine from one of the booths somewhere behind him.

A shrill female voice cursed the president and all of his relatives.

"Shut up. All of you," barked the terrorist. "No one will be hurt if you stay seated and remain calm. If anyone—and I mean anyone—makes a move, I will kill that person. Do you understand?"

There were hushed murmurs about the dining car. Hunt's ears still rang from the sound of the automatic weapon the man had fired into the jukebox, silencing Elvis Presley as he rocked the jailhouse.

"I said, shut up!"

The terrorist was young, mid-twenties, a wiry build, but taut, fit. His weapon was a Heckler and Koch 9mm automatic. By his voice, Hunt believed him to be one of the men he'd overheard in the baggage car. His eyes darted right and left, he shuffled from one foot to the other and held the weapon at a slightly peculiar angle. This was not an experienced combat vet, but likely a kid caught up in some radical political group that had crossed a very big line. Hunt wondered how they'd gotten weapons onboard. Security, post 911, was strict. There must have been an inside connection. If he'd been closer to the man, Hunt might have made a move, but he was seated in a booth beside Dana and separated from the terrorist by perhaps twenty-five feet. There was no chance of getting to him before he squeezed off a round.

Hunt leaned closer to Dana, whispering yet keeping his lips ventriloquist still. "Don't make eye contact with this guy. He'll want to make an example of someone."

The terrorist jerked his head to the right. "You! What are you doing there?"

"Nothing," came a gasping voice from behind Hunt and to his left. "Just... need my... inhaler."

"Don't reach into your pocket," barked the fanatic as he pulled the trigger.

There was the echoing *tat-tat-tat* of automatic weapon fire, the sound of a body tumbling to the floor, and an eruption of screams and cries. The young mother slid her son to behind her in the booth, the Asian man looked down and away. Hunt thought he saw the man tap some keys on his computer. Emailing for help perhaps? A nearby woman gagged as if ready to vomit.

Hunt and Dana were unarmed, but both were skilled at hand-to-hand combat. If the terrorist came close, there might be a chance to intervene. As they were seated side-by-side, Hunt, who was at the aisle, would be the one to engage. Dana would need to be quick if she meant to assist in any way. But the kid wasn't giving them the opportunity. He just stood there staring, silently taunting the crowd, daring anyone else to challenge his authority.

Hunt's sense of duty screamed at him to check on the victim. Dana was skilled in emergency medical procedures. If the man was alive, she might be able to stabilize him until help arrived.

If help arrived.

"Shut up!" cried the terrorist, his brown eyes wide, almost crazed. It seemed he'd emerged from his near stupor to realize that the room had once again fallen into a frenzy of screams and curses. "All of you—shut up!"

The crowd quieted to muffled whispers, though several people wept uncontrollably. The terrorist casually raised his gun barrel toward the ceiling, and cocked his head, affecting an air of confidence. Despite his posturing, the kid was nervous, frightened of what he'd just done. Hunt could tell by the twitch of his wrist, the subtle tremor in the legs, the wide, nearly panicked, look in his eyes and the long, almost desperate pause after the victim had fallen to the deck.

"Now," said the kid. "You know I'm serious. This train has stopped. No one will disembark. I am not alone, but have several colleagues moving about the train, each as willing as I to kill. Each willing to die for our cause."

No one doubted this. Already, they'd heard gunshots and screams erupt from the next car to the rear.

"Everyone just stay seated. If you do as you're told, no one else will be hurt." The terrorist scanned the crowd as more sounds of mayhem echoed from the adjacent car. "I will not be in this car continuously. If I or one of my colleagues returns to find anyone missing, we will kill someone."

At this point, the door behind the terrorist slid open and another armed man emerged. The kid seemed relieved as he said, "This man is going to collect your cell phones and all electronic devices. Don't try to hide these from him unless you're suicidal. Your cell phones: lift them above your heads—now people!"

*****

The terrorists left the dining car soon after collecting the electronic devices. Obviously, there were not enough of them to maintain a constant presence in every car. That was significant, and might allow the Huntingtons an opportunity to mobilize countermeasures. Dana had examined the victim. Four rounds to his chest. He'd died instantly. The miracle was that no one else had been hit by a stray bullet. The terrorist had appeared nervous, and by his very baring, Hunt could tell he had no actual military experience. But he was obviously a competent shot. Hunt would remember that when next they encountered one another.

The collection experience had been invasive and demeaning, frightening the passengers further, and causing several women to weep. The young terrorist maintained his position, Heckler and Koch at the ready, while his companion, a middle-aged man of perhaps five foot ten, frisked every passenger thoroughly—the women especially so.

Afterward, Hunt had borrowed a travel blanket from a passenger, covered the body, and slid it under one of the tables and out of the aisle. It was a tight fit, and he'd needed to curl the form into a fetal position, but at least it was more or less out of sight and less a constant reminder of what had just occurred. After this, he returned to Dana, sitting opposite her as the frightened passengers whispered and fretted amongst themselves.

"The train's moving again," she said.

Hunt nodded. "Yeah. The roadblock was lifted. No hostage negotiations that I could tell. No contact from a SWAT team. Weird."

"I'm sure they threatened to detonate the bomb."

Hunt shrugged. "Maybe, maybe not. Knowing that there's a bomb onboard, why would they let this train pass? By doing so, they're endangering additional lives."

Dana nodded. "If they were allowed to detonate in a crowded station or within a heavily populated area the death toll could be far greater." She paused for a moment and then asked, "Did you get a look at the bomb?"

"Nah. My view was obstructed. I don't know if we're talking firecrackers, C-4, or thermonuclear."

Dana's clear blue-violet eyes narrowed in thought. "If we had a smart phone, we could coordinate our actions with the FBI or Homeland Security, perhaps photograph terrorists and email intel to the authorities for identification purposes."

Hunt shrugged. "There's got to be laptops, phones, iPads, whatever we need in the sleeper cars."

Dana nodded. "I'd be surprised if the terrorists left those untouched."

"True, but even if they went through each room, they might have missed something."

"I suppose it's worth a try. But, we'd best hurry. This train can't be much more than two hours from Denver."

Hunt scooted out of the booth and rose. Dana did the same. There was an immediate flurry of protests from the other passengers.

"Hey! What are you doing?"

"That terrorist guy said we had to stay in our seats."

"You're going to get us killed!"

Hunt thought of the body lying crumpled and bloodied under a table. It was amazing there wasn't outright panic.

Hunt held up his hands signaling the crowd to quiet. "Whoa, whoa, whoa. Calm down. The last thing we need is to draw attention to this car."

"Where are you going?" shouted a man, short, balding, wearing a Nike sweatshirt and blue jeans.

Hunt didn't want to reveal their plan—what little plan there was—and so simply said, "I need to use the john."

Now there was another voice. "The rest of us need to do that too. But, none of us are going to risk our lives for it."

There were murmurs of agreement.

"I think you'd better tell them," said Dana.

"They'll panic."

"They're already panicking."

Hunt nodded. He didn't really want to reveal much about himself or Dana for fear the information might get back to the terrorists. Likely, they'd both be executed as a precaution. But, it was that same information that might calm these passengers, offering them some hope. "Alright," he said. "Everybody listen." Hunt made his way toward the front of the car and then turned to face the group.

The griping continued as if Hunt had said nothing.

"Listen!" he barked.

At this, the crowd settled some, but there were angry stares and muttered curses.

"Okay. I'm going to tell you something, but I need you all to remain calm. Do you understand?" Hunt scanned the space. "My name's Marc Huntington. I'm former U.S. military, a sergeant major from Delta Force, an elite special ops unit. My wife, Dana, is former MI6. That's like the British CIA. Earlier, I overheard the terrorist's plan and notified security. Believe me when I say, they have no intention of releasing us to safety."

"What is it you know?" asked the Asian man who had had the laptop computer.

"There's a bomb on board. They plan to detonate in Denver."

As expected, there were cries and shouts. It took Hunt and Dana nearly two minutes to calm the crowd again to the point where they could speak. "Please," urged Dana. "Please refrain from drawing attention to this compartment."

"Listen," said Hunt. "The authorities have been contacted. That's why there was a roadblock back there. But, we're on the move again, which means something's gone sideways. Now, Dana and I have the experience to deal with this, but we need you to keep quiet so the terrorists don't suspect anything. This needs to be the car they check the least. Got that? Spread out. Take our seats. Chances are we won't be missed."

There was a general murmur of consensus. The young mother asked what Hunt and Dana planned to do. "We'd rather keep that to ourselves," said Dana. "The less each of you knows, the safer it is for all of us."

"We're already pretty deep," said the balding man.

"Then let's not make matters any worse," said Hunt. He then turned and addressed the Asian man who'd had the laptop. "What's your name?"

"Topher. Topher Barnes."

"Okay, Toph. You were on your computer when the terrorist came in. It looked like you might have tried to send an email off—maybe some sort of S.O.S."

Topher shrugged, offering a twist of a grin. "I tried, but wasn't able to finish and send without being seen."

Hunt nodded. "Fair enough. Nice effort, though." Offering the guy a quick pat on the shoulder, Hunt turned to Dana. "We'd better have at it."

*****

Hunt and Dana made their way to the nearest sleeper car, and were going through one of the suites, which was essentially two bedrooms combined. Even so, space was tight. Fortunately, this was only three cars distant from the dining car, but still they'd been forced to explain themselves to frightened passengers in each car as they made their way through. These people were hostages. They were terrified and volatile. The more people that knew about the Huntington's efforts, the more likelihood that the terrorists would discover what they were attempting. But, it was very difficult to move about a train without being seen. So far, they'd been fortunate not to encounter any terrorists. If they did, their excuse would be that they needed to use the restroom.

Another interesting—but not surprising—element was that they'd seen no American Cry staff since the onset of hostilities. Hunt hoped this simply meant the employees had been captured, and not that they'd been executed. Hunt felt for them. These were just people trying to do their jobs. They had nothing to do with whatever misguided cause drove these lunatics.

Dana slid an open piece of luggage to the side. "I've found nothing in any of these bags. How about you?"

"A pretty cool video game and a negligee you would just rock in." He paused, sifting through a small travel bag, but finding nothing. "Why don't we split up? I'll take this side of the aisle, you take the opposite. This is taking too long."

"Agreed," nodded Dana. "Be careful."

"Yeah, you too."

Hunt gave Dana a quick peck and then moved into the narrow corridor and turned right toward the next sleeper compartment. The terrorists had obviously searched each of the rooms as evidenced by the unlocked doors and luggage strewn about the diminutive rooms. If neither Hunt nor Dana found a phone or computer within the next five minutes, they'd move on to plan B. Whatever that was.

Glancing back to make sure Dana wasn't watching, Hunt slipped a hand into his pocket, withdrawing two Oxycontin pills, popping them dry. The migraine hadn't surfaced, but he felt the need. Just in case. No use risking one hitting at such a time.

Excuses.

Nothing but excuses.

He'd always considered addicts to be weak and morally bankrupt individuals. There was no excuse. These people got themselves hooked. They should have known better. Their faults entirely. Now he found himself traveling that same road. Frightening.

But, not frightening enough.

Not yet. Not so much as to cause him to seek help—or to even tell Dana. He was strong. He could handle this.

For now, he needed to remain focused.

The next room over was a standard bedroom and had a small bench-like seat which converted into a bed. As well, as a second bed which folded down hung against the wall. Somehow, they'd even managed to squeeze in a shower. As with the previous rooms, clothing was tossed about. Hunt went immediately to the luggage, feeling along the fabric for something concealed in one of the small outer pockets and then repeated the process on the interior of the piece. He then moved to the bathroom area. Perhaps the terrorists had missed a phone lying on the sink rim or toilet seat. Nothing. In all, it took less than two minutes for Hunt to determine that this room had nothing of value.

Already Hunt's mind was sifting through options, attempting to determine his next course of action. If he found no means of contacting outside help he needed to either subdue the terrorists or, at the very least, stop the train in an unpopulated area. The second, he believed to be the easier of the two. Emergency breaks could be thrown. The problem was that the terrorist would respond negatively to such an action and he still didn't know how many fanatics were onboard. Likely no more than ten. If there were, he would have encountered sentries in at least every other car. As it was, he'd been through three cars without sighting a rebel.

Even so, should he successfully stop the train, the terrorists would likely kill passengers in retaliation. Hunt had dealt with hostage situations in the past; he knew what must be done, but he and Dana were unarmed and facing an unknown number of combatants presumably spread over the length of the train.

Hunt moved to exit the cabin and nearly walked directly into Kelvin Donnelley. "Huntington!" smiled the thief. Donnelley stood roughly six foot one to Hunt's five-nine. "Rifling through passenger luggage—heh?" asked Donnelley in his rapid-fire speak. "And here you were so self-righteous. Demanding that I return. That diamond. Hypocrite!"

Donnelley chuckled and stared down into Hunt's face, his gaunt features contorted with a curious grin. Hunt now realized that two armed men stood just beyond the doorway. Obviously, they were with Donnelley. Hunt recognized neither, and so added these to the total number of terrorists he'd seen. "Hanging out with the terrorists, Kelvin? What's your connection to all of this?"

Donnelley twisted his head as if trying to readjust his neck and then licked his lower lip. His eyes were bloodshot but vicious. Twitching and constantly shifting, he seemed nearly bursting with pent up energy. "Terrorists? Nah. No. I prefer the term, patriot. Like Jefferson. Madison. Washington. Ushering in a new era. Freedom for a land gone astray."

What a bunch of bunk!

"You're a common thief, Kelvin. A thief and a thug."

"Thief! Yes. But, ah, more." Donnelley sniffed and then cracked his neck again with a quick cock to the left.

Hunt took a step closer. Donnelley's guards tensed, but didn't fire. "You really planning to detonate a bomb in Denver, Kelv? Hundreds could be killed."

Donnelley giggled. "A bomb? Yeah. That's right. A bomb. Let's say a bomb. Heh. Don't worry. You won't be there."

With that, Donnelley nodded and then stepped aside. Both gunmen raised their weapons. "Come with us," smiled Donnelley. "It's time you disembark." He paused to grin. "How fast we going? Forty? Fifty? Fast enough to split your skull. On impact. Heh! Don't worry. I'll take care of sweet little Dana. She'll experience. A real man. Who knows? She might even thank me."

Chapter 7

Paris France

Jonathan Thorpe exited the taxi, paid the driver, marched across the two lane road, and slipped into the narrow space between two red brick buildings. Emerging on the back sides of the shops, he turned right, angling across a cobblestone alleyway where he strolled into a small bakery. Having entered through the rear, he found himself in the kitchen. Apologizing profusely for his "mistake," he made his way across the cluttered space while quickly donning a beret he'd carried in his day bag, strolled through a swinging metal door and into the retail portion of the establishment where he immediately exited.

Here, he hailed another cab, giving the driver instructions for an address only two kilometers distant. The past hour had been a flurry of activity: his narrow escape from his Winchester residence, a short ride on the tube, a call to a pilot he'd kept on retainer for such situations, the airport, a quick stop at a locker in a rented hanger, and now evasive maneuvers in Paris. It was unlikely the client had tracked him—yet. But, another confrontation couldn't be far distant.

Thorpe continued to ponder the situation. Obviously, the mystery man had hacked into his computer, learning that Thorpe had been digging into his dealings. But that he'd responded by sending two thugs to eliminate him stunned Thorpe. He'd anticipated a forced meeting with the client, pointed questions, perhaps even threats. But, it perturbed him that lethal force had been ordered at the onset.

Who was this man and what was he hiding so zealously?

Well, Thorpe knew some of what was hidden. He'd been forced to participate in a certain acquisition as repayment for his release from prison. But even still, Thorpe only possessed a very small piece of the overall puzzle. His knowledge could be considered a threat, true. But in revealing what he knew he'd be implicating himself as well.

Thorpe knew that he must uncover the client's secrets and use them as leverage. Otherwise, his body would likely be found floating along the Thames, bloated and bruised.

Unacceptable.

The cab pulled to a stop.

The address was for a residential street. There were currently no other vehicles on the lane. A woman of perhaps sixty walked a well-trimmed poodle. Two lanky teenage boys stood talking beside a twenty year-old Peugeot. Thorpe paid the driver, tipping him well but not excessively. He didn't want to stand out in the man's mind.

Waiting until the cab had rounded the nearest corner, Thorpe crossed the street and proceeded up the lane. Two blocks later he turned right, strolled past six homes and then walked up the drive of the seventh where he rang the doorbell. The home was small, but well kept, the neighborhood in decline. A car passed by, and Thorpe glanced down and away. He'd not gotten a look at the driver, but couldn't risk making eye contact if the vehicle was in fact there for him. He hated this, living in paranoia, and would not allow it to continue. The client may have initiated this bloody battle, but Thorpe would bring it to an end.

Degare Laurent came to the door nearly two minutes later. Upon seeing Thorpe, Laurent said, *"Deranger,"* meaning trouble. And then waved Thorpe in, pointing toward the tiny living room adjacent the foyer. The room stank of stale tobacco, though the aroma of fresh baked bread danced about the nearby kitchenette. Thorpe seated himself on a cream-colored love seat dating from somewhere in the mid-seventies. His host settled into a stiff-looking wood-backed chair opposite him.

Thorpe was surprised at how little Laurent had changed since he'd seen him last some seven or eight years prior. He was older of course, easily into his seventies now. But he still had the posture of a career commandant. His brown eyes had faded some, but the perpetual glint had not strayed far. His white hair was thin and untamed, only wisps remaining, but his eyebrows remained midnight black and as bushy as a Saint Bernard's winter coat. His form was slighter than Thorpe remembered, and his clothes hung loose on his frame, though they were still neatly pressed and in immaculate condition.

"Vous avez nerf," said Laurent after a prolonged silence.

Thorpe smiled and shrugged. "Yes, well, I suppose you're correct. I have nerve. That, it seems, is one of my few failings. Though, some might consider it a strength."

"As always, the thief, he speaks out of both sides, eh?" said Laurent, now switching to English.

"You look well," said Thorpe. "Especially considering Claudette's passing."

Laurent scoffed. "*Betise*! That was three years. She was weak with grief. It was better for her this way. You and I, we are men. We go forward. Now, what is it, your need?"

"Need? Well, yes, I am, I suppose, in a bit of a situation."

"That much is a given. *Continuer*. Proceed."

"It seems I've run afoul of a rather powerful man."

"His name?" asked Laurent.

"Ah! You see, there lies the difficulty. The man is an apparition of sorts. He doesn't exist. Not, at least, as far as any traditional channels are concerned."

"And what have you done to anger this apparition?"

"By attempting to determine his identity, mostly. Likely, he fears I might uncover much more."

"Mmmm. And your connection to him?"

"He is… was, I suppose, a client. I procured certain items which he desired."

Laurent nodded and snorted. "This man Thorpe who comes to me, he thinks so highly of himself, but still he is just the thief." The Frenchman stroked his chin as if he wore a beard. "And so you steal things for this client you do not know. What things did you burgle?"

"Artifacts, paintings, a fossilized skull."

"Trinkets. This is all?"

Thorpe hesitated. "There was one other. Something I'm not at liberty to share."

Laurent nodded silent and long, his pale brown eyes intent on Thorpe as he contemplated the scenario. He wouldn't press, at least not yet. "You are in fear for your life?" he asked finally.

Thorpe nodded.

Laurent drummed his fingers on his right thigh. "If he has sent you into hiding, it is not because you seek his identity alone. He fears you may uncover a greater secret. And this fantastic *mystere*, this hush-hush, is why the man lives as a specter. Discover this and you will have the what? The leverage needed to remain a living person, eh?"

Thorpe stared at Laurent but did not speak. He'd come with a specific purpose in mind, but now, sitting face-to-face with the man after so many years, he wondered if he had the right to draw him into this tangled maze. Thorpe's involvement in his life had already cost him a daughter. What could motivate this man to help Thorpe in his time of need?

"*Vous pense trop.* You think too much," said Laurent. "You've come to ask me some *faveur.* Allow me to make the decision for myself."

Thorpe nodded, making direct eye contact with the wiry Frenchman. "The last time we saw one another, you were still well connected. You've now been retired from the *police judiciaire* for several years. Your channels, are they still open?"

Laurent pursed his lips. "Some persons that I trained or led, they are still active. But, why should I aid the thief?"

"For the same reason you aided me before. While, true, I tend to skirt the law, we both know that in the scheme of things, I do not harm the greater good. The baubles I procure from the disgustingly rich are well insured. Only egos are truly damaged. But this man, my client, I now have reason to believe might be a danger to society at large."

"Then why not bring your information to the police instead of to a retired *carcasse*?"

Thorpe grinned and shook his head. "You know the answer to that, Degare. I have a dubious relationship with law enforcement. As well, seeing as I've had dealings with this man, I would bloody well prefer not to be implicated further."

"But here you flee, you hide. All because you make inquiries, and now you ask me to do the same. Have I not already made enough of the sacrifice for you?"

Thorpe leaned forward, resting his elbows on his upper thighs. "If I could change what happened to Adeline, I would do so. You must know how dear she was to me. But, the past is beyond my control. It's only the present that I may influence. I come to you, not as a friend—I couldn't presume so much due to our history—but out of respect and honor."

"*Foutaise! L'homme parle foutaise.* You come to me because you are a frightened little *chien*. At least have the decency to be honest in your speech."

"No," said Thorpe, this time with a tight edge to his voice. "This is not rubbish and I am not a dog. I may not be entirely innocent in this enterprise, and I will admit, the man has placed me in peril. Are my motives selfish? Bloody hell, yes. But, there is a greater good here. And on that you will simply need to trust me."

"This I do not do, to trust you. Convince me otherwise if you believe it can be done."

Thorpe's jaw went tight, his eyes became slits. "I recently spent several months in Diyarbaki prison. I believe this man to have been instrumental in my imprisonment. He also arraigned for my release, but on the condition that I perform a certain task. This was something in which even I would not normally have dealings."

"You've alluded to this thing once before, what is it?"

"No, no, no. You see, I'm not prepared to implicate myself further. This much you will take on faith, that the man is dangerous, and not only to me. Now, are you willing to perform one more deed for the greater good, or have I wasted my time?"

Laurent chuckled. "The greater good. When have you ever cared for the greater good?"

Thorpe leaned further forward, his gaze intense, his chocolate eyes narrow and unrelenting. "Will you help me?"

Laurent did not answer right away, but seemed to contemplate for long moments before finally nodding and saying, *"Oui. Je vais vous aider."*

"Brilliant!" smiled Thorpe, who now fished in his pocket, withdrawing a computer memory stick and handing it to the Frenchman. "Everything you should need is here: photographs of the man, of his properties, along with addresses, a brief history of some of his dealings. How long will it take you?"

Laurent shrugged. "I do not know. Give me a day at least."

"Best make it quick," said Thorpe as he rose to leave. "I'd prefer to have the information in time to prevent my untimely demise."

"And I should contact you how?"

Thorpe handed Laurent a folded page. "I've created a new email account. False name, utilizing a public computer only. It should be safe for at least one information transfer."

With that, Thorpe marched across the room, down a narrow hallway, through a tiny kitchen, and out through a rear exit into a narrow stone alleyway.

Chapter 8

Somewhere in Colorado

It was hidden in a man's shoe and obviously overlooked by the terrorists: a smart phone, a Droid, the latest model by the look of it, plenty of memory, internal GPS, digital compass, Wi-Fi, camera and video capabilities. The thing might have proved quite handy if Donnelly hadn't entered the small cabin just then.

"Hello, Dana," he said as he leaned against the door frame, his wavy brown hair slightly disheveled, his gaunt face rather tense as if in deep concentration. He was a tall man, not unattractive for his age, but rather peculiar both in appearance and bearing. "You'll want to hand me the phone." Donnelley ran a finger twice across his nostrils then stepped forward extending his hand as if expecting Dana to hand him the device.

Dana shook her head. "So sorry, Kelvin. But, I need to contact authorities concerning the terrorists. Hunt was telling the truth about that bit."

"Really, Dana. That guy? Your husband? A face like his? He must bring home a hell of a paycheck. Caught a hottie like you."

Hottie? Donnelley was referring to her as a hottie? "Yes, he is indeed my husband, and no, the paycheck has nothing to do with it." Donnelley had a peculiar look in his Kelly green eyes. Dana recognized it as lust. "Now," she added. "I must locate my husband in order to coordinate our efforts with the authorities."

Donnelley grinned and chuckled. "That easy? A terrorist cell. Don't you think, heh? They might be more difficult to defeat than that?"

"It's a beginning. Now, if you'll please excuse me."

Dana moved to step around the man, but he adjusted to block her way. It was a small space. There wasn't much room to maneuver. "Nah, nah, nah," quipped Donnelly in his rapid-fire speech. "You started something earlier. Got me all excited. Left me wanting. Not good. Time to pony up, heh? Show some integrity. Give me what you promised. I guarantee you'll enjoy it."

"I promised you nothing, Kelvin. You can't really still believe that anything might happen."

Donnelley offered his quirky grin. "Oh, it will happen. Seems to me, I'm in complete control. Of the situation."

He stepped forward, reaching out as if to put his hand on her breast.

"You bleeding plonker!" shouted Dana as her knee came up into his groin, followed seamlessly by a quick chop with her right hand to the back of his neck. Dana was already to the doorway as Donnelley hit the floor. The bloody beast had actually intended to force himself upon her.

Turning left, Dana meant to locate Hunt, but there was an armed terrorist making his way in her direction. Shifting to the right she saw that a second armed man guarded that door. The only positive aspect of this situation was that neither was likely to fire for fear of hitting the other. The man on the left was both closer and slighter of build. Dana made a quick decision and charged this man, catching him entirely off guard.

The corridor space was extremely tight, making it difficult for Dana to utilize her hand-to-hand combat skills and so she dove at him, striking mid belly with her right shoulder. The terrorist folded at the waist and the two tumbled to the floor. Somehow, the gun did not discharge, but the terrorist, a young man of no more than twenty-five years-old, would not release the weapon.

Dana had only seconds before the next man intervened and so grabbed the gun with both hands, and though the terrorist retained his grip, slammed the butt against his face three times in rapid succession. Just as it seemed his grip might loosen, Dana received a brutal kick to the stomach. Fortunately, it was partially deflected by her elbow and so she retained her hold on the weapon. A quick glace told her who she now faced.

Donnelley.

Why was he assaulting her instead of the terrorists?

Dana jerked the weapon free of the terrorist's grip, the momentum of the pull causing the barrel to jab upward striking Donnelley mid-gut. The second armed man had since approached, but the space was so confined as to prevent him from interfering.

Donnelly stumbled back, connecting with this man as Dana jabbed the first terrorist in the throat, then attempted to thrust him in the direction of the two other men. But, he was too heavy, her angle awkward, allowing her no true leverage. Instead of ramming the others, the young man folded over, his upper body flopping onto Dana. Somewhere in the maneuver the assault rifle fell free of her grip and tumbled out of reach.

There was a sharp tug at the back of her head as Donnelley grabbed a fist full of her hair, pulling her to her feet. She had no choice but to comply, coming upright in quick stuttering steps. Still, she whirled around, intending to strike him in the face, but again the restrictive confines made the maneuver difficult and Dana struck the bulkhead rather than the man.

He slapped her hard across the face, causing brilliant colors to dance before her eyes.

Another slap and then another. He wasn't giving her the opportunity to reorient. Despite her athleticism and training, the man still doubled her in weight. A prolonged struggle would surely end in his favor. Still, Dana attempted to strike her aggressor.

Now, the first terrorist was on his feet, grabbing her from behind.

"Pull her into this cabin," ordered Donnelley, as he yanked on her hair, directing her to the compartment where she'd found the phone.

He was giving orders to the terrorists. He was one of them.

Donnelley slapped her again, hard, causing her vision to go momentarily black. He threw her harshly on the narrow bed. "Whore!" he screamed. "Filthy lying whore! I'll give you what you want, heh. What a filthy whore always wants."

To Dana's horror, Donnelley began undoing his belt. She was still disoriented from the several blows to the head. Her movements were slow, unsure. My God, he intended to rape her! He truly intended to rape her.

"Boss, we don't have time for this." It was one of the terrorists, the one who had come from the right. He was a middle aged man, Caucasian, an apprehensive expression on his unshaven face.

"Won't take long," said Donnelley. "Hold her down, heh? Little Asian whore. Won't take long."

Despite her near vertigo, Dana was already scrambling from Donnelley's reach, flaying right and left, looking for something to use as a weapon or some miraculous way to squeeze past the three men who crowded the tiny box-like cabin.

"Mr. Donnelley, really, we have a schedule to keep. We don't have time for…"

"Hold her down!" Donnelley twitched, whisking his finger across the base of his nose, his eyes wide, nearly crazed.

Both terrorists squeezed past Donnelley, descending on Dana, grappling with her, pushing her down into the mattress. She kicked the older man in the upper thigh with little effect. She'd been aiming for the groin, but everyone was in motion, it was difficult to be precise about anything. There was a large handbag perhaps two meters distant, maybe it was heavy enough to use as a weapon, or perhaps there was something usable within. Still, pinned as she was, two meters might as well have been two kilometers.

Dana landed a half dozen solid blows, but in the end, the two pinned her down in such a way as to allow Donnelley access to her. The younger terrorist seemed jumpy, agitated as he pressed Dana's right arm and thigh firmly against the mattress. Constantly licking his lips, glancing one direction and then the other, he looked excited, maybe even eager to see the main attraction. The older man refused to meet her gaze, perhaps reluctant to be party to the assault, yet he held her firm and relentless just the same.

As the initial plan had called for Dana to appear seductive, she still wore a short black and red skirt worthy of the Las Vegas nightclub scene. Now, she regretted that choice more than she could have ever imagined, for Donnelley was able to pull her panties off with only three sharp tugs. She pressed her legs tightly together, but Donnelley jerked them apart with such ferocity as to rip a muscle in her left thigh. A gasp of pain escaped her lips, but already, she determined this would be the only sound of weakness. She would not weep and beg.

"Don't fight him," whispered the middle aged terrorist as Donnelley smacked her twice in the face, hard and merciless, and then lowered himself onto her. Still the man refused to look her in the eyes. "Just get through it," he added. "Just get through it."

Dana spit in his face.

Donnelley laughed as he entered her, giggling like a schoolgirl as he struck her again and yet again before settling into his rhythm.

Now, he was supporting himself with his arms on either side of her. Dana twisted her head hard right. Bit into his left wrist. Yanking the arm free, he smacked her across the face with his right fist. And then again and again. Donnelley giggled and cursed, pressed and pulled, struggling to accomplish his deed. The minutes dragged on. He persisted, his face red with anger and joy. Dana struggled with consciousness as he twitched and grunted, striking her from time to time, causing her vision to blur and blood to seep from her lips. She tried desperately to take herself somewhere else, even if only in the mind, somewhere far away and distant from here. But the reality was too horrid to flee, too constant, too immediate.

*****

After the rape, Dana was bound and then escorted to one of the baggage cars. Apparently the terrorists had disposed of any luggage that had been stored here because the car was simply an empty space with sheet metal walls and ceiling. The train's crew was present. Dana assumed this was all of them, thirteen employees in total, but she really didn't know what the full compliment should be. Each was bound and seated upon the cold metal deck. Some wept, a couple talked, others sat in the cold isolation of their own thoughts. As Dana entered, each turned to look at the battered women in the ripped and barely concealing red and black club skirt. It was clear to all present what had oc-curred. One woman shrieked at the sight of her. "Oh my God. They're raping the passengers. Oh my God!"

Dana closed her eyes, attempting to force the images of the past half hour from her mind. She could not dwell on personal tragedy, not now, not with a bomb onboard. There would be time for that later—a lifetime of time, she supposed. Did anyone ever really recover from something like this? She imagined not. Some piece of this day, of this event, would travel with her every moment of every remaining day.

But, in order for there to be remaining days, she must survive this one. And that meant preventing the bomb's detonation. Could she even think of that now? Could she even care? Was it worth it, continuing to live? Perhaps it would be better to allow the terrorists their gambit, to simply huddle against the cold unforgiving wall with these frightened strangers and let happen what would happen. Who could blame her? What more could be expected of her after what she'd been through? Surely, even Hunt would understand.

Hunt.

How could he ever get past this? Their relationship had already undergone an incredible strain when he'd learned she'd hidden her previous marriage to Jonathan Thorpe from him. They were only recently becoming the couple they had been before. Could their tenuous bond sustain another such blow? She honestly didn't know. Intellectually she knew that none of this was her fault, that Donnelley and his men were entirely to blame. But intellect and logic were only part of the equation. She had to live with the emotion and despair. And so would Hunt. He would, as well, know that Dana was the victim, that no blame rested on her. And he would say as much. She was certain that he'd do his very best to be loving and supportive. But, what would his heart say? Would he still be able to look at her has he had before? Would he still want to caress her, to touch her—to make love to her?

And if he did still desire her, could she let him come to her as a husband? Right now she couldn't imagine being touched by a man—even Hunt. Her skin seemed to creep from her bones at the very thought of physical contact. She became cold, goose bumps appearing across the landscape of her arms. A shiver traversed her spine. Should she even go on? Was there any reason to go forward? If she had to live with this burden for the remainder of her days, was that a life worth living?

Dana exhaled sharply, shook her head. None of these questions were for now. If she was to withdraw into her own private hell it would need to wait for another day, because if she didn't do something soon, she'd be denied the choice on how or even if to carry on from here.

"Donnelley," she said, though she could not meet the man's gaze.

"Yes? Wanting some more?"

Dana had to fight every urge to charge the disgusting pig. "No thank you. I'd prefer a real man next time, not some twitchy coke head."

Donnelley snorted and ran his finger across the base of his nose, narrowing his eyes.

Dana forced herself to appear confident and above all that had happened. "Do you really believe that you hide it so well? Dilated pupils, nervous energy, even muscle spasms. You're a long term user. And now I learn that you're a bloody terrorist and rapist as well. How do you get this motley crew to follow you?" A pause. "Do they know you have trouble keeping it up?"

Dana should have expected the blow, but she was still too shaken from her ordeal to think things through to their logical conclusions. The backhand caught her entirely off guard, connecting at the left cheek and causing her to stumble three feet back to against the shiny unforgiving wall. To her credit, she did not fall.

"My entertainments? Heh. My own concern. And for your information, we are not terrorists."

Attempting to steady the swaying room, she said, "Well then, what do you call it?"

"Patriotism. Something a whore would know nothing about."

Dana's eyesight was blurry. She'd taken too many blows to the head, endured too much in such a short interval of time. "Patriot? Bloody delusional. How could bombing this train be considered patriotic?"

Donnelley clucked his tongue and cocked his head, first to one side and then the other. "Bomb? Right. Your husband thought it was a bomb."

At this moment, the middle aged terrorist that had held Dana down during the rape moved to Donnelley, whispering in his ear.

"I will tell her what I damn well want to tell her!" shot Donnelley. "I'm in charge. Not you."

Moving quickly, Donnelley marched over to where Dana stood, stepping to within inches of her, his breath was stale with tobacco and Dana had to force herself not to retch. Just the proximity to this beast made her want to scream.

"It's not a bomb," he said in a hushed giggle. "No, no. Heh. So much better. The plague, my little whore. The bubonic plague." He grinned and then licked her on the cheek with an enthusiastic giggle. Dana tried to head butt him, but he danced away too quickly.

Bubonic plague? How had this lunatic put his hands on bubonic plague? Was he even telling the truth? How could she know?

"Denver, heh? Just the beginning," he added in his quick staccato speak. "Passengers on this train. Proceed to Chicago, Cleveland, Washington DC. A very big message."

The man was off his onion and there was nothing Dana could do about it. But more troubling still, he had said this in front of the train crew. With this knowledge any one of them could potentially forestall the spread of the pathogen. Donnelley might be nutters, but he wasn't stupid. He had no intention that these people would live long enough to reveal his true plan. As it was, they were probably only kept alive so long as they might be needed for any train-related issues, mechanical or otherwise.

"Oh, oh, oh," said Donnelley with a grand twitch of his lips. "Nearly forgot. This is interesting. Very interesting. Your husband. Mister GQ himself. Has disembarked the train."

Dana's stomach took yet another severe twist as she said, "But, the train hasn't stopped moving."

"Why no. It hasn't." Donnelley giggled and twitched.

Chapter 9

The Swiss Alps

Dr. Marion Dietz did not like to be rushed. Her work was unique, ground-breaking in every way. If she was to accomplish her goal, her name would forever rank among the medical and scientific greats such as Bernard, Virchow, Watson, and Koch. None could claim a greater accomplishment. And yet, her employer was pushing for a public display this very week. Fourteen workable applications already, field testing underway even this day, and yet still he desired a more visual, a more dramatic exhibition of her work. The man was not a scientist and seemed uninterested in her objections. His timetable had little to do with science, but was politically and personally motivated. What little science the man engaged was peppered with occultism and pagan mysticism. Dietz was not at all pleased with this dilution of proper protocol, but had been forced to endure the man's intrusions in order to proceed with the project. There, after all, would be no project without the test subjects this man had supplied. And in truth, she would never have breached this admittedly peculiar area of her discipline if not for the rare and unusual material supplied by her employer. She had little room to complain, and she grudgingly accepted this. There were worse ways to spend the waning years of one's professional life than making groundbreaking advances. Dietz finished logging a note on her computer, took a long sip of Barenjager Honey Liqueur and rose from her cluttered work station. Just a few sips to keep her warm inside, never enough to effect her performance in any way. It was time to check on her most productive subject.

Dietz glanced through the Plexiglas barrier before her. The subject was lying unconscious on a table in a small isolation room crammed with monitors and equipment. Her heavy eyelids were closed, but fluttering as if in some weird syncopation. By appearance she was a woman in her mid-thirties, African in heritage tinged with what appeared to be a smattering of Middle Eastern. She was rail thin, weighing only eighty-seven pounds and was skeletal in appearance. Her black hair was thin with several gaps where one could clearly see her flesh beneath. Her cheek bones were high, her lips full and broad. Her teeth were uneven with an unusual amount of decay for someone of her near youthful appearance, and the nails, both finger and toe, were unkempt, broken and yellowed. Dietz could sympathize with this. Her own nails were rather displeasing to the eye. She'd simply never had time for or interest in such extravagances as polish and manicures.

But, this woman was not truly youthful. Not even remotely so. At least, not according to all Dietz had learned. The subject's actual age was astonishing at the very least, and if not for scientific evidence supporting her employer's claims to the woman's history, she would not have believed it.

Before entering the room, Dietz donned a level A hazmat suit: extra-large view window with FEP face shield, butyl gloves and liners, double storm flap, and boot flaps. Despite her numerous years working with such equipment, the space suit, as she called it, was cumbersome and irritating. Of course, she understood the need. Archebacteria fusion 27A had the potential to be quite deadly.

Dietz completed her routine examination, checking the subject's vital signs, as well as the latest lab results. The woman was physically stable, but comatose. And truly, there was no need or desire for any of the subjects to ever wake. Sad. Truly sad. But necessary; as were so many sacrifices made for the advancement of knowledge. But, she should feel no remorse where these subjects were concerned. If not for the bacteria, all but one would have died long ago. It was the strain that vitalized their forms. Mindless, yes. Eternally immobile, true. But alive. And this was the miracle. Alive.

Moving to the corner of the small cube-like room, Dietz approached a video camera mounted on a tripod. Adjusting the aim and focus, she set the camera to record before stepping forward, turning toward the lens, and squaring her slightly rolled shoulders. She then stated her name, the date and time, and the subject's identification number. The subjects were all anonymous and so the woman was known only by this number. "I will be working with subject thirty-seven for the second time this week," said Dietz. "I've increased the saline drip in order to flush undesirable toxins from her system and thus create a more palpable environment for the incubation of archebacteria fusion 27A. As of this morning, gestation time has decreased by another thirteen percent from this subject's previous evaluation. My hope is for a similar reduction today."

Dietz then strolled from the view of the lens and once again to behind the camera, then zooming in on the subject.

The eyelids fluttered.

The left side of the face twitched.

These were not conscious motions, but reflexive in nature.

After some five minutes the chest heaved.

A subtle flutter of movement undulated beneath the skin.

Amazing, the tenacity of the microbes.

Dietz moved periodically to within the camera's view, checking vital signs, adjusting the drip, recording data. Her hands trembled with excitement. The implications of this project were astounding. She only hoped that she was up to the task, that nothing such as that which had occurred in New York would once again rob her of her success. "I've now increased the A.B. 27A drip," she said aloud as she twisted a valve which initiated the flow of pale violate liquid.

Dietz clasped her gloved hands together, desiring to pick at her nails, to pull free any jagged corner she might find as she observed the process from behind the camera. She hated the gloves, the suit, the prison-like quality of the shiny protective folds. Necessary. All was necessary. A foul habit anyway, picking the nails like a nervous school child.

From this point forward things would move quickly.

Subject thirty-seven shuddered.

Facial tics scampered across her features.

Skin rippled.

A sharp intake of breath.

A gurgling sound from deep within the throat.

Leg spasms.

And then waiting. Always waiting.

Twenty-two minutes now, and finally the body shuddered.

The unconscious head jerked from side-to-side.

A thin trickle of blood escaped the right nostril. This was not unprecedented, but was a natural part of the process. Dietz grinned as the subject's tongue lulled from the right side of the mouth.

Fingers extended and then curled, repeating this movement, faster, faster.

The legs pulled upward as if in an attempt to meet the chest, but leather restraints prevented all but the slightest movement.

The head jerked up left, down right repeatedly in weird diagonal jolts. It amazed Dietz that the woman did not damage herself with such harsh movement. That would be such a shame. She hoped this would never occur. Somehow, Dietz knew that she would be the one to bear the fault for such a mishap.

The fingers extended, curled, extended and Dietz found that she was mimicking the action.

The body shuddered.

The knees bent, but only as far as the restraints would allow.

The fingers extended.

The head jerked.

The knees bent.

The body pitched and jerked.

Again, the desire to pick at her nails. Surely there was some scrap that demanded attention, some piece to twist and pull, to suck and chew.

No. There was nothing to fear here. This was simply a test subject, comatose, safely strapped into place. Dietz silently chastised herself for her unease. It was terribly unprofessional.

Cautiously, Dietz stepped to the side of the camera allowing the subject to remain alone in the lenses view.

A particularly violent jerk.

The bed stuttered forward a full three feet.

Dietz forced herself to stand firm in her position, her right hand instinctively moving toward her mouth, where it was stopped by the plastic mask.

Again, the subject's violent thrusts caused the bed to move.

Dietz eyed the heart monitor. The rhythm was increasingly erratic. Under other circumstances she would discontinue the experiment, sedate the patient, and bring her into a normal sinus rhythm. But the circumstances were such that normal human compassion must be put aside. Science stipulated it, the thirst for knowledge and achievement demanded it. This was all usable data.

Another lurch. Dietz felt a subtle tremor in her limbs. She'd never believed her employer's explanation as to the nature of the bacteria withdrawn from the ancient fossil; this could not be as the man believed. And her science had proven as much. She took comfort in this fact. All of this could be explained scientifically. She'd analyzed the material, grown cultures, catalogued it, modified it to fit a specific need. Knowledge, logic, learning, discipline, these had granted this opportunity, this success, not mysticism or the occult. But now, right this moment, witnessing the scene before her, even a scientist could find cause to wonder.

Movement. Another violent jerk. Gagging. Retching.

There it was. Emerging from both nostrils and lips to be captured by the plastic receptacles strategically placed at the orifices, the precious mucus. Amazing how Dietz had been able to accelerate the growth—exponentially. The production of cells, of gestation, of reproduction.

Wonderful.

Terrifying.

Again, Dietz lifted her hands as if to pick at a nail.

"You seem agitated."

The voice coming through the speaker startled Dietz nearly causing her to jump. She turned to see the Collins woman, the master's sweet little attack dog. She was smiling through the Plexiglas, obviously pleased at the shocked look on Dietz' face. At roughly five foot four, Collins was much smaller than the somewhat gangly Dietz, but still the scientist was uncomfortable with the woman. She was scrappy, over confident, seemingly eager for confrontation.

"Yes," said Dietz after a moment's pause. "The subject's vital signs indicate that she is in a state of distress." Why did she feel she needed to explain herself to this woman? Dietz tired of the constant oversight from the ill-equipped.

"Joshua is curious," said Collins after a moment. "The twelve subjects, do you have them prepared for transport?"

The twelve subjects.

She still couldn't believe her employer hoped to demonstrate their success while the results were yet preliminary. "I've made preparations," said Dietz. "As I've told our employer, this is a delicate, experimental process. I've advised against a public spectacle."

Collins shook her head and smiled. "Honey, y'all can tell him anything you want to tell him. But, he's got his schedule and he intends to keep it. I suggest you check your priorities. Do you want to see this project through to its conclusion, or would you rather someone else take over and receive the credit?" The smaller, younger woman smiled, winked, and then turned, exiting the room without another word. Dietz decided that she truly hated Tina Collins.

Chapter 10

Somewhere in Colorado

After his capture, yet before Donnelley had located and attacked Dana, Hunt was dragged forcefully to the back of the train. One of the terrorists—there were four now and he hadn't seen which—had pistol whipped him with three sharp strikes to the temple, causing him to struggle against unconsciousness as multi-colored spots danced before his eyes.

Hunt was slow to respond. He was a better fighter than this and knew that if was on his game he could take these clowns. They weren't military. He wasn't even sure they were trained in any form of combat, hand-to-hand or otherwise. Their only advantage was in numbers and weapons. Hunt was disgusted with himself for allowing them to surprise him and tried to shake away the vague but persistent unevenness in his head.

He'd struggled as they dragged him through two sleepers, five cargo cars (one of which contained the train's crew, bound and subdued), and finally to the caboose which was decorated in red, white, and blue, and made to resemble a car from which Lincoln was rumored to have given speeches. There was no back door, but simply a small landing and a flag-draped railing. Hunt had elbowed the terrorist to his right smacked the back of his head against the one directly to the rear, and kneed one almost directly left. Still, it was evident that the sheer weight of their numbers alone would soon force him through the narrow opening and onto the metal and stone surface zipping furiously below them.

Options racing through his brain, Hunt determined that he might be forced to make the move himself, throwing himself from the train in such a way as to increase his chances of survival. He judged the train's speed at something under fifty miles per hour, perhaps as tame as forty. The terrain varied from sharp stony drop-offs, to coarse cracked asphalt, to grassy rolling plains. Hunt hoped he could hold out long enough for the next relatively forgiving surface to slip into view.

He twisted and crouched as the four men pressed upon him, maintaining a low center of gravity and causing one man to nearly slip past him to press against the metal rail that was the only barrier between them and the surface below. Hunt felt an additional surge of adrenaline. If he could force one or two of these men off the platform, his odds of survival increased exponentially.

Jabbing the man in the gut, he simultaneously took a hit to the left shoulder by another terrorist. He belted the first man again and then again, now pushing him against the barrier, tipping his torso at such an angle as to cause him to nearly tumble end over end. The terrorist's eyes went wide with fear and Hunt felt he just might get the guy over the edge and onto the rushing stone and metal below.

But Hunt was pummeled with several more blows: head, torso, even groin. The hatchway area was tight. The crowd of men densely clustered. He couldn't even distinguish which strike had come from whom. Hunt twisted, landing a fierce jab to the man pressed against his back. This was all the opening the endangered terrorist needed and he pounded his head into Hunt's upper chest and throat.

What minimal advantage he had found lost, Hunt winced at the increased barrage of hits and jabs. He was now pressed firmly against the barrier as the men attempted to spill him over and onto the harsh ground below. Wincing with pain, he caught a glimpse of green to one side. He had but a moment to make the decision. Retain some small fraction of control and perhaps survive to return and aid Dana, or tumble directly onto the unforgiving track and stone. Startling the thugs, he'd wrenched free with a violent tug, barreled into the nearest man, and flung himself and the screaming man over the railing. He was aiming for a grassy embankment hoping to avoid the sharp stones and cold hard metal of the track and its bed.

They hit once, the startled terrorist between Hunt and the ground. They bounced, hit again, and then, releasing the man, Hunt curled into a tight ball, arms cradling his head, knees pulled up to just below the chin, and rolled down the embankment, bouncing and thudding. There were some stones, and plenty of uneven ground. The embankment was perhaps twenty-five feet in length and he came to rest on a narrow dirt road adjacent what appeared to be an apple orchard. Every inch of his frame screamed in protest at the abuse, but Hunt couldn't allow himself the luxury of tending to his physical needs. Spitting dirt and blood from his lips, he scrambled back up the slope in a frantic half run half crawl, making his way to the terrorist.

The man was semiconscious, moaning and cursing under his breath. Hunt slapped him on the cheek. "Wake up," he commanded. "Talk to me, you lousy S.O.B." Hunt wanted to question him, to find out who these people were, what their true objective was, and hopefully learn something that could help the authorities to rescue the hostages and prevent detonation. More than anything he wanted to free Dana. Selfish, true, but human to the core. "Wake up!" shouted Hunt, slapping him again.

The man's eyes fluttered, he spit blood onto the grass beside him. He was probably five or six years younger than Hunt, somewhere around thirty. His hair was blond, eyes blue. There was a narrow gash on his right cheek and blood trickled down onto his bushy goatee. "You're one crazy mother," he said with a pained smile. "God, that hurts."

"Who are you people? What's your objective?" asked Hunt.

"Screw you!" shot the punk, his small mouth twisting in bitter defiance.

Hunt had no time or tolerance for macho bravado and slammed his fist into the side of the man's throat, just to the left of the Adam's apple. The terrorist screamed. "Talk to me or I'll make hell and damnation seem like a decent option." Hunt drew close, face meeting face, a harsh whisper spilling from his lips. "I'm former Delta Force. I know dozens of torture techniques that I'd just love to take for a spin. Care to test me?" Delta Force operatives were not trained in torture, but the punk didn't need to know this. To emphasize his point, Hunt grabbed a narrow twig from the grassy slope and slowly inserted it into the terrorist's ear. A sharp jab and the eardrum would puncture. Hunt didn't have the time or patience to utilize the sixteen interrogation techniques as outlined in Army doctrine or to follow protocol of any sort. This was a quick in and out situation. Get what information he could and then act with speed and diligence. He no longer represented the US military, protocol be damned.

"Alright, alright, alright," cried the guy. He was still too weak and disoriented from the spill to offer much resistance and continually arched his back in pain. The man had taken a couple of serious hits on the way down.

"Your name," barked Hunt.

The thug hesitated, grimacing with pain. Hunt was straddling him, his left arm pinning the guy's right arm and his hand holding the head in place. With his right hand, he pressed the stick just a bit further. "Will!" screamed the man. "My name's Will."

"Will what?"

Only a moment's hesitation this time. "Cooper. Will Cooper."

"Sounds almost as plain vanilla as John Smith. We'll get back to that later. Who do you work for?"

"Donnelley."

"That much I've figured out. What's the organization? What is it you hope to accomplish?"

"We're..." he hesitated only briefly. "Freedom fighters."

"Freedom fighters? You live in the freest country on the planet. What is this really about?"

"Freedom. Really. This country's all screwed up. You've seen it. They're bankrupting us, man. Bankrupting us and then grabbing power. It's like we're in a prison state."

Hunt shook his head at the idiocy. "If that's what this is about, you people are morons as well as psychopaths. Spend a few weeks in Afghanistan, Iraq, Libya, then we can talk about liberty." Using his left hand, Hunt pressed the man's head tighter against the ground, eliciting a subtle whimper. "What's the name of your group? Are you home grown or tied to a foreign entity?"

The terrorist hesitated. Hunt pressed the stick further into the ear and received a screaming shriek for his efforts. "Americans, man. Americans," blabbered the terrorist. "Get that thing out of my ear! Please, man. I'll tell you what I know."

"Name of your organization?" asked Hunt, withdrawing the stick only a hair.

"The RPA."

"RPA, what's that stand for?"

"Revolutionary Patriots of America."

"Never heard of it. Is Donnelley at the top of the pyramid, or is this just one cell in a larger group?" Hunt helped the man answer with subtle pressure to the eardrum.

"Ow! We're a cell. Just a cell. God, I hurt. I think you broke my back."

"If you're still feeling pain, your back's not broken. Who's in charge?"

"Don't know. It's secret, man. Really."

The man was regaining his strength. Hunt could feel him trying to move beneath him, and so he withdrew the stick, smacked him hard across the face with his right fist, and then reinserted the twig. "I need answers," shot Hunt.

"I know, I know. Donnelley's the highest guy I've met in the group. Honest. I don't know any names above him."

"How does he receive his orders?"

"Phone, I guess. I see him talking to someone on his phone."

"What is your mission? To bomb the train or the Denver train station? I heard talk of Denver."

A peculiar expression flitted across the terrorist's features, there and then gone. "Denver. Uh, we hit Denver."

"Give me a timetable."

The man actually smiled. "Why? What can you possibly do? We're both out of the game, man."

"Not entirely. I can contact authorities. Feed them intel."

Here, the man laughed before wincing with pain. "You go ahead with that. See how far it gets you."

Hunt's stomach took a dive. Something was terribly wrong here. "What are you getting at?"

"The authorities. They're not on your side. Not all of them at least. Why do you think that blockade was lifted so fast?"

Hunt had pondered this. There was no way that Homeland Security, the National Guard, the FBI, whichever organization had taken point on this, would allow the train to move on. Not at the risk of hundreds of more casualties should the train reach a major station and detonate. Hunt pressed the stick further into the ear. This all rang true, the explanation about the blockade, government involvement, even the terrorist's smug attitude when bragging about the group's clout.

"Which government entity has been compromised?" he hissed.

"Ow, ow, ow! Stop that!"

"Which branch?"

"All of them. All of them, man. The feds, the military. Ow! You may not have heard of us, but you will. This isn't the only operation in motion."

Maintaining the pressure on the eardrum, Hunt slid his left arm to where it rested across the man's windpipe. If half of this was true, the implications were terrifying. Multiple terrorist attacks set in motion, unknown targets, and the very entities that were designed to eliminate such threats compromised to the point where they were implicated in the events. Hunt didn't know where to begin. "What else do you know?" he asked. "Who else other than Donnelley can you give me?"

"Only the guys on the train," gasped the man. "My own cell. I don't know any others."

"What are the other targets?"

"Don't know. They wouldn't tell us in case one of us got caught, we couldn't spill."

That made sense. "Alright," said Hunt. "Here's what we're going to do. You're going to tell me where you meet, who first contacted you about the group, what your ultimate goal is. Names, dates, addresses, the works. After that we'll part ways. But if I in any way sense that you're holding out on me, you lose the hearing in one ear and then the other. Got that? I don't have time for games."

Hunt had no means of recording the interrogation, no paper and pen, no recording device, even his cell phone had been confiscated during the raid, and so he committed as much as possible to memory. Most of the information was nonspecific, a warehouse in east Detroit, a guy named Benjamin. But, these were at least the first pieces of the puzzle. With luck, this meager information would lead to more substantial intelligence.

Ultimately, Hunt used his ever present yo-yo and the terrorist's own belt to bind him, leaving him lying face down on the narrow dirt road adjacent the track with a large stone of perhaps sixty pounds resting on his back. The stone, he knew, would be toppled within minutes, but its purpose was simply to further delay the terrorist from gaining his freedom and contacting his higher ups. As well, Hunt confiscated the man's cell phone. He'd have the call memory and address book thoroughly investigated. With any luck, it could lead the authorities to the people at the center of this thing.

But, which authorities? Who could be trusted? Local police, most likely, but they wouldn't have the resources or authority to operate beyond their jurisdiction and as soon as they moved up the chain it was likely one of the compromised entities would take notice.

*****

Hunt made his way along the train track figuring it would eventually meet with civilization. The terrorist's phone had been deactivated, likely as soon as Hunt had pulled him from the train. This group was fast-acting and effective. They tolerated no loose ends.

He was alone with his worst possible companion—himself—and his mind flitted from one uninviting topic to another: Dana's deception in hiding her previous marriage, his growing dependence on Oxycontin, the events in Iraq. He'd tabled this issue—Iraq—at least as far as any active pursuit, though Dana regularly nettled him about it, wanting him to pursue the information given to them by Jonathan Thorpe, information which might exonerate Hunt of any wrongdoing. He wasn't entirely sure why he hadn't yet acted on this intel. He intended to, or so he told himself. But, there was another, deeper, side of him which was comfortable letting it lie. He supposed that if he was to be honest with himself he'd admit that he was afraid of what he might find. Thorpe—of all people—had given him reason for hope. Perhaps he hadn't been at fault, perhaps that child he'd killed really had been the suicide bomber and not an innocent. Perhaps he'd really had no other options.

Due to the bomb blast, his memory failed him on this account. But, Thorpe's information granted Hunt the opportunity to once again live with himself. He didn't want to do anything to destroy that fragile balance. If he pursued this new information, if he sought to clear his name, what if he found that it was nothing but a cruel joke? What if he learned that he really had acted irresponsibly and cost his men and that child their lives?

Someday he would need to face that possibility.

Someday.

Not today.

Hunt had walked about two miles when he saw the crop duster. It first appeared as a bright yellow spot in the clear blue sky, trailed by a string of white/gray which spread out, descending upon the orchard below. Initially, Hunt didn't think much of it, but as he continued forward, simply following the railroad track, hoping to eventually meet up with some form of civilization, he noted that not only was the duster remaining in his vicinity, but it was low enough that the pilot just might see him if he made a spectacle of himself.

He ran along the track waving his arms, shouting, though he knew there was no way the pilot could possibly hear him. In a moment of inspiration, he lifted the terrorist's cell phone toward the sun with hopes that it would glint and draw the man's attention. It took nearly ten minutes, but eventually the plan worked and the pilot brought the plane down in a narrow field only a few hundred yards from Hunt's position.

The man was heavier than most pilots Hunt had known, with a belly large enough to be used as a serving tray and a rump that served as its own sofa cushion. He was unshaved and rather odiferous, but Hunt was ecstatic to see the man. There was already a plan forming in Hunt's mind—a rather extreme plan, but one none-the-less. If he was to believe what he'd been told by the terrorist, he couldn't trust anyone with even minimal information, and so, at least for the time being, was forced to act alone. Perhaps this plane could put him back in the game.

"I hope you've got a real disaster going on for all the running around, screaming you're doing," said the pilot as he approached Hunt, who had sprinted to the landing sight and was now severely winded. "Its gonna be a pregnant bear getting my Thrush up and outta here without clipping a tree or two in the process."

"Yeah. Emergency. You could say that," huffed Hunt. "Listen, I need you to fly me somewhere and fast."

The man shook his head slowly. His gray beard nearly glimmering in the midday sun. "This here isn't a charter plane, Mister…"

"Huntington. Marc Huntington. You can call me Hunt. Listen, you see those train tracks over there? I was just thrown from a train by terrorists who have a bomb onboard. I need to get back onto that train."

The pilot screwed his face. "Um, Mr. Hunt, sir, if there's a bomb on there, don't you think it might be better to stay off the train?"

Hunt stepped forward, invading the older man's space. "Here's the deal. My wife's on that train and there's no way in hell I'm leaving her to deal with this alone. I'm former Delta Force, skilled in hostage situations. Those radicals have compromised government agencies. I can't take this through traditional channels."

The pilot contemplated this for a moment and then nodded. "Then I guess you'd better tell me what you're thinking. Cause it sounds to me like time's a factor." Extending his hand to shake, he added, "William Roberts. Unfortunately, due in part to my Alabama twang, some take that as cause to call me Billy Bob. People I like call me Robbie."

"Well, Robbie, let's check out this plane of yours."

Chapter 11

Dana watched as Donnelley paced the room, pausing at the bulkheads, deciding whether to turn left or right, pivoting mid stride, as he spoke into his phone. She could only hear one side of the conversation, but the man was clearly agitated. His face twitched, he continually whisked his index finger across the base of his nose. As always, his speech was quick and short, even more so now. The terrorist was obviously talking with his superior.

"Yes... I understand... No. We kept the woman. Former British intelligence. Hostage. The man. Delta Force. He's been eliminated."

Dana wasn't sure how Donnelley had learned of their backgrounds, most likely from frightened passengers.

"No," continued Donnelley. "Bio-weapon. The passengers know nothing... Yes. Just after I disembark... No. It was the Huntington man that alerted security. They called the authorities... No, we have been careful... Huntington thought it was a bomb. The passengers know nothing. They'll be released. Each carrying the plague, heh? It will spread... Yes. Long live America."

Donnelley disconnected, shoving the phone into his right jacket pocket. He wiped his nose, clucked his tongue, and marched to where Dana sat against the cold metal wall, kicking her harshly in the side. "Whore! You and your husband have caused me..." Here, he trailed off, apparently not quite sure what the Huntingtons had caused him. Again, he shouted, "Whore!" before turning aside.

Pain shot through Dana's torso. She was still reeling from the events of the past hour, but tried to pull her mind into focus. The man was agitated just now, having obviously been dressed down by his superior. It looked like he was in need of a hit, his addiction muddying his judgment. If Dana nettled him just so, she might gain useful information. But, could she do it? Could she converse with this man? Look him in the eye? Pretend that she didn't want to rip his balls off and feed them to a pack of ravenous wolves? God, she just wanted to sleep, to welcome simple oblivion for even an hour. She needed to escape the memories, the humiliation, the sense of helplessness. The rape, though an hour past, seemed to continue for as long as she was in this man's presence. That horrid,

horrid monster. She shivered. Not from cold, but from fear. He could do it again. He could do it right now, right here, in front of all of these witnesses and there wasn't a bloody thing she could do about it.

Stop!

She had to keep her wits about her. The lives of hundreds could rest in her next actions. Hunt was either dead or gone. He would not be here to help. And that was a situation that she in no way had allowed herself to accept or contemplate. One thing at a time. She had no real information on Hunt. A pitch from the train was not necessarily fatal. Hunt knew to drop and roll. The man jumped out of planes; surely he could handle a toss from a moving vehicle. No. Deal with Hunt another time. Do not grieve. He was likely alive. Perhaps injured, but alive.

Her thoughts went back to Donnelly. He was a beast. She'd see him gutted by the time this was through, but for the moment her task was to keep her emotions in check and learn all she could. As much as her every fiber screamed in protest, she needed to dialogue with the man, coax information from him. She swallowed, blinked, attempted to focus just above and to the left of his head, granting the appearance that she was meeting his gaze, but avoiding it none-the-less. "Your boss didn't sound too pleased with your performance," she said with as much calm as she could muster, though still, there was a quiver to her tone. "Too bad that."

"What you talking about, whore?"

"Hunt got word to the authorities. Your superior blames you."

God, she wanted to rip his eyes out.

Donnelley turned to face her, tilted his head at a peculiar angle and said, "Your husband was mistaken. Incorrect information." He cocked his head sharply to the left eliciting a loud crack. "The police will look for a bomb. There is no bomb. The bio-toxin canister—not obvious. Eventually find it. So what, heh? The passengers will be gone. The plague spread."

"Right. Long live America," she said mimicking his closing salutation to his boss.

"Whore! What do you know?"

Anger was rising within her. Dana struggled to maintain composure. "I know that a raping coke head scum spreading a deadly disease across the country will not cure any ills."

Donnelley whirled, strode to her, and slapped her before kneeling to speak face-to-face. "Little whore! You have no right." He twitched, giggled. "The United States will not suffer. Too much. There's an antidote. It will be distributed."

"Boss, we can't talk about that." It was another of the terrorists, an older man, perhaps sixty years old or better. Olive skin. Salt and pepper hair. "You know the drill."

"Shut your wop mouth, Billy." He paused. "Shouldn't you be with the mechanism?"

"Everything's set, boss. I'm just sayin'..."

"I know. What you're saying. Not your job to say it, heh? Let me deal with my little whore. She's ready. To give me candy."

Dana's entire body shuddered. Not again. Please, not again. She didn't know if she could take another rape. She couldn't!

The man named Billy stepped forward, his posture erect, his tone firm. "The mechanism's in place. You'll want to look at it. You know, give it your seal of approval before we proceed."

Donnelley clucked his tongue. "Billy, Billy, you want her yourself. Don't you? I don't blame you. She is a hottie. Tell you what. After I'm done with her, she's yours. My gift to you." Donnelley giggled.

The terrorist named Billy shook his head. "Nah, Boss. I just want you to look at the set up. That's it. Just doin' my job."

Donnelley nodded, twitched, and then punched Dana hard in the stomach: once, twice. She tumbled sideways, curled into a fetal position. He grabbed her already torn top, ripping it free with two sharp tugs, exposing her breasts. "Be back for you, little whore. Be back."

He rose, following the terrorist Billy from the car, a crooked grin on his gaunt face.

Tears erupted. Dana simply could hold them back no longer. Her body racked with sobs. He planned to do it again. He was going to do it. She knew he was going to do it. And then he was going to pass her around to all of his filthy friends. There was nothing she could do to stop them. Not a thing. She was bound, unable to use her limbs, unable to utilize her training and experience. Donnelley would have his thugs hold her down again. Despite her training, despite all that she'd learned and done. This one half-crazed drug addict could have his way with her and there was nothing she could do to prevent him. She'd never felt so small, so helpless, not even as a child. It was as if he'd robbed her of all that she was, of who she had been, that she was no longer herself, but rather, his plaything only.

There was a voice. Beside her. At first she started, nearly screaming. But then it registered that this was a female voice. One of the imprisoned crew. A fellow captive. Another woman. She opened her eyes, forced herself to look. It was a young woman, in her twenties: blond, freckled, with tortoiseshell glasses. Linda, she believed her name to be. They'd spoken some while the terrorists had been otherwise occupied.

"I'm sorry," she said. Linda had a raspy voice, as if she might be struggling with a cold. "Are you alright?"

Dana hesitated and then nodded. "Bloody bastard's a brut. But he hasn't broken anything."

All of the captives were bound both hands and feet, and so Linda was not able to move to help Dana as she struggled to right herself again to a sitting position. In truth, Dana wondered why she even bothered. She was fully exposed in front, and with her hands bound behind her back, she could do nothing to cover herself. A fresh wave of shame flushed her face and she considered curling back into a fetal position and letting events take their natural course. But, no. If Dana succumbed to her depression, Donnelley would win. And that was simply unacceptable. Dana glared harshly at one of the male hostages that seemed to be fixated on her breasts. Embarrassed, he averted his gaze. "We've got to get free," whispered Dana, hoping to keep the conversation between she and Linda for now. "I'm unsure of how much further till Denver, but I know we must be free by then."

"You mean because of the plague?" asked Linda, following Dana's cue and keeping her voice to a whisper. "Do you think they actually have real bubonic plague?"

Dana nodded. "There are militarized strains. They've never been used beyond a laboratory, but they exist." Dana decided to refrain from expressing her belief that, due to their knowledge of the plague, Donnelley likely planned to kill everyone in this car before fleeing the train. He simply couldn't risk word of the plague reaching authorities before it had spread. Especially, since it was he that had spilled the information.

"How would these freaks get their hands on something like that?" asked Linda. She was obviously terrified, looking not only for information but comfort from a fellow human being.

Dana shook her head. "I don't have enough information to speculate."

Linda nodded. She was young, scared. Somehow, despite what had happened to Dana, the young woman was looking to her for encouragement.

"Listen, the worst thing we can do his panic. Also, don't make eye contact with Donnelley. He's volatile; you don't want to draw his attention. Let me deal with the bloody puke. He's already focused on me." She paused, and then addressed the room with as much confidence and authority as she could muster. "Listen to me. Our window of opportunity is narrow. Start working on your binds. They're only bleeding duct tape. Someone must be clever enough to slip free. All we need is for one person to get loose and then help the rest of us. Hurry now. We don't know when they'll return."

Dana wasn't sure that she believed any of this, but at least it gave them hope. And who could say? Maybe someone would gain freedom in time to affect the outcome. She doubted it, but where there was life there was hope. At least, she used to believe that.

Chapter 12

The Swiss Alps

He sat in his grand octagon-shaped bedroom. There were no windows. Any guest to the room might wonder why, in this magnificent setting, high in the alps, amidst nature's wonders, someone would desire bedchambers devoid of a view. But any first time visitor would have other, more troubling, questions as well. Most people found the dozen or so glass tanks containing various reptiles off-putting. As well, the three flat screen televisions puzzled most, each continually featuring classic situation comedies, the combined sound creating a tangled cacophony of laughter, japes, and dialogue. The absence of lamps often caused wonder, all light originating from either the previously-mentioned television sets or from the blazing circular fire place at the center of the room. Though, the photographs and artwork depicting dead and mutilated bodies likely caused the most trepidation.

He understood this. Depictions of scenes from Auschwitz, Rwanda, Jamestown, in truth, he was sometimes disturbed by these same images. That acknowledged, it was also the act of facing his unease, confronting that which terrified him, that made him strong.

There was something on his feet. Movement. A coral snake, perhaps four feet in length, slipping across his naked flesh. Bending, he reached down, gripping the writhing creature just below the head, he brought it up to stare eye-to-eye. It was a beauty really, thick alternating bands of black, rust, and white, its black eyes empty as eternity, its form undulating in his grasp. Kissing it lightly atop the head, he gently dropped the snake to the hard wooden floor and then moved across the room, in the process, glancing at one of the screens. Golden Girls. Hmph. A gaggle of randy biddies. He supposed that might have been humorous in another time. Another screen featured M-A-S-H. Simplistic moralization decrying the evils of war. Nonsense. Ah! The third screen featured Seinfeld. He enjoyed locating the Superman logo sure to appear in each episode.

Seating himself, on the floor beneath the Golden Girls screen, back against the wall, he stared across the space to the naked form lying on his circular bed. The woman was about thirty years of age, long dark hair streaked with blue dye, three red rose tattoos on her abdomen. There was a thin, barely discernable line of blood on each cheek. She was lithe, perky, dull. "I... have no use... for you," he said after several uninspired moments. "P...lease leave."

The woman appeared frightened of him, her eyes wide, her movements a series of quick jerks and darts as she gathered her garments and slipped silently across the room and through the doorway. He supposed she hadn't enjoyed sharing the bed with his beautiful reptilian companions.

Not surprising, really.

He grew tired of his sporadic bedmates. Perhaps it was time to settle contentedly into solitude rather than continuing to seek fulfillment through other human beings. Apparently, that aspect of life was eternally elusive to him.

So be it.

Affection. Love. Companionship. These were the follies of lesser men. No wonder he found them so alien, so disconcerting.

So evasive.

Reaching to a teak end table perhaps four feet distant, he clasped a tumbler filled with buttermilk and brought it to his lips.

Tart. Thick. Viscous.

The events were now underway. The beginnings of them at least. So many years in preparation. A lifetime really. And in truth, lifetimes before his lifetime. No. Not for this specific series of events, but for the cause, for the destiny.

He brought his tongue out, nearly touching the base of his nose and then slowly, he slid it around to the left, and then down, and then right along his lower lip. Slow. Deliberate. Sensuous. Every remnant of his creamy treat savored. The buttermilk. He loved it so.

He pondered his own contemplation.

He had strived for this moment, for this time, these events. He had given body and soul, and then soul again. He was committed—fully. Every fiber of his being dedicated to the cause.

Another sip.

He whisked a meandering strand of light red hair from his pronounced brow.

It was true. What he had been taught to believe.

He knew it must be true.

He'd dedicated everything to this goal, to this purpose.

The woman's infectious words. "What does one do when he comes to the culmination of a dream and finds that dream wanting?"

What does one do when a belief held so dearly, a conviction that has infected every breath of life turns to vapor?

It wasn't that he no longer believed in his goal, his destiny, his heritage. It was that he no longer knew if he believed in these. And by questioning his foundation, wasn't that the same as abandoning it?

No.

Not yet at least.

If nothing else, the sheer momentum of his entire life would send him crashing through those next few days.

And then the weeks, and the months, and the years beyond.

Perhaps.

But, what if that momentum waned. What if the fissures in his foundation became visible?

How would his brother respond? And not only his brother. So many others. All dependent on him. All looking to him for leadership, guidance, and strength. He had been groomed for this time—literally bread for this purpose. How could he now doubt the validity of his life's experience?

A long gulp of buttermilk. He allowed it to languish on his tongue before slipping down his throat like a weary serpent to its cave.

There was a knock on the tall oaken door.

He smiled at the interruption. It was likely best that his contemplations conclude. Nothing of value could come from such thoughts.

"You… may enter," he said, not bothering to rise.

The door opened and a woman strolled in: light of skin, mid-forties, auburn hair spilling over broad shoulders. Katrina.

"Oh!" she stopped mid step. "Sir, I'm sorry. I didn't realize you were…"

"Naked?" he offered.

"Yes. Excuse me. I'll come back after you've had a chance to dress."

"No... need," he said. "H...have you never seen a... naked man?"

"Well, yes, but..."

"Then you... are seeing nothing that is... new. What is it that you n...need?"

Katrina regained her composure almost immediately, squaring her shoulders, meeting his gaze with her piercing green eyes. She was strong, this one. Reliable. Full of resolve and vigor. Dedicated to all he had set in motion. Hers was a belief in all he professed.

What does one do when he comes to the culmination of a dream and finds that dream wanting?

He proceeds as if never there was a doubt. Too much had been invested, too many people were dependent on that dream's fulfillment for a trivial thing such as uncertainty to cause this man to falter.

"The event," said Katrina. "The U.S. event. There have been complications."

Nodding, he rose, unfolding his lean, athletic form, ignoring her discomfort at his undress. "What level of complication? Is it critical or... less s...so?"

"Passengers somehow learned of the threat and contacted authorities."

"And... our contacts within the... infrastructure? Were they able to contain the s...situation?"

"So they say, yes. I've been informed that everything is now proceeding as planned."

He nodded and then sipped off the remainder of his buttermilk. She was rather pretty actually. A bit severe perhaps, but otherwise comely. Strange how he'd never noticed. "Then... why are we h...having this conversation?" he asked, his expression neutral.

Katrina appeared flustered. Good. That was as it should be. She was dedicated, loyal, but no one in her position should be allowed to feel at ease. That could breed pride and self-assurance. And while he meant the woman no ill will, it was paramount that separation be maintained. Lonely. His was a lonely life. But necessary.

"Well," she stammered. "I, um, thought you would want to know."

He simply stared at her for several moments before handing his empty tumbler to her. She was near to the top of the organization, at least nearly as close as someone not of the blood could rise. But again, she must never forget her place. Hierarchy was so very important. "Thorpe," he said at last. "Any w…word on Thorpe?"

She waited a moment, perhaps gathering her thoughts, or maybe determining how best to state that the issue was not yet resolved. "That is in process," she said, her voice even and unemotional. "I have assurances that the matter will be resolved shortly."

"What of Bedford?"

"Exactly as she has been. We are confident at that end."

"Collins?"

"In transit."

"Very… well," he said, offering the barest hint of a grin. "You may leave."

She nodded and turned to go. As she reached the doorway he called to her. "Katrina."

"Yes," she said, turning to face him.

"Your… dress today. V…very n…nice."

Chapter 13

Colorado

The Rockwell S2R Thrush Commander was not a large plane, though unlike many crop dusters, it did have space for one passenger. Nor was it a biplane, but rather the wings were situated low toward the base of the fuselage. A forty-four foot wing span, single prop, she was a solid vehicle. The two side hatches open, wind raced across Hunt's face and the Pratt & Whitney engine hummed steadily as he scanned the track below for the fleeing train.

Hunt still wasn't sure about his plan. At the very best it was foolhardy, at worst lethal and ridiculous. Robbie seemed a decent enough pilot. He'd flown in Vietnam. Any combat experience, even decades gone, was a plus, Hunt supposed. Military background. The man got it. But still, the maneuver was tricky and Robbie's capabilities untested. That said, the move wasn't entirely unprecedented. Hunt's Delta unit had practiced parachute landings on moving targets such as trucks and trains. But that was a much more controlled approach. The better chutes could get a guy to within a square foot of his intended target. This jump would be much less precise.

But Hunt didn't have time for other—safer—options. They were less than an hour outside of Denver and Hunt had to be on that train as soon as humanly possible.

He saw it now. Not far ahead. A long silver snake making its way northbound, at its head, an old fashioned steam engine. Hunt knew that the thing wasn't truly powered by steam, but was rather made to give the classic appearance while a modern engine propelled it. The train was a showboat on the exterior as well as the interior. "There it is, Robbie!" said Hunt, pointing ahead and to the left. "How close do you think you can get? Above it I mean, so I can hop out of the plane and onto the top."

"Your wife, she don't mind being a widow too much does she?"

"Yeah, yeah, I know. I've been watching too many Indiana Jones movies."

"I was thinking Mission Impossible, but yeah, you got the point."

"You have any better ideas?"

"Yes, sir, I do. Go to the next train station. Buy a ticket. Walk through the door."

If only it could be that simple.

"Nice idea, Robbie. But that train's going to blow through every station till Denver. And by then it'll be too late. As much as I hate the idea, I've got to board while she's still moving."

"And again, we can't bring the authorities into this, why?"

"They're compromised. Maybe not every agency, but I don't know who I can trust. A blockade was already lifted due to this breach. That took some major pull and likely an extensive cover up. I can't risk a repeat. If I contact the wrong people, this thing could go far south. We're just too close to the target to get another shot."

Robbie nodded. "I didn't do nothing quite this dicey back in 'Nam, but since then I've done some stunt flying, county fairs, that kind of thing. I'll get down to within about three feet of your train. But the wind whipping through those mountains, that's pretty unpredictable, and even if I match the speed, that means you hopping out with the wind racing by at fifty MPH. Even a three foot drop, you could take a nasty tumble."

Hunt stared straight ahead, focusing on the train. "That'll have to do. I don't see that I have another viable option."

And with that, Robbie nodded, scratched his stubble, and then banked left, swooping down in pursuit of the fleeing train. The Thrush had a top speed of two hundred miles per hour and so caught up with the locomotive in just over a minute.

Climbing out onto the wing proved perilous enough. The wind buffeted Hunt, nearly knocking him free as he clung tightly to the door frame. The plane lurched with a particularly brutal gust of wind and Hunt was nearly flung off. If one of those hit while he was jumping he'd likely wind up under the train. There really was no good angle for the jump. It wasn't like he was on a bi-plane where he could grab onto the struts from the upper wing. Ideally, he'd move more to the back of the wing before leaping, but that would mean letting go of the door frame, and once that was released, Hunt would be blown right off of the tenuous platform. No, what he'd need to do would be to leap from his current position, further forward on the wing than he liked. This would cause his inertia to be more horizontal than vertical. Instead of hopping directly down onto the train from a mere three feet above, he'd be leaping past the wing and then down onto the metal surface below, likely tumbling into a roll.

He couldn't afford to roll.

Whatever he did, he would need to maintain a stable position upon impact. Too much momentum and it would be all over. But this was for Dana. In no known universe could he take the safe route and allow her to be killed or badly injured. She'd been captured once before, in Brazil, and though he'd maintained a professional detachment, the concern had nearly ripped his heart out. Not again. Never again.

They were just about into position now, just a little lower. "That's it, Robbie," hollered Hunt. "Just a little bit more."

Another gust of wind, nearly throwing Hunt off to the right.

"You okay, Mr. Hunt?" shouted the pilot.

"Yeah. Those gusts are killing me though. Wish I had something to deflect the wind."

The pilot hollered something in response but it was lost in the rush of air.

They were there now. Robbie nodded, giving Hunt a thumbs up signal. The Thrush wobbled slightly side to side against the barrage of wind surges, but the man was a competent pilot. He was doing Hunt right.

Hunt crouched, surveying the surface below him. He knew from experience that he needed to be prepared, but also that unnecessary delays increased rather than decreased anxiety. Better to just take the plunge.

A quick breath.

One last nod to Robbie.

And Hunt leapt.

He hit the surface feet down, his momentum carrying him into three running steps, but the end of the car was only a few feet distant. Hunt tried to slow himself, but nearly lost his balance. Rather than tumble off the side, he dove forward, sliding on his belly.

The maneuver almost worked but inertia was not in a friendly mood and Hunt tumbled off the end of the car.

*****

Donnelley returned to the car, pacing and glaring, raking his hands through his hair and chuckling softly. Dana fought to restrain the shudders that erupted about her form, but only managed to minimize the quiver. The beast was accompanied by a young man, mid-twenties, average height, rather wiry, but not insubstantial. This man had a nasty looking Kalashnikov assault rifle slung over his shoulder and carried a metal case about the size of a shoebox in his right hand. He seemed nervous as the dozen or so sets of eyes followed his every movement. This now made seven terrorists that Dana had seen since the onset of the situation.

"You can't do this," shouted one of the captives, a middle-aged man named Benny. He was a conductor, recently separated from his wife of over twenty years. Dana had had the opportunity to acquaint herself with many of these people during the past hour and found that she liked the man's easy going personality and charmingly off-center sense of humor. Benny was stationed in Denver and was set to meet with his estranged wife for dinner this evening with hopes of reconciliation. He'd seemed more nervous about the marital encounter than at his current status as a hostage.

Donnelley ignored him.

"You can't do this!" shouted Benny a second time. "We're American citizens."

"Meaning what?" shot Donnelley. "You're an American. That make you special? It should. It should. But, there are no patriots any more. Well, there are. But they die. Most of you just sit. In your recliners. Vote the most charming candidate into office. Serves you right. What you're getting. Serves you right. Today you get to really serve your country. Anyone here proud of that? Heh?"

No one responded. Donnelley's wide-eyed stare held them in check.

Donnelley whisked a finger across the base of his nose and marched to where Benny leaned against the shiny metal wall. "You up to the task, black boy? Want to be a patriot? Die for your country?"

"Mister, I just want to get home to my wife. I don't want anything to do with your racist crap or your phony cause. I just want to see my Dessie."

"Dessie? That's her name? Dessie?"

Benny nodded. "Yeah. Desiree. She goes by Dessie." Now that it was out, the conductor seemed regretful that he'd spoken her name aloud, like he'd somehow soiled or endangered her.

Donnelley clucked his tongue and marched a tight circle around the center of the car. The younger terrorist stood off to the side, clutching his metal box and staring intently at his boss. "Dessie, Dessie, Dessie," said Donnelley. "She your whore? Good little piece of dark meat, heh? Wanna share? When we get to Denver. Wanna share?"

Cursing, Benny scrambled in a futile attempt to stand, but the restraints made him clumsy. Donnelley simply put his foot on the man's forehead, giving a hard shove, and the enraged conductor tumbled back against the cold silvery wall. There were other shouts of protest, but Donnelley ignored these with a subtle giggle and cluck. "Nick! Nicky, Nick, Nick, Nick," he said, turning to the young terrorist. "Please turn our dark skinned friend into a true patriot, heh?"

The terrorist named Nick stared wide eyed at Donnelley.

"The gun, Nick. Use your gun."

Still, Nick hesitated.

Donnelley stepped forward and snatched the metal case from his hand. "Show these people. What it means to be a patriot, heh? Now, Nicky. Do it now."

Nick took a tentative step forward.

Benny scooted back, cowering against the wall.

"No, Nick!" shouted Dana.

"Whore!" shot Donnelley. "Stay out of this!"

"Nick, you don't need to listen to this bleeding fool. Don't you see, he's gone crackers!"

Others joined the protest as Donnelley kicked Dana in the side, causing her to stumble sideways. Blinding pain from her abdomen.

"Are you a patriot, Nick? Heh? Are you?"

There were shouts and screams from about the room, but Dana was curled in pain, eyes squinted, knees against her chest. She heard but did not see.

The gun burst was defining.

The screeches and squeals of horror that followed even more so.

"Bloody bastard," groaned Dana.

"No, my parentage, little whore, is quite legitimate. Yours I would question, though."

Dana sucked in air. "Maybe you're legit. But, do your parents know you're a murdering rapist pig?" She knew she should goad him no further. She was in no position to defend herself; he could quite possibly harm her further, kill her, or worse, rape her again, but she couldn't stop. She needed to feel some small level of control in her life, needed to steal some of that power back from Donnelley.

The terrorist clucked his tongue. "Cute. The whore has spunk."

Dana was still writhing on the deck. The hostages were screaming and crying. Nick, the newly christened murderer, was shouting for everyone to shut up. There were tears in his voice. He was near panic. It seemed the lad was just now learning what it really meant to be a terrorist.

There was a metallic clink followed by several clatters. Donnelley had opened the metal case and was fishing around for something.

"Ah, ah, ah," he said. "Here it is, here it is. Heh." There was a shuffle of movement and Dana felt a sharp tug on her hair as Donnelley pulled her back into a sitting position. He held a small plastic inhaler in front of her, of the type an asthmatic might use. "This," he said. "This, heh, well, I think you know. Don't you?"

"Plague," said Dana, her voice barely audible.

"Mmmmm. Yeah. That's the stuff. Pretty potent too. Concentrated. More so than the strain in the train's ventilation system. Plague, you see, was not originally an airborne pathogen. Got it from rats. Fleas. I wonder how soon the symptoms will occur."

"Don't..." said Dana, her voice barely a whisper.

"Oh, yes. My little whore. Wish we had time. For another round. Too bad."

Again, he pulled her hair, this time cocking her head back sharply. While his right hand held her in position, the left hand struggled to force the nozzle between her clenched teeth.

He sprayed.

She felt the liquid on her lips. He sprayed again. She could taste it. My God, she could taste it! Furiously, she spit. But as she did, he spritzed again, this time getting a significant amount of the mist into her mouth. Dana coughed and hacked as Donnelley let go and stepped back.

"Good, good. Heh. Anyone else? Hmm? Anyone?"

The room went suddenly quiet. All were worried about exposure.

"Huh! No one." There was a short pause, and then, "Nick, these people have all volunteered to be patriots. Would you assist them?" He turned, once again facing Dana. "But, leave the whore alive. She needs to suffer."

Donnelley moved toward the hatch. "Oh! And, Nick. Do you still have that knife? The one you carry in your pocket?"

"Um, yeah."

"Good, good. Cut out her tongue, heh? We can't have her telling tall tales. About us. Can we?"

With that, he opened the door and strolled through.

Even as the door closed, Nick slowly lowered his gun, inhaled sharply, bit his lower lip, and followed orders.

Chapter 14

The terrorist Nick stood staring in disbelief at what he'd just done. Dana recognized the onset of shock. She almost anticipated to the moment when he started to vomit. Television and movies, gory as they may be, don't prepare someone for the real thing. There's a separation with the media. These are not real people, not real situations. The blood is manufactured by Maybelline, the wounds made of latex. Not like this, dead eyes—real human eyes that blinked and darted only moments before—staring blankly ahead, bodies opened, organs revealed. And the stench of feces. Bowels often release upon violent death. The scene was horrific. Where moments before the car had been populated by over a dozen frightened souls—people with families, lovers, lives—now there was only the remains of what had been.

Nick stood quivering, vomit still clinging to the corners of his mouth. The Kalashnikov hung loosely in his grip. The terrorist had never looked so childlike as he did in that moment. His soft unlined face seemed never to have known the caress of a twin blade. His clear brown eyes were moist with suppressed tears. His arms quivered visibly. He seemed smaller now, less substantial, but infinitely more dangerous. Nick had crossed a line from which there was no return. If not before, he was now totally invested in his cause. It would be the only way he could live with himself, to hold to the lie that what he had done was worthwhile and noble, that despite all logic, he was one of the good guys.

Dana fought to suppress her own shudder. Bound, half naked, beaten, and raped, she could do nothing but stare blankly at the carnage before her.

Nick shuddered once and then again. Finally, he wiped the puke from his lips with a violent swipe of his sleeve. Turning as if to leave, he seemed almost surprised to see Dana hunched against the wall. He paused, nodded, and then began to dig in his pocket. He was searching for his knife.

Dana's stomach leaped and twisted.

"Nick," she said as calmly as she could manage. "That was very difficult for you. That much was obvious." She had to relate to him on a human level if she was to prevent him from maiming her. "Best you sit for a moment, steady yourself."

There was a weak moan from somewhere at the far end of the car. Someone else was alive in here. Barely, it seemed, but alive at least.

Nick ignored the sound and seemed to study Dana.

"There's something I need to do," he said.

"I know what you've been told to do," said Dana. "That doesn't mean it's what you need to do."

He stared at her, focusing on her exposed breasts. How she wished her hands were unbound so that she could cross her arms before her. Strange. Bloodied corpses all about, the threat of an impending attack, and she thought of modesty. Humans were a bloody peculiar lot.

"What I've been told to do is what I need to do," he said in a lifeless monotone. Dana got the impression that he was trying to convince himself as well as her.

There was another moan from across the car. Weaker this time.

"Look around the room, Nick. You've already proven yourself. You've killed for the cause. You've made your contribution."

The terrorist shook his head like a little boy. He did not look at what he'd done.

"Nick, think about it. What's to gain by maiming me? I'm already infected. I'm going to die." She prayed this wasn't so, that somehow the aerosol plague had been defective or that her body had been strong enough to fight it off.

"Donnelley said for me to do it," said Nick. Dana thought she might see a tear at the corner of the young man's eye.

"Nick, I understand, you're fighting for a cause. You're obviously committed. You've already done more than anyone should expect of you. But, think about Donnelley. Is he as committed as you? Does he really represent what you stand for? He raped me, Nick. Brutally raped me. Is that patriotism? Is that why you're here risking your life, so your drug addict boss can rape defenseless women?"

Nick did not respond.

"Donnelley was talking to a superior on his mobile earlier. Do you really believe that person would be happy with Donnelley's performance? He allowed security to learn of your plot. A blockade was put in place. How troublesome it must have been to persuade the authorities to let the train pass? The risk of exposure must have been incredible."

There was another moan. This time Dana could identify the voice as female. She wanted deeply to check on the woman, to offer aid, but knew that she could not break this moment.

"Nick, I'm going to die. Allow me to do so as a whole person. For God sake, look at what he's already done to me."

Nick looked down, perhaps ashamed at what had been done, perhaps steeling himself for what was to come. "I've got to."

"Why? Why must you? Do you truly believe Donnelley's going to come back in here to check your work? Do you think he's man enough to look at the carnage? I believe not. You were told to carry out his plan because he doesn't have the belly to do it himself."

"You'll tell everyone about the plague."

"Of course I will. But it will be too late. The authorities believe there's a bomb aboard. As soon as this train reaches Denver, they'll evacuate the passengers. That means the last place they'll get to will be baggage compartments. By the time I can open my mush, the virus will have already spread."

The knife was now in Nick's trembling hand, the three inch blade extended.

"Blimey, Nick, you know I'm right. Think, lad. Think."

The terrorist took a tentative step forward.

Dana tensed. He was going to do it. No matter what his brain told him, he was too frightened to disobey his boss. My God, he was going to cut her tongue out.

"Nick!" shot Dana. "You know I'm infected. I swear to God, if you come close to me I'll spit a gob right in your mug and you'll be as infected as I am. Don't you dare doubt me on that."

He hesitated.

"I'll spray your eyes, your mouth, and to boot, I'll bite your bleeding fingers off if you try to stick that blade in my mouth. I'm a bloody rabid Rottweiler, I am."

"You won't tell anyone?"

"Like I said, by the time they get to me it will be too late for warnings to do any good." Dana prayed this wasn't true, that even if some passengers had disembarked, that they'd still be detained for questioning thus limiting the spread until she could get word to someone with the clout to hold them.

"Donnelley will kill me." He sounded like a little boy.

Dana shrugged. "Perhaps, if he finds out. But I will infect you. That is a guarantee. If you come much closer, you will die young, and horribly. It may not be today. But it will be soon. Militarized viruses are designed to act quite quickly."

The young terrorist fiddled with the knife, made to step forward, hesitated.

"There's no shame, Nick. Only on Donnelley. He's the one that's off his onion. Look about this place. You've done your bit."

"But, if he comes back in here…"

"I'll tell him I tried to bite you, that there was no way I'd let you within knife range."

Nick nearly swallowed his lower lip as he contemplated her words. Slowly, he turned to leave, and then, just as Dana began to believe that she had actually talked him out of it, he turned and marched purposely toward her, giving her only a moment to react. Instinctively, Dana twisted to her right and rolled into his shins with all the force she could muster.

He wobbled.

She flipped about, and raked her legs around to his lower claves causing him to fall awkwardly to the deck.

Still, the knife was in hand.

Bound as she was, there was no opportunity for subtlety. Shuffling quickly, Dana head butted the startled terrorist, once, twice. The pain was great. So much so that she thought she might lose consciousness before Nick. Still, she butted him one last time. The terrorist fell backward with a half muttered curse. Dana scrambled over him positioning herself so that her belly covered his mouth and nose, blocking his air supply.

Nick's frantic arm came up, the knife still clutched in his grasp. Dana did not hesitate, but bit him hard in the forearm. The blade fell free, landing on the rubberized surface with a dull clatter.

Nick shuddered beneath her, squirming hysterically to gain breath.

Dana bit again.

A muffled shout from beneath.

Nick's left arm came from behind Dana, snatching her hair and jerking her head back.

But the terrorist's angle was wrong. He caused pain, yes, but couldn't manage the leverage to pull her away.

His right arm, now free of Dana's jaws, flitted about the floor, blindly searching for the fallen blade. Dana could see the knife. It was a good arm's length beyond his reach.

He yanked again causing Dana to emit a tiny squeak of pain. Still, she refused to scream, not willing to relinquish control. She may have been victimized, but she would not live as a victim. Never.

She pressed harder against him. Harder.

Near suffocated, Nick's grip was loosening now, his stifled screams of protest all but gone.

Another thirty seconds and his arms fell limp, his body shuddered and then stopped writhing. Dana remained put, pressing, pressing. There was no movement below, but still she remained. All of the anger, all of the hatred and humiliation of the day consumed her. Never. Never would she be put in this position again. These vile terrorists would pay, every bleeding one of them. They would suffer, they would die, they would rot.

Finally, she rolled off of the unmoving form, arms still bound behind her back, legs strapped together at the ankles. Glancing to Nick, she saw that his chest still rose and fell. Dana didn't know what to think of this. A part of her wanted to finish what she'd started. Suffocate the scoundrel. But, no. Not yet at least. The man deserved to die, true. The carnage about the car attested to that. But he was incapacitated and she was still bound. Better to free herself. Likely,

Nick would not be unconscious long. Whatever move she was to make would need to be executed with haste.

Scooting across the hard rubber surface like an inch worm, Dana made her way to the fallen knife.

Three inch serrated blade, mother of pearl handle. Dana turned her back to the thing, and searched for it with her fingers. Her arms were bound at the wrists with duct tape. The material was far too strong to pull apart by strength alone, but if she could get the blade in hand, it wouldn't take much effort to cut through.

Scooting about backwards, clutching with bound wrists, it seemed an eternity before she finally located the knife, blade end first. It was amazingly sharp and only a whisk of a touch left her right index finger bleeding. Cursing, she fumbled about, finally gaining a grip on the handle.

She glanced at the fallen terrorist. He remained unconscious, his breathing steady. The moaning from the far end of the car had ceased with an eerie finality.

Carefully, Dana attempted to turn the knife so that she could cut the duct tape, but her positioning was awkward. The knife clattered to the floor.

The terrorist moaned.

Dana scrambled for the blade.

In her haste she tumbled sideways.

Again, she snatched a glance at the terrorist. He coughed.

Dana righted herself.

There. She'd found the blade.

Carefully, carefully, she turned it.

Bloody hell! She'd cut her back.

Nick moaned again.

Now, the blade was positioned. She drew it forward, back, forward, back. It was difficult to tell if she was making any progress.

The terrorist's eyes fluttered, but did not open.

Frantically, she sawed at the stubborn gray tape.

Another cough from Nick.

She could feel some of the fabric tear. But not enough. She was still bound.

Nick's eyes fluttered again. He mumbled something.

Dana yanked at the tape, attempting to rip the remaining strands free, but she'd not yet cut through enough of it.

Nick rolled onto his side. He was staring at her.

Dana clutched the blade, sawing back and forth. Several times she stabbed her own back.

Nick cursed her as he heaved a deep breath.

Dana continued battling her restraint.

Nick moved unsteadily into a sitting position.

Just a little more. Dana could feel the final strands of the fabric giving way.

Nick raised the Kalashnikov, pointing it at Dana, the barrel lulling from side to side.

There was no thought involved, only sheer survival instinct. The blade flew from Dana's newly-freed hand, sinking into Nick's upper chest. It didn't hit his heart, but rather the musculature to the right of his left shoulder. The still-dazed terrorist tumbled sideways with a loud scream, the automatic weapon slipping from his grasp as his right hand shot to where the blade now protruded from his flesh.

Dana's feet were still bound. She scrambled to the fallen rifle, grabbed it by the stock, and swung it with all her might, catching Nick in the jaw with the still-warm barrel.

He faltered, but did not fall. The bloodied knife was now in his hand. He was too close, within striking distance.

Dana pulled the trigger.

Chapter 15

Hunt grabbed, and clutched, and pulled, somehow finding enough hand and footholds to prevent soaring off of the racing locomotive. Eventually, he managed to reenter the train through a hatch atop one of the baggage cars and now cautiously entered a passenger compartment. He needed to learn what had happened since his departure, find Dana, and together make a plan. There was a general surge of chatter and questions tossed in his direction. Windblown, bruised, and dirtied, all eyes turned toward him as he moved up the narrow corridor.

"Hi ya, folks," he smiled in an attempt to dispel some of their anxiety. "Sorry to drop in unannounced. I know that's a social snafu. Anyone care to tell me what the terrorists have been up to?"

Quiet murmurs, but no response.

"Anyone at all? I won't tell the teacher—honest."

A young man stood up, average height, rather thin, unruly brown hair, jeans, T-shirt. He stepped forward with a bit of a limp, but was strangely serene considering the circumstances. A cocked head and a wry grin, he scrutinized Hunt. "You don't look like the cavalry. Who are you?"

"Marc Huntington. Just a passenger, but I'm former Delta Force. I'm experienced in hostage situations and have already taken these thugs on once and lived to tell about it. Can you give me a hand Mister...?" Hunt paused, awaiting a name.

"Joey McIver."

"Great, Joey McIver. What can you tell me?"

"Not much. We're pretty isolated here. One of them marches through every few minutes, always armed. I think they're mostly trying to intimidate us and make sure we behave."

"Every few minutes? Can you be more specific?"

"Eight to eleven minute gaps. I've been keeping an eye on that."

"How many minutes since the last walk through?"

"Six."

Hunt nodded. He only had another couple of minutes before the next terrorist arrived. "Is it always the same man?"

"No. I've identified three so far. They don't speak and I really don't see much commonality between them. You know, different ages, different clothing. No women, though. And all Caucasian. I guess that could mean something."

Interesting kid. Very observant. "You have a military background, Joey?"

The kid shrugged. "Short stint. I spent several months in a coma. Medical discharge."

"Sounds like a story I'd like to hear sometime. I've seen five terrorists so far, but have no way of knowing if your three were any of the ones I've already encountered. It'd be nice to know how many we're facing." Hunt scanned the room. Frightened faces, every one of them. At any moment one of these people could crack and cause a real problem. Hunt returned his attention to McIver. "Have they made any additional threats, let leak any information?"

"No. Like I said, these guys don't really say much of anything."

Hunt nodded. "Okay. Got it." He gazed at McIver, assessing him, and then spoke in a near whisper. "Listen, you seem to have it together, but I don't think it's a stretch to say that you're not physically up to taking on these guys."

McIver shrugged. Obviously still recovering from whatever trauma he'd experienced, he was in agreement.

"But, my take is that you have a level head. If I'm going to stop this thing from going down I've got to move quickly. Can you keep these people calm? A few of them look like they're ready to lose it."

McIver offered a crooked grin. "I've already been doing that. But some of them," he angled his head toward a middle-aged, heavyset woman three rows up. "Some of them are going to panic no matter what anyone does."

The kid was right. Hunt had already identified the woman—hyperventilating, flushed, wide-eyed—as a potential problem. "Understood. Just do what you can. But, for now, get back in your seat. We're almost to your eight minute mark."

McIver nodded and turned, making his way back to his seat. Hunt scanned the area. Four rows back there was an empty seat beside a woman, brunette, caramel highlights, hazel eyes—calm.

"Hi. I'm Marc. Can I slip into this seat?" Hunt always found that it put people at ease if he introduced himself. It helped to make a human connection.

"Christine Aisenberg. You like Kiss?" she asked noting Hunt's black concert T-shirt. "I'm more of a Springsteen gal. Throw in some Green Day and Pink."

"Small talk about favorite bands during a hostage crisis," smiled Hunt. "I like your style, Christine." He turned to her and spoke softly. "There's going to be a terrorist walking through here within the next three minutes. Can you keep your cool if I make a move?"

She studied him for a moment. "Do you really know what you're doing or are you playing cowboy with our lives?"

"Ninety percent one, ten the other. You okay with that?"

"It depends which one's the ninety percent."

Hunt smiled. It was amazing how cool some civilians could be during a crisis.

The forward door to the car opened. Hunt lowered his head, not wanting to draw attention to himself by making eye contact.

Almost before the terrorist had stepped into the car, the heavyset woman McIver had identified as a potential problem began to shout and point toward Hunt. "That man! He's not one of us! He just came in. That man! Don't blame us. It's that man! I had nothing to do with it."

Hunt was also amazed at how horrible some civilians could be during a crisis.

The terrorist was one Hunt recognized from earlier: mid-thirties, six foot, pudgy, but solid if Hunt remembered correctly. He held a Heckler & Koch semiautomatic assault rifle. Hunt only had seconds to make a plan of action. The terrorist was still too far up the aisle for him to engage as planned.

McIver intervened. "Aunt Judith, stop that." The young man was out of his seat now. "She's always saying something crazy."

The terrorist turned toward McIver giving Hunt his opening. "Excuse me, Mr. Terrorist," said Hunt as he marched up the way. "Any chance of getting a bottled water? I'm kinda parched from being tossed from the train."

The man turned toward Hunt a surprised look on his full rounded features, but the corridor was tight, and Hunt was prepared. He landed two solid blows to the terrorist's one, but in the scuffle the weapon discharged a round, the sound nearly deafening in the tight space. The car erupted in panic, people out of their seats, attempting to flee the tube-like space. Two more jabs to the thug. A twist, a flip. The terrorist tumbled across a seat occupied by a screeching mother and daughter. Hunt chopped him hard at the base of the neck and then jerked the man by his shirt collar, dropping the now unconscious form to the floor with a hollow thud. In less than five seconds the H & K was in Hunt's possession.

"Joey! Don't let anyone leave this car!" he shouted this to McIver. To the crowd he hollered, "This terrorist is down. Please. Do not panic. The situation is under control." It seemed a silly thing to say. They were already panicked. Glancing down the way, he saw that Christine Aisenberg had blocked the rear exit. Good for her. At least he had a couple of level-headed allies here. "Listen!" he shouted again. "You need to calm down. Depending on how close the other terrorists were to this car, they may or may not have heard the gunfire. If they walk in here and everyone's out of their seats they may open fire." He paused for a moment, allowing the concept to sink in. "Now, please, return to your seats." He gazed about at the stricken faces. Most were regaining composure. Several wept. One overweight gentleman nearly swooned but recovered with a disjointed stumble. "Okay. Good. Good. Now, was anyone shot?" This was Hunt's most pressing concern. He prayed that innocents weren't injured due to his actions.

There was a general murmur as the passengers looked from one to another. After a moment there was a voice from behind. "This lady here. She was hit."

The crowd became more agitated again. There were the first murmurs of returning panic. "Stay calm. Stay calm," said Hunt as he squeezed past the passengers to see what had happened. "Who was hit? How bad?"

"This woman here," said someone.

And Hunt saw her. Elderly, black, maybe seventy years old or better. And tiny. Frail even. Blood soaked her flowered blouse at the left shoulder. "I didn't want to cause a ruckus," she said in a tiny voice. "Seems you already had enough problems on your hands. But you tell that loud mouthed fool that I'll have some words for her. Shouting like that. She should be ashamed of herself."

Hunt smiled. The woman had spunk. "Hello, ma'am. I'm Marc. How badly are you injured?"

"It's just a flesh wound," she said. "And stop with that ma'am nonsense. You'd think I was old. Call me Mattie."

People never failed to amaze Hunt. They were never quite as predictable as one might expect. "May I see your wound?" he asked.

Mattie nodded and pulled her blouse back with obvious effort, revealing her shoulder. It appeared the bullet had entered just below the collar bone. There was no exit wound. The bleeding was bad, but not so much so as to indicate a severed vein or artery. "Okay, Mattie. You're going to have a heck of a sore shoulder for a while and a doctor will need to extract that bullet. But I think you're going to be fine. For the time being, we need to stop that bleeding."

"Well, I could have told you that much," said Mattie with a weak smile.

"Yeah, I'm sure you could have." Hunt turned to address the crowd. "Anyone here have any medical training?"

Christine Aisenberg stepped forward. He was actually surprised at how tiny she was now that he saw her standing, no more than five feet tall it seemed. "I'm not a medic, but I worked in a hospital during a Nor'easter. We had to evacuate to another facility due to flooding."

"Okay, Christine. Good to know. Find something to stop her bleeding, something to use as a compress. I need to get moving if I'm going to do us any good." Turning toward the front of the car, Hunt hollered. "Jocy, is the terrorist still unconscious?"

"He started to stir a little. I gave him a kick to the forehead. He's out."

"Good man. Use a couple of belts, maybe a necktie. Bound him. Stick a sock in his mouth. Maybe put a hat on his head so his buddies don't recognize him as easily. Set him in a seat. Try to make it look like he's sleeping. It's been a few minutes, no terrorist action. I don't think they heard the shots. But, if I'm going to make a difference, I need to get moving."

Chapter 16

The fallen terrorist's Heckler and Koch in hand, Hunt made his way through two more passenger cars and several sleepers unhindered. No terrorists were visible and this troubled him. Where were they? What were they up to? His fear was that the terrorists were assembling for the final push—the detonation of the bomb. He was torn between his need to locate Dana and the urgency of the impending bomb blast. By all logic the explosive device was paramount. With luck, he'd stumble across Dana along the way.

He found her in an empty baggage car amongst a scene of brutal carnage. Perhaps a dozen bodies, all clad in American Cry uniforms, were scattered about the perimeter of the space, each bound with duct tape, each bullet-riddled and bloody. Dana was wearing a man's bloodied uniform jacket over her top and binding an injured terrorist with a belt. The young thug had been shot in the right thigh and also had what appeared to be a knife wound in the upper chest.

Dana was bruised and bloodied, her face and lips swollen, her left eye black and puffy. There were abrasions and cuts. She'd taken quite a beating.

At the sound of Hunt's approach, Dana whirled, aiming the terrorist's Kalashnikov at his chest.

"Whoa, whoa, whoa. It's me, hon. Point that thing another direction."

For a moment it seemed she didn't recognize him. There was a dazed expression on her heavily bruised features. Dear God, what had these beasts done to her?

"Dana, it's me."

She seemed to come to herself then, nodding almost mechanically. "Hunt... Um, Donnelley claimed to have thrown you from the train." Her voice was small, barely audible. So unlike Dana.

"Yep," said Hunt. "True enough. Now I'm back." As he approached, she shrank away, as fearful as an abused mutt. "Honey, what did they do to you?"

She paused for a moment as if thinking. Her eyes were glassy and seemed unfocused.

"Honey?"

"Plague, Marc. I'm infected with the bleeding plague. Don't come so close."

"Plague?"

She nodded absently, still not entirely engaged in the conversation. "Bubonic plague."

Bubonic plague. Was that what this was about? Had they somehow gotten their hands on a strain of the stuff? And Dana, how was it that she'd become infected?

"Kelvin Donnelley's the leader," said Dana in a listless tone. "At least the leader of this cell. He answers to someone higher. It's not a bomb, Hunt. They're planning to release a militarized strain of the plague on this train just before it reaches Denver."

Hunt understood the strategy immediately. "And then the passengers disembark, at once spreading the pathogen about the country as they board connecting trains to other cities. Has it been released yet?"

Dana dazed at nothing. "I don't believe so."

"And you. How did you get infected?"

Her eyes averted his, instead landing on the hard rubber surface below. "Donnelley," she said quietly, as if the name itself was some foul and dangerous incantation. "He forced a dose on me through an inhaler. He…" And here she broke off, seemingly losing her train of thought.

Hunt took a step closer. She backed away. "Honey, what did he do to you? You've been beaten. Your clothes are torn."

"He… They… Beat me rather severely. That's all. They got the jump on me. Tight confines. No maneuverability. Just beat me. That's the sum of it."

"Aw, honey, I'm so sorry." Again, he tried to step closer, but she cowered.

"Hunt, the plague. I don't want to infect you. I…" She hesitated for a moment, apparently formulating her thoughts. "I… don't know the incubation period. But, clearly the plot is that the passengers spread the plague through contact with the public at large. That suggests this strain has been designed to infiltrate the system and become actively contagious within a very short span. They've engendered it as an airborne variety intended to be distributed through the ventilation system."

"You're injured," he said. "How badly? Is there anything broken? Are you able to move with me as we search for the devise?"

Another hesitation. "I… don't think I'd be much use. I'd… slow you down." She dazed off at the metal sky for several moments, her eyes unblinking, her mouth set in a firm line. "Go after Donnelley," she said at last. "Find the devise. Stop the train before Denver. I'll interrogate this bloke." She kicked the bound and injured terrorist at her feet. "If I learn anything of relevance, I'll locate you."

She was broken. Dana's ever-resilient spirit, her verve, the very core of who she was, this was damaged at some fundamental level. Hunt could see it in her downward gaze, sense it in her soft, hesitant speech. The exposure to the plague, he supposed could be the cause. Certainly she understood that without proper medical treatment this could prove fatal. But Hunt had no time to contemplate the issue, nor to minister to his wife, though, at his core, that was all he desired to do. This thing had just escalated to another level. Not only were the passengers on this train, or even those at the Denver station, endangered, but anyone who came in contact with any of them as well. If Hunt didn't do something now, this could lead to a major outbreak.

Finally, Hunt nodded. Dana was right. In her current state she would likely be more of a hindrance than a help. Hunt hated the thought of leaving her at such a time, but found no other option. "Will you be okay?" he asked.

Dana offered no words and no hint of a smile. Instead she simply raised the Kalashnikov as if to say that anyone who troubled her further would get more than they bargained for.

There was an awkward moment. Averted eyes. Unspoken words. Finally, Hunt turned to leave.

"Marc?"

"Yes?"

"Donnelley says there's an antidote. The plan is to spread the plague and then offer the cure. Most likely at some political price. The filthy pig calls himself a bleeding patriot."

"I'll find that antidote if it kills me," he said, his heart troubled in ways he could not yet identify.

*****

Hunt found the terrorists in a cluttered baggage car near the rear of the train. There were six of them now, situated toward the back. Hunt cracked the forward door to the car just slightly, hoping to eavesdrop on their conversation without risking entrance to the space. He was amazed that they didn't have a sentry at this entrance. Definitely no military discipline here. He wondered if there were any others, perhaps one in search of the missing man Hunt had felled soon after returning to the train. Straining to hear, Hunt managed to make out much of the conversation despite significant external noise as he crouched in the small and unsteady space between cars.

"Billy. Everything prepared?" asked Donnelley to one of the older men. Hunt could see about a third of the man's face and took him to be in his early sixties. Judging by his Jersey accent, Hunt believed him to be one of the original two he'd encountered in this same car earlier this morning.

"Yeah. The devise is linked to your remote. Just press the button."

"And our travel arrangements?"

"We're ready to disembark," said another, younger, voice. "The Blackhawk awaits your signal."

Blackhawk? How did this group of misfits get their hands on a Blackhawk helicopter? Whoever their government contact was, he certainly had some clout: calling off a blockade, securing a military bird. This was a serious player—or players. It was quite possible that more than one official was involved. The blockade alone would require significant clean-up on multiple levels. In the post nine-eleven world, one did not simply override a mobilization on suspected terrorist activity. At the very least the train should have been boarded and inspected.

"Good, good, good," said Donnelley in reference to the Blackhawk. "We'll depart. Let's say five minutes, heh?"

Five minutes. Not much time. Donnelley would activate the bio-toxin immediately after departure. There wasn't really any choice but to stop the attack at this end.

This meant a frontal assault. Hunt had been in numerous life and death situations. He'd had to kill before. He'd never cared for it and still struggled with the memories of those missions. Some military men treated killing almost like a video game, keeping score of their kills, boasting of their battlefield exploits. To Hunt killing had always been a necessary evil—with the emphasis on evil—and deadly force should only be used when all other options had been exhausted.

He was now in such a position.

There was no time to locate and disassemble the device; there was no unit awaiting his call. No one would race in to surround the terrorists and convince them to surrender peacefully. These men were armed; they'd already demonstrated their willingness to kill. Hunt had no option but to attack quickly and lethally. The consequences of waiting could be the lives of hundreds.

Hunt adjusted his position, rubbing a cramp from his right calf as he assessed the situation. Donnelley was holding the remote detonator and also almost certainly knew the placement of the lethal devise. The others may or may not know details beyond their own parts in the scheme. Hunt would need to subdue Donnelley in order to prevent his activating the devise, while keeping him alive for interrogation. But in order to get to Donnelley, Hunt would need to disable the others. He'd been first through the door in similar operations and knew he could likely take three men out before they could react.

But first through the door implied that a team followed close behind. Hunt had no such luxury this day.

He would roll left, take out three, dive behind a stack of metal containers to his right and tend to the next three, injuring Donnelley in the process. Very tricky. If even one of these men was skilled, Hunt might not live to initiate the second maneuver.

It occurred to Hunt that, now a civilian, he had no obligation to take such a risk. But Dana was infected. Donnelley might be the only one with a cure. And what of the hundreds—potentially thousands—of people who might become infected if this thing was released?

Hunt grimaced. There was no use in self-delusion. Yes, he was concerned about the spread of the plague. But this was about Dana pure and simple. Would he still do this if Dana hadn't been infected? Maybe. Possibly. Most likely. Still, it was her troubled, emotionless face that he saw in his mind's eye, her vacant stare, near lifeless voice. And he knew that however cruel it might seem, he would do whatever it took to save this one all-important person. The rest of the world be damned.

The joint connecting the two cars was flexible, making it difficult to remain still as the train maneuvered over the winding track. Twice, Hunt nearly fell. He wished he had a flash/bang to toss in ahead of him. The distraction could be invaluable. This doorway was clumsy, making it difficult to enter and get off his initial three bursts before the men could react.

Hunt closed his eyes, visualizing the assault, walking through each motion in his mind, anticipating the response time, the chaos, the retaliation.

A deep cleansing breath. Another.

Eyes open now. Alert. Prepared.

In one swift movement, Hunt swung wide the door, rolled, and fired the first three burst. Diving to his right, Hunt avoided the first round of return fire. He was behind the metal containers now. Bullets pinged and echoed as Hunt scrambled further forward, his right calf cramping, he nearly stumbled.

Hunt released another burst. Another terrorist down.

Return fire. Wide, unfocused.

Hunt rolled, aimed, fired.

There was the soft thud of a body tumbling to the deck, the clank of the man's weapon, and then only the steady droning clatter of the train's perpetual motion.

Total elapsed time: less than seven seconds.

Hunt remained low, scanning the scene from behind a stack of Samsonite, easily locating five fallen terrorists—and no Donnelley. A quick scan of the room and Hunt confirmed his fears. The rear hatch was cracked open. The weasel had scurried away, letting his cronies take the heat. Taking a quick inventory of each fallen form, kicking weapons away, confirming that none were stirring, Hunt then raced toward the exit.

A sudden shuffle.

A shot.

Hunt dove left, returning fire almost before he'd identified his target. The wounded terrorist did not survive his second encounter with Hunt. How had the man recovered his weapon so quickly? Hunt blinked, reacquiring focus. Damn it! He was not entirely on his game.

Scrambling to his feet, the terrorist's Heckler and Koch in hand, Hunt raced through the two remaining cargo cars and then the caboose. He was just in time to see Donnelley scrambling from a rope ladder into the retreating Blackhawk. Immediately, Hunt opened fire, but still the bird arched away, disappearing to the east.

Hunt had failed. Dana would likely pay with her life.

Chapter 17

Dresden Germany

Resisting the urge to scratch at his false mustache, Jonathan Thorpe looked right and then left, inserted a key into the rear door of a tall blond bricked office building, twisted, pushed, and entered into a dark and musty back hallway. While still mid-day in Colorado where, unknown to Thorpe, Marc and Dana Huntington battled terrorists upon a speeding train, it was eleven-thirty pm in Germany. He took the lift to the fourth floor. It creaked and moaned in a grinding metallic protest. The lights flickered in a kind of surreal dance. But, eventually the door opened and Thorpe stepped onto a tightly woven green and gold carpet, turned right, again glancing suspiciously from side-to-side, before finally entering an office suite on the left. Thorpe's fingers danced across the small keypad just within the door, reactivating the alarm system.

He was now standing in a small unremarkable foyer area, the law offices of Hirsch and Goldstein. The law firm did exist and calls to this office went through, but were routed to the firm's other office located across town. In actuality, this was one of Thorpe's safe houses.

Thorpe studied the room, his milk chocolate eyes scanning the furnishings and floor. It had been six weeks since he'd been here, and the place was in desperate need of a good dusting. But, dust was Thorpe's ally. It revealed foot and finger prints along with other unwanted disturbances. It tickled his nose, and, in truth, Thorpe was a bit of a neat freak, but it served his purposes. Suppressing a sneeze, Thorpe grinned. To all appearances, the place was undisturbed.

Thorpe now strolled to behind the large reception desk, reaching underneath, his fingers located yet another keypad. He entered a six digit code and then turned and opened the door located to the rear left of the desk. Here he entered his diminutive but functional residential suite, turned and tapped in a third code on a pad found just within the doorway.

At times it all seemed like paranoia and clandestine nonsense worthy of an Ian Fleming novel.

At times.

But not at this particular time.

As it was, he'd have been thrilled to have a platoon of commandos or a bleeding tank.

It took nearly five minutes for Thorpe to inspect the suite, examining every lamp, lifting every cushion, running his fingers along the frame of each painting, ensuring that everything was as it should be. Even so, he was unsettled. He'd used three different aliases throughout the course of the day, switched flights unnecessarily twice, worn several outfits, and even donned a wig and false mustache. Yet still he couldn't escape the feeling that the mysterious client knew exactly where he was at all times.

Paranoid, true, but just so much so as to be useful.

Thus far he believed paranoia was the single element that kept him alive.

Thorpe blew breath harshly from between his lips and, raking his hands through his hair, strolled to the large window overlooking the city. He was situated on the Elbe's northern bank and gazed out over a cluster of domes, towers, and spires. The buildings were stately, regal, some even mischievous in design. It was a spectacular view, especially at night when the moonlight and city lights conspired to bath the architectural peaks and valleys in a golden radiance. Thorpe loved the view and fully understood that it was a bit of a sensation that it existed at all. In early 1945 Allied forces reduced large portions of the city to smoldering debris. Thousands were left homeless, but still the city survived.

Well, Thorpe was thankful for that. Art and architecture, both were meant to outlast any given individual, political movement, or even generation. Human beings were temporal, art had the potential to last, if not eternally, at least well beyond the span of a lifetime, and to inspire and influence so many more than could a person. It was a paradox, thought Thorpe, that people, who by and large were rather dull—with obvious exceptions such as himself—could create pieces of true brilliance and lasting beauty. It was these, he supposed, that justified human existence at all. Art, in all of its forms, aspired to something greater than the day-to-day struggles of survival and petty grabs at significance. Even science for all its wonder was suspect. Today's pet theory would be disproved a decade later and present day science would soon seem arcane and foolish to the learned men of the next generation. But art, architecture, fine literature and music, those could be appreciated for generations to come—at least by those clever enough to recognize the value of such. The common rabble would simply ignore these in favor of their video games and heavy metal music, but there were always those precious few who recognized rare and evasive brilliance.

Thorpe shook his head and chuckled humorlessly.

Useless drivel.

He was on the run, his life endangered, and here he stood contemplating the nature of humanity. He was a peculiar lot, he supposed. Superior, true, not beholden to the petty morality of his inferiors, but peculiar none-the-less. So be it. That, in essence, was the temperament of an advanced intellect. The very nature of his existence was abnormal when compared to someone of a more common mind. Thorpe created his own purpose, developed a truth unto himself; finding no need to rely on the bumbling and restrictive ethics and expectations which defined so many lives. He should revel in his peculiarity not dismiss it. But now was not the time for philosophy. Now was a time for decisive action.

Pulling the silly mustache from his face and shoving it into his pocket, Thorpe moved away from the window with its stunning view and to a small oak desk situated on the far eastern wall. Beside the desk was a utilitarian-looking safe, gray, boxlike, uninspired. Thorpe inserted a key, punched in a code, and then opened the door. He then withdrew a sleek black laptop computer. This act reminded him of the girl, Liza. This had all begun with one of his computers. She had died because he had somehow allowed a PC to be compromised. Thorpe closed his eyes, breathed deep. Nothing could be done for the girl. She, like each deceased person, like every generation before, was gone. Harsh, but true. Still, a shame, he concluded.

He shook his head.

Focus, Jonathan. Focus.

He needed evidence, concrete and verifiable: facts and files, photographs of the mysterious client, incriminating tidbits which he could distribute to safe boxes throughout the world. Information that would be released upon Thorpe's untimely death. Thorpe needed some ironclad assurance policies. With the information he'd already uncovered, if he could just spend a day on this he could likely identify enough verifiable illegalities to detour the man from ever going after Thorpe again.

He opened the laptop staring at the dark and lifeless screen. The last time he'd logged onto one of his computers his files had been offloaded and his location compromised. A girl had died as a result.

Dare he power up?

Yes. There really was no option, was there? This computer contained software that could help him breach even the most secure networks, government sites, military, law enforcement. He needed that access, needed that power if he was going to survive beyond this day. He still didn't know exactly what he had done to cause a lethal reaction from his former client, but the course was set. He had no alternative but to act. And besides, it was unfathomable that the man could have compromised all of Thorpe's computers. Good God, he wasn't even in the same country now. There was no evidence to indicate that this safe house had been discovered. A functional dose of paranoia was acceptable under the circumstances, but must be repressed when it became debilitating.

Thorpe grinned at the absurdity of his own contemplations and pushed the power button.

The computer hesitated a moment, seemingly weighing its response to his action before finally coming to life. The screen flickered and then faded, only to reappear seconds later, the Microsoft Windows logo gleaming bright and colorful. Thorpe released his breath. He really mustn't allow himself to become so fearful. True, fear was a biological reaction to exterior stimuli, but it was also a choice. He could choose how to interpret that stimuli and thus regulate his response. If he interpreted a hesitation on the part of the computer as a potential danger, his body would respond in kind, sending adrenaline racing through his system, causing him to become jittery and muddle brained. If he chose to consider the hesitation as nothing more than an extra couple of seconds during boot up, he would remain calm. Thorpe was in control of his emotions, he possessed the power.

Thorpe picked up a narrow black remote control which sat atop the desk and aimed it at a stereo system situated on the far wall. Depressing a button, he selected Elliot Fisk, a classical guitarist, and then returned the remote to its spot as the fluid tones of nylon strings danced about the room.

Finally focused, Thorpe inserted the memory stick he'd removed from his now-destroyed Winchester residence computer, typed in a code, and connected to the internet via a complicated series of relays. Certainly he was secure. No need to fret.

His adversary was American; that much Thorpe knew. As well, he owned property in Switzerland, Hong Kong, Germany, and God only knew where else. Thorpe also had several photographs of the man and a list of known associates, many of whom were high-profile political figures from several powerful nation states. With such an abundance of information and with the considerable resources available, Thorpe had every confidence that he would succeed in his quest.

Four hours later, Thorpe was pacing before the computer, digging through his memory, searching out new options.

Two more hours, minor progress. Three more associates, two previously unidentified front corporations.

Another hour and he had a name: Joshua Tull.

Thorpe had yet to locate biographical information. There was no record of the man's birth, no education or employment history, no credit or medical records. No law enforcement or intelligence agency had compiled data on the man. How could a man with connections at such high levels of government remain a ghost?

The only possible conclusion was that all data, all files, had been erased. And for that to occur, it would mean that this was a man of some significance. Thorpe stirred a cup of now lukewarm tea and then stood, cup in hand. Perhaps he was working off of the wrong assumptions. All official records seemed to have been deleted, but what of more mundane sources? Tull might not appear in Scotland Yard's system, or MI6's database. The CIA may have nothing on the man, or even the Federal Trade Commission, but what of the New York Times or the Washington Post? What about the bleeding Podunk Gazette or whatever local newspaper covered events near the man's childhood home? Joshua Tull was American. There were likely news stories from before he'd attained true significance, perhaps high school or college graduation, maybe some sort of local award. Tull was intelligent, powerful. Those of this ilk rarely moved through life unnoticed. If Thorpe could find even a tidbit from Tull's youth, he could likely follow the thread into adulthood, where he could then uncover the deeper secrets.

Thorpe set his now-empty tea cup aside and reseated himself at the computer, a new vigor in his posture. He was onto something. He could sense it. One could put up obstacles, one could cause a delay, but it was quite difficult to truly stymie Jonathan Thorpe.

His initial search produced several Tulls, five of which were Joshuas, one of whom had military connections, but none of which was his man. He also discovered a furniture factory which bore the name Tull, a classic rock outfit named Jethro Tull, and a Tull's Food Emporium in northern Nebraska.

But, what was this?

A professor at a Virginia University.

Not the same man, to be certain: too old, too plump. But the resemblance was unmistakable: The light red hair, broad mouth, pronounced brow, and angular face. Based on the relationship to the man standing beside him in the photograph, he was quite tall as well. Again, like Thorpe's man who must be six foot four or five by American measurements.

This man was a relation, perhaps a father or an uncle, maybe even an older sibling. Thorpe noted the date on the picture, 1994, nearly two decades gone. Still, this was the connection. This was the true starting point. From here he could learn much about the man. Thorpe copied and pasted the name into the search box: Linus Tull.

Again, he was beginning with next to nothing, but now at least he'd found his thread. Now, Thorpe would prevail.

Another hour and the blood fled Thorpe's face as if in shame.

Bloody hell! What had he done?

Thorpe rose, crossed to the window and stared out over the scenic dawn. This was lunacy, pure and simple. This was conspiracy at a global scale, hundreds of thousands of lives endangered, political systems corrupted from within, poised for simultaneous collapse. And who this man, these people, believed themselves to be, absurd, deranged.

And ridiculous.

This could not be. The entire thing was a ploy, a set-up, designed to mislead anyone who dared dig so deep. What Thorpe had uncovered was far too widespread, far too ambitious to be founded in truth.

Thorpe studied the spires and columns of the brilliant architecture before him. His emotions were his to control, his intellect at his command. He would think this through, discover the rationality within. He could formulate a course of action, sift through the lies and implications, reconstruct the hidden data and innuendo. This, he could do. What he had discovered had been a lie, a falsehood. There was no other sane conclusion.

Thorpe turned, intending to return to the computer.

"Hello, Johnny, darlin'."

"Tina!" Tull's commando. How had she found him? How had she entered without his knowledge?

"Close your mouth, Johnny. Keep the fireflies out. I'm thinking you and I, we have a thing or two to discuss."

Chapter 18

The Swiss Alps

Joshua Tull paced the large octagon space he used as a bedchamber. The blaze from the circular fireplace at the center of the room hurled dancing shadows against his gaunt and pale features. He was dressed smartly, black silk shirt, open at the collar, charcoal jacket of Italian design, matching slacks, snakeskin boots, the skin taken from a creature that had once been his pet.

There was a complication.

He both loved and despised complications.

They made life so much more interesting, offering a break from the mundane, from the perfect execution of all that he had planned.

But, then, they were so… complicating.

Tull stared at one of his three television screens. Lucy and Ethel were stomping on grapes at a vineyard. Such silliness we use to entertain our weary minds. Is our race truly so shallow? Do we not desire anything more stimulating to aid us through the long wicked days?

He turned marching toward the great circular bed. "Katrina," he said into his Bluetooth.

"Yes, sir. He'll be on the line shortly. His secretary is getting him. She says he's concerned that the line could be unsecured."

"Our… c…conversation will remain p…private. He can be assured."

"I have already conveyed that, Mr. Tull. I also added that any undue delay would be looked upon most unfavorably. The man has a wife as well as a son. I've arranged for them to be followed as there might be need of additional motivation."

Tull's face broke into a broad grin. Katrina was a fine woman: sharp, spirited, ruthless, perhaps even a bit bloodthirsty, while still level-headed. Peculiar that he had never invited her into his bed. Perhaps one day. The woman truly did deserve reward for her efforts. Personally, he was not of the bloodthirsty sort, but he recognized the need for and value of those who possessed that certain verve. Yes. Katrina was a fine specimen.

Tull turned, now facing another screen. Cheers. A comedy about people with no purpose in life other than to sit at a bar and poison their brains. Human beings could be so mindless, so simple.

"The senator is on the line," said Katrina.

"Mr. Fagundes," said Tull. "It seems... our arrangement has g...gone afoul."

Fagundes didn't immediately reply. Most likely due to the abruptness of Tull's statement. The man was a politician, and as such, accustomed to certain social and professional protocols and courtesies. "Sir, the arrangement of which you speak... Are you certain that our line is secure?" His English was heavily accented. The man was a buffoon, too lazy to have properly learned a dominate tongue.

"I have more to lose f...from an... unsecure line than do you, Fa...gundes. You were... saying..."

"Um. Yes. The arrangement. This is my concern. In my good conscience, it is not in the best interest of my people that we proceed. To grant such power to that unworthy scoundrel Henriques, it would be obvious and catastrophic."

Tull turned to the Cheers screen, watching Shelly Long berate Ted Danson. Such a shrill woman. He didn't understand why Danson's character didn't simply kill her. That, he thought, would have been a humorous episode. "Fagundes, did I hear you c...correctly? You do... not believe our arrangement to be... in the interest of y...your people?"

"Sir, you must understand my position."

Tull grinned as he turned to face a screen featuring an episode of Barney Miller. "Ah! It is... not I that needs to understand. Allow me to clarify... my position. You represent a c...country of over 200 million... people. You are increasingly industrialized, y...yet over a quarter... of your population still lives in... poverty. These people are highly s...susceptible to disease and... contamination which would... ultimately spread to the broader p...population."

"I understand all of this, but..."

"Based on our… models, a global pan…demic could reach t…two million dead in just… over a week. Of course, the… source countries would s…suffer the heaviest fatalities… initially. Currently, and due to your previous efforts on our behalf, Brazil is… not a source country."

"Yes. I understand this all. And please remember my contribution some months past in aiding you with certain exports of some concern. Without my help, you would not have been allowed to leave my country with those bodies."

"After the second week, s…seven million dead," said Tull, his voice even, perhaps even cheery. "Third week… 18 million, then 33 million. Shall… I go on? The model is quite fascinating. Perhaps I could… send you the visual representation. I'll have one… specifically of Brazil… forwarded. The spread rate of an aggressive… strain is quite captivating."

"No. That is unnecessary. I understand."

"There is… a cure. And after the initial surge, a… vaccine will also be… made available in certain nations. Assuming your… continued cooperation, you… will have access to these. The contagion would… not have the opportunity to gain hold or to decimate your land. Again, that… assumes your cooperation. D…does that sound as if… it might be in the best interest… of your people?"

"Sir, you must understand. If I help to elevate Henriques to a position of power, I will be finished."

A selfish little mongrel, this one. Why was it that so few people of true character ascended to substantial power? Certainly there must be some flaw in the human psyche, some malevolent gene that buries the best most genuine individuals in menial positions such as caregivers and therapists while relegating the national good to those who desire position solely to further their own ends.

"And if you… don't concede," said Tull. "Millions of your citizens will die. It will… be leaked that you had it… in your power to p…prevent the horror. Think, Fagundes. It is… not a strength of yours, but… think. Which is in your… best interest?"

Tull disconnected the line, not allowing the man to respond. Tiny, vacant mind. Such an incredible waste of flesh. The man should never have been permitted to reproduce.

"Katrina?"

"Yes, sir."

"You heard?"

"Of course."

"Follow up on... the conversation. P...prepare for... a Brazilian event, but... watch Fagundes. I believe he will have... a change of heart. And then, perhaps, this evening, join... me in my bedchamber. It is... long past due that I... reward you for your efforts."

A pause and then a nearly silent, "Yes... Mr. Tull."

Chapter 19

Colorado

Hunt popped two pills, balled and then opened his fist repeatedly, and paced the small space frustrated and concerned. It had been over two hours since he'd seen Dana and at that point she had seemed listless and mostly unresponsive. All of the passengers along with two surviving crew members who had not been in the baggage car for the mass execution had been taken for screening to a small clinic some forty-five minutes outside of Denver. Hunt had been separated from the others, tested for the plague, and questioned twice already by men in surgical masks concerning his role in the day's events.

But, Dana.

He needed to know about Dana. Was she really infected? Had the substance Donnelley sprayed into her mouth truly been the plague? He still held out hope that perhaps it had been a ruse, that it was a ploy and that she was fine. The CDC was involved now, so obviously the threat was taken seriously, but Hunt had no idea what was being done to contain the bio-toxin and prevent other attacks.

If only they'd let him see Dana.

Hunt paced to the far wall and, for what had to be the tenth time, reached for his yo-yo. It was gone. He'd used it to bind a terrorist. He supposed he'd get another one. Foolish, probably. Childish, undoubtedly. But it was a calming device and he'd had that purple Duncan since childhood.

Silly! All that had happened and he was contemplating yo-yos.

Hunt stared at the vanilla wall before him and thought about just how crazy the world had become. Homegrown terrorists, fanatics bombing their neighbors because they disagreed with some Washington official that would likely be voted out of office during the next go around. Didn't people get it? The system was already in place. All we need do is use it the way it was meant to be used. But people rarely looked at the obvious. That was too mundane. These lunatics didn't want to follow the issues and back candidates that reflected their views.

These people didn't want to run for office or help garner support for favorable legislation and policy. These people wanted grand plans and bloody revolutions. Well, the USA had already suffered through that. Now it was time to rely on the systems established as a result. And if the system needed a little tweaking now and then, so be it. That was the natural evolution of society. But, nothing good would ever come from attacking innocent civilians simply to make a point. Hunt had been to countries where freedom was truly repressed. He would have loved to have dumped this band of idiots in Afghanistan or Iraq. Then they'd learn what true repression could be. Though, he doubted that Donnelley or any of his crew could have survived long in a truly hostile environment.

But, Dana. My God—Dana.

Hunt crossed the room again, and then again, and again.

Bare.

Sterile.

Not even a bad hotel print on the wall.

Only a Formica table and three chairs.

He glanced at his watch. Two minutes since the previous glance.

He turned, walked toward the wall, reaching for his missing yo-yo.

A woman entered the room. Not a doctor, most likely law enforcement of one breed or another. She was perhaps fifty and, unlike most women her age, had allowed her short curly hair to go salt and pepper rather than opting for dye. She was round but not obese: Face, body, nose, eyes, everything round. Dressed in a tan sport jacket that might have looked at home on a used car salesman, baggy navy blue pants, and white Reebok sneakers, she carried a small blue and white Igloo cooler which she placed on the narrow rectangular table at the center of the room. Hunt found it difficult to get an immediate read on her. Definitely not FBI, too informal and relaxed for that. Local perhaps. She didn't have the polished cookie-cutter look of a Fed. "Sergeant Marcus Huntington," she said, glancing over wire-rimmed glasses to read his name from a file. Her voice was warm in tone, her accent slightly southern.

"You can drop the sergeant. I'm no longer active. And the only people who call me Marcus are trying to sell me things I don't need."

She flipped through the file, scanning it. No doubt she'd already absorbed its contents. "Yes you are inactive," she said with little interest. "Your exit from the military was rather abrupt, not entirely voluntary." She studied him for a moment before continuing. "My name's Bedford. I'm with Homeland Security. You may have noticed that I'm not wearing a surgical mask. The doctors have cleared you. You're not infected."

Homeland Security. Federal, but not FBI. Still, the woman seemed an odd fit. "Glad to hear it," said Hunt. "But I'm more concerned about my wife, Dana Huntington. Do you have information on her condition?"

Bedford plopped the file onto the surface of the table, tugged on a plastic folding chair, and sat down. As she did so, she removed a small digital audio recorder from her right jacket pocket and set it beside the folder on the table. "I'm sure the CDC will answer those questions. I'm here for another purpose."

"I'm sorry, Mrs. Bedford, but I've been going crazy in here. Dana believes that she's been infected. I need to know if that's true, and if so, what can be done to cure her."

"It's Bedford, Marcus. No 'Mrs.' No 'Ms.' No title, just call me Bedford. I find that keeps things pure and uncomplicated."

Hunt had noticed a wedding ring on the appropriate finger, but could care less how the woman chose to be addressed. "Fine, fine. Bedford. I need to know about Dana."

"Then I suggest you answer my questions directly and succinctly. The sooner we're done here, the sooner you can speak with the medical professionals about your wife."

Hunt stared into her pale gray eyes, clear and emotionless, only partially obscured by wire glasses, and, after a moment's hesitation, marched to the table, pulled out a chair and sat directly across from the woman. "Okay, Bedford. What do you need from me?"

Not responding, she opened the cooler and withdrew a sandwich wrapped in wax paper. "Turkey and Swiss. It's been a long day. Are you hungry, Marcus?"

Hunt shook his head. "No thanks. Not much of an appetite right now."

Bedford shrugged, unwrapped a portion of the sandwich and took a bite. Chewing with the right side of her mouth, she stared at Hunt for a moment and then pressed the record button on the digital device asking, "Why were you on that train, Marcus?"

"I was a passenger."

She smiled. Her mouth was small, her smile even more so. Her cheek swelled with food. "Yes. You and your wife were passengers. Why don't you tell me the purpose of your presence on the train?"

"You've got a file on me, so none of this is secret. We recover stolen property for a living. A jewel thief by the name of Kelvin Donnelley was on the train. He'd stolen a pretty valuable rock named the Stonemeier diamond. The reward offered was substantial. We were there to retrieve the diamond."

"And you and Mr. Donnelley, had you ever met before?"

"No."

"Did you manage to retrieve the diamond?"

"Again, no. I learned of the terrorist plot before we'd had a chance to complete our operation."

Another bite of bread and turkey followed by several rapid chews. "And you were unaware of the plot prior to boarding the train?"

"Of course I was unaware."

She swallowed. "When did you first learn of the plot?"

"Seven forty-two AM. Mountain time."

Bedford chuckled. "That's very precise, Marcus."

"We were in the midst of an operation. There was a time schedule. I entered the baggage car at seven forty-one with the purpose of changing into a porter's uniform as part of our ruse aimed at Donnelley. I overheard two men discussing the plot. At the time I interpreted their plan as involving a bomb. It wasn't until later that I learned of the plague."

"Why didn't you notify the authorities?"

"I did. It took some persuasion, but I convinced security to investigate. The terrorists were gone from the baggage car by the time security arrived. I'd heard the men's voices but not seen their faces. I couldn't identify them."

"And so, knowing the potential threat, you did nothing?" Bedford sounded incredulous. She took another bite. The sandwich was half gone.

"I urged train security to contact the officials, FBI, Homeland, something. Again, after some persuasion, they made the call."

"To which agency?"

"I don't know. By then I was out of the loop. But it should be pretty easy to figure out. They barricaded the track, stopped the train—for a while at least."

Bedford swallowed. "There was no call, Marcus. Nothing came until after you pulled the emergency break—after you'd killed several passengers and the supposed terrorists had fled."

Hunt stared at the woman, attempting to read intent in her cool gray eyes. He'd interrogated people. He knew the techniques. Did she really think he was involved or was she simply tossing out feelers in an effort to trip him up? "I killed terrorists not passengers. Are you telling me that you have no record of the train having been stopped by a barricade and then allowed to move on minutes later?"

Her expression was even, her soft round features unreadable. "Several of the passengers mentioned an unscheduled stop. Most assumed it was some mechanical issue. None mentioned a barricade."

That made no sense. She was either misinformed or purposely skewing the questions in order to gauge his response. Hunt stared at her for several seconds. He hated conspiracy theories, thought they were for fanatics and losers. "Donnelley indicated that there were connections—government connections. The kind that could order a blockade released and the incident erased."

"That sounds like fiction, Marcus." She lifted the sandwich, took another bite.

"Yeah, well, sometimes my whole life seems like a fiction." He paused. "Listen, I don't buy into conspiracy theories any more than you do. I've found that the simple solution is usually the correct solution. That said, Donnelley is working with someone else, someone who gives him orders, and, yes, someone with governmental clout." Hunt leaned forward on his elbows, meeting Bedford's gaze directly. "I'm not saying the thing is widespread, but I am saying that at least someone in a position of power is pulling strings. Put the pieces together." Hunt held up a finger. "One, the blockade was withdrawn without any official record of it. Though, if you can figure out where we stopped, I'm sure you could find some locals that saw something—maybe cops or highway patrol. Two, Donnelley escaped on a Blackhawk helicopter. I didn't get the tail numbers, but it was a Blackhawk. I can verify that."

"But, you're the only witness to this supposed escape. No one else saw the copter."

"Three," said Hunt ignoring her comment. "Militarized Bubonic plague dispensed through canisters connected to the ventilation system, and, in my wife's case, by a handheld inhaler. You have verified the plague by now, right? It was released on the train practically before Donnelley clawed his way into that bird."

Bedford didn't nod, but simply said, "You already know the plague was real. You and every passenger have been tested."

"That's my point. No one picks up Bubonic plague at a Seven-Eleven. Only someone with connections—high level security connections—could get to that stuff."

Bedford studied Hunt, a curious expression, possibly fear, maybe contemplation danced across her face. "Kelvin Donnelley is a thief. From what I've read, with the exception of a couple of recent larger takes, he's mostly small time. Can you help me out, Marcus? How is it that a common crook is heading up a terrorist cell with access to a militarized bacteria?"

"That's your job, not mine, Bedford. I've probably got the same background info on Donnelley as you. But here's what I can say. As unstable as he is—and he is unstable, I'm guessing cocaine abuse, possibly some other underlying issues—he was able to get automatic weapons past security, two varieties that I saw: Kalashnikov and Heckler and Koch. Maybe you can track him through his arms dealer. As well, he brought the mechanism aboard to release the plague. For him to have done this, he had to have connections either with the railroad or with government security."

Bedford wiped her mouth with a paper napkin and nodded for him to continue.

"He had a cell of seven to nine men, various ages and backgrounds, but all, to the best of my knowledge, American. They knew how to operate their weapons, but most had no military training. These were civilians united around some crazy cause. To me they looked like a band of misfits. I'm thinking someone knew how to feed on their insecurities and need for significance, and pulled them in as pawns. As well—and listen to this because I'm not sure that anyone really let this sink in when I explained it earlier—one of the terrorists told me that this was only one of many strikes. I explained this to the National Guard when they first arrived, also to the FBI. Now I'm talking with Homeland and I'm still not sure anyone's sent word up the ladder to raise the alert level."

"Well, Marcus, I can't speak for anyone else, but I'm still in the process of assessing the situation. Tell me about your interaction with the terrorists."

Hunt sighed. "May I please check on my wife's condition?"

"I'm sorry, Marcus," she said, laying her palm on his as would a country doctor when delivering a cancer diagnosis. "I understand your concern. I have very real concerns of my own. But we have a situation, and like it or not, you're in the middle of it. Tell me the truth and tell it succinctly and you're more likely to see your wife sooner rather than later. Now, your interaction with the terrorists?"

Hunt massaged his temples with his fingertips and tried not to scream at the woman. "I'm sure you've read my written report. The FBI, a guy named Millken, already went over that with me."

"Walk me through the high points." Bedford set the remaining portion of her sandwich on the wax paper, wrapped it, and put it back into the Igloo.

"At first we didn't know Donnelley was involved. In fact, I interrupted our operation to recover the diamond because of what I'd learned. I even told Donnelley about the terrorists."

"And his reaction?"

"He played it cool, didn't give anything away."

"Go on."

Hunt spent the next forty-five minutes going over the details of the day ending with his pulling the emergency break and then racing through the train yelling like a lunatic in an effort to evacuate the train before anyone could be infected. Bedford interrupted frequently with questions. "How is it you returned to the train after being thrown free?" "Why did you use deadly force on the men in the baggage compartment?" "How could you be sure that all of these men were terrorists?" "Did you learn who they were working for?" "Where were the weapons stashed?" "How much has your wife told you of what happened to her?"

Finally, Hunt shook his head. "We're repeating ourselves, Bedford. I've told you everything I know. Now may I please see my wife?"

"Some of the passengers were under the impression that you were one of the terrorists," said Bedford. The woman was relentless.

Hunt shrugged and sighed. "Maybe they did. Especially after I'd gained a weapon. But I'm sure you've already interviewed most of them. You must have testimony indicating that I fought against these thugs. So why are we wasting time? There might be other attacks under way as we speak."

Here, Bedford leaned forward, turning off the recorder as she did so. She stared hard into his eyes, her soft round face an unreadable mask. When finally she spoke, her voice was slow and deliberate. Something was up with this woman and Hunt couldn't quite figure out just what that might be. "I've spent so much time with you, Marcus, because I needed to get a read on you. I've read your file: both your statements from earlier today and the non-classified portions of your military record. It seems you left under a bit of a cloud."

"I did," said Hunt, again massaging his temples. He was jonesing for another Oxycontin but suppressed the thought. Later. Soon. Not yet.

"It also seems like all of the allegations against you didn't quite add up, the testimony was sketchy, the evidence incomplete, yet still you resigned."

Hunt buried his face in his palms, inhaled deeply, and then lifted his gaze. "I'd been injured. You can tell that just by looking at me. I had some memory loss—still do. I haven't fought this thing because the plain truth is that I don't remember what happened. But, you can believe this. What they say, that's not me. I am not a child killer. I am not a loose cannon. I would not lead men into combat while inebriated. I've learned a few things since, from other sources. It appears my actions were not quite as the official record would indicate. There will come a day when I fight these lies. But not today, not until I have my proof. Not until I've regained enough of my memory that I can stand before a board of review and give a truthful and complete testimony. Now, if it's all the same with you, I'd like to see my wife. I'm worried about her."

She stole a glance at her wristwatch, a gold Citizen with a black face, and then stared at him long, her gray eyes glinting in the florescent light. "I believe you, Marcus. And for the record, that's what this was about. I wanted to learn if I could trust you. This thing might get ugly. Already there are those saying that you cracked in a hostage situation overseas, killing a child and losing two of your men, and now, in another hostage situation, you've murdered several passengers."

"And that's not true."

"And I said that I believe you. It doesn't mean everyone else will. And even if they do, you're an awfully convenient scapegoat."

"Maybe so. But, I'm just a witness."

Bedford rocked her hand in front of her in an iffy motion. "Well, yes and no. You're a witness. You have no official involvement, but Marcus, you took out nearly the entire cell." Pausing, she glanced at her watch and offered a small grin as she then folded her hands before her on the table. "Like you, I'm not a fan of conspiracy theories. But, I find it incomprehensible that something like a blockade could be swept away so quickly. For all official purposes, it did not happen."

"And?"

"The passengers are frightened, their testimonies contradictory to one another. This is to be expected. But it's obvious the train did stop and then resume travel a short time later. Considering all that's happened I'm inclined to believe that you are correct and that there was in fact a blockade."

"Which leaves us where?"

Bedford shrugged a down home shrug. "That, Marcus, is the who-wants-to-be-a-millionaire question."

"And why are you telling me this? My role is done here."

"It is. But, like I said, you're a convenient scapegoat. You could be pulled back in." She paused as if contemplating how much more to say. There was a strange quality to her expression as she continued. "Someone from above is manipulating this thing. Until we determine who, things could get sketchy." Bedford reached into her left jacket pocket and withdrew a business card, sliding it across the table to Hunt. "Just in case there's a need."

They stared at one another. "You said you believe me. How do I know that I can trust you?"

She shrugged, smiled. "You can never know, you can only hope."

Hunt stood. "I'm going to assume I'm free to go."

Bedford nodded. "I see no reason to detain you further. The FBI ninnies wanted to hold you, but I'll override them." She paused for a moment, seemingly contemplating her next statement. "I know you're concerned about your wife. She's been through an awful lot. Be gentle with her."

Something in Bedford's tone, in her clear gray eyes, made Hunt pause. He was just formulating his question when the lights flickered and then went dark. Five seconds later, the fire alarm blared.

Chapter 20

Dana was infected.

She laid semi reclined in a hospital bed enclosed within a clear plastic tent. The symptoms had already taken hold—much faster than what the doctors had expected: fever, headache, chills. Her stomach felt as if it had turned inside out. She retched but had nothing left to vomit. There had been uncontrollable diarrhea, the last bout being laced with blood. Several physicians had examined her. She was the first to display symptoms, most likely due to the method by which she'd become infected, but other passengers from the train had begun to show the beginning signs. Fourteen were symptomatic thus far, twenty-seven tested positive for the bacteria. If Hunt hadn't managed to evacuate the train so quickly the infection rate would likely have been much greater.

Hunt.

He would be here soon.

They were questioning him, she knew, but that would only go on for so long.

But then what?

She hadn't told him the worst of it. The plague, yes, he knew of that, knew that it could be fatal. But… the other thing. How would he react? She trusted him. He would be supportive. He'd tell her that everything would be alright and that none of it was her fault. And deep down she knew that he would be right in this. What happened to her was not of her own doing. It was something beyond her control. So, why did she feel filthy? Why did it repulse her to touch her own skin or to look another person eye-to-eye? Had any of this been her fault? Could she have fought harder? Could she have somehow damaged Donnelley in such a way as to prevent the attack? No. Yes. No! Absolutely not.

Maybe…

Her clothing… She was dressed provocatively, intentionally dressed to seduce.

No!

Still not her fault, not her blame, not her guilt.

Women dressed provocatively every day. Enter any night club and Dana's attire would seem commonplace, perhaps even tame by some standards. Men were not mere animals, not irrationally subject to urges and instinct alone. Men might have urgent drives, but they also had minds. They had the power to suppress their desires. Regardless a woman's attire, there was no excuse for rape.

So why did she feel so despicable? Why did it seem this had redefined her, reformed the very basis of her being? Dana closed her eyes, attempting to clear away unwanted emotions and to bring logic forward.

But what of Hunt's emotions?

Would he be able to suppress the emotions that he would surely feel, to act on logic and intellect alone and stem his fury and disdain? Would he ever be able to look at her the same as he had before, or would this forever change their relationship?

Should she even tell him?

Could she?

And if she didn't, what then? She'd lived with one secret for the first three years of their marriage, that of her previous marriage to Jonathan Thorpe. Hunt had not handled it well when he learned of her deception. If this became a secret, what then? Would he forgive her if it should later be revealed? And could she keep such a thing from him? What if she'd contracted some disease from Donnelley? Dear God, what if she'd been impregnated? How could that be explained away? But, at her core she knew she must hide this. Hunt was a military man: trained in combat, even-tempered, logical, even brutal when necessary. But that was Hunt the soldier. She knew the man beneath and he was a person of deep emotion and principle. This would affect him. There was little doubt of it. He would never look at her the same. It was in his make-up. Hunt could see shades of gray, yes. He'd acknowledge them, react to them, but he was wired to see things in black and white. This was where he was most comfortable. This was his default mode. Shadowy imperfections, tricks of fate, soiled souls, he struggled with these. It wasn't that he had no compassion, quite the opposite. But, Hunt broke issues down to their most elemental form. He would see Dana as either pure victim or pure guilt. Likely, victim. She didn't want to be viewed as either. She'd never been a victim. She didn't want to think of herself as one now.

He would try to fix this. That was his way. But this was a thing that could never be fixed. At some level this would always be with them, no matter how many years went by, no matter how many future experiences separated the event, this would forever more be a defining event.

But, what she needed was for him to see her as his love, pure and true. Not a victim, not someone damaged or soiled, or in need of fixing, but simply as his love. She needed this more than anything.

But, even this perfect thought repulsed her.

The thought of him holding her was as revolting as the kiss of a viper. Hunt was not the guilty party, but he was a man, and at this moment she couldn't endure a male presence. She wanted desperately to see him, to hold him, but simultaneously could not bear the thought.

What a pathetic mess she'd become.

Dana steeled herself.

Enough with the girlish emotion.

She was a survivor, an intelligent and single-minded individual. It was time she evaluated her course instead of wallowing about in self pity and shame. The plague and the attack by Donnelley, these were both issues at hand. She would deal with them as such. As to Hunt, she would deliver such information as she felt appropriate at such time she deemed it necessary.

The lights flickered and then went dim.

There was the faint smell of smoke.

The fire alarm blared.

The back-up generator kicked in. The lights came back on, but dimly, casting a pale light across the room.

There was commotion in the hallway beyond Dana's room.

And then a gun shot, and another.

Screams.

Chaos from down the hall.

Dana ripped the tape from her arm, dislodging the IV needle as she did so. Pulling the plastic tent to the side, she swung her legs as if to rise from the bed.

Her head swam.

Her stomach twisted and lurched.

She hadn't realized how severe the symptoms had become. Maybe it was because she had remained still, or perhaps because she'd been so wrapped up in her thoughts. But Dana was unsure if she'd be able to stand, and even if she did, how many steps she could take before collapsing. She'd been infected for what, thirteen hours, fifteen at the most? Should she be this sick so soon? She didn't think so.

Another gunshot, this one closer.

The screams persisted. There was the sound of running footsteps.

The smoky smell became thicker. There was no doubt. The clinic was under a full-scale attack.

Dana rose, faltered, steadied herself.

Who would attack a clinic?

No. The question was, who would attack a clinic peopled with the survivors of a terrorist attack?

Someone who wanted to cover up the fact that the attack had taken place.

But, she had no time to contemplate this further. She was cornered if she remained as she was. It took seven steps for Dana to make the door. After the initial three, she'd nearly tumbled forward from nausea and weakness. Placing her hand against the doorframe to steady herself, Dana closed her eyes and took three deep breaths. Alright. Fine, she was bleeding deathly ill, but she didn't have time for that just then. It would just have to wait. Before opening the door, Dana tried to visualize the layout of the place. The building was single story, most likely no more than fifty beds, perhaps less. The main entrance was to the left. She assumed that would be covered and anyone caught fleeing through there would be shot. The gunshots had come from the right. Logic would dictate that she flee left. Again, not a wise option. Better to do the unexpected. Better to press toward the commotion instead of away. The fire might have been meant to eliminate evidence, both human and material, but it would also cause survivors to flee the scene. The terrorists would anticipate this and post sentries at the exits.

Another burst of gunfire from the right.

Renewed screams from that direction.

Dana was likely a bit daft, but she exited her room and turned toward the right, continuing to use the warm vanilla wall for support. Smoke was present, creating a filmy haze before her eyes, but was not yet overly thick. The blaze was apparently still in the early stages.

A wave of vertigo washed over Dana but only paused for a look-see. If anything, it seemed she might be gaining strength. Perhaps being up and about helped. Or maybe this was the lull before the category five Bubonic hurricane.

Racing footsteps; coming her direction.

Dana ducked back through her doorway and watched through the narrow rectangular window just above the door handle as a young woman raced past, the sound of pursuing footsteps not far behind. Dana recognized her as one of the passengers from the train: a small woman, blond, mid twenties. Dana noted a wheeled tray of the type used to serve meals to patients. It was situated just behind her. Grabbing the tray, she opened the door, and pushed it into the path of her pursuer. The thug tumbled and cursed as he collided with the tray. Dana was upon him immediately. A quick kick to the soft spot beneath and behind the jaw line. Dana was barefoot now, wearing only a hospital gown, but even so, her practiced attack sent the man tumbling. The terrorist had carried a Kalashnikov semiautomatic. Dana snatched it up and quickly and fiercely bashed the man in the left temple with the stock of his own weapon. The terrorist fell limp and bloodied.

A burst of gunfire.

Dana moved down the corridor in pursuit of the sounds.

Tufts of drywall dust flittered above Dana's head as rounds struck the wall.

She dove left, rolled, returned fire. All thoughts of illness or incapacitation were gone. Dana was in combat mode. The natural autopilot of adrenaline took over. Scrambling to her feet, Dana raced forward in a low crouch ignoring the unfamiliar weakness in her limbs. There was a terrorist directly ahead, gun raised, legs spread in a firing stance.

Dana fired first.

One dead terrorist.

In Dana's mind it was a dead Donnelley.

They were all Donnelley.

The heat was greater now as Dana turned the next corner to find three men holding two dozen people at gunpoint as raging flames drew ever closer to the trapped innocents. Flames danced from behind and the terrified hostages had a clear choice: face the fiery blaze or a barrage of bullets. Two people were already down as a result of gunshot wounds, one male, one female. They lay sprawled amidst the crowd of frantic victims, their mingled blood, a slippery puddle creeping ever closer to the others. One of the thugs turned at the sound of Dana's approach, his face taut with tension and excitement, his eyes narrow with bloodlust. Dana didn't hesitate. Her aim was true.

Three more dead terrorists.

Three more dead Donnelleys.

Another man emerged from the left, barking orders, shielding his eyes from the heat of the ever-increasing flames. How had Dana missed him? Coughing and squinting, she adjusted and fired.

Yet another dead Donnelley. But, still it wasn't enough. The corpses seemed to leer at her. They giggled. They grunted in exertion as they sought to violate her.

Movement from behind. Dana whirled and fired.

Hunt dropped to the floor.

Chapter 21

Hunt and Bedford moved cautiously in the direction of the commotion, Bedford having produced a pistol from a holster located at the small of her back. The Homeland Security agent had already tried to call for back-up. Her phone found no signal. Somehow cell coverage had been blocked as were the clinic landlines. Once again, Hunt was reminded that these guys were heavy hitters. Whoever the Revolutionary Patriots of America were, they had remarkable resources at their disposal.

"There's heavy smoke up ahead," said Bedford.

"Yeah. And plenty of commotion," said Hunt as he paused at a corner. "Before we launch into this thing, give me some operational stats. How many agents are on site and how many clinic security guards?"

Bedford studied Hunt for a moment as if contemplating the wisdom of sharing any of this with him. Finally she said, "Three Homeland agents, myself included, two FBI, four local law enforcement. The clinic probably had one, maybe two of their own. I can't imagine a small rural place like this having more."

"No National Guard, only a handful of plain clothed agents. That's pretty meager considering we were all victims of a major terrorist attack. How soon can we expect reinforcements?"

Bedford shrugged her down-home shrug. "The terrorists were all dead or fled. I don't think anyone really expected them to come after the survivors."

Hunt wasn't comfortable with the answer but let it go. "The cell on the train was decimated. So this attack confirms our conclusion that the Revolutionary Patriots of America are much larger than one cell. What's our locale? Just how isolated are we? How many exits? Where are they located?"

Bedford offered a small grin, more of a smirk really. "Four exits, two of which, the east and west, are public doorways. There are two employee-only doorways on the north side of the building. As to our location, we're fairly well isolated. That was intentional. Less opportunity for contamination, less visibility. The goal was to contain both the disease and knowledge of the attack until this was sorted out."

Hunt nodded, but didn't like it. A larger facility in Denver would have been better prepared to handle both security and medical requirements. "Who made that call? Homeland? National Guard? The Fibees?"

Bedford offered another of her customary shrugs. "It wasn't my call, Marcus. I'm just following orders."

In other words, she either didn't know or wasn't telling.

They were getting close now. The heat of the blaze was greater, the sounds of gunshots and commotion more pronounced. A young woman ran past, small, blond, mid-twenties. Hunt had seen her on the train. He thought of stopping her for questioning, but she was frantic and thus likely unhelpful.

They rounded another corner and found an unconscious man sprawled on the tile floor, blood and swelling on his left cheek. He'd been hit with something heavy and likely with some force behind it. Dressed in black operational gear, he was likely a terrorist.

Hunt recognized the room number nearest the thug as Dana's and so marched toward the door, opening it. Empty. Now, where had she gone? He turned back to Bedford who was just rising after inspecting the unconscious man. There was sweat on her face. The heat was becoming greater by the moment. "I think this is far enough, Marcus. You're a civilian. I know you have a military background, but I can't endanger you further. I'll engage the menace. Why don't you search the rooms for patients? Some might need help in fleeing the building."

Hunt shook his head. "Nah. That's the room they put Dana in. I need to find her before I do anything else."

"If she's not in her room, she's probably fled."

Hunt glanced down at the unconscious form on the hard tile floor. "If I know Dana, she's the one who knocked this guy senseless and probably headed into trouble not away from it." He paused and offered a wry grin. "She's rather high maintenance that way."

A burst of gunfire from forward and around a corner.

Shouts.

Another burst.

Both Bedford and Hunt raced toward the sound of the commotion, Hunt feeling naked without a weapon. Dear God, he hoped Dana wasn't taking fire. Who knew what condition she'd be in by this time? He hadn't seen her for several hours now, but his last image was of her being led almost zombie-like into the room he'd just left.

Hunt rounded the corner just slightly behind and to the left of Bedford.

Three things happened simultaneously: Dana whirled and fired, Bedford cried, "Homeland Security, drop your weapon," and Hunt dropped into a controlled roll coming to rest only five feet before the startled Dana. At that last instant recognition widened Dana's eyes and she pulled the gun off target sending the deadly burst into the ceiling tile, some of which fell in shattered fragments.

But, Hunt had seen something that Dana had missed. One of the felled terrorists behind and to Dana's right was alive and reaching for his weapon. Hunt made to convert his roll into an attack, but just as he came within striking distance the man's head exploded in a spray of pink/red mist.

Dana stood, legs spread, a firm grip on her weapon.

There was a moment of near utter stillness and then, as one, the two dozen or so hostages raced forward, fleeing the flames, and nearly trampling Hunt and Dana in the process. Somehow Bedford disappeared amidst the commotion, but Hunt didn't think of this at the time.

"Come on, Dana," said Hunt, extending his hand. "We've got to go. Those flames are out of control."

But Dana pulled away, cradling the Kalashnikov like a lethal lifeline. The flames were just visible, the glow pulsing from around the corner, and the smoke was getting thick. They weren't in mortal danger yet, but the threat was imminent.

Blinking sweat from his eyes, Hunt hollered, "Dana! Come on!"

She seemed to reconnect then, perhaps truly seeing Hunt for the first time. And then, as if just remembering the plague, she turned her head away covering her mouth and nose with a sleeve.

Hunt coughed. The smoke density was becoming a factor. "We need to get moving, hon. You up to it?"

Not waiting for a response, he grabbed Dana's free hand, stole a quick glance back at the dead terrorists, and led her up the hallway. Had she done that? Had she taken all of those men out? As an MI6 operative, Dana had weapons training, but to the best of Hunt's knowledge she'd never before used lethal force. But, the expression on her face when she'd eliminated that last man—pure hatred, loathing even. It seemed, in that moment, she'd gone to an entirely different place.

There was a nurse's station at the intersection of two corridors. At this, Dana found a surgical mask which she immediately donned as well as a set of green scrubs. As Dana had been garbed only in an open-backed hospital gown, she immediately pulled on the loose-fitting attire before silently rejoining her husband. Another minute and they came upon the unconscious terrorist adjacent the room Dana had recently occupied. Hunt paused, stared down at the still form, and then bent, feeling for a pulse.

"Hunt, what are you doing?" Dana's voice sounded incredulous.

"This man's still alive. We can't just leave him here to burn."

Dana scowled at him. "The bleeding beast deserves what he gets."

This was a woman who volunteered at the local homeless shelter and carried McDonald's gift cards to give to every bum on a street corner looking for a handout.

Hunt held her gaze for a moment and then turned, grabbing the man first under each arm pit, and then, hefting him over his shoulders, marched past Dana toward the north side of the building. According to Bedford, there were two employee exits there, and the blaze was presumably still in the southern end of the structure.

They reached another intersection and discovered flames coming from the eastern corridor. The blaze was more widespread than Hunt had realized. A small group of people raced toward them from the north. Even though they all wore surgical masks, Hunt recognized some as passengers from the American Cry. "You're Barnes, right?" said Hunt to a young Asian man toward the front of the pack. "We met on the train. What's the situation in that direction?" Hunt nodded toward the north as he said this.

"Fire. Flames. But no one seems up to a barbeque," quipped Topher Barnes. He held out his hand, offering Hunt a surgical mask. "You'd better take this. Some of the people have been infected. I found a box of masks in a closet."

Hunt carefully set the still unconscious terrorist on the floor and accepted the mask, slipping it over his mouth and nose. "Good thinking, Topher. Any sign of the clinic staff or of security personnel?"

"Nope."

Hunt nodded. Again, none of this seemed right. Where were the doctors and nurses? Where was security? Where had Bedford made off to? Had she been attacked, carried away by the rush of panicked patients? There were too many holes in the scenario.

Judging from the glow, the flames from both the south and east were moving quickly. The two northern exits would be unavailable, and the western doorway was far enough north as to be inaccessible. The terrorists had obviously started fires at various points in the building with the intent that no one would escape alive. It was quite likely they'd lay in wait outside as well, guns at the ready.

But, Dana had taken some of them out. They might not have the manpower to cover all possible contingencies. Still, Hunt wished he'd thought to grab one of the fallen thug's weapons; then both he and Dana would be armed. "Alright," hollered Hunt to the panic-stricken crowd. And then he outlined his plan. There were some protests to his commanding tone, some people simply frightened and panicked, but Hunt spoke with the authority of experience and no one else was rising to the occasion. There was little time for debate and Hunt took charge, giving assignments, directing the frightened survivors, and generally keeping things moving in such a way as to dispel panic.

He assigned three lookouts, instructing each to slip through an open window and to a designated position near the edge of the tree line. Each made it out of the building without incident. The windows to the clinic were not secured in any way and Hunt was able to simply slide each of the two open and then knock out the screens. They were in a two-bed examining room on the west side of the low one story building. The clinic was nearly square except for a small alcove at the southwest corner. The parking lot wrapped around the south and east sides of the structure, and from his vantage point, Hunt could only see three vehicles, two compact cars and a Regan era Ford Pick-up. It was past midnight and there were no sounds of passing traffic. The clinic was set back off of a two lane road adjacent a small wooded area at the base of a tall hill. Upon arrival, Hunt had noted that over the rise was a trading post/tour depot with two buses in the lot. He'd located a mechanic amongst the survivors and instructed him to hot wire both buses. The survivors were to split into two groups which would then travel in opposite directions where they would, once clear of immediate danger, seek medical attention.

Topher Barnes, the first to climb through the window, positioned himself adjacent a shed situated slightly north, Joey McIver, at the edge of the wooded area, and Christine Aisenberg behind the pick-up to the south. No one had cell phones as these had not yet been returned, but Hunt was able to see each from the window and had given basic hand signals to use for communication. There had been some debate over going back to retrieve the weapons from the slain terrorists, but the blaze had already progressed well beyond that area. In truth, they had no more than fifteen minutes before the place was engulfed. The people coughed and held towels or clothing before their eyes, nostrils, and mouths. Many screamed and shoved, positioning themselves closer to the windows. The scene was chaotic and it was a battle to keep people from fleeing through every window and risking gunfire from hidden terrorists. Hunt could get these people to safety if only they'd keep their heads.

Dana was getting back into the game and moved about, giving fearful victims menial tasks to keep them occupied while asking if they'd seen others. There had been far more people on the train than the few huddled in this small space and Hunt had already determined to look for other survivors once this group was safely off.

"There's still no fire department response," said Dana now at her post at the second window. Her bruised and swollen face was hard to read behind the surgical mask, but her eyes were narrow with concern and anger.

"Yeah," said Hunt as he helped an elderly man over the windowsill. "Somehow they're blocking all communications from this site."

"I would think the smoke would have alerted someone on the outside," said a wiry woman of about fifty.

"Yeah. Too dark for anyone to see the smoke," said Hunt. "Maybe the glow of fire, but nothing yet." Hunt assumed the terrorists had somehow orchestrated the slow response, but he didn't verbalize this.

The elderly man, thin, salt and pepper hair, with a Stan Lee mustache, raced toward the tree line in a half jog half hobble. From there, he could move left, right, or continue forward. McIver was charged with directing the group to disperse before making it up the rise. Anything to make it difficult on the terrorists.

There was a loud crash from the hallway to the rear. The ceiling had collapsed. Sparks flitted wildly and a metal strut cartwheeled into the room causing the crowd to scatter.

"We've not much time," said Dana in a flat, emotionless tone.

Hunt ushered the next person forward, a pear shaped woman of about thirty. "What's your name, ma'am?" asked Hunt.

"Dorothy," said the woman with a tremble. She looked agitated and unnerved. Several blisters were visible on her skin. "That was my grandfather just before me."

Hunt nodded and smiled, hoping to calm the woman. "Just take it easy, Dorothy. You're almost free of this." He patted her on the back and then helped to steady her as she stepped on the chair Hunt had placed before the window. Even through the fabric of her clothing, he could feel that she had a very high fever.

Hunt signaled the lookouts for an all-clear, receiving three affirmative responses.

Finally, there were sirens in the distance, eliciting a few stifled cheers. If the terrorists hadn't yet fled, now they most certainly would. Still, Hunt didn't want to be here when the authorities arrived. He—and the other survivors—needed to take control of the situation, otherwise they'd likely be gathered together once again and somehow he didn't think anyone would survive that go-around.

"Alright, Dorothy," he said, attempting to move the woman along. "You're clear to go. Don't worry. Dana's got you covered with the gun. Just crouch low and run straight for that young man at the tree line." He pointed toward the shadowed figure of McIver.

The trembling woman stepped up onto the molded plastic chair and from there placed her right foot on the windowsill.

"Very good, Dorothy. You can do it."

She trembled, blinked several times and then slipped from her perch and onto the gravely ground below. Immediately, she hollered as if in severe pain.

Dana continued to scan the area, one side to the other, the gun barrel moving right and then left. A terrorist might see this as an opening.

"Dorothy, are you alright?" asked Hunt. "Did you injure yourself?"

Dorothy blinked, obviously attempting to focus. "Ankle. I think I broke my ankle."

Hunt was immediately out of the window and crouching beside her. There was no swelling yet. Likely, she'd just sprained it but there was no way to be sure. Without comment, he scooped her up, moving in a crouched jog toward the tree line. Hunt could see McIver waiting, scanning each way, watching for movement. Hunt was almost to cover when he heard the burst of gunfire. His instinct was to dive to the ground, but he still held the woman and so crouched lower yet, racing forward, pressing, pushing.

But there was something wrong.

The gunfire had not come from the exterior, but rather from the interior of the building. Depositing Dorothy with McIver, Hunt sprinted back toward the building. There was another burst of rounds.

One of the passengers, a man, young, overweight, scrambled through the window, rolling onto the ground and then stumbling to his feet.

"What's happening?" hollered Hunt as the two raced toward one another.

"A terrorist! Came in through the hallway," huffed the man.

Another man scrambled through the window, and then a woman after him, running blindly over the gravel surface with no regard for potential threat. Hunt made the building in time to see Dana standing over two dead terrorists. The one Hunt had carried into the room and one other. Though they were both obviously dead, still Dana aimed her gun at them. Blood and brain matter dripped from the wall. Hunt was pushed aside as the remainder of the patients pressed and clawed at one another, scrambling two at a time through the window and into the open. Dana remained still and silent, staring blankly at the carnage, the Kalashnikov still trained on the shredded meat that had, only moments before, been human beings.

Chapter 22

Bedford sat on a service road overlooking the flaming clinic from a vantage of perhaps five hundred yards. She was situated behind a small copse of trees and seated in her rented Ford Focus eating a turkey and Swiss on sourdough. She tapped her iPhone. "Bedford?" came a male voice almost immediately, rather thin in tone, but authoritative still, aged with decades of whiskey and cigarettes, it was amazing the voice's owner still lived.

"It's me," said Bedford into the phone.

"Well?"

"Not much change since my last report fifteen minutes ago."

"Survivors?"

"Twenty-seven at last count. All patients, no staff, no insurgents."

"The circumstances?"

Bedford fought the urge to sigh loudly into the phone. How many times could the man desire to hear the same information? "The same as in my previous report," she said. "Most were lost in the first wave of the attack. Marcus Huntington helped a small group to escape through a window and then made his way about the structure, entering the building on three separate occasions from different openings, in order to help another dozen to escape."

"And the combatants?"

"As I told you—all dead at the hands of the Huntington woman."

The high raspy voice offered a subtle cackle. "Spunky little jackal, that one."

"The woman was severely beaten and sexually assaulted by Kelvin Donnelley. She's still in shock. If you ask me, she's taking her anger out on anyone she sees as connected to Donnelley. I'm not sure I blame her."

"She could be arrested and charged with premeditated murder."

Bedford shook her head, still gazing down upon the scene below. "No. Most people would think her a hero for eliminating the hostiles and assisting her husband in freeing the endangered civilians. I doubt anyone would testify against the claim that these were acts of self-defense. Besides, she's been infected. A concentrated dose. Chances are she won't live to see the end of the week."

A heavy exhalation. "True. Regrettable, but true. Huntington, the man I mean, can we use him?"

Bedford stared out over the still-burning structure, watching the firefighters try to bring the blaze under control. The building was a loss as had been the plan—damn it! "Marcus? He's obviously resourceful."

"That much I knew. The question is, can we use him?"

"He's not gullible."

"He would be of no use to us if he was." A pause, and then, "As I see it he's unusually motivated. His wife is dying. I would guess he'd use any means necessary to acquire the antidote. His quest, and what is revealed through it, might be quite helpful to our cause."

Our cause.

These days there were far too many—all, it seemed, conflicting. But Bedford had to focus on one alone. Despite the consequences, her course was set.

"Very helpful." Agreed Bedford. "Tina Collins? What's the latest on her?"

A sigh. "That one? The situations complicated. I'm missing more facts than I possess. Let it go."

"I'm not entirely sure that's a healthy attitude where our asset is concerned."

"Bedford, don't play naive. Our asset is off grid. Whatever happens will happen. This is too big to blindly assume that no one will be lost."

"I'm not a schoolgirl, sir. My concern pertained to information lost should the asset perish, not to the person's well-being." She paused and then added, "Have you gotten anything on Peeves? Anything that can link him?"

"No. There's no proof. Nothing more than suppositions."

"Andrews?"

"Same answer, Bedford."

"Gant?"

A cackle. "You are a good girl. You know that?" And then he hung up.

Bedford stared ahead for several moments, nearly mesmerized by the pulsating glow of the blaze, and then slipped her left hand into a jacket pocket, removing a photograph of a young man. Her hand trembled.

Chapter 23

Dresden Germany & Virginia USA

Jonathan Thorpe had drugged Tina Collins almost a day ago now, he supposed. Though the time zone change tossed his sense about some. It really had been his only option—drugging her. He simply could not trust the woman. She'd entered his safe house—how she'd done this, he still couldn't be sure. She'd said they needed to talk. And so they'd talked.

"Johnny darlin', I'm not really sure why I'm here," she'd said, crossing the room to gaze out over the Dresden skyline. "Nice view. The apartment's a little cramped for your snooty tastes, but you're on the run, aren't you?"

"Yes, well, pleasantries aside, just why are you here, Tina? Do you mean to take me back to Tull, or perhaps kill me? Killing me is an option I suppose. There's already been an attempt. But, you knew that didn't you?"

Collins chuckled. "Ya'll finally learned his name. Johnny, you're landing yourself smack into a world a trouble." She turned to face him. Her dark skin glinted in the artificial light. She really was rather striking. Skinny as a bobbies' night stick, but striking still. "And yes," she added. "I should take you back to Joshua. Either that or kill you straightaway. But… Let's just say I'm not too sure I want to do either."

"And what exactly is that supposed to mean?"

"I'm a woman, darlin'. We're a fickle breed. I'm also allowed my secrets. But, I'll tell you what. I'll give you the opportunity to convince me not to pursue you—at least not until circumstances call for it."

Thorpe seated himself on the corner of his desk. "Yes, I suppose, that sounds wonderful and all, but dare I ask what it is I must do to achieve this wondrous grace, why would you offer it, and how in bloody hell am I supposed to trust you?"

Collins laughed. She had a magnificent smile. "Johnny, Johnny, always assuming you're in control of the situation. Let me put it this way." In a quick, fluid motion, she reached behind her back and produced a small Glock semiautomatic. "I need to know all of what you've learned about Joshua. After that, I'll make a decision." She cocked her head. "And if I get the notion you're holding out on me, well…"

Collins winked.

Damn the woman!

Thorpe met her gaze and then stood, moving toward a small foldout couch at the far end of the room. Collins wouldn't shoot him. Not yet. She was capable, he knew this from experience. He'd seen her coldly execute her former partner, Haas, when his increasingly irrational actions had endangered her cause. But, she didn't yet know what Thorpe had learned or with whom he might have had communications. She was playing something here and he didn't yet know what that might be. But he was confident that until such time as she felt he'd become more a risk than an asset, he was safe. "I've some bourbon if you like. Otherwise, tap water is the best I have to offer." He lowered himself onto the sofa. "Feel free to help yourself."

"I'm not thirsty, Johnny darlin', and you're stalling."

"If you'd planned to shoot me the deed would be done, so why don't we at least make this amicable? Pour me some bourbon, please. It's in the cabinet. The tumblers are below, and the ice cubes are where you'd expect. Then sit down. I've no problem telling you what I've learned. I'm sure none of the information is unknown to you."

Surprisingly, Collins chuckled, slid the Glock back into its holster and did just as Thorpe had suggested, pouring his drink and then seating herself on a blue and green patterned reclining chair opposite Thorpe. It took her a moment to situate, her expression indicating that she wasn't quite comfortable, but finally she smiled and said, "Have at it, Johnny."

With each new revelation, Collins stunning features became tauter, her eyes and broad full lips narrow. She had no idea that someone could have learned so much that had been hidden so well. She'd underestimated Thorpe. This was a good thing, but it also meant she would not do so again. "Now, allow me to ask you a thing or two," he said in conclusion.

Collins shrugged. "I guess you can give it a try, darlin'. But, you might not find me so forthcoming."

"Then, perhaps we should begin with something simple. I've uncovered significant information. How much of it is true?"

No smile. No feigned warmth or surprise. "Far more than you'd care to believe. And there is more that you may never unearth."

"That is quite appalling. You must know that. Is Joshua Tull insane?"

"Define insanity."

"Damn it, woman. I'd appreciate a real response."

"And I warned you that I'm not at liberty."

"Very well, tell me what you can tell me."

Collins blinked and then rubbed her eyes. "What you've already uncovered, Joshua believes it all. Including the more fantastic elements of the scenario."

"And you're a party to it. You believe this as well? You support his scheme?"

She blinked again, several times in rapid succession. "I... Joshua is... I'm involved..." She paused. Rubbed her eyes again and offered a weak smile. "Johnny, you little brat, you drugged me. It was the chair wasn't it? That little prick I felt when I sat down."

Thorpe matched her grin and raised her a shrug. "One cannot be too careful."

Several blinks, a shake of the head. "Oh, Johnny, you arrogant fool. You... should have trusted me." Another shake of the head. It seemed she might topple forward.

"Well, of course, trust is all nice and sweet, but, Tina dear, you pulled a gun. I saw what you did to Haas. Even if we had some level of mutual confidence, it wouldn't extend that far."

"Listen," she said, her voice now thick. "You... can trust me because I didn't kill you. And, think about it, Johnny. You hafta know I was supposed to."

"Then why not kill me? It's not as if we've had some stellar relationship."

"Ignorant fool," said Collins. She offered a weak smile and several blinks of the eyes, shaking her head as if Thorpe had missed something obvious. "Things aren't exactly as you might think they are. But, I gotta tell you..." Here, she drifted off.

"Bloody hell," snapped Thorpe. Of course the drug would take effect right when she was about to reveal something of import. He rose, strolled to the sink, filled a glass with cool water, returned to Collins, and tossed the liquid in her face. "You were saying?"

Collins sputtered and spit. "What?"

"You were about to tell me something. It seems it might have been of value."

Collins blinked, rolling her head. She wouldn't remain conscious for long.

"Come on, dear. What was it that you so desperately wanted to tell me? I'm sure it wasn't concerning my stunning features or winning smile."

Several blinks and a cough. "Multi-layers…"

"I'm not following."

Collins shook her head violently, blinking, trying to regain focus. Thorpe felt more and more the idiot for luring her to sit in that seat. Collins had information. "More… important to… you. Dana Huntington… infected."

"Dana? Infected how? What is she infected with? How is she involved in this madness?"

And Collins told him, at least the basics of it. And then she was out, not to regain consciousness for several hours. Much too long of a wait considering what Thorpe had just learned.

*****

The Virginia afternoon was unseasonably hot, the temperature something over eighty degrees. Late September, nearly October, and it was as muggy as a devil's armpit. Thus far, Thorpe had been unable to reach Dana. As well, he'd researched the thief-turned-terrorist, Kelvin Donnelley, during the flight and had yet to get a lead as to his locale. Peculiar fellow. Not the type Thorpe would have imagined having a hand in something so large or extreme. It truth, he seemed a rather average hoodlum. Another peculiarity was that Thorpe had found no reports public or otherwise indicating that there had been a terrorist attack aboard a Denver-bound train. That could mean one of two things: either this group was as powerful as his research would indicate and had contained any public or official knowledge of the event or Collins and Tull were pulling one over on him and there had been no such incident.

Thorpe found that possibility almost as absurd as the conspiracy theory. He had dealt with Tull, interacted with him, even contributed—albeit unknowingly and under coercion—to this event. No. Something had happened. There had been an attack. Perhaps not all that he'd been told. But the core, that was a definite.

As much as he hated to think that such an operation could exist, it was even more unsettling to think that he could be duped so handily. Something big was in motion, Dana's life was endangered, and dear God, Thorpe had been the one to contribute the means. He couldn't have known, of course. How could he? But still. That particular theft, Tull's intent was clear. There was only one reason someone would want militarized bubonic plague. How could he have been so selfish as to go along with such a thing?

He was weak, of course. His will had been broken in that Turkish hell. He'd been willing to do anything to escape that madness.

Thorpe cursed his own weakness and turned a corner, driving slowly past the large Victorian estate owned by Linus Tull. Thorpe had learned that the man was in fact related to Joshua. They were siblings, though separated in age by nearly a quarter of a century, and the product of different mothers. The two, it seemed, were not close in any familial way, but as to their associations and apparent motivations, were cut from the same cloth.

Thorpe had already identified the security system and breached the records of the company which had installed it, accessing the exact placement of each piece of the system, and downloading the layout of the home along with schematics and codes for the system. He allowed himself only a wisp of a smile. Dana had developed most of the software he still used for such operations.

Dana.

Thorpe continued to the end of the block, turned the corner, parked, and turned off the ignition. A daytime breach was incredibly risky, but there was little option. Reportedly, Linus Tull was reclusive, rarely leaving his home, sometimes even going more than a month without so much as strolling about the grounds. He had a security detail of four armed men and a highly sophisticated electronic system.

The electronics was the easy part. Thorpe was a master at this and could have the entire system disabled in less than sixty seconds. But the human element, that was unpredictable. Thorpe had little time to learn their routines, to know which men were likely to break pattern to have a smoke or to use the restroom, which might sit about and chat or watch the television, or which were more aggressive and likely to use lethal force.

In addition to the practical considerations, Thorpe was still contemplating his source: Tina Collins. Was her information valid? The few snippets he'd been able to verify proved legitimate, but there was much that he would need to take on faith. And Jonathan Thorpe was not a man of faith, that was, unless one counted faith in one's self. There he was quite devout. But even if Collins' information proved truly reliable, the next question became, why had she revealed what she had? What was the motivation? Was she acting on Joshua Tull's orders, again using Thorpe as a pawn, or had she, for some as yet unknown reason, betrayed her employer? And if so, to what end? Thorpe believed she found him rather attractive—as did most women—but his ego wasn't so inflated as to allow him to believe she'd done it out of some adolescent bid for his affections. Collins was a professional. She'd proven this at multiple levels. So why confide in Thorpe? What was the gain? Was this her move or something initiated by Joshua Tull?

He was on the grounds now and so refocused his thoughts to the task at hand. The fence had been easy. Already, he'd shorted the perimeter sensors, quickly inserting a tiny black component no larger than a box of playing cards, which tricked the system into maintaining a stable reading regardless of breaches or disturbances. The estate was lightly wooded, offering sporadic cover. Following a line of low hedges, Thorpe moved closer to the sprawling mansion in a low crouch. There were three cars in the drive, only one of which Thorpe knew for certain belonged to Tull. Thorpe was concerned that the man might have visitors. Again, the risk of a hastily-prepared daylight operation. If not for Dana, he would wait. Nothing else was so pressing. But he needed to find the specifics on the bio-toxin: how it had been mutated, and what could be done to cure her.

He spotted the first guard almost immediately. Strolling along the west side of the building, his posture was relaxed, but his taut expression and darting eyes told Thorpe that the man was alert and prepared for action. Thorpe moved closer, cautiously, breath nearly held. Once within ten feet of the man, Thorpe silently reached into his hip pouch and withdrew a small gun, checked it in three quick motions, and then aimed and fired.

The tiny tranquilizer dart hit the man at the base of the neck. Thorpe was there to grab him before the now-limp guard could fall to the ground and cause a disturbance. Quickly dragging the unconscious form to behind the line of shrubs, Thorpe paused, contemplated the man's weapon, a Beretta sub-compact pistol, snatched the gun and moved cautiously toward the west side of the home. He preferred to avoid lethal force, but if what he'd learned was true, neither Linus Tull nor any of those in his employ would hold the same reservations where he was concerned.

Locating a gray metal box attached at the base of the structure and hidden behind a wall of vegetation, Thorpe picked its lock and then went to work on the wiring, clipping a red and then a green line and then inserting a narrow plug which contained a specialized chip of Thorpe's own design. He then connected another small unit to the first by way of additional wiring and then withdrew a matchbox sized remote from his pocket and punched in a code. Two lights blinked green. All function was suitably compromised in under a minute.

Glancing right and then left, Thorpe stood, moving quickly along the wall to a door leading to a corridor adjacent the study. By all logic, Tull's computer would be in that study. This was the target. Thorpe picked the lock and entered. No alarm. Brilliant. His countermeasures appeared to have worked. He turned left down the long hallway carpeted in deep reds and golds. There was artwork on both walls. Familiar in style. These were not pieces he'd seen before, but the similarity to the collection of Joshua Tull was amazing. These two half brothers, separated in birth by a quarter of a century, raised in different states by different mothers, had nearly identical tastes. Very peculiar. Thorpe found it difficult to believe that the influence had come from the father. It could have, he supposed, but the man—now deceased for almost twenty years—had been an unremarkable man. A banker, he'd made a rather substantial income, but Thorpe had found nothing to indicate any keen fascination in this peculiar occultic mode of art, or of much else for that matter. No community service, no awards of achievement, nothing of note. The man had lived, worked, reproduced, but otherwise left very little mark beyond a rather healthy inheritance. He'd not married either of the two women who bore his children, but rather contributed to the boys financially and from a distance. It was not clear that either of the children had had any actual contact with the man. Thorpe paused, examining a Hieronymus Bosch painting depicting an angel being held at the ankle by a taloned hand and dragged into hell. Thorpe had obtained a companion piece for Linus Tull's sibling.

Quite peculiar.

Thorpe moved forward only another ten steps before pausing again.

Voices. Female. Spanish speaking. Thorpe's hasty research had been incomplete, giving him the number of security personnel, but not other staff such as maids and cooks. The door to the study was only perhaps fifteen paces forward, there were no interior doorways behind him. The two women were apparently situated around the bend and to the right at the end of the corridor. Thorpe made the decision to go for the study doorway. He could only hope the room was unoccupied. Bursting in on Tull or a guard would be much worse than encountering two maids.

Quickly, he made the door, picked the lock, and slipped inside. The room was dark. An interior space, the study had no windows. The lights were on a fader and Thorpe slid this up only so much as he needed to navigate the area.

The room was of about five hundred square feet and littered with strange occultic artifacts and images. As predicted, there was a computer on the desk. With any luck it would be the one containing the needed files. Thorpe inserted a disk into the drive and a memory stick into a USB port. The disk began to whir and Thorpe saw the computer come to life. Six asterisks appeared in the password box, the computer blinked and then Thorpe was in.

There was no time to sift through the files to determine which were of value and so Thorpe opened the program he'd just installed, selecting the "download all" option. Again, the disk whirred. A window opened, showing the progress of the download. The disk whirred some more, hesitated, and then resumed. A red block appeared on the download graph and then another. The memory disk flickered blue. The disk whirred. Another red block on the chart.

"Come one, come on," hissed Thorpe. It seemed the program was bogging down. He'd never known it to take so long. Four minutes already and it was barely a third of the way done.

Another red block.

The memory stick flickered.

Two more minutes.

Too slow. Much too slow.

Thorpe's stomach tightened. Why had he suddenly become jumpy?

Voices. Two of them—male.

And footsteps.

Coming closer.

Another red block.

The memory stick flickered.

Closer.

One of the voices belonged to a man advanced in age, the other, young.

Another red block.

They were almost to the door now. Thorpe considered hiding, but there really was no time, nor was there a suitable place. Simply put, he was exposed.

The memory stick flickered.

The download was barely more than halfway to completion.

The footsteps ceased.

The voices continued.

The door handle turned.

Thorpe withdrew the stolen Beretta as Linus Tull and a young sullen-faced man stepped into the room.

Tull smiled at the sight of Thorpe, no surprise in his expression. Like his half-brother, he was tall, perhaps six foot five inches. He had light red hair and angular features. Again, like his sibling, he had heterochromia, each eye of a different hue, one green, one blue, these situated beneath a pronounced brow.

The age difference was noticeable but not as much so as Thorpe might have supposed. "Well, look at this," said Tull, his voice rich and full. "I know you. Well, not exactly. But I've read your file. Thorpe. Sit down. Sit down. You've done a tremendous amount of traveling in the past twenty-four hours. The jetlag must be horrendous."

Thorpe returned the grin. "Thank you for your concern," he said. "But, all of those hours on a plane, I'd just as soon stand. I'm sure you understand."

Tull nodded and shrugged, taking a sip of deep red liquor and strolling toward a couch at the far end of the room. His companion remained silent and positioned in front of the door. "I hope you don't find me rude if I sit. The old bones, they no longer appreciate prolonged activity."

"I don't suppose I'm in a position to consider anything rude. I am, after all, the intruder." As Thorpe could no longer aim toward both, he kept the gun trained at the younger man. There was a bulge under the left armpit, a shoulder holster.

Tull shrugged. "Put that gun down and we'll call you a guest. You work for Joshua, after all. I'm sure we can extend some courtesy."

"Yes, well, that's lovely, but your beloved Joshua has taken it upon himself to have me murdered. I'm not particularly pleased with him."

"And so you come to me. Well, I suppose that shows your resourcefulness. Joshua picked a good man, it seems. How much, exactly, have you learned?"

"Well, I suppose I've discovered enough to make you conspirators uneasy, but not enough to prove a damn thing."

A chuckle. "Yes, that is the way it goes, isn't it? And what you've learned, do you believe it?"

"Ah! Well, there, you see, it becomes difficult. I'm not yet convinced that even you believe it all. And if you do..." Thorpe shrugged.

"If I do, I must be crazy, is that it?"

"Well, either way, I think you're a bit batty, but yes. What I've found, this clandestine movement of yours, you're basing it on the premise that you're some master race destined to rule the world. Were you and Hitler friends when you were young?"

Tull offered a hearty laugh. "I'm not quite old enough to have shared a childhood with Adolf. Besides, the man was a lunatic, perceiving only a fraction of the truth. If he'd only allowed himself to believe, if he'd embraced the opportunity given him instead of corrupting it for his own ends…"

"Ah! Yes, of course, as opposed to you."

Tull leaned forward, elbows on his knees, hands clasped loosely before him. "The difference is that our claim to superiority happens to be valid."

"Right. Yes. Of course. Because you believe you were sired by some mythical supernatural being?"

"Eh, mythical, no—well, not exactly—but, it seems you've learned the crux of it."

"The crux being that you and Joshua are among a race of superior beings. I'll admit, I'm skeptical about your parentage. It's unlikely that Theodor Tull was your father. You and your brother are both tall, with light red hair, and those peculiar eyes. Tull shared none of those characteristics. He was rather squat and dark. And the similarities cannot be attributed to the maternal side, as you do not share the same mother. This aside, I'm sure that whoever fathered you, he was entirely human." Thorpe paused for a moment. "What troubles me is that it appears the two of you are not alone. There are dozens of you spread about the globe, each with similar features, most of whom are powerful, but far from obvious. Very peculiar. Care to elaborate? I'm thinking, cloning perhaps?"

Tull chuckled. "Cloning. Of course, you would retreat to science. Science is safe. It can be explained. It blots out that which we find disconcerting. But, consider my advanced age, Mr. Thorpe. Do you really believe cloning to have been a viable option at the time of my conception? No. Science was not yet advanced in the area of genetics. But, Mr. Thorpe, it does seem you've learned a great deal. I'll be honest, that troubles me." With that, Tull nodded toward his companion, and Thorpe had only a moment to dive behind the desk as the first barrage of bullets flew through the space he'd just occupied.

Scampering around the heavy mahogany desk, Thorpe emerged on the far side, squeezing the Beretta's trigger.

Bloody hell! The safety was still engaged.

Thorpe scooted back, avoiding yet another burst of fire. Waiting a three count, he then popped up and, before the young man had an opportunity to get a bead on him, unloaded two shots into the guard's right kneecap. The guard tumbled forward, dropping his gun as Thorpe snatched the memory stick from the computer, raced forward, grabbing the man's fallen weapon, and then kicking him sharply in the face. The guard tumbled sideways, cradling his kneecap and moaning in pain. Tull was barely off of the couch, cell phone at his ear, by the time Thorpe made the doorway. Reinforcements would be only moments behind.

Due to Thorpe's precautions, no alarm had yet sounded, but between Tull's phone call and the echo of gunfire the staff had certainly been alerted. Instead of turning left out of the study, and retreating the way he'd entered, Thorpe turned right, racing down the dimly lit corridor and then making another right at the end of the hallway. Pulling the small remote from his pocket, he depressed a red button. A dull pop and whoosh could be heard from the west side of the building. Thorpe's charge had detonated. Soon the building would be smoke-filled, and flames would threaten the structure. The staff would be forced to decide between chasing him and saving the estate. Thorpe was betting that Linus Tull would choose the estate. The problem was, with his resources, Tull would likely locate him within hours.

Thorpe was almost to the eastern door to the building when he encountered two armed guards racing toward him. Wanting to avoid lethal force, he fired the Berretta at the light fixture above their heads. It burst in a splay of glass causing the two to shield their eyes with their hands. Thorpe leaped through an adjacent window, shattering it and rolling clumsily on the grassy ground. Scrambling to his feet, he raced toward the already-breached perimeter fence as bullets whizzed past. He'd almost made it to the barrier when the bullet found him.

Chapter 24

Las Vegas Nevada

Hunt crossed the small waiting room to the vending machines where he purchased a Mountain Dew and a Snickers bar. The breakfast of champions, he supposed. It had now been two days since the attack and nothing made sense. He'd done his best to help the other survivors of the Colorado clinic blaze to escape, but had heard nothing of them since.

Curious.

Frightening.

As for Hunt, he and Dana had slipped from the clinic, veering south along the ridge until connecting with a major thoroughfare where they had then taken two consecutive taxi cabs, ultimately arriving at a small airfield where Hunt chartered a plane to Las Vegas, their city of residence. Retrieving Hunt's car at the airport, they'd not returned to their plush high-rise condominium on the Las Vegas Strip, but drove directly to a small clinic in the Summerlin subdivision on the far west side of the valley. The facility was run by Dr. Jerry Byers, a retired Army doc Hunt had known while in the service. After a bout of hefty persuasion, Byers had agreed to admit Dana with no official record as to her stay.

And now he simply remained put.

Byers was doing his thing and Hunt was stuck in the tiny torturous mind numbing cage of a waiting room. The clinic was not designed for inpatient care and so admitting Dana as such had been an anomaly. It was early morning, before regular business hours, and Hunt had the place to himself. He slid two Oxycontin onto his tongue, sipped his Mountain Dew, flipped through year-old magazines, listened to old Kiss songs on his MP3, and glanced occasionally at the high definition television mounted on the cream colored wall.

Mostly, Hunt worried about Dana. About her being infected with the plague.

Was that his fault?

Had there been something else he could have done?

He remembered having been sluggish, his mind just a little out of sorts. If he'd been one hundred percent would it have made a difference? Would he have been able to stop them before Donnelley got to Dana?

The answer was a vapor, unknowable and therefore infuriating. He would never know for certain if his weakness had brought this thing about, and so, as with Iraq, he would carry the guilt.

Hunt massaged his temples.

Something was going on with Dana. Something beyond the plague, something beyond even the beating and the mass execution she'd witnessed. The ruthless manner in which she had disposed of the terrorists at the Colorado clinic. One of the men had been unconscious, unarmed and injured—no discernable threat—and still she'd gunned him down. Hunt had tried to talk with her about it while in transit, but she'd remained silent, distant, staring out of the car window, only responding to Hunt's questions with rudimentary replies. She often glared at him, her eyes narrow slits over the surgical mask she wore. Any mention of Donnelley or the terrorists was met with bursts of profanity. Hunt wondered if more had happened than Dana had revealed and he asked her this directly but she'd denied any such occurrence. "I was brutally beaten and infected with the bloody plague, isn't that enough?" she'd nearly shouted.

Dana had been intentionally infected. She could very well die. Add to this the fact that she'd been forced to witness the cold-blooded execution of the train crew after she'd survived a vicious pounding. Hunt had no business questioning her behavior. Combat-hardened soldiers sometimes cracked after lesser events.

Something caught Hunt's eye.

On the television.

A breaking story.

Hunt grabbed the remote control, increasing the volume as he pulled his MP3 earplugs free. An apparent terrorist attack in Chile. Plague, released in a crowded bus station in the capital city of Santiago.

Still listening to the report, Hunt rose and began to pace. This was the third terrorist attack in two days—not including the Denver-bound train: London, Beijing, and now Santiago. Each had utilized the plague. Each had been highly visible with no attempt to hide the event. His mind now fully engaged, Hunt clicked off the facts:

Each attack distributed the pathogen through a similar system.

Each event was on a different continent.

Each was apparently perpetrated by previously docile homegrown cells, who, based on the nature of the attacks, were somehow highly funded and well connected to their respective governments.

But, the Colorado attack was different. There was a full on effort to hide the incident. Whoever was behind this had made every effort to obliterate any knowledge of the event.

Why?

The purpose of any terrorist activity was to create fear. And fear could not be accomplished if no one was made aware of the incident. This had nettled Hunt from the beginning. Bedford's assertion that the RPA had attempted to cover up the attack didn't wash. Why go to such lengths to hide what they'd obviously worked so hard to achieve? Even an unsuccessful event could cause terror. The very fact that the attack had been staged, that only by the merest chance had it been diminished—not even stopped completely, people had been infected—would cause nearly the same level of panic. Maybe the question shouldn't be why cover it up, but rather who? If these attacks were all connected, and logic dictated that they were, why handle the Colorado incident differently? The answer: The terrorist group wouldn't. The difference was that someone else—some other entity—was suppressing this thing.

The government?

If so, this was very disturbing, because innocent civilians had been killed in that clinic fire. Was the U.S. government willing to slaughter dozens of its own citizens simply to keep a lid on this thing?

Chugging a gulp of Mountain Dew, Hunt stared up at the television screen. Over three hundred and fifty exposed in Chile. What was the angle? Who had coordinated these attacks by separate groups, each seemingly with its own agenda? The faction claiming responsibility in London had claimed political reasons, the Beijing group, religious, the Santiago cell had yet to be identified.

Donnelley and his bunch had been disenfranchised patriots, but their rational was thin and poorly conceived.

And Donnelley himself. The man just didn't seem capable of orchestrating such an attack without considerable assistance. He was obviously an addict of some sort, prone to emotional outburst and physical manifestations such as twitching. Someone was pulling his strings.

Jerry Byers strolled into the waiting room: white lab coat, clipboard, typical physician. He'd tossed on about thirty pounds since Hunt had known him in the service, but still looked fit for a forty-five year old suburban guy. Like Hunt, he still kept his dirty blond hair in a military-style buzz cut and had the vigor of a man who put in his hours at the gym. "Hey, Jer. Tell me some good news," said Hunt as he turned to face the man, his fist clenched and jaw tight, despite his casual approach.

Byers met his gaze. "I can give you good news, but I'd rather give you the truth."

Hunt's stomach took a dive. By nature, Byers was an optimist. It was practically a religion for him. The man almost always found some reason for hope and a smile. Not so in this instance. "Hit me with it, Jerry."

Byers offered a barely perceptible nod. "As we've discussed, Bubonic plague is a bacteria, it multiplies quickly in the bloodstream and often attacks the lungs. Traditionally, it's treated with a course of antibiotics. I've got your wife on Streptomycin. It's had absolutely zero effect."

"Is there something else you can give her?"

"Gentamycin is the other option, but I'm not hopeful. This is a militarized variant. As such, there's a specific drug, an antidote, which needs to be administered. Ordinarily, these are manufactured by the same group developing the modified strain."

Hunt massaged his left bicep. The thing was cramping. "You're saying that here, in the U.S., we're developing bio-weapons?"

Byers angled his head. "Not as such. Labs are tasked to develop the weapon in order to then generate a cure so that when lunatics from overseas create the stuff we're prepared."

Insane. The world was insane.

"Alright. So, administer the cure."

Byers hesitated, his lips pulling into a tight and narrow line. "You see, Hunt, there's a problem. We've matched the bacteria in your wife's system to a variant on file at the CDC."

"Okay. And?"

"Their samples are missing—along with the antidote."

Hunt stared at him for a minute, contemplating the ramifications. Someone had breached security at the CDC. Not an easy task by any means. They'd taken the antidote, meaning they wanted complete control, either intending for the bug to spread uninhibited, or for them to use the antidote as a bargaining chip to further their ends. "Can more antidote be manufactured?" he asked.

A slow shake of the head. "Not without access to the bacteria."

"Dana's got the bacteria in her blood."

"Hunt, I'm a run-of-the-mill physician, not a research scientist. I wouldn't know where to begin."

Hunt turned, pacing one way and then the other. "The CDC could do it. Send them samples."

"I'm in contact with them on that, awaiting a response. To be honest, they seemed very cautious, maybe even suspicious of my inquiries."

Hunt balled his fists as if to punch someone. Too many unnecessary road-blocks. "I'm guessing the CDC didn't manufacture the weaponized plague. That had to happen at a military facility. Can the CDC gain access to the antidote through that end?"

"I'm looking into that as well, but we've got to be realistic. I've no clear-ance. It could take me days—if at all!—even to learn where it had been manu-factured."

Hunt marched to within inches of Byers. "You're telling me there isn't much time."

To his credit, the doctor met Hunt's gaze. "At the rate the symptoms are accelerating, I'd say Dana has forty-eight, maybe seventy-two at the outside."

Hunt couldn't accept this, not so easily. "But the CDC, they know who manufactured it. Can't they apply some pressure? This is life and death, Jer. We can't just sit back and let her die."

Byers appeared as if he might lay his palm on Hunt's shoulder in a comforting gesture and then chose against it. "I didn't say anything about sitting back and letting this thing happen. You have to know I'm on it. I'm just telling you the facts. Now, I'm going to get back on the phone and see what I can get in motion. Are you going to be okay?"

"Yeah. What choice do I have?" A pause. "But, um, my meds, you have any on hand? I've been on the road for a few days, running low."

Byers eyed Hunt for a long moment, his clear green eyes sharp behind his metal-framed lenses. He said nothing.

"What?"

"We've known each other a long time. I've been treating you for several months. There are some things, Hunt. Since you've been here with Dana. Behavior, mannerisms, your overall demeanor."

"Meaning what exactly?"

"The Oxycontin, how frequently are you taking it and in what dosage?"

"Damn it, Jer, I don't need this right now."

"Are you experiencing insomnia, anxiety, muscle or bone pain?"

"I'm really not in the mood for..."

"I've observed your restlessness and involuntary leg movement. You're constantly massaging your limbs."

"Jerry! My wife is dying!"

Byers remained silent.

"Okay, maybe I'm upping my usage a little. It's under control."

Byers nodded. "Those things can be seriously habit forming."

"I get it, Jer. Like I said, under control." Hunt reached for his absent yo-yo, silently cursing its absence. "This isn't a good time, Jerry. Not with Dana... Give me some grace, huh?"

Another nod. "After this is done, we look into your situation—agreed?"

"Yeah. Agreed."

"I'll give you a five day script, no more."

Hunt nodded. Chastised like a child. Avoiding Byers' gaze, he glanced toward the hallway leading to Dana's room. "Can I see her?"

"We're running tests. My nurse will come for you when Dana is prepared to see you." With that, Byers gave Hunt a pat on the back and retreated into his office, leaving Hunt, once again, alone in the waiting room.

But Hunt wasn't about to sit by and let events unfold in whatever messed up way they might land. Already he was speed dialing a number he hadn't used since just after Brazil. He wasn't quite sure how Colonel Lucky Lindell would respond to the call. In some ways Hunt felt his former commander might hold him responsible for the death of his son the previous February in Sao Paulo. Lindell had only spoken with Hunt once since the funeral and that call had been purely perfunctory. But, Hunt couldn't let hurt feelings or even bitter mourning prevent him from making the call. Lucky was at the Pentagon. He was in a position of power. By all logic, he could get things done.

Hunt was on hold for several minutes. When finally he was put through, it wasn't Lucky Lindell's rich and authoritative voice he heard, but rather that of a young woman. "Colonel James Lindell's office. Lieutenant Corina Meeks speaking."

"Corky?"

A pause. "Yes?"

"Corky, it's Marc Huntington."

"Hunt?"

"Yeah, Cork. I didn't know you were still working with Lucky."

"I was just recently reassigned. Lucky pulled some strings."

"He's good at that," agreed Hunt. He still didn't know the full story, but apparently Lindell had moved behind the scenes after the events in Iraq, most likely saving Hunt from undergoing a court martial. Lindell looked after his people. "Listen, Corky, I don't mean to be rude. I'd love to catch up with you sometime. But I've got a situation here. I need to speak with Lucky."

"He's out, Hunt. Unavailable."

"Till when? This is time sensitive."

"I don't know when he'll be back. There's a situation."

"I'm going to take a wild stab and say it has to do with the recent terrorist activity around the globe. Santiago, maybe?"

"Hunt, we're friends. You know I'd tell you if I could."

"Uh-huh. Let me ask you this. Is Lucky's office aware of the terrorist attack on a Denver-bound train two days ago?"

"Hunt, what are you talking about?" Her voice held a mixture of surprise and skepticism.

"Homegrown terrorists released militarized bubonic plague."

"How did you come across this? We haven't heard a thing."

Hunt gripped the phone tightly. If the Pentagon wasn't aware of the event something was seriously short-circuited. And what of Homeland Security and the FBI? Both agencies had had personnel at the clinic prior to the fire. How had this information not made it to the Pentagon? Two and two did not equal four with this thing. "I was on the train, Cork, caught wind of the plot and notified train security. They called it in. There was a blockade set up—I think National Guard, but don't quote me on that. The blockade was lifted almost immediately. No one even boarded the train to investigate the report."

"That doesn't make sense."

"Yeah, well, there's more." And Hunt went on to detail the events of the past forty-eight hours.

"So, you're thinking there's more than one party involved," said Corky after listening quietly throughout Hunt's explanation.

"It's the only thing that makes sense. All of the other attacks have been made public."

"All of the other ones that you know of," cautioned Corky.

Hunt's gut went tight. "Are you saying there have been more events? Does your office know something?"

"I wish we did, Hunt. Not that I could reveal it to you. But, no. I have no such knowledge. I was just postulating an idea."

"Okay. Good point. If there was one cover-up, there could be others. But, listen. I need a favor. This is a biggie and I can't take no for an answer."

Hunt thought he heard a subtle chuckle. "Same old Hunt. What do you need now? A new yo-yo?"

"Actually, that would come in handy. I bound one of the terrorists with my yo-yo string. I need a replacement."

"The worst thing, Hunt, is that I believe you. Now, what is it you want? I need to move on this information."

Hunt thought for a moment. "Okay, a couple of things. The leader of the terrorist cell escaped the train on a Blackhawk helicopter. Wanna tell me how a homegrown terrorist cell gets its hands on a Blackhawk?"

"Go on."

"The terrorist leader is a small time crook named Kelvin Donnelley. I need your help in finding him."

"Hunt, you're a civilian. This isn't your responsibility."

"He infected my wife with the plague, Cork. From what I can gather, he's got the antidote."

There was a pause on the line. When Corky spoke again, her voice was quite. Hunt had been afraid she wouldn't take well to this. He and Corky had been close—intimately close—at one time. "You have a wife?" She said finally. "I remember a certain morning in San Lucas when you insisted irreparable horrors would visit you if ever you settled down with one person."

"Yeah, Cork. People change." Hunt waited for a moment before continuing. "Listen, I'm sorry if this makes you feel slighted or something, but it is what it is. Now, back to the point. Donnelley's answering to someone in a position of power. The Blackhawk, the cover-up, the plague, those other attacks around the globe. All of that, and there's no official investigation, no one even trying to catch this guy. Whoever is behind this obviously has the ability to manipulate our defenses. I can't just sit around and wait for the government to get into the game while Dana sits in her death bed. The doc gave her forty-eight hours, Cork. Three days max."

"That's horrible, Hunt. I'm so sorry." A pause. "Isn't there a treatment? I'd have thought…"

Hunt cut her off. "It's a militarized variant. The normal antibiotics don't cut it. Jerry Byers is treating her. He's already checked with the CDC. The antidote, along with their samples of the strain have gone missing. Donnelley taunted Dana with the cure. It makes sense that he would have it. I need to find this creep. I also need to find out if that antidote is sitting in some lab. Jerry has no clearance. He's just a civilian and they're stonewalling him. I need your connections, Cork. Lucky's connections."

It seemed Corky contemplated this for a moment. "Hunt, I want to help. I do. But, I don't have clearance for some of this either."

"Lucky does."

"He's unavailable. Hunt I told you that."

"Damn it, Corky, my wife is dying. Government agencies are obviously compromised. That means it's up to me."

"And so you called your old flame to help you save your wife."

Hunt held his temper, though his inclination was to scream. "Corky, you're bigger than that and you know it. Besides, I called Lucky, not you."

He heard her sigh. "You're right—of course. I'll research this Donnelley and check into the theft at the CDC. I'll need Jerry Byers' contact information so I can coordinate on the plague antidote. I'll see if I can find a trail for you to chase."

"Good. That's good. We need to go beyond the CDC, though. If they don't have the antidote we need to find the lab where the bug was produced. My guess is they'd have a sample."

"I'll find the lab."

"Thanks, Cork. This means a lot to me."

"You really love her, don't you?"

"Yeah, Corky. I fell pretty hard."

Chapter 25

Dr. Marion Dietz moved about the large cluttered space, carefully inspecting each of her subjects individually before repeating the process almost immediately. The transatlantic flight had been a worrisome experience. Transporting such fragile and precious subjects with quite specific needs was difficult by any standard, but there had been turbulence and even in a converted 717, space was tight—twelve hospital beds along with medical equipment including hazmat compartments and gear. At one point, after a particularly dramatic dip, three of the beds had collided. None of the subjects were injured—they were all strapped tightly in place—yet still, two IVs were pulled free and equipment needed to be reset.

Twelve.

One dozen subjects, each a living breathing incubator harboring the most amazing bacterial strain ever developed both in nature and the lab, each at some stage in a prolonged coma, or more accurately, hibernation. In some instances, exceptionally prolonged. In the case of the very old ones, even she had seriously wondered if the process would work. Her scientific mind had difficulty accepting the truth of it all. Yes, it was science that preserved these people, but not science as she knew it; and in the mind of her employer, Joshua Tull, not science at all. Yet then, why enlist her if he believed the process to be entirely beyond the scope of the empirical? The man was inconsistent and unreadable as well as tyrannical and compulsive.

She knew that theoretically these specimens should not be alive. Bacteria had been known to lie dormant for centuries, as had viruses—even for millennia. The B-permians strain found in Southern California, was purportedly 250 million years old. Even a plant, Lomatia tasmanica: 43,000 years old. But, complex, multi-celled organisms? Mammals? Human Beings!

It was the bacteria that provided the miracle: invading the system, slowing the bodily functions to near nonexistent, while simultaneously preserving the tissue by providing hydration and minerals it absorbed from the surrounding atmosphere. These unicellular microbes invaded the DNA of the host, initially slowing the system to a state of deep hibernation and then sustaining the host for remarkable durations. It was an amazing piece of nature. Once Dietz had been made aware of and then given the opportunity to view this astounding assortment of subjects, she'd been offered the magnificent task of nurturing—and even improving upon—the natural strain.

The strain.

The bacteria.

Joshua Tull had acquired this. Two variations of the same genus, one benevolent, one malign, had been discovered growing within a fossilized bone in South America. How Tull had known of the bone's existence—not to mention the dozens of comatose forms located in a nearby cave—remained a mystery. But he had sent a team to retrieve these and as soon as the subjects had arrived, Dietz had set about the task of analyzing the unique bacterium.

She knew Tull's motives were self-serving, but the opportunity to head such a project had been too great to ignore. If these two bacteria could be manipulated properly they might be used to put patients in a state of suspended animation until cancer, or possibly Parkinson's, or a dozen other horrific maladies, could be treated or cured. This was what earlier scientists had hoped cryogenics could achieve; but this was something already existent in nature.

The problem, of course, was that the sister strain was monstrous in its capabilities.

And this was the strain that interested Tull.

But, he had agreed to fund her research on the benign strain once Dietz had completed the task at hand. So much good could be done. Dietz was not so foolish as to believe the ends justified the means, that granting Tull a modified version of the malignant archebacteria, enhanced in its communicable properties through fusion with another strain, in this case, Yersinia pestis, better known as Bubonic plague, could ever undue the harm he intended. But, eventually, once this new plague he sought to unleash had been tamed, once the fear and anger and desperation had subsided and life returned to normal, then, when the benign strain was in use and saving lives, then the world would recognize the gift they had been given. The potential benefit to humankind was astounding. Perhaps Dietz would be well remembered regardless any connection to the events of this week.

Her lips quivered, only slightly. Involuntarily. Reaching into her pocket, she withdrew her flax: Barenjager Honey Liqueur. Her true and loyal friend. No judgment. No condemnation.

A tiny sip as she gazed across the space—an old airplane hangar. There was plenty of room, all of the necessary equipment. But the pressure to bring this project to completion was near unbearable.

Another sip.

Dietz moved to the second closest patient, draped in clear protective plastic, by all appearances a "young" dark-skinned woman of perhaps seventeen to twenty years of age. The first time Dietz had seen her, the subject had been attired in the loose fitting robes and jewelry usually associated with ancient Egypt. It staggered Dietz' mind to know that, based on test results, this woman was over four thousand years old.

Astounding!

She'd come to Dietz, as they all had, not only comatose, but to all appearances dead. And it was these patients, those held a breadth away from eternity that could incubate and even multiply the malignant strain. It was almost as if nature had developed the one strain in order that the other might flourish. Still, if Dietz could one day determine how to revive these or, perhaps, newer, much younger, subjects infected with the benign strain, then medical history would be made. This would be a workable, beneficial accomplishment.

But, not that. Not now. This time was for the other.

Another, longer, sip.

Still, this woman, this subject showed promise. Dietz had pursued her own goals while simultaneously tending to those of Tull. It had taken months, but Dietz had brought this woman to a seemingly near-conscious state. Not only had Dietz tended to her from a biological bent, administering measured doses of the benign bacteria, rehydrating her system, monitoring the steadily progressing vital signs and testing blood and tissue samples for signs of unwanted side effects and/or rejection, but she also put this, and each other patient through a daily physical therapy routine in an effort to stretch, limber up, and strengthen muscles not used in centuries. Skin creams and oils had been applied to the flesh, revitalizing skin that had long ago lost its elasticity. Dietz had had help of course, a top-rate staff of over two dozen physicians and therapists, many who, like her, had once been considered amongst the best in the world. Only one of her staff had accompanied her on the journey though, a forty-six year-old physician named Natalie Pierce.

There was a sound from behind, and Dietz turned, assuming she'd see the other doctor.

It was not Pierce.

"Joshua! I hadn't expected you."

Tull's thin humorless lips pulled into a taut grin as he sipped buttermilk from a lead crystal tumbler. "If I announced my... every coming," he stammered. "I... would never catch anyone in... mischief." He nodded as if this explained everything.

Dietz forced a smile, attempting to meet his peculiar gaze. "There is no mischief to be found, Joshua. As always, I'm on task—all the more so considering the time limitations." She paused and then added, "There are butter cookies on the lab table if you're interested."

Tull stared at her as if contemplating her statement, his heterochromatic eyes revealing nothing of his intent.

"The subjects are progressing," she said after determining that he was not about to speak. Habitually, she tugged at one of her yellowed fingernails. "But, I will reiterate that I believe your timetable to be unrealistic. The gestation period of the newly reengineered strain is still questionable, the results uncertain. Are you sure you wouldn't like a cookie?"

Tull cocked his head back. It seemed almost he was sniffing the stale air of the retasked hangar. "Hmmm... One... must leave time for one's pleasures," he said.

"Excuse me?"

He grinned, now leering at her bosom. "You claim that you... are always on... t...task. One must leave time for one's pleasures."

He stepped forward. Dietz knew that men did not find her attractive. For one thing she was sixty-two years old and likely looked a few years older yet. But, even as a young woman she'd rarely caught a man's eye. She was too tall, her shoulders rolled, her hair thin and her complexion uneven. Many found her mannish: large, often scabbed hands, hollow long face unadorned with make-up, she was anything but feminine. Still, it was obvious what Tull desired.

Stepping to her left, she said. "I'm sorry, Joshua. I am not one of your play-things. Unlike Miss Collins, I am not willing to play the whore simply to gain favor."

Tull shrugged. "Playthings. You… could be… mine. I could be yours. The… distinction is unimportant." He sipped his buttermilk.

Dietz moved around the table which held the young Egyptian woman, keeping this between she and Tull. "This is our most promising subject," she said in an effort to redirect his mindset. "Aside from the sixty year-old male that has been in hibernation less than a year, that is."

Following Dietz around the plastic-draped bed, Tull set his now-empty tumbler on a nearby tray. "Most… promising? They should all be promising. That is why we selected this… particular dozen."

Dietz pulled at her nail, circling the bed and monitors even as Tull strolled around to where she had just stood. "I meant only that, of the twelve, this particular subject has produced the most output. The gestation period is less than in the others."

"I don't sleep well," he said, still following her, slow, yet deliberate, his gaze unblinking. "T…terrible spells in the night. But, that… said, even I who would relish a full night's rest, would not… desire a centuries long slumber. How curious it must be."

"I'm certain it was not her choice, Joshua. This is a complex medical situation. Will you please stop following me around this patient?"

Offering a wry grin, Tull did as requested, pausing near the patient's head. "No. It is not her choice to sleep. She has fled so… long ago. A peculiar thing, life." Tull angled his head as if in contemplation. Again, it seemed he sniffed the air. "They will be ready?"

"Well, yes, but…"

"And so your task… is near complete. Be happy, Marion. It will soon be… time for you to p…play." He stepped forward and, not giving her time to react, kissed her gently on the forehead, and then turning, strolled casually from the room without a backward glance.

Chapter 26

Hunt still had trouble seeing Dana's beautiful features so swollen and bruised. She lay semi-reclined in the hospital bed, a plastic tent covering the upper half of her body. Dr. Jerry Byers had been trying to get her temperature down since their arrival, but still she'd leveled off at just under 103. She was experiencing severe headaches, nausea, delirium. He'd never seen her so gaunt or unresponsive. It was early evening now and Dana had been in and out of consciousness throughout the day. When she was awake, she alternated between some slight semblance of the woman he knew and a silent, sullen, bitter form.

It seemed their connection had somehow been severed, that their comfort in one another, their very oneness, had been compromised. Hunt feared she might be attempting to distance herself from him so that he wouldn't take it so hard if she died.

If so, that was foolish thinking. If anything this would make it all the worse.

Pulling his earplugs free, Hunt turned off his MP3 player and wrapped the plugs wire around the device. Normally he used music—most often the classic rock band Kiss—to keep his mood up and his adrenaline flowing. Today, even songs like Detroit Rock City and Strutter did nothing but annoy him. He felt helpless and disconnected. He needed to do something, in some way contribute to Dana's recovery. Hunt was not good at waiting.

Dana coughed.

Her eyes fluttered.

Consciousness!

Hunt stepped forward. "Hey, Sweetie. How you feeling?"

She coughed again, deep, hollow, the rattle of death at the doorstep. "Isn't it obvious?"

Their eyes met through the plastic tent.

Cool. Emotionless. How could he feel so disconnected from the love of his life? He fiddled with the MP3 player in his pocket wishing for his yo-yo. "Um, an old Delta Force buddy who works in Lucky Lindell's office is checking into both Donnelley and the antidote at the CDC. We're doing all we can, hon. Something'll break on this thing."

Dana stared calmly at her husband for perhaps fifteen seconds before speaking. When she did, her speech was interrupted by hacking coughs. "It's not you, Hunt. I don't want you to think that it is. But, I can't have you here right now. Go home if you must. Go track down the antidote if you feel the need to be useful. I'll call you when I'm ready for you to return."

"But, honey. I need to be here for you."

"No you don't. Not now. I need to be left alone. That's the bloody awful truth of it. I can't have you here. Now go."

Her expression was firm.

But her eyes were moist.

They stared silently at one another for more than a minute before she said, "Hunt, go. Please. Just go."

Hunt stood firm for another several seconds, simply staring through the plastic tent at Dana's battered face. Finally he nodded and turned to leave without another word. In his gut he felt something had happened just then. Something of finality. Something irreparable. And for the life of him he just couldn't put all of the pieces together.

Stopping only momentarily at the reception desk, Hunt confirmed that Doc Byers had his cell number, and then marched out into the hot Nevada heat. His was only one of four cars in the parking lot: a 1973 Volkswagen Thing, yellow, with a rendition of the movie poster from John Carpenter's 1982 horror classic, The Thing, painted on the hood. He'd never seen the movie but loved the wordplay. Dana hated the car the same way she hated his love of the band Kiss. In her eyes the car was a beast and the band a circus, in Hunt's, both spoke to his personality. True, both the car and the band dated to before his birth, but they were part of what made him the irresistible goof she'd fallen for.

He sat alone in the lot staring west toward Red Rock Canyon. He'd proposed to her out there, at the top of one of the peaks. He'd promised to never leave her, that he would be there for her always—no matter what. But now, at a time when she would need him the most, she pushed him away.

Why?

And what should he do?

What did she want him to do?

Not wait. Not that. Not anymore. He couldn't just sit waiting for something to happen. He needed to be in motion, to do something. Anything. Not knowing his destination, Hunt turned the ignition key and then threw the decade's old car into gear, turning right onto Town Center Drive, he proceeded south to Charleston Avenue where he turned westbound toward Red Rock Canyon. Already, he was dialing a number.

"Lieutenant Corina Meeks." Her tone was one of annoyance at being disturbed.

"Corky, it's Hunt. What ya got for me?"

There was a slight pause and then, "I'm still working on this, but… Listen, Hunt, I don't know how much of this I should reveal. You're a civilian."

Hunt emitted a frustrated grunt. "We both know you're going to give me this intel, otherwise you wouldn't have gathered it."

"Still, if anyone learns that I've given this to you…"

"Then I'll testify that you gave it to me under duress. Cork, I'm really not in the mood for games."

A sigh. A shuffle of papers. "Okay. Well, you're right. There is some sort of cover-up going on concerning the Denver-bound train. I can't confirm that it was terrorist in nature, but something happened."

"I already know what happened. I was there. Anyway, as intriguing as that all is, my first concern is the antidote. What's up on that front?"

Hunt could hear Corky tapping on her computer keyboard as they spoke. "About three months ago, four vials of militarized plague were checked out of a bio lab outside of Dallas."

"Checked out? Someone can just check out bio weapons like videos at Blockbuster?"

"It's not that simple. There are clearances, permissions, protocols, quite a bit of red tape. There must be a specific reason for the transfer as well as a clear chain of possession. But, the short answer is yes. In rare instances, it can occur."

"Alright. Tell me the rest."

"These vials were returned, but it has since been discovered that the plague itself is missing. A harmless substitute is now in the vials. The antidote is gone too."

Hunt's stomach felt like a rock: hard and cold yet capable of shattering into a thousand pieces. "I assume you've confirmed that the antidote at the CDC was also stolen."

"I'm afraid so."

Hunt drove past the Red Rock Casino, over the 215 expressway, and onto the last stretch of road before the state park. The view was stunning, with jutting red and tan cliffs and desert brush, but Hunt could care less. "Do we know who took the vials from the Dallas lab?"

"The lab tech that checked them out went missing three days prior to the discovery. No sign of him so far."

Hunt pulled a green spiral notebook from the glove compartment and clicked a ballpoint pen. "Uh-huh. Give me the name, Cork. I track people down for a living. I'll find the little twerp."

Several taps on the keyboard. "Alvin Johnson, twenty-eight, graduated with a masters from MIT in oh-nine. He'd been with the lab for only four months at the time of the incident."

"Sounds like Mr. Johnson was sent there on a mission. We'll want to check his activity between 2009 and his acceptance to the facility. Look into his associations, see if we can trace him back to Donnelley and his crew."

"Is that an order, Sergeant Huntington?"

Hunt chuckled. "Sorry, Cork. My mind's just racing. But, yeah. I think it'd be a good idea to check his recent activity."

"Agreed. Listen, Hunt. I've got some intel on Kelvin Donnelley."

"I'll take whatever you've got."

"His younger brother was stationed in Afghanistan. An E-8. Career man, just about to hit his twenty and out. He was killed by friendly fire five days before his deployment was to conclude. His commanding officer, a Colonel Steven Calhoun, was court-martialed, charged with incompetence and negligence."

"Incompetence? From a colonel? That's rare."

"It seems the man was having some medical issues he'd failed to report. Forgetfulness, mild dementia. He'd seen a doctor and learned he was experiencing the early symptoms of Alzheimer's but never shared the diagnosis with his superiors. The symptoms were still relatively minor and sporadic, but still his decision-making ability had been compromised, and thus, the deaths—plural— could have been easily avoided had the man acted responsibly."

"Uh-huh. And?"

"Calhoun was granted a presidential pardon after serving less than two years. It seems the man had some rather important friends."

Hunt nodded. "Okay, that speaks to Donnelley's hatred toward the current administration." He slowed, pulling the little car into a tight u-turn, eliciting honks and colorful gestures from fellow motorists. "One more thing," said Hunt. "You mentioned the Denver cover-up. Care to elaborate?"

Corky hesitated. "It's more a feeling than anything else. You know, averted eyes, sudden changes in topic."

"Got it. Wanna give me names?"

"Not yet, Hunt. Let me do some more digging."

"For now, I can live with that. Let me know if you learn anything else. I'm going to track down Alvin Johnson."

Disconnecting, while simultaneously pulling onto the 215 eastbound and toward McCarran Airport, Hunt began an internet search on his back-up smart phone—his newer model having been taken by Donnelley's crew and never returned. With luck, he'd know his destination by the time he reached ticketing.

*****

Dana refused to cry.

She'd been violated, abused, degraded at a level she never before knew possible. But, she would not lie here and play the victim. She was strong, or so she told herself. Most of the time she even believed it. Strange, a deadly disease ravaged her body and all she could think about was the... violation.

No. Not mere violation. Rape.

It was a rape. She needed to acknowledge this. No lesser words, no skirting of the issue. She had been raped and that was now a part of her history, a part of who she was now and who she would be from this time forward.

That was, assuming she lived beyond the week.

And no matter how strong she was, she'd come to realize that she would never see the world in quite the same way again. She'd been absolutely powerless to prevent the act. Her will, her freedom, her own body, all were at the mercy of those disgusting beasts. And what was to stop it from happening again? How could she know, assuming she was somehow cured, that some other pig wouldn't force himself upon her? How did she know that all men weren't simply lying in wait, only holding onto civilized behavior out of sheer societal necessity? How could she be certain that they couldn't see what had happened to her? Could it be that they'd recognize her as broken, used, that she was available for the taking? Wouldn't they know? Wouldn't everyone know? Surely it had to be obvious.

Doctor Byers didn't know—or, at least, pretended not to know. She simply couldn't confide this secret to a man. Even to a doctor. It would make her vulnerable, exposed. She'd told the Homeland Security agent, Bedford—a woman. But, she'd sworn her to secrecy. Bedford was not to tell Hunt.

How could Dana ever tell Hunt?

And why should she? This was her body, her life. She had a right to secrets.

And where had Hunt been when it happened? Why hadn't he been there for her?

Dana stopped. She would not follow that train of thought. Hunt had been caught in a battle for his life. Or so he'd said. Thrown from the train. But not exactly. In truth, he'd jumped from the train before the terrorists could push him. He'd done it in order to maintain some control, lessen the risk of serious injury. He was looking after his own skin.

Enough.

That was unfair.

Still, he should have been there for her. He should have found some way. The same way he should be here for her now.

But, she'd sent him away.

Still, he should have known she needed him to stay.

Dana was seized with a convulsive hack. If her stomach hadn't already been empty she would have relieved it of its contents.

Wiping spittle from her mouth with a tissue she caught sight of her wedding ring. Hunt was a good man. He was her man. But, he was a man, still. He was her partner in life, but not in this. In this she was alone. Entirely alone. Forever alone.

Chapter 27

Appleton Wisconsin

Hunt popped the hood of his rented Jeep Wrangler and pretended to inspect the engine as he studied the small yellow house directly across the narrow street. Tan brick and rubber siding. A late model Toyota in the driveway. A Weber grill visible in the backyard. Four middle school aged boys played running bases in the cul-de-sac three doors north. A twenty something year-old woman walked a Shetland sheep dog to the south. An elderly woman watered her lawn while periodically hollering at the boys that they'd, "Better not trample my azaleas while chasing that god-awful ball." It was a typical Midwestern morning of the kind that peppered Hunt's boyhood memories. He'd been an Indiana lad—a Hoosier. The summers may have been a notch warmer, but the setting was the same, right down to the rust-spotted cars in the driveways and the chain link fences between the lawns. Hunt would even bet that each refrigerator contained a pitcher of sun tea.

Alvin Johnson really hadn't been that difficult to locate. He wasn't a skilled criminal and was very poor at covering his tracks. In fact, prior to the incident at the Dallas lab, his record had been clean with the exception of a speeding ticket at the age of seventeen. Fifty-six in a forty-five MPH zone. The guy wasn't exactly Bin-Laden.

So, why steal the plague?

Johnson's politics were vanilla, just slightly left of center, pretty much average for a guy in his twenties. There was no record of his having attended even a single political rally, much less joining any fringe groups. He hadn't had a serious love interest in three years, so it was unlikely a girl had led him down the path. He had some debt—not insurmountable—but enough to make life increasingly uncomfortable. Until recently, he'd been a month behind on all of his bills and had even had his car repossessed, though, through payday loans, he'd managed to scrape together the cash to get it back. Three months ago he suddenly caught up on all of his obligations, but aside from this there were no other obvious signs of a cash infusion. No new cars or lavish lifestyle. No tropical vacations or real estate deals. He'd simply paid his debt to current and moved in with his sister, though his official address remained in Dallas.

Still, Hunt was guessing money was the motive. Someone had offered Johnson a substantial sum for the bio-toxin. Johnson had just had the good sense to keep the majority of his take out of circulation. Hunt had learned that just after returning the now-useless vials, the man had given notice at the lab, and then dropping promptly from sight. He'd obviously hoped that the theft of the plague would go unnoticed for an extended duration and that by the time it was discovered, he would be beyond suspicion.

Foolish.

Amateurish.

Someone had gotten to this man. Hunt intended to learn just who that might be. Kelvin Donnelley had dropped off the radar and if Hunt was to find the cure, he needed to start here. It was just past two p.m. and no one had yet left the house. Johnson had come to live with his older sister, Lucy. The woman was divorced, no kids, and worked as a cashier at a nearby supermarket. Hunt had hoped she'd have an early shift so he could have Johnson to himself, but that wasn't going to be the case.

So be it.

Johnson, himself, was still unemployed. But, of course, he didn't need a job right now. He'd been paid handsomely for the bio-toxin that now threatened Dana's life. Hunt felt no pity for Alvin Johnson.

Strolling to the front porch, Hunt rang the doorbell. He'd thought of dressing as a cable guy or a vacuum cleaner salesman, but just didn't want to bother with anything elaborate. Dana had only a day or so left to live and he'd already wasted far too much time sitting around waiting. It was time for quick, decisive action.

He rang the bell again and then saw a woman peek through the curtains to his left. Brown eyes. Wide. Darting. Good. Let her check him out. Dressed in a black Kiss Destroyer T-shirt, blue jeans, and Reeboks, Hunt didn't look like a Federal agent or a cop. Though, he did hope she hadn't had a good look at the left side of his face. The scars were off-putting to a lot of people.

The curtains shifted back to their former position. A moment later he heard a muffled female voice. "Who are you? What do you want?" Even through the partition, he could hear a subtle quiver in her tone. Hunt's internal alarm flashed red. His gut told him something wasn't right here.

"Yeah. Sorry to bother you. My car stalled in front of your house and my cell phone's out of juice. Any chance I can borrow your phone to call Triple-A?"

A moment's hesitation. "I'd rather not. Why don't you try someone else?" She was obviously frightened. It would be logical for her to fear that her brother had been tracked to her home. But this had a different feel, like a fear for one's own life. Hunt had experience with people in such situations; there was a different kind of urgency than with other fears.

"Done that already," he said. "You're the third house I've tried. Not a very hospitable neighborhood, I guess. You sure I can't use your phone? I don't even need to come inside. I'll just stand here on the porch. It'll take two minutes max."

"I really think you should try someone else." Hunt could barely make out the words through the door. She seemed to be speaking through gasps and quivers.

"Really? Okay. I get it. Don't open the door for a stranger. It's the world we live in these days. Mind if I grab a drink from your hose? It's getting hot out here and since my car's stalled I can't use the air conditioning."

There was a pause and then. "Um... Sure. I guess the hose would be fine. I'm sorry."

"Yeah. No problem. Where's your hose?"

"Oh. Um, to your right. Just around the corner."

"Got it. Thanks."

Hunt turned, descending the steps. He would use his trip around the side of the house to scout the back entrance and then to create an opportunity. But, the sister. Why so frightened? Something was seriously wrong in there.

Bypassing the coiled hose, Hunt strolled around to the backside of the house where he found scattered flower pots, three lawn chairs, a grill, and a cracked and empty birdbath. Both the screen and wooden doors were open, the frame broken. Someone had forcibly entered the house, most likely only just recently.

It all came together.

Hunt withdrew the Browning single action pistol he had holstered at his tailbone, and moved slowly through the open door and into the kitchen. There was a kettle of tea boiling on the stove, an unfinished bowl of granola on the table, and an orange tabby, back arched and ears laid flat, cowering in a corner.

Hunt saw them almost immediately. A single male, aged 35-40, dressed in tactical gear, his left arm wrapped across the woman Hunt had seen at the window, his right hand aiming a weapon at Hunt.

The first shot hit the wall behind where Hunt's head had been only a second before. He dove and rolled smoothly into a crouched firing position, but the intruder pulled the woman back and forth in random jerks making it impossible for Hunt to get a clean shot off without endangering the hostage. The man fired three more bursts as Hunt dove to his left behind a large oak china cabinet. A picture frame exploded on the wall behind him as the bullets struck. The cat screeched and ran to the opposite corner. The pot of boiling tea leaped and then tumbled with a graceless twirl, spilling brown liquid across the linoleum floor.

As with the insurgents at the Colorado clinic, this man was different than the terrorists Hunt had encountered on the American Cry. He was no amateur, but rather a skilled combatant. His poise, his handling of the weapon, even the gear he wore, all spoke to his professionalism. But he wore no insignia, he attacked civilians. If not a terrorist then what?

Scrambling to his feet, back against the cabinet, gun held before him, Hunt heard the man and woman move further up the hallway and around a bend. The woman whimpered and the cat hissed as Hunt peeked out from behind the china cabinet. He could not see his opponent and so moved forward in a cautious crouch, the Browning held before him.

Glancing to his left, he peered into an open bedroom, but heard a door open and then close from further forward and so quickened his pace.

The rumble of an automatic garage door.

The opening and closing of car doors.

An engine starting.

Hunt raced up the narrow hallway and turned left into the cluttered laundry room. Pushing the door to the garage open, Hunt first saw the blue Toyota pulling clear of the driveway before his eyes settled on the fragmentation grenade on the concrete floor ten feet in front of him.

Hunt dove left just as the grenade exploded sending flaming shrapnel through the opening he'd just occupied. Clear of the doorway and protected by the laundry room wall, he was not hit by the brunt force of the blast, but still, was knocked from his feet, slamming against the unforgiving dryer before tumbling to the vinyl floor.

His vision went white and then black.

He shook his head, causing puffs of dust to billow from his form.

The blackness was now populated with brightly colored spots.

He shook his head again, vision returned. Coughing, he spit dust and matter from his mouth. He felt like he'd been hit by an entire defensive line—shades of his college football days.

Not allowing the luxury of time, Hunt quickly assessed himself: a couple of moderate lacerations, a few bruises in the making, the potential onset of a migraine headache, but otherwise it seemed he'd survived the event.

Several more blinks and he rolled to a sitting position, back against the white Whirlpool washing machine. He withdrew his phone, punched 911. Time was critical. The woman, Lucy Johnson, was only useful to the man as a hostage. Once he considered himself clear of danger, he'd likely execute her without hesitation. She only had minutes to live and Hunt was in no position to initiate pursuit.

Hunt had a sharp tactical mind and had noted the Toyota's license number upon first arriving at the address. He gave the car's make, model, approximate year, the license number, and the last location and direction of the vehicle to the 911 operator, explaining that he'd seen a man force a woman into the car at gunpoint and race away. He had reason to believe the man's intent was to kill her shortly and urged immediate pursuit.

He then disconnected, not allowing the operator to question him further. Due to sophisticated software, his phone could not be traced, but, seeing as there had just been an explosion at this address, he knew police and firefighters were likely en route.

Rising slowly, still blinking away the floating spots from before his eyes, Hunt peeked into the garage. A couple of small fires. Nothing that was likely to spread before the fire department arrived. A portion of the west-facing wall had been blown away, but the structure appeared sound. The damage could have been much worse.

His steps unsteady at first, Hunt regained his bearings as he left the laundry room, turning right at the narrow hallway, and then right into the first bedroom. He'd seen the open door when moving past it before, but, at the time, had been concerned for Lucy Johnson's safety.

A young man Hunt assumed to be Alvin Johnson lay on the floor in a widening pool of his own blood.

He was not yet dead.

Hunt knelt beside him, still blinking away tie-dye splotches from before his pupils.

There was a gunshot wound to the right bicep, another to the upper chest, left side, too high to have hit the heart. Johnson was on his back, but based on the pooling blood, likely there was an exit wound near the shoulder blade. Hunt slapped his face causing the semiconscious man's eyes to flutter. "Alvin Johnson?"

No response.

Another slap.

"Johnson!"

A groan of pain.

"H… help me. I'm shot."

Hunt leaned close, forcing Johnson to meet his gaze. "Know this. My wife is dying of that plague you stole. If you don't give me the information I need, I'll let you lie here and bleed out. Do we understand one another?"

Johnson moaned, narrowed his eyes, and then nodded. He was not a pro. There would be no bravado.

"Who paid you to steal the plague?"

"Are… you the police?"

"Does it matter who I am?"

A slow shake of the head. "Stop the bleeding… Please!"

"I'll think about it. Talk first."

A nod and a shudder.

"The antidote to the plague, do you have it?"

"No."

"Where is it?"

A cough. "No… idea. Gone. Months ago."

Damn!

"Who was that man? Who just tried to kill you?"

"Don't… know."

"Do you know who sent him? What organization?"

Johnson shook his head. "Please. The bleeding."

"What do you know about the terrorist group, the Revolutionary Patriots of America? Do you know where they base their operations?"

Johnson narrowed his eyes as if in confusion. "I don't know about any terrorist group."

Interesting. Was it possible this idiot had no idea what the plague was to be used for? Could anyone be that clueless? "Then, who was it? Who paid you to steal the plague? Who did you give it to?"

"Thor…"

"Thor?"

"No… Thorpe. A British guy named Jonathan Thorpe."

Chapter 28

Hunt sat in a small café on County Road 88 just outside of town and some ten miles from the Johnson house. He'd heard approaching sirens while still interrogating Johnson and had slipped away before the authorities arrived. Normally, he would have no problem giving a statement or helping in any way, but again, the terrorist attack was being covered up at some pretty high levels. He might well be detained while the local police attempted to verify his story—a story that could not be confirmed. Likely, he'd have been held as a suspect in Johnson's shooting, the grenade blast, and who knew what else. Dana's life depended on his locating Donnelley and securing the antidote. He had no time for nonsense.

Dana. She wouldn't even accept his calls.

Hunt had communicated with the doctor, Jerry Byers. He'd confirmed that Dana's condition had worsened, but stated that she was still conscious and coherent. There was no explanation as to why she'd shut Hunt out. He couldn't imagine what he'd done to cause this reaction and so tried, with some difficulty, to shut thoughts of Dana from his mind as he focused on the problem at hand.

Sipping on a Pepsi, Hunt glanced about the narrow and nearly empty café: two visible employees, a teenaged waitress and a thirty-something year-old fry cook, unshaven and gangly, who worked harder at flirting with the spunky little waitress than he did at flipping burgers. There were three customer beside himself: a middle aged man of Mediterranean descent who paged through a fishing magazine as he sipped coffee and nibbled on cheesecake, a college-age male wearing a Green Bay Packers Jersey and relishing a double bacon burger while bobbing to his iPod, and a businesswomen chugging an energy drink as she tapped on her HP laptop computer and nibbled at a salad.

In an effort to remain clear of complications, Hunt had ditched the rented Jeep—which he'd secured under an assumed name—and then rented a second car from a different agency under yet another name. Likely someone had seen the Jeep parked in front of the Johnson house and possibly even seen him depart in it. The explosion had drawn several neighbors out of their homes to stare wide-eyed and gape-mouthed at the damaged structure. He'd taken the precaution of exiting through the rear, and circling the block, coming to his vehicle from the opposite side of the street, but he was a stranger in a tight-knit neighborhood community. Someone would remember him. He could only hope that no one had given a solid description. His scared face would be a telltale feature for any who knew to look for it.

As a precaution, he'd changed clothes and donned a just-purchased Milwaukee Brewers baseball cap, but even so, he wouldn't want to remain in town for long. Still, he required time on his laptop to do research and felt comfortable with a half hour layover in the café for a quick bite and some web searching. He was just south of the regional airport and could be there and airborne in under an hour should he find a clue to pursue.

Clicking into a document, he scanned the information he'd accumulated on Donnelley: Fifty years old, a native of Florida and a rabid Dolphins fan. Eldest son of Irish immigrants Colin and Shannon Donnelley. A bachelor degree in mechanical engineering from Florida State University. Two younger siblings, one brother, one sister. The brother, Colm, had been killed in Afghanistan. It was assumed that the government's handling of the events surrounding Colm's death, in particular the pardoning of Col. Steven Calhoun, had caused Donnelley to seek retribution.

Hunt took a long sip of Pepsi, a bite of his patty melt, and then looked further back. He needed something more, something that spoke to connections or actions relating to recent events. Donnelley had been married to his college sweetheart, Julia Frasier. They'd divorced four years later after she'd learned of his numerous affairs, some of which, it seemed, may have been nonconsensual in nature. No official charges had ever been placed, but complaints by female coworkers had been filed. Hunt had already contacted the former Mrs. Donnelley. She'd been angered at even the mention of his name and swore she hadn't seen him in over twenty years. No she didn't know where he might hide, yes, she'd prefer he'd leap off of a very high cliff onto jagged rock and die a horrible agonizing death, thank you, goodbye.

Before turning to criminal activities, Donnelley had drifted from job to job. Apparently, he was highly skilled as a mechanical engineer, but socially

volatile, having confrontations with other employees at every jobsite. Eventually, he'd left the field to take a series of retail positions. His career as a jewel
thief began at age thirty-four after he'd worked for a jeweler for six months
during which time he'd stolen several diamonds, replacing each with a stone of
lesser quality. Eventually, he was suspected and fired, though no concrete proof
had been found to connect him to the thefts.

Another bite of his sandwich and a swish of Pepsi.

He researched the Revolutionary Patriots of America. To all appearances,
until a few months ago the group existed only in the most elementary sense.
Based out of rural Michigan, it was a rightwing militia group with less than two
dozen members. It seemed mostly they drank beer, shot tin cans off of tree
stumps with Uzis, and griped about how much better things would be if they ran
the government. How had Donnelley connected with them? How had they come
to have high-level government connections at the level Hunt had witnessed over
the past two days?

The answer was simple. They couldn't. Not so quickly. These yahoos were
a front organization, patsies too ignorant to realize they were being used to
further someone else's agenda. On the flight from Vegas, Hunt had researched
the RPA along with each of the cells credited with the recent terrorist events
overseas. Each was similar. Tiny, loosely organized groups had suddenly
become well-funded and apparently given an opportunity to forward their
misguided agendas. The only real difference was that the American incident had
been covered up.

Who was behind these attacks and what was their ultimate agenda? And
more importantly for Hunt's purposes, how did Donnelley fit in, where was he,
and did he truly have the antidote or was that in the hands of his superiors?

And what of Thorpe?

How did that smarmy weasel fit into all of this?

From what Hunt knew of the man, he was almost always motivated by
money. Hunt's guess was that Thorpe had procured the bio-toxin and its
antidote for whatever organization drove the RPA and its foreign clones.

Hunt's fingers danced across the keyboard searching for evidence of
Thorpe's recent whereabouts. If the Brit knew that Dana had been infected,

likely he'd lead Hunt to the antidote. Hunt couldn't believe Thorpe would knowingly allow Dana to perish if he had the means to prevent it. As much as Hunt despised the fact, Thorpe still had feelings for her. Maybe those emotions could be used to save her.

After which Hunt would beat the rodent to a bloody pulp for his part in releasing the plague.

Hunt's phone chimed.

It was a blocked number. Hunt's phone was unlisted. Curious, Hunt took the call. "Yeah. Who's this?"

"Marcus?"

Hunt recognized the woman's voice immediately. "Bedford."

"Well, aren't you perceptive?"

"How'd you get this number?"

A hearty chuckle. "I'm with Homeland Security. We have a resource or two."

"Okay, dumb question. Please tell me you have the antidote."

"The antidote, no. A lead on Kelvin Donnelley, quite possibly."

"Donnelley. Are you moving on him?"

A pause. "Marcus, listen, I know how important this is to you. You're concerned for your wife…"

"Don't beat around the bush, Bedford. Are you moving on Donnelley or not?"

"We are not. And the reason is quite simple. By all official accounts, the terrorist incident in Colorado never took place."

Hunt tightened his fist about the phone. "We both know that it did."

"Yes, we do. And that's why I've contacted you. Barring an official acknowledgement of the incident, no government agency can move on the man. But, you're no longer connected to any governmental body. I've done some research on you, Marcus. You're a licensed private investigator as well as a registered fugitive recovery agent—a bounty hunter. Though, you use neither license in any traditional sense. As I see it, you can legally pursue Mr. Donnelley better than can I. As long as you don't break any laws, we can't stop you from chasing Kelvin Donnelley with hopes of retrieving that stolen diamond. If you happen to learn the location of the antidote in the process, all the better."

Hunt considered this for a moment. "You're with Homeland. You witnessed the attack at the clinic. You have knowledge of the attack aboard the train and yet there's still no official acknowledgement of the incident." Bedford did not respond to this and so Hunt continued. "The RPA is obviously the pawn of another, more powerful, group. Unlike the domestic attack, none of the incidents oversees have been hidden from public or governmental view. I'm gonna take a wild leap and guess you're not being straight with me."

"Now, now, Marcus, you are a feisty one. Yes, I've withheld details, and will continue to do so. You must understand, I'm simply not at liberty to disclose the sum total of my knowledge."

"And if I refuse to cooperate?"

"Well, then you'll lose valuable time. I don't think Dana would appreciate that. And quite honestly, neither would I. She really is quite a little darling and she's been through more than you can imagine."

"And what do you gain, Bedford? This isn't all about Dana, not from your perspective."

"We get Donnelley, maybe even the remaining stores of the plague and antidote. Now, I'm sure you're familiar with the concept of a win-win scenario."

Hunt considered this for a moment. "There's another player here. Someone is squelching all knowledge of the incident. I'm beginning to think that maybe you're involved in that. You conveniently disappeared during the clinic fire. You haven't verified either incident to your superiors. Maybe you have an interest in this thing that goes beyond your professional capacity. Am I getting warm?"

"Marcus, time is tight. Will you follow Donnelley's trail or should we consider your wife a lost cause?"

"You know I'm going after Donnelley. But, unless you're straight with me, once this is over, I'll be investigating you. And know this: I'm very good at investigation. I still have friends at the Pentagon. And I'm not afraid to dance with the media. Are we clear?"

A warm chuckle. "Very. Listen, Marcus. You don't know me. I don't expect you to trust me like you would your mama. But I'll give you a tidbit or two, enough that you know I'm on the side of right. Will that settle your little squirming conscience?"

"Go on."

The sound of a chair sliding across wood. The rustle of Bedford sitting. And then, "You're correct. The Revolutionary Patriots are pawns. Donnelley answers to a much more dangerous organization. International. Small, but very ambitious and influential. Don't ask me for details; it would be a waste of breath."

"And the cover-up? That didn't originate with that group, did it?"

"No. It didn't." A pause. "Listen, Marcus, we've identified high-ranking officials both in the U.S. and abroad who are either involved with or coerced by this shadow movement. Again, high-ranking. When I tell you that I need to tread carefully, I'm telling you the God's honest truth."

"Yeah. And?"

"There is a group, I guess we could call it the opposition, a counter movement. Code name: White Eagle. Very loosely organized. No official capacity whatsoever. There are representatives from several different sectors: CIA, FBI, judicial, political."

"Homeland?" ventured Hunt.

"Plans have been laid, people put in place," continued Bedford, ignoring Hunt's interruption, "Those within the government community who have learned of the shadow and seek to contain it are moving to subdue them before they can gain further influence."

"Stop talking around the issue, Bedford. Admit it. You're part of this White Eagle or whatever it is."

"That may be true."

"Then give me something I can use. I'm not ready to join the Oliver Stone conspiracy club just yet. Make it simple for me. What's really happening?"

A chuckle. "There's nothing simple about what's happening. Let me say this. Yes. White Eagle learned of the impending attack and sought to cover up the terrorist event."

"You learned of the attack beforehand. It sounds like you have access within the group."

A long pause. "We… do have a person on the inside, yes. That said, if you catch Donnelley, you cannot tell him that I've revealed this to you. That information cannot get back to his superiors."

Hunt thought for a moment. Why would he tell Donnelley anything? "Alright. You have intel. What's the play here?"

"The shadow group was hoping to cause widespread panic within the U.S. and several other key countries, destabilizing the governments in order to better position their own people waiting in the wings. By disrupting the U.S. event, we've preserved our position even as chaos ensues throughout the other involved nations."

"So, when the train was stopped by the blockade, what happened?"

"We first learned details of the event when the National Guard set the blockade in place. Our contact had indicated that something was on the horizon, we knew of the plague, but had no knowledge allowing us to move preventively."

"And when the blockade was lifted?"

"That was the shadow organization using their influence to complete the attack. Within an hour word had spread throughout Washington that the reported attack had been a hoax and that no further action need be taken."

"But the cover-up, including the clinic fire?"

"That was White Eagle. They - Alright, we - piggybacked on the shadow group's initial cover-up. They'd intended to hide the attack only long enough for the event to occur uninterrupted. We suppressed it entirely, thus eliminating its effectiveness. As you know, a terrorist event cannot strike terror if no one knows of it."

"You're telling me that representatives of the U.S. government were willing to burn down that clinic, to murder innocent citizens in order to keep this attack quiet. You're telling me that those people Dana killed were not terrorists, but government officials masquerading as terrorists? Do you have any idea what you've started? The survivors will speak out. The families of the dead will seek explanation."

"Marcus, consider the alternatives. Have you followed the news? Have you seen the widespread panic in Hong Kong and Chile? By suppressing knowledge of the event, we've spared the U.S. from similar outbreaks of madness."

Hunt shook his head. "Nah. Bedford, I'm not buying it. We experienced nine-eleven. If anything we became stronger, more unified."

"I'm not asking you to agree with our methods, Marcus. What I am asking is that you do exactly what you already intend to do. Locate Kelvin Donnelley and retrieve the antidote. The only difference is that after you've done so, would you please be so kind as to bring him and the antidote to us?"

It really wasn't much of a decision. Bedford had information Hunt needed and likely Donnelley could help her people squelch additional terrorist activity. Though, in his gut, he knew there was more to it. They probably wanted Hunt for plausible deniability. There was no connection between Hunt and Bedford or any of her cohorts. Still, this thing just didn't quite ring true. Something wasn't adding up and he couldn't quite nail it to the wall. Damn, he wished his muddled head would get in the game.

"Yeah," he said finally. "Give me the lead. I'll get Donnelley for you."

Chapter 29

Dana stared at the ceiling through the clear plastic tent that protected others from her disease. The symptoms were consistent but the severity came in waves. Mild nausea would suddenly wrench at her stomach causing her to curl into a fetal position. Coughing fits would seize her with such fervor that it seemed her very lungs would rip free. The fever dipped and spiked, ranging from just over 100 degrees to nearly 107.

For the past several minutes there had been unusual traffic in the hallway beyond her room. More movement, urgency in the voices, perhaps some indignation. She'd heard one elderly man proclaim that, "Doc Beyers better have a fine excuse for this nonsense." Another voice demanded the return of her copayment. It seemed everyone was moving in the same direction—toward the exit door. It was still early afternoon and surely far too soon to close up shop for the day. Something was seriously amiss. Dana knew she was the only in-patient, that no others were kept overnight, and wondered if the commotion had anything to do with her condition.

Bedford entered her room at just after three-thirty pm. The Homeland Security agent appeared slightly winded and perhaps a bit distracted as she ambled toward Dana, her round cheeks red, her eyes wide and drifting from side to side behind her wire rimmed spectacles. "Mrs. Huntington, Dana, I'm sorry to disturb you but, ah, you know how it is."

Dana focused on the woman's clear gray eyes. "Agent Bedford, there's been quite the commotion beyond my door and now you're here, three states distant from our last encounter. Care to elaborate?"

Bedford smiled. It was warm, comforting, the type of smile one could trust—and therefore Dana did not. "Well, Dana, you seem sharp as a shark's tooth. I'm glad to see that. It would be better for you to be coherent at this stage." She now stood directly to Dana's left, hands clasped casually before her.

"And what stage might that be?" asked Dana.

"We're going to move you to a more secure, a more advanced facility."

Curious. Dana's understanding was that she was to be kept away from official channels for fear that those compromised by the terrorists would learn of the survivor and make an attempt on her life. "Is Hunt aware of this?" she asked.

"I spoke with Marcus earlier."

"And Dr. Byers?"

"He will make no objection."

Dana narrowed her gaze. "Where is Hunt now?"

"In the Midwest. Following a lead on Kelvin Donnelley."

The Midwest? Not even in the same state, but across the country. She had told him to leave—ordered him really—but she hadn't anticipated that he would take it quite so literally. She was dying and he was off traipsing about...

In search of the cure.

Yet, still...

"And this clinic, the commotion from the hallway?"

A twist of the lips en route to a welcoming smile. "Oh, that. The staff evacuated the other patients. Your condition is still pretty volatile. We couldn't risk you infecting others or being seen by anyone who might be tied to the terrorists."

"How would terrorists know to look for me here?"

"Well, we're hoping they don't. But, the fact is. I found you—and it wasn't that hard. You're in your city of residence in a clinic run by your husband's old army buddy. It doesn't take a Sherlock Holmes or even Columbo to put that much together."

Dana stared at the woman. She had a point. It would have been much better to seek treatment in a locale not otherwise associated with either her or Hunt. Dana staved off a coughing fit, steadied herself, and then asked, "But, we know that government agencies—quite possibly including your own—have been breached. How do you propose to protect me?" Dana's slight form shuddered as the hacking cough overrode her will.

Bedford leaned forward, her expression serious. "Well, Dana dear, we've taken that matter into consideration and are doing our best to ensure your well being. But the fact is that we need access to you."

Well, that sounded terribly ominous. "Access?" asked Dana, now wiping spittle from her chin.

Bedford seemed to contemplate for a moment, stroking her chin with her fingers as a man might stroke his beard. "Let me see how best to put this. The bacteria, the plague, this disease you have, it's more than you've been led to believe."

"It's the bleeding bubonic plague. How much worse does it need to be?"

Bedford glanced around as if contemplating what to say and then met Dana's gaze. "Well, I'm not sure just exactly how much of this I should tell you. There are those who would get their shorts all in a bind. But I'm thinking you have a right to know—the basics at least. The bubonic plague. They're using that as a carrier for the real whammy, another, more troubling element that's been imbedded within the plague's genetic matrix."

"Care to elaborate?"

Bedford closed her troubled eyes, nodded, and then told her.

Fifteen minutes later a horrified Dana was rolled out of her room, down the narrow hallway, through the now-empty waiting room and into a waiting ambulance. As she was whisked past the nurse's station she noticed something quite unsettling on the floor behind the counter. Blood. Not much. Only a couple of drops. It was almost a miracle she'd seen it at all. But even in her current condition Dana had a keen eye for detail. An attempt had been made to clean it away, as evidenced by the near invisible pinkish streaks leading to the droplets. But, Dana was certain. Something had happened here. Something unseemly, something Bedford was unwilling to disclose.

Chapter 30

Paris France

While still early afternoon in Las Vegas, it was nearing nine pm in Paris as Degare Laurent flipped up the collar of his wool overcoat and tugged his felt beret so low as to nearly conceal his faded brown eyes. The early autumn air was brisk and a slight mist of precipitation dusted the boulevard, but it was neither the dampness or the temperature which chilled his frame. At seventy-two, he was still spry and his senses had not yet dulled. True, the short term memory was not as he remembered it to be, but he'd had none of the more dramatic effects of age he'd witnessed in many of his generation. The mind: that was the key. The body could wither away, but if one still possessed his mind he still possessed himself.

Looking from side to side, Laurent crossed the street three doors shy of the intersection. Traffic was light in this neighborhood and besides he didn't want in any way to be predictable. He'd thought of utilizing his automobile, but determined that it was much more recognizable than was a pedestrian. A vehicle had license plates. Much too easy to track. But, a lone person on foot, especially once among a crowd, ah, here a man could find refuge. He'd thought of seeking assistance, perhaps calling the police, contacting his former precinct, enlisting the aid of former comrades, but decided against this course of action. Perhaps after he'd learned more, after he'd gained some solid information which could be acted upon. For now, well, all he would accomplish would be to elicit questions he was not yet prepared to answer.

No. For now, this was a thing he must do alone. But, what it was he must do, this he was not sure. He'd contacted the thief, Thorpe, via secure email, giving him all he'd learned.

Secure?

Well, there was secure and then there was secure. Laurent had very little confidence that true security existed in this technically hyper-evolved time.

From what he'd learned in the past twenty-four hours nothing was quite as it might appear.

Glancing right and then left more frequently than was wise for a man attempting to remain inconspicuous, Laurent came to the intersection, veered left and then crossed the adjoining street. Cursing his nerves, he thrust his fists into his coat pockets and marched eastward. He wasn't even sure that anyone was interested in him, much less following him, but he had the sense that he must be on the move. Maybe it was that Thorpe had been so fearful, that the egocentric thief had been found and then attacked at one of his residences. Perhaps it was Laurent's own age which stymied him. As a younger man he'd never worn a mask of fear. He had known fear, true. What man with both military and law enforcement experience had not? But, knowing fear and wearing it like a straightjacket were two entirely different things. This irrational terror that nettled his bones, that tugged at his elbow, and whispered in his ear, this was a stranger to him, an unwanted pest to be shooed away like a mangy cur. He had no need of it and worst yet, it distracted him from more practical lines of thinking.

Laurent had determined that he would contact his eldest son, Frederic, and ask him to secure transportation under his girlfriend's name, thus, in theory, eliminating any obvious connection to the elder Laurent. But, even this, he would not do until further distant from his residence and with a disposable phone that he'd yet to purchase.

This man that sought Thorpe, he was connected to others. There was an organization, no, more better, a movement. This man, these people, they desired power for themselves, but not in a traditional sense. They were all connected, apparently by blood, though they were spread about the globe. But it was not position or fame which they coveted, but rather the ability to manipulate those in such positions. Why attain an office from which one could be ejected when one could control the procession of men and women who held said office from a safe distance and never fear reprisals? Their politics were peculiar, their beliefs fanciful, and their methods deadly.

What Laurent had learned, well, these people, these sons of the gods, as they referred to themselves, had been responsible for numerous deaths over a span of decades. Yet still they had remained hidden, only faint shadows to disperse on the breeze. Could such a group exist in reality?

Laurent turned another corner, now leaving the residential subdivision and entering a commercial area of the arrondissement. Here he felt less exposed. There were people walking about, chatting, entering and exiting business establishments. One could get lost here, or lose someone, a tail perhaps. Again, looking right and left, he proceeded forward. While on the residential through-ways he had seen no evidence of an observer, yet, still he felt that creeping unease, an indefinable sensation, that constant and unfamiliar irritation. There was no evidence, not even a hint, and yet he knew—he knew! Someone was nearby. Someone knew that he had learned that which was not meant to be learned.

Laurent scoffed.

Foolishness!

The follies of an old man.

It was Thorpe. This man, this thief, trouble, it seemed to follow him. Had Laurent not already lost far too much as a result of this man? Why had he once again allowed himself to be drawn in by the thief? Had he not learned?

And now. Now Laurent did not know whether or not to trust his own instincts. Was he the idiot, fleeing shadows and changes in the breeze, or was there a true threat?

The threat in broad terms, he supposed, was real. But, the specific threat to him at this moment, that was the seat of his doubt. Was it possible that these people could know of him already? Could they have learned of his prying, his investigation at the behest of Jonathan Thorpe and tasked someone to subdue him this quickly?

All logic told him that, no, they could not. And yet, here he was, skulking about, acting like a fugitive. And in his heart, the threat was real.

He was now before a small bakery with metal tables and chairs situated on the front walkway. The door to the shop was locked, but he could still see Sophie, the baker, moving about within. Short, round, always busy, forever scolding her customers through a grin and a wink. Laurent frequented the shop and had an easy going business relationship with the woman. He respected her and even enjoyed her well-meaning complaints about his waistline and age spots. Though only in her early forties, she was a widow and had run the business alone for the four years since her husband's untimely death as a result of lung cancer. She was a good woman. Honest. Hard working. Not beautiful, but with a spunky charm that brought her many suitors. Mostly they walked away with nothing more than pastries. Perhaps she would allow him entrance. Maybe he could hide away in there while she tended to her day-end duties.

She had moved to the back now and was thus obscured from sight. Still, he knocked on the glass door. What foolishness. Certainly, he should leave and return home.

He knocked again.

Why was it he was now more anxious than ever? Had he seen something that had registered subconsciously, but had not yet clawed its way to the surface of his mind?

Why had she not come forward? Could she not hear his knock?

Now he was certain. He could not say why, could not give a rationale for his fear, but he knew—he knew!—that he was in danger. Someone was here. Someone was watching, waiting for just the right moment to strike.

He knocked again. Louder. More insistent. Still, Sophie did not show herself. Did she think him an irritant? Was she afraid that he was here to force her to reopen for business, to sell him a croissant though the register was closed? There. A shadow moving about. Was that her? It must be her. He knocked again, urgently. He must get inside.

There was a sound from behind. A voice. American. Female. Young. Speaking in English. "Sir? Monsier? Is there a problem?"

Laurent turned. It was a young woman. Late twenties or early thirties. African American. Thin—too thin, but attractive still. She appeared concerned. "Yes, yes," he said in heavily accented English. "I am sorry. I did not mean to create the scene."

The young woman nodded and then looked at him as if with some recognition. "Not a problem at all, darlin'. It is you, isn't it? You are Commandant Laurent, right? It's been so long. You probably don't remember me."

The girl knew him! "Yes," said Laurent cautiously. "It is I. I must apologize, but I do not remember your name. We have met, you and I?"

The young woman smiled a wonderful seductive smile, nodded, and then Tina Collins pressed a five inch blade into Laurent's abdomen.

Chapter 31

Hunt stood staring out over the gently undulating Lake Michigan. Though he stood more than two blocks distant, he could see the colorful sailboats which dotted the blue expanse, the jet skis that bobbed and weaved. Cars raced past on Lake Shore Drive. Bicyclists and skateboarders zipped around pedestrians and motorized vehicles alike. It was a warm, late September day, the lake air was fresh and pure, the breeze a lover's caress; the city was vibrant, alive, and Hunt was too uptight to appreciate any of it. He'd grown up just over the Indiana/Illinois border less than an hour from where he now stood. The place was practically home to him. But he felt alien and disjointed.

He'd tried several times to reach Jerry Byers at the clinic. No one had answered the first seven times. On the eighth, it was a police officer that picked up the phone. The man had been curt and unhelpful. The clinic was closed until further notice. Hunt might want to look into finding another physician. It was only when Hunt stated that his wife was a patient there and should still be on site that the man showed interest. Obviously, something had happened, for the officer began probing Hunt for information while offering none in return.

Hunt disconnected the call.

Again, Hunt tried to reach Dana. Still no response. Was this because something more had happened to her or because for whatever reason she still didn't want to speak with him? Bedford as well had fallen off grid. She'd gotten him this far—to Chicago—but it had taken him nearly another full day of leg work to track Donnelley to this locale. Now Friday morning—the Colorado event had been Tuesday—Dana had no more than a day left by Byers' estimate. And Bedford had become unavailable. Was she simply too busy to take his calls, or had she too taken to avoiding him? Too many questions. Zero answers.

Hunt punched another number. This phone was answered. "Corina Meeks."

"Hi ya, Corky. It's me. How's the digging?"

"Hunt, you wouldn't believe the resistance I'm getting."

Hunt turned gazing at a blue and white speedboat making its way along the shoreline. He didn't like the level of concern he heard in Corky's voice. "Yeah, Cork. No surprise there. Listen, something's happened in Vegas. Jerry Byers' clinic. Cops are onsite and giving no details. I can't reach Jerry. I can't reach Dana. Could you play detective for me?" Hunt hated throwing all of this on Corky, but had limited options.

"Sure, Hunt. I'll poke around. Where are you?"

"Chicago. Following a lead on Donnelley. Though, to my knowledge, he's had no prior Chicago connection."

"How did you track him to Chicago?"

"Homeland security agent named Marjorie Bedford. In fact, do me favor. Run a background check on her. She's involved in this thing. According to her, on the side of truth, justice, and the American way, but I have my concerns. Apparently, she and some others have joined together to undermine whatever conspiracy they've uncovered. The group goes by the code name, White Eagle. I'd like to know if she has any skeletons lurking about."

"Well, you are demanding, aren't you?" The tone was stern yet playful.

"Sorry, Cork. Stressful times."

Hunt could now hear Corky writing with a pencil. "Bedford. You said the first name was Marjorie? M-a-r-j-o-r-i-e."

"Right. See what you can find for me."

"Alright, Hunt. Give me a sec. I might have something for you." Hunt heard quick, skillful keyboarding. "Yes. Okay. Las Vegas Metro police were dispatched to Beyer's clinic on reports of suspicious activity. Nothing more on that yet."

"Nothing? No reports filed? No back-up called?"

"Give me another minute." Again, Hunt heard the rapid fire tapping of Corky's keyboarding. "Oh…"

"What, Cork?" Her voice sounded troubled.

"Like I said, no reports filed as of yet, but… Hunt, the coroner was sent to that locale last evening."

Hunt's entire form stiffened. His lips moved but no sound escaped. She couldn't be dead. Couldn't! The disease, the plague, it was working quickly, but this wasn't the disease. Whatever had happened, the clinic had been shut down, officers dispatched, Byers was AWOL. This was something else. The terrorists. The RPA or maybe those pulling their strings. Dana might still be alive. Likely, she was a captive. But she might still be alive.

"Hunt?"

"I'm here, Cork. Thanks for the intel."

There was a pause on the line and then, "You know I'm here for you. I mean, if anything happens to your wife. I mean…" There was a long pause. "I'm still here."

Hunt took a long breath. When he spoke, it was not in response to Corky's statement. "Anything else, Cork? Anything on Donnelley? I'll be moving on him in less than five minutes."

"Sure, Hunt. Um… I didn't mean to… You know…"

"I know what you meant, Corky. You have anything?"

A few more taps of the keyboard and, "Yes, I do. I think I may have found Donnelley's Chicago connection."

*****

Hunt moved slowly down the narrow corridor of the century-old high-rise condominium situated just east of the Magnificent Mile neighborhood of Michigan Avenue. Plaster walls, oak door frames, antique-style elevators, and paisley carpeting. His Browning was not yet in hand—there was too big a chance that he might encounter a passerby—but it was at the ready, holstered at his tailbone, hidden under his untucked denim shirt.

Hunt hated the politics of this thing. He—a civilian—was tasked with securing the terrorist because government agencies had been compromised. This wasn't an episode of the television show, "24." There shouldn't be a mole in every situation room. These people were supposed to have contingencies for such things, systems in place to ensure that such a scenario could never play out at such high levels.

In theory, Donnelley was holed up in a condo just up the hall. It was owned by a Marvin Davies. The name was false. Hunt couldn't know if the actual owner was Donnelley himself or one of his superiors, but the Davies legend barely withstood a basic credit check much less intense scrutiny. Even as Hunt moved up the corridor he wondered if Donnelley had the antidote with him or had passed it on to someone else. Either way, Hunt felt confident that he could wrest the information from him given only a few moments alone. Donnelley would likely not enjoy the encounter.

What concerned Hunt was that he had no way of knowing if Donnelley was alone. It was possible that other terrorists had joined him. He hated relying on incomplete intelligence, but time had not allowed him another option.

There was movement up the hallway. A couple exiting their condo. The man appeared to be in his mid to upper fifties, and was dressed sharply with a designer suit and high dollar watch, likely a Rolex. The woman clung vigorously to his arm and kissed him several times on their short trip to the elevator. She seemed a quarter of a century his junior, blond, busty, vivacious. The perks and curse of the wealthy, he supposed. Hunt couldn't quite understand what two people separated by such a significant age gap could share in common. Still, what did he know? He had a wife only four years younger than he and things still managed to go sideways more often than not. Maybe there was something to throwing logic and social conventions out a high window and walking in the face of sanity.

The giggling and smooching couple was now onto the elevator. Hunt was alone in the hallway. Donnelley's unit was the next on the left. Hunt reached back, patting his pistol. He knew it was there but was comforted at the touch of it. Glancing in both directions, Hunt pulled a fiber optics scope from a large Velcro pocket on his pants. The thing looked like a long black tube, 2 mm in diameter, with a viewing lens something akin to the eyepiece of a telescope. This scope could be slipped under a door or through nearly any crack and afforded Hunt an amazing view. Even in low lighting, the scope boasted nearly 9,000 pixels per 1.5 mm. Very sharp. Very detailed.

Hunt knelt, sliding the scope under the door. Moving it slowly right to left, he was able to see all of the living room area and a portion of the kitchen.

The terrorist was not visible, though a thick haze of tobacco clouded the space. Someone was obviously there.

Hunt took a moment to study the layout. The rooms were large, the décor sparse yet tasteful. And pricy. Even at first glance, Hunt could tell that nothing in the room had come from Wal-Mart. Donnelley's hideout was high rent all the way around.

There was a movement in the hallway from behind. Casually, Hunt shifted just slightly, moving to tie his right shoe. A completely innocent activity and one that would explain why he was kneeling on the floor. It was a woman, Hispanic, mid-forties, dressed in business casual. Hunt nodded to her offering a smile and a, "Have a good day," as she made her way past him and to the elevator.

Giving a moment after the elevator door closed, Hunt then returned to the scope. He caught a glimpse of someone—it looked to be Donnelley—crossing from left to right across the room and then out of sight. The man wore only boxer shorts. Hunt had not been able to secure the layout of the unit, but determined it likely that Donnelley had just returned to the bedroom after visiting the kitchen. The man was obviously not dressed for company and Hunt had not heard even muffled conversation from beyond the door. Likely, he was alone.

Without further hesitation, Hunt removed a lock picking kit from a pocket, setting it on the tightly woven carpet and opening the small canvas pouch. Since his injuries in Iraq, Hunt had suffered frequent and severe migraines. These had diminished his concentration, making it hard for him to focus on detailed tasks such as picking. But, these had subsided some in recent months and Hunt found that, though he was not as quick as he had been in his Delta Force days, he was again becoming adept at the skill.

Lifting the scope, he studied the room again, determining that the area was still unoccupied. Setting the scope aside, Hunt then slipped the picks into the keyhole. Hunt would have only moments to complete the task or risk Donnelley reentering the room prior to his entrance. Maneuvering the needle-like tools, Hunt gave a twist, but the locking mechanism did not release. Steadying himself, he tried again. This was not a difficult task. Thirty seconds. This should take thirty seconds!

Another slip. Another twist. A subtle click. Hunt exhaled. The lock had released.

A ping.

The sound of a sliding door.

"Excuse me. Excuse me!"

It was the Hispanic woman. She'd just exited the elevator, now carrying several pieces of mail, and was marching in Hunt's direction.

Hunt smiled, rising while still maintaining his hold on the brass doorknob. "Hello again. Just fixing the lock," he said as he opened the door and slipped inside, locking the door behind him, and leaving his scope in place. The game had just become more complicated. Likely, security would be notified.

Turning toward the living area Hunt watched as Donnelley stepped to before him, cigarette in hand, still wearing only his boxers. Obviously, he'd been alerted by the sound of voices followed by the rushed opening and then closing of the door.

Hunt withdrew his weapon as he suppressed a cough. The room was a haze of stale, blue-gray smoke. Disgusting habit for a disgusting man.

Donnelley smiled, his deep-set eyes red, his face twitching as he proceeded to speak. "That's your plan, heh? Shoot me? Or maybe just to threaten me?" He paused, clucking his tongue twice. "Think about it, Huntington. Think, think, think. Avenging Dana's honor won't do her any good. Not without the antidote. She is alive, still, heh?" A subtle cock of the head as he studied Hunt. "Yeah. Alive. But, not much longer. What'd they give her? Another day? A few hours?"

Hunt remained as he was, the gun trained on Donnelley's chest. Having been seen by the woman, he had very little time and couldn't afford to be diverted from his task. "I'm here for the antidote. That's it. Give me that and I'm gone."

"Like that? Just like that?" A pause. A grin. "You don't know, do you? The little whore didn't tell you." He stepped closer, ignoring the weapon. "I guess it's up to me. Fill in the gaps. We had some fun. Me and the missus. Heh. Feisty one, your little Asian whore. Good though. Tasty. She... Heh! Pleasured me good. I thought she would have told you."

"Liar!" Hunt barely kept his index finger from squeezing. The man's claims were ridiculous. Absurd.

But…

Dana's behavior since the train.

Her reluctance to see Hunt.

It almost seemed…

Donnelley grinned, swiping an index finger across the base of his nose. "Liar? Hmm. Yes. When I need to be. But not now. Not about this." He turned away, strolling toward the couch.

"Stay right there," barked Hunt.

"Or what? You'll shoot me? Not without the antidote. After—yeah, of course you would. But not yet, heh?" Donnelley flopped onto the couch landing in a semi reclined position. "It's not here. I'm really not that stupid, you know. It's safe. Someplace you can't go."

Hunt stepped forward, weapon still drawn. He didn't know what to believe, didn't have time to process Donnelley' claims, to separate the truth from the lies. And so he remained focused on the task, not allowing himself to be goaded into emotional turmoil. "Where is it?" he asked. "Where's the antidote?"

Donnelley glanced to the end table beside the couch, jabbed his cigarette onto a brass ashtray and then picked up a pack of Camels, withdrawing a smoke, and then slipping it between his lips.

"Donnelley! Where is it?"

Donnelley lit the Camel. "Hmm. Thought I'd answered that one already. It's not here. Remember me saying that? I do."

"Take me to it. I swear, Donnelley, I'll shoot."

"Then you'll never find the antidote. The whore will die. You'll be arrested for murder. Nah. Not, worried, Huntington. There's no gain in shooting me. Not yet, heh?"

Hunt stepped forward into the stench of Donnelley's smoke. "No gain in killing you—agreed. But, in shooting you…" Hunt pressed the barrel of the gun against Donnelly's right kneecap. "The antidote, Donnelley."

There was a sharp knock on the door, followed by a shout. "Security!"

Donnelley chuckled, simultaneously clucking his tongue. "Well, this is interesting. I guess we don't have much time. To come to an agreement. Do we?" He blew smoke in Hunt's face.

"Security!" came another shout. "Is everything okay in there? We had a report of an intruder."

Donnelley grinned.

Hunt withdrew the weapon. If he fired now, security would be on him in seconds. The antidote would be lost to him. Dana would die.

Donnelley clucked his tongue again, still chuckling. "Just a minute," he called to security. "I'll be right there." And then to Hunt he asked, "How much do you love her, heh? What would you do for a whore?"

Hunt's mind was racing as he contemplated his options. They were few, and none concluded with him gaining the antidote through this encounter.

"What would you do for her?" repeated Donnelley. "I want to hear you say it."

"Anything. I'll do anything."

Donnelley smiled and took a long drag on his Camel. "Does that include releasing the plague in a public place?"

Chapter 32

Hunt hesitated before climbing the dozens of steps leading into Chicago's famous Field Museum. The place seemed almost a castle or perhaps an austere house of government with its four great pillars at the entrance and its stately stone façade. Visitors from all over the world made their ways up and down the concrete steps. An elderly couple nodded and smiled at Hunt as they descended. A group of early elementary grade school children, fresh off the orange and black bus and each wearing a lime green T-shirt emblazoned with the school name and mascot, scampered up the way, eager to see dinosaurs and mummies, to dream of thrills and adventures as only children can. Hunt remembered taking field trips here himself as a schoolboy. How many innocents were in this mammoth building? How many could become infected?

After entering the building and paying for his admission, Hunt marched through the ticketing area, past two enormous charcoal gray elephants, stuffed and forever engaged in a motionless scene of battle, and was then confronted by Sue, the largest and most complete Tyrannosaurus Rex skeleton ever discovered. She was crouched as if poised to strike, her immense jaws and teeth fierce and formidable. Hunt watched as a father comforted his preschool-aged son who seemed terrified at the awesome sight, cowering away and whimpering. It seemed the child resisted—but only just barely—the temptation to suck his thumb. The school children scampered to the thing in a wave of lime green exuberance, hooting and cheering, shouting cries of awe and wonder as their adult chaperones sought, with little success, to bring the group under control. How many of Hunt's fellow visitors could imagine that the simple backpack he wore contained something far more deadly than this spectacular monster ever had been in life?

Hunt scanned the vast hall, searching for signs of Donnelley. He would be here, Hunt knew. The man would need to have a visual on his reluctant recruit. In no way could he trust Hunt to follow through on this ghastly mission without hands-on direction. The main hall was long and narrow, almost regal in design. Roman style columns seemingly stood guard along both sides of the hall. A pair of two-story tall totem pools manned the entrance. Two evenly-spaced rows of arched openings were situated at the upper level near the lofty ceiling and offered Hunt a shadowed glimpse onto the second floor.

Where was the man? Where was Donnelley?

There was a commotion from behind. Another surge of children—these wearing bright orange shirts—raced across the marble floor. Another field trip. Another busload of unsuspecting innocents.

Hunt turned away, forcing his mind off of the children and onto Dana.

Everything for Dana.

Nothing mattered but Dana.

Hunt's phone chimed. Utilizing his Bluetooth, he answered. This was a pre-arranged call.

"Heh, Huntington. There you go," said Donnelley in his staccato speech. "Circle back. Toward the T-rex. Place yourself. The heart of the crowd."

Donnelley obviously had a vantage, and likely it was one of the second story openings, but these were shadowy and were at such a distance as to make identification difficult. "You do realize they're mostly children," offered Hunt.

"And that means what? That they're innocent? Heh. Have you forgotten childhood? Kids are cruel to weaker classmates. Cruel and spoiled." Donnelley's speech was punctuated by giggles and clucks. The man was truly unhinged, or at the very least, either riding or coming down from a high.

Hunt scanned the arched openings lining the hall. Surely Donnelley was on the upper level gazing down on him, but where was the man? "You really trying to justify this, Kelvin? You think that just because kids tease each other they deserve death? You're one twisted sicko."

A chuckle and several clucks of the tongue. "The bio-canister is in the backpack. Leave it unzipped. I'll discharge the plague remotely. Once the gas is deployed I'll tell you where to find the antidote."

"I know the drill, Donnelley. How could I forget?" Hunt moved further from Sue the T-rex, still scanning the upper level as he made his way past the elephants and through the great hall. "Listen, Donnelley... Kelvin. I know about your brother."

"Colm? You're trying to use Colm against me? Stupid, Huntington. Stupid." Donnelley paused and Hunt heard a sniffle and then a belch. "Do you want to see your little whore again?" he asked after a moment? "Heh? You want to go back? Taste my leftovers? You'd better turn around. Do exactly what I say."

"Yeah, yeah. Got it. Listen, if it's stupid for me talk about Colm, how about Colonel Steven Calhoun? Wanna talk about him?"

A pause on the line. "What do you know? About Calhoun?"

Ah! Was that a reaction? "I know you blame him for your brother's death. I know he was pardoned and that you blame the government for that injustice. I know he's your reason for coming to Chicago. He left the military, came here. The man works security in this building. You can feed me all the lofty psycho patriotic crap you want, but we both know this is about simple, sadistic revenge. I wonder, do the other members of the RPA know your true motives? Would they still follow you if they did?"

"You think you know so much, heh? My revenge on Calhoun. Yeah, that's part of it. So what? It still fits the big plan. Still wakes our country. From apathy. Yeah. No conflict, Mr. Delta Force reject. This is about America. Resetting her course."

"Through the deaths of thousands of innocents? Do you have any idea how many people will die if that plague spreads through a city this size?"

"No. I haven't given it a thought." A chuckle and a cluck. "Of course I'm aware. This is a revolution, Bozo. Time to, heh, do your part."

"Ever think of a more conventional way of making your point? You know, running for office, infomercials—suicide?"

"Heh! The soldier boy thinks he's funny. Just remember who screwed whose wife, heh? Just remember."

Hunt clenched his fist. There was nothing to be said—yet. But, soon. Plenty needed to happen soon.

"Turn around, Huntington. Toward the crowd. Do it now or the deal is off. The little whore is waiting for her antidote. Can't keep her waiting."

Silently, Hunt turned, gazing down the massive hall at the dozens of excited children. He took a step forward. And then another. And another. "I'm obviously not going to get out of this alive. Not being this close to the plague when it's released. Even if you give me the antidote, Dana gets it first. You mind telling me who you're really working for? You know, the people behind those attacks overseas? Maybe what this is really all about?"

"Funny man. Heh. That you'll never know. No one will. Now, stop. Yeah. Right there. Walk in a circle. Around the brats, around, around. That's it. Yeah. Good. And now it's time."

Hunt heard the click of the mechanism as Donnelley activated the canister remotely. There were easily two hundred school children within a fifty foot radius of him.

Chapter 33

Unknown location

Dana blinked.

She blinked again.

And then coughed.

Her mucus was thick, coppery sweet, a mixture of sputum and blood.

She was disoriented and found it difficult to concentrate. There was a buzzing in her brain, the sounds of a thousand insects.

Or maybe even a thousand voices.

Again she blinked, this time focusing on the wall before her.

Focus.

Concentrate.

Maintain control of your own mind.

Another cough, this one racking her already battered core.

She ached as she never had before. Every fiber of her frame felt as if it had been stretched, and torn, and battered. Even a simple act such as scratching her nose was an excruciating effort.

Dana focused on the plain vanilla wall before her. The surface was blank, unadorned with even a cheap print or a dated photograph. There was no furniture apart from her hospital bed. But, the room was not empty. She was attached to equipment. There was the steady beep, beep, beep, of the heart monitor. An IV fed her fluids through a vein at her right wrist. There were sensors of some sort positioned about her head, torso, and legs, and connected to a device situated on a metal cart which displayed readings that Dana could not interpret through the plastic tent surrounding her. There was no window, and so she could see nothing beyond her room.

She hacked again, her throat raw and dry. She might actually be willing to kill someone for a simple glass of water.

Time seemed a constant swirl. How long she'd been in this semi-delirious state she couldn't know, but at some point she noticed a figure beside her. She had not seen the door open, had not perceived the woman as she'd approached. How long had she been standing there? A minute? An hour? Dana blinked in an attempt to clear her vision. The woman wore a green surgical mask and scrubs. Latex gloves covered her hands.

"Well, hi there, Dana. It looks like you're with us again."

"Bedford?" Dana's voice was nothing more than a hushed croak.

"That's me. Hard to tell past the mask, I know."

"Water?"

A shake of the head. "No. The best I can do is ice chips." Bedford slipped a small Dixi cup filled with chips under the plastic tent. "I know you're probably wanting something more substantial, but doc's orders." She shrugged as if to say, "You know how it is."

Dana sucked on several chips and asked, "Where am I?"

"Safe."

"That's no bleeding answer."

Bedford shrugged. "It's the best one I've got. Should I ask how you're feeling or is that a plain dumb question?"

Dana slipped another couple of chips onto her tongue. "Why was I taken from the clinic?" She was thinking of the blood she'd seen behind the counter at the clinic. The other patients being dismissed. No sign of Jerry Byers or any of his staff. She would not let Bedford know that she'd seen this. But, she knew her situation was tenuous.

"As I said before, we feel your particular, what do you want to call it—ailment? We think your ailment will be better treated here."

"My ailment?" she said. "You make it sound like the bleeding flu." Dana closed her eyes, still coming to grips with the horror that infected her. Not only the plague, but the Amazon bacteria as well, the one they'd encountered in Brazil. Bedford had explained that some monster had tied it to the plague, genetic manipulation, a better way to kill thousands, perhaps millions. Dana had seen the result of this pathogen firsthand. She'd watched as Dr. Gregory Milton slipped into a coma so deep some would call it suspended animation. She'd stood helpless as Andrew Lindell's temperature rose and rose, bringing with it first madness and then death as his very skin popped and burst in a sizzling ooze. This was the bacteria carried within the fossil, the skull which had been discovered in the Amazon. After lying dormant for centuries, exposure to air and light had apparently activated the monstrous germ. And now someone sought to spread this deadly horror, to use it as a weapon of terror.

And she had been infected.

Not just by some random terrorist. This had been Donnelley. It wasn't enough that he'd raped her, that he'd robbed her of all dignity or even her will to live. But, then he'd cursed her with one of the most horrific deaths imaginable.

She would kill him.

That was all that was left to her. Donnelley's death. After that, she would allow herself to succumb. Perhaps she'd even help the process along. It was too late for her. Too late for anything. She'd sent Hunt away. And though she longed for him, she was also repulsed by the thought of even the most innocent intimacy. She was damaged beyond repair. Better to eliminate the cause of so much pain, perhaps even do some good in the act, and then be done.

But, even one last act might be too great a task. Her condition was poor, and in truth, she wasn't even certain she had the strength to traverse the room unaided.

But, she would find a way. This she knew as a certainty.

There was movement. Bedford. She was slipping a tissue under the tent. Dana hadn't even been aware that she'd been crying.

"Yes. Thank you," said Dana as she accepted the kindness. "Any progress? A cure perhaps? An antidote which can be mass produced should this beast be released on the general populace? That is why I'm here I assume. My continued existence would be a plus, but really you need my blood for your experiments."

"Those questions are for the experts. I'm just making a social visit. But, sure. A cure wouldn't be so bad, would it?" And Dana knew right then. Maybe it was the tone of her voice, maybe the too casual response, but Dana knew that Bedford's intent was for Dana to spend the few remaining hours of her life in this tiny box of a room.

Well, that just wasn't going to happen.

Chapter 34

Chicago Illinois

Hunt stood on the vast concrete steps of the Field Museum staring up at a near cloudless sky and breathing in the cool lake breeze. He still wore the backpack containing the deadly canister and his mood was somber. Visitors, both adult and children, continued to come and go, chatting and laughing, oblivious to any potential danger. Hunt wiped his brow, closed his eyes, and thought once again of Dana. Precious, unpredictable, infuriating Dana. He simply couldn't lose her. He was a strong man. He'd survived combat, lost men under his command, had been disfigured by a bomb blast, even been wrongfully accused of leading a mission while under the influence, but the thought of going on without Dana, that was worse than any scenario he'd ever faced. It was a possibility he refused to accept.

He glanced at his watch. Nearly fifteen minutes since he'd emerged from the building. Why hadn't Donnelley called? Had he evaded Hunt yet again? Hunt knew he couldn't trust the man, but had been forced to follow his lead. He was certainly a fool for believing that Donnelley would follow through on his part of the bargain, but hadn't been left any real choice. He'd demanded to see the antidote before committing to the task. Donnelley had refused. He'd insisted that Donnelley remain visible during the operation, that they have an established meet point. Donnelley had laughed. Hunt was at the mercy of a morally bankrupt individual with psychotic tendencies and substance abuse issues. And yet, despite the man's many flaws, he somehow continued to maintain the upper hand.

Hunt wasn't even sure of how to next proceed. If Donnelley had skipped out on him, the chase would resume, but Dana simply didn't have enough time left for that to occur. Likely, she was now into her final few hours. There was no room for further hindrances. As it was, he still didn't have a locale on her. Corky had now confirmed that Jerry Byers, two nurses, and a receptionist had been found dead at the clinic. But, there was no sign of Dana. Hunt's phone chirped, bringing him back into the moment.

"Donnelley?" he said into his Bluetooth.

"Didn't think you'd do it, Huntington. Soldier boy's a killer at heart, heh?"

"I did what you asked, Donnelley. Where's the antidote?"

A giggle and a cluck of the tongue. "The antidote. We'll get to that, heh? In time."

Hunt scanned the area, looking for a sign of the man. It was unlikely he'd remained within the museum and risked infection. Still, he was probably nearby. "No more games, Donnelley. Dana doesn't have much longer and if she dies, I'm coming after you. And know this, I've found you once, I can do it again. If she dies, you won't survive our next encounter."

"You found me because Bedford sent you. Like an attack dog."

What did he know about Bedford? How could he know that she'd given him the lead? "I'm serious, Donnelley. If Dana dies, so do you."

"Ha! Heh! Tough soldier boy. Don't worry. You'll get the antidote. I have my own reasons for giving it to you. But just remember, I own you now. Own you to the soul."

"Oh, yeah? How's that?" Hunt began making his way down the long broad stairs, still scanning as he went, looking for someone watching him while simultaneously speaking on a phone.

"What you just did. People are going to die. Lots and lots of people. All your fault. Security tapes will prove that. And I can point the authorities to your doorstep."

Hunt scanned left and then right. Two gulls were pecking at spilled popcorn. A young woman made her way down the steps with a baby carriage. An elderly gentleman sat on a step, resting before he continued up the way. "We'll tackle that issue later. How do I know it'll work?"

"What?"

"The antidote. How do I know that what you're giving me is the real antidote?"

A chortle and a sniff. "You don't. Do you? Guess you'll need to trust me."

"Not likely, Donnelley. I'll have it tested before Dana gets a drop. Just remember what I said would happen to you if she dies."

"Yeah, yeah. Rambo comes after me with a vengeance. Stop right there."

Hunt had just reached street level. In order for Donnelley to know this, he had to have a visual. Hunt scanned the shifting crowd with renewed intensity. The man was close. Very close.

"Turn left," said Donnelley. "See the ice cream vendor?"

"Yeah. I see." It was just ahead, a portable stand.

"Tell the kid you're picking up a package for the Asian whore. Heh! Keep your phone on. I want to hear you say it—Asian whore."

Hunt clenched his fists, still scanning the pedestrians. If he caught up with Donnelley, he'd likely kill the man.

"Go on. Go on," urged the terrorist. "I wanna hear you say it."

Hunt looked toward the colorful stand as he moved forward, but focused on the parking lot beyond. There, standing between a black Volkswagen Jetta and a Ford SUV, was a man, tall, slightly rolled shoulders, salt and pepper beard, an obvious overbite. He was leaning on the Jetta, a phone to his ear as he gazed in Hunt's direction. No surprise there. Fearing that Hunt might try something en route, Donnelley had insisted they take separate vehicles. He'd followed Hunt to the museum in that car. Hunt turned his head slightly as if looking at the ice cream stand, but kept his eyes on his query. Donnelley wasn't walking away from this thing if Hunt had anything to do with it.

Now Hunt was in line at the stand behind a family of five: mom, dad, two boys, and a girl, all of the children elementary aged. He wondered if this family had been in the museum while he'd been in there. The little girl looked up at Hunt. He smiled at her. She turned away, probably frightened by his scarred face. Hunt had grown accustomed to this reaction from children, but still, at some level, it hurt. He'd always liked kids and hoped to have some eventually.

Now, the father was paying for the food. One of the boys had already dropped a dollop of chocolate ice cream onto his yellow T-shirt. The mother was wiping him off, the little girl staring at Hunt and hugging her mother's leg.

Finally, it was Hunt's turn.

"Say it. Say it," urged Donnelley.

Hunt smiled at the twenty something year-old guy manning the stand. "One of my idiot coworkers left a package for me. He wants me to say something crass to get it. You gonna make me say it or can you just give it to me?"

"No, Huntington. Say it!" barked Donnelley in near panic. This freak really liked his games.

The kid glanced down at the counter, looking embarrassed, and brushing a greasy brown lock from his forehead. "He said he'd only pay me if I made you say it."

"Yeah, well, the guy's an idiot. That thing he wants me to say, it's about my wife. That package you're holding, it's her medicine. How much is he paying you?"

The kid seemed to contemplate this for a minute, screwing his peach fuzz face into a contortion of concentration. "Fifty bucks," he said at last. The real number had probably been twenty.

"I'll give you a hundred if you hand over the package. It's important. She really needs her meds."

Hunt withdrew the money and handed it to the kid as Donnelley swore in his ear. Apparently uncomfortable by the entire exchange, the young food vendor shrugged as he handed Hunt a brown paper bag containing a small vile of yellow liquid. There was a fruit basket on the ledge and Hunt snatched an apple before turning away. Antidote now in hand, Hunt turned and began strolling toward the parking lot, purposely angling slightly to the left of the terrorist and tilting his head downward as if examining the contents of the bag.

"Where are you going?" asked Donnelley, a twinge of concern in his tone.

"My car. You have a problem with that?"

A pause. A snort. And then, "There's only enough antidote for one, Huntington. You need to choose. Who dies, you or your wife?"

"Broken record, Donnelley. I told you before, Dana gets the juice." Hunt continued toward the parking lot, angling around a young couple walking two schnauzers, and targeting the aisle to Donnelley's left, to all appearances, oblivious of the man.

"Heh! Noble. It's easy now, before the symptoms kick in. Then we'll see who gets the antidote." A few seconds of silence and then, "I know you've seen me. Capturing me won't help you any. You already have what you need."

Hunt smiled at the man, Donnelley was in motion now, both men moving in the same direction, a row of cars separating them. "The choice is even easier than you think, Donnelley. There will be no symptoms and therefore no choice to make."

"Heh?" Donnelley quickened his pace, scattering a small group of gulls.

Hunt matched him, the cool lakeside breeze invigorating him. "The plague. It wasn't dispersed." Hunt was aware of Donnelley's every movement, watching his eyes, his hands, even his stance, knowing that though there were metal detectors in the museum, his opponent had had plenty of time to retrieve his weapon while Hunt stood waiting on the steps. With luck, he was wise enough to avoid firing in a public venue. Donnelley had to know there was a heavy police presence in and around the museum campus. Opening fire would not lead to a favorable outcome.

Donnelley stopped, pivoted, began moving back in the direction of the Jetta, his hands still empty except for the phone he held. "But, I pressed the remote. I heard the hiss of the gas. Through the phone. As you walked around those brats." His voice was quick, jittery.

Hunt turned as well, still matching the terrorist step for step. "Yeah, well, things aren't always as they seem. I clogged the nozzle with super glue when you first gave me the backpack. Remember when I was readjusting the straps to make it fit? I slipped in a quick slight-of-hand. You stood and watch as I disabled your weapon and didn't have the sense to figure it out."

"Liar. Why would you have glue?"

"I always carry it. The stuff's great for sealing battlefield injuries. Almost as good as stitches."

"I don't believe you."

"Yes you do. You said yourself you didn't think I'd do it."

"But I heard the gas disperse," Donnelley's tone was tinged with anger and panic.

"Yeah. The hiss, well…" Hunt blew air softly from between his lips, tongue pressed against his bottom teeth. The effect was that of a subtle hiss. "Sounds real, doesn't it?"

It was then that Hunt made his move.

Donnelley had frisked him, taking his Browning and his knife, but this didn't leave Hunt without resources. In one swift movement, he hurled the apple at the man like a major league pitcher losing the final pitch of a no-hitter. The apple struck Donnelley on the right temple. Momentarily stunned, he took a clumsy step back, dropping his phone. Hunt raced toward the man and was only ten feet away when the gun appeared.

Donnelley fired wildly as Hunt dove behind a 1960's era red Mustang and heard the loud tone of bullets piercing metal.

The idiot!

There were kids nearby.

Now, weaponless, Hunt crouched as he raced around the Mustang and toward Donnelley, still keeping vehicles between them. Not only did he need to protect himself, but he couldn't risk the backpack being hit and the plague released.

"We had a deal," barked Donnelley. "We had a deal! Calhoun was in that hall. I saw him. He should be infected!"

Donnelley squeezed off three more rounds.

There were shouts and screams from all sides. Someone hollering for Donnelley to stop. Hunt saw a police officer racing up the long lakefront walkway which stretched between the Field Museum and the Shedd Aquarium.

Hunt changed directions, moving around the opposite side of a forest green Toyota as he slipped the backpack from his shoulders and hid it under the car.

Donnelley fired again, but the shot was wild. The man was allowing emotions to rule him, thus causing his accuracy to suffer.

Hunt was close now.

Another three feet.

He lunged.

The gun discharged.

The brown bag slipped from Hunt's grasp.

More shouts from beyond as the round furrowed the asphalt.

Rolling into Donnelley's shins, Hunt toppled the terrorist, immediately straddling him. Donnelley sought to bring the gun to bear, but Hunt ripped it from his grip, tossing it far to his right.

His fist came down.

Again, again, again.

The raw emotions flooding his mind.

Donnelley's abuse of Dana—his claims to have had her.

The plague.

The attacks on public locales.

But, mostly Dana.

He pummeled the man, Donnelley's face becoming bloody, his nose broken, cheeks swollen, Hunt's rage so great that he didn't hear the police officer barking orders. So lost was he in his haze of rage that he nearly took a swing at the two officers as they pulled him free of the man.

Coming into his head, Hunt allowed them to subdue him. Immediately, they slammed him face to the concrete, pulling his hands behind his back. Hunt stammered something about Donnelley being a terrorist, and then finally took in the scene about him. Five police officers, guns trained on him and Donnelley. "Okay, okay," said Hunt. "I get it." He eyed the brown bag containing the antidote some ten feet away on the ground. Whatever happened he had to retrieve the bag. Dana's life depended on it. "He's a terrorist," added Hunt. "I just prevented a bio-attack on the museum."

The antidote.

Somehow he had to get to the antidote.

"Actually," said Donnelley, who was similarly pinned to the ground. "There's your terrorist. I'm with Homeland Security. Like to see my credentials?"

Chapter 35

Unknown location

Dana knew that if she was to make a move it would need to be soon. Her strength had waned and likely would continue to do so. She'd determined that this was not a traditional medical facility. True, she was in what appeared to be a hospital room with all of the equipment one would expect, but aside from that, nothing seemed as it should. Even this naked room spoke to the fact. Hospital rooms had television sets, widows, even subtle adornments on the walls. This had none of these. As well, she heard no announcements calling for doctor so-and-so to room such-and-such, no nurses made periodic checks, there was no foot traffic beyond her doorway. Even the minimal food they'd offered had been microwavable fare—nothing cooked in a kitchen or delivered on a rolling tray.

No. She was in a facility of some sort, but it was not a hospital.

She was a lab rat.

And while, yes, she wanted to do her part to inhibit the spread of this bloody disease, she felt the cause would be much better served in a place of her choosing, in the open, where her fate was known not only to those of her choosing but to the public at large.

Her fate.

In her eyes this had already been determined.

This would be the end of her. And that was for the better. Life with all of its agonies and trials no longer held appeal. All she sought was peaceful oblivion. No memories, no fears, no Donnelleys.

But, not here. Not with Bedford or those she served. The Homeland Security agent—if indeed she was—had killed Jerry Byers and his staff. Innocents. Bedford could not be trusted and thus this facility could not be trusted. Dana would make her way to a legitimate facility, tell the physicians what she knew and then…

Find a few handfuls of meds and pop the bloody things. Then they could have all of the blood they needed from her, do whatever testing needed to be done. She was not a coward. She would have done her part.

Dana knew that there was a cart just beyond her doorway. She'd seen it when last the physician had visited. The cart contained medications. This was Dana's first goal, to reach the cart.

Summoning her strength, she pulled the covers back, exposing her legs and torso. Her legs were bruised, a remnant of the rape. She shuddered as she slipped one leg and then the other under the plastic tent and off the side of the bed. Lowering herself slowly, she slid, belly against the mattress, until her bare feet connected with the cool tile floor.

She had so little strength and so paused, still draped across the bed, fearful that should she attempt to support her own weight she'd tumble to the ground unable to move.

The buzzing in her head seemed to increase with exertion.

Bloody distracting.

Closing her eyes, she concentrated on the task at hand, focused, willed herself to move.

There. She'd slid a bit further, allowing her legs to support a portion of her weight.

Now a bit more.

The legs trembled, the left more so than the right.

But, yet, she had not fallen.

A little more, a little more. Now she supported the majority of her own weight.

Pathetic!

She was becoming excited about standing against a bed with all the finesse of a ten month old.

Dana turned slowly, slipping from beneath the tent and maintaining a hold on the bed with her right hand while pulling monitoring sensors and the I.V. needle free with her left. She now faced the doorway. How far was that? Perhaps five steps, maybe seven?

A surge of deep hacking coughs overtook her, nearly causing her to stumble, but she sustained her balance. This illness, this bloody disease was of Donnelley.

Donnelley would not win.

It was ten shuffling agonizing steps to the doorway but she made it. Dana was pleased to find that it was unlocked. Likely, they thought her incapable of an escape attempt. Still, not exactly high security considering the deadly pathogen racing through her bloodstream.

The cart was there. Again, no need to lock things away, Dana was a near corpse. Surely she couldn't find her way to these meds.

Her first act was to find a thermometer. It was of a modern sort, the type one stuck in the ear.

104.7 degrees Fahrenheit.

She was bloody fortunate not to be delirious. Still, she'd seen what this bacteria had done to others, literally burning them from the inside out. At some lunatic level, she was lucky she supposed.

At some lunatic level.

Next, she shifted through the numerous items on the cart, examining each, looking for something quite particular. She found it after perhaps a minute's time. Epinephrine. Synthetic adrenaline. Energy. Strength.

Hope.

Nearly stumbling as she prepared the injection, Dana prayed the stuff would have the desired effect. If it could only give her enough of a boost to get her out of this place, beyond Bedford's control, that was all she asked.

Jabbing herself in the upper thigh, Dana nearly screamed as the surge of medication rushed through her system.

Yes, she could sense it already—the difference—building, growing, dispersing. It wasn't perfect by any means. She still felt deathly ill. The buzzing in her brain continued—if anything increased—but there was a renewed strength in her limbs. They ached, they quivered, but they supported her.

For now at least.

Gazing about, she found that she was alone in a long and narrow corridor lined with doors.

Barren.

Devoid of life.

The plaster walls were a yellowed white, the vinyl floors white with flecks of pale gray, some stained yellow or brown. Even the wooden baseboards were painted a soulless white.

And old.

The building had an old feel about it: the light fixtures, the plaster walls, even the thick musty odor—not a dirty or mold-laden smell, just old. And vacant. Not a creature was stirring…

She wondered what this building had been in life: a school, a boarding house, a hospital or clinic? It seemed both too enormous and too mundane to have been a private residence.

She tried the door adjacent the room she'd just occupied. Locked. The next, locked as well. The third, unlocked. She wasn't quite sure what she was looking for, perhaps some clue as to where she was, maybe a weapon—a cure! Anything. Any small piece to the puzzle. She knew her time was limited. Her little energy boost would not last too terribly long and there was the risk of being seen as well, but she hoped to, if at all possible, leave with some usable information.

The room was a small office. There was a metal desk and vinyl chair. Atop the desk, a tabletop computer. Elsewhere in the room, a three-door wooden filing cabinet, and a closet door. The file drawers were empty as was the desk. In the closet, she found a men's wool overcoat, an empty leather satchel, and a pair of men's rubber galoshes. She took the coat and the satchel. Dana was not modest, but the thought of traipsing about in an open-backed hospital gown was less appealing than sporting a man's coat that trailed near the ground.

There was a nail file, two pieces of spearmint gum, and a small spiral notepad in the right pocket of the coat and a wad of used tissue in the left. The notepad was entirely blank, but Dana used the nail file to unscrew the computer and remove the hard drive. In an unlocked and unoccupied office, it likely contained nothing of use, but at least she was making an attempt. Slipping the hard drive into the satchel, she exited the room, glanced left and then right, and returned to the cart. Here, she grabbed the remaining two doses of Epinephrine, and a handful of other meds, and tossed them in with the hard drive. There were three surgical masks folded neatly on the second tier of the tray. Having no desire to spread the bleeding disease, she took one of these and put it on, slipped the others into the satchel, and then moved slowly down the corridor. Already, she felt the lethargy returning. Twice she nearly stumbled for no reason other than her own weakness.

Her limbs ached. She was racked with constant fits of coughing, often accompanied with spats of blood. Her vision was blurred, and that blasted buzzing in her brain nearly drove her to scream.

At the end of the corridor was a metal door. She'd made it all this way without seeing a single individual. Bloody fortunate, that, but concerning as well. Why the isolation? The disease perhaps. This was obviously not a proper medical facility. Perhaps she was contained for fear of the contagion.

The stairwell was dark and narrow, illuminated only by a single bare bulb one floor above Dana's location. There were three additional floors below her, each becoming darker as she distanced herself from the light source. The stairs were of concrete and so didn't creak, yet still Dana slowed as she reached the bottom flight.

Another metal door.

Did it lead to the out of doors—to freedom? Or did it perhaps lead her into a meeting place filled with enemies?

Slowly, silently, she twisted the cool brass knob. A chill skittered across her spine, perhaps the result of air movement, perhaps due to her fever and fears. A sliver of light invaded the stairwell. The door only open a crack, Dana could not yet see anything of use, but heard no voices, no movement.

She pushed it just a touch more.

Still nothing.

It seemed the stairway led to a small foyer or waiting area. She could see the arm of a leather couch, an oak end table, a throw rug, all on a hardwood floor of narrow almost golden planks. The place smelled of cigar tobacco and mildew. Rather disgusting, really.

A fit of coughing. If anyone was present, they now certainly knew of her presence. Hoping to hold onto what slim element of surprise she might still hold, Dana pushed the door the rest of the way open.

Empty.

Cautiously, she stepped forward, alert to every sound.

There were two corridors leading from the room, each near identical to the other. Still, she had found no windows, no exterior doorways, nothing to even hint to whether it was day or night. She chose the corridor on the left for no reason other than the fact that it was the nearer of the two. She knew she must keep moving. This building was not unoccupied. Certainly she would come across someone soon and didn't want to be caught in the open when that occurred.

The hardwood floor was cool on her bare feet as she tried each door along the corridor, cautiously twisting each knob. The first five were locked. In the sixth, she found a corpse.

The woman was still attached to machinery, the same monitors and whatnot that Dana had been tethered to only minutes before. The aged face was drawn and white, the skin peppered with blisters burst and draining. The Amazon strain, there was no denying the symptoms. Dana recognized her. They hadn't spoken, but she'd been both on the train and at the clinic in Colorado, traveling with a younger man, possibly a son. Apparently at least one of the buses carrying the survivors had been captured.

By Homeland Security?

Or by Bedford?

Dana was less and less likely to consider the two one and the same.

Making a quick search of the room, she found nothing of use, and so moved back into the corridor.

In the next room she found Matthew. As with the woman, she recognized him, but had never shared a prior conversation. He was perhaps thirty years of age, something over six feet tall, with receding blond hair, nearly straw-like in color. His eyes were sunken, his face hollow, and his fever similar to hers. It took a bit of doing but she managed to shake and jostle him into consciousness. She debated on whether to inject him with one of her two remaining doses of epinephrine and decided against it. She meant in no way to be selfish, but wanted these available should the need arise. She could always give him a boost later.

"You were on the train," he said after hurried introductions. "And at the clinic. You were like Annie Oakley on steroids with that Uzi." He shook his head, apparently attempting to better focus.

"It was a Kalashnikov."

"Yeah. Whatever. I just don't ever want you angry with me."

The bloke had a smarmy sarcastic way about him, but Dana didn't outright dislike him. Just a bit of an oddball, she supposed. "How long have you been here?" she asked.

"That's kind of hard to tell when you're in a state of delirium. How about a reasonable question?"

"Right. How did you come to be here and how many people have you seen?"

Matthew was still seated on his bed, the plastic tent pressed behind him. He teetered from side to side. "Yeah, we were stopped maybe a half mile from the clinic in Colorado. A couple of monkey goons in space suits dragged me into an ambulance and sedated me. No idea where the others are. That was a good time. I'm definitely looking for more of that action."

The man's sarcasm really was rather intolerable. "And your experience here? What type of treatment have you received? Have they done any experiments, told you anything? Have you any idea how many people are here?"

"Well, the lady sure is full of questions."

"Please, Matthew. Every minute we remain endangers us further. I'm attempting to determine how to proceed."

"Yeah, sorry. I'm not really that big of a jerk. There's something about dying a horrific death that doesn't set right with me. Go figure."

Dana simply stared at the man. How did he find the energy to be so flippant?

"Alright, yeah, treatment, I don't know what they've been doing. It's not like they've told me anything. They come in, take a few gallons of blood, poke me a few times, take my vitals, mumble between themselves, and leave."

"They? How many?"

"Usually just two. A man and a woman, doctor and nurse, I'm guessing."

"Usually two?"

"I've seen one other. A lady. I'm going to say she's in her fifties. Biggish woman. Round. Not medical. She asks the other two about my condition."

"Bedford."

"Excuse me?"

"Her name's Bedford. Supposedly she's with Homeland Security, but I've my doubts. This facility is in no way official."

Matthew began coughing uncontrollably. She'd noticed sweat beading on his brow.

"Matthew, are you alright?"

Between coughs, he managed a sly grin and said, "Oh, sure, I'm ready to compete in the Olympic Games. Can you grab my dumbbells?"

"Alright. Stupid question. Are you capable of an escape attempt?"

He shrugged. "I don't think I have much choice. I'm going to say they're not trying to cure me; they're just trying to learn from me."

Astute observation. Most likely accurate.

"Alright then. Let's have a go at it."

Dana stepped forward, taking Matthew by the hand and supporting him as he slid off of the bed and steadied himself. He was quite hot to the touch. Only three minutes before he'd seemed the same temperature as Dana—and she had a fever of one hundred and four.

They moved slowly, Matthew placing his palm on Dana's shoulder for support. The physical contact with an unknown male caused Dana to nearly scream, but she forced down her emotions. This man was not an attacker; he was just as much a victim as she.

But he was a man.

And men raped women.

A man had raped her.

Other men had held her down, forcing her to comply.

She couldn't be this close to him.

She just couldn't. It seemed her skin crawled away from her bones. Her heart thumped and stomped in violent protest. Her vision blurred.

Abruptly she pulled away leaving the man to support himself.

Startled, Matthew stumbled to the floor. "What the hell?"

"I... I'm sorry. I... I just can't. I..."

She had no words, only emotions, images. Donnelley, his filthy tobacco breath hot on her as he thrust, again, again. The twisted leer. The quirky overbite. The bloodshot eyes and twitches and ticks.

Dana turned, leaving Matthew flopping about on the floor, trying to right himself though he didn't have the strength. It wasn't his fault. It wasn't! But, she couldn't be that close to him. Not that close. He wasn't a Donnelley. But, how did she know? How could she know? Matthew could be a rapist. He could be faking it, pretending to be ill.

Not with that fever. He couldn't fake that fever.

He could be waiting for the right moment, maybe waiting for companions to come and hold her down, to take her, defile her.

Rubbish!

Nonsense!

She was smarter than this. She was not the emotional sort. This man needed help. He needed her help.

She took a tentative step toward him, began to reach down, to offer her hand.

No!

She couldn't do it.

Not now. Not yet.

"I'm sorry. I'm so sorry."

"Lady, I don't know what your deal is, but I'm pretty well stuck."

"I know. I know. I just..."

Dana turned, exiting the room without stopping to consider that the corridor might be occupied.

She could hear Matthew calling after her, pleading, sobbing. "Lady! Please! Lady! I'm going to die in here! Lady! Come back! What did I do? Lady—please!"

Twice, she nearly turned around. Twice, she nearly showed compassion to a fellow victim—to a fellow human being. And twice she turned away. Twice she ignored her conscience. Twice she buried her rationale in favor of bubbling fear. Tears spat onto the cold vinyl floor, and still Dana moved on, ignoring every other doorway, ignoring Matthew's cries as they became no more than a dim background noise. Dana simply moved forward, step by painful step. She would never see Matthew alive again.

Chapter 36

Chicago Illinois

Donnelley led a handcuffed Hunt through the double glass doors and out onto the sidewalk adjacent a narrow tree-lined street. The terrorist's nose was bandaged where Hunt had broken it, his left eye was swollen, and his lip split. Hunt felt a chill race his entire length as the cool late September breeze tickled and darted about him in subtle swirls. He wasn't quite sure how close they were to the lake, but he still smelled its presence on the air: fresh, moist, vibrant. Not stuffy and thick like the air he'd been breathing within. They'd spent the past two hours at a police precinct, Hunt having spent the majority of this time locked in an interrogation room as Donnelley convinced the authorities of his credentials as an agent of Homeland Security.

How had he pulled that off?

Hunt knew Donnelley's background, he'd read his file. The man had never done any government work, much less with an anti-terrorism division. He was a run-of-the-mill thief now turned terrorist.

The whole thing was ludicrous.

Unless Donnelley's dossier had been a fake.

No.

In addition to the information Dana had compiled, Hunt had also received intel from Corky Meeks at the Pentagon. His information had to be correct. There had to be some scam here. And Donnelley himself, his demeanor, his caustic attitude, his substance abuse, there was no way he could be connected with the government. Who would hire him? Who could trust an addict with anything important?

Hunt abused a substance.

No.

That was different. His was a prescribed medication. Maybe he wasn't using it quite as directed, but he wasn't a cokehead like Donnelley, he wasn't a junkie.

Donnelley was scum, plain and simple.

Hunt was simply… experiencing momentary substance-related difficulties. There was a difference.

"That was fun—heh?" said Donnelley through a gloating smirk. He paused to light a Camel and then blew a cancerous cloud into Hunt's face. "Keep it moving, soldier boy." He gave Hunt a sharp shove between the shoulder blades.

"I admit, you surprised me, Donnelley. I'm wondering how a low-life like you managed to forge those credentials."

"Forged? Heh! You really don't have a clue. Do you?" Donnelley gave him another shove. "Keep going. I'll have a car waiting for us. Just a couple of blocks up."

Passersby glanced at the handcuffed man before averting gazes. They were outside of a police station; this couldn't be an unusual sight.

"We need to go back to the museum," said Hunt.

"Heh?"

"The antidote. I dropped it during our scuffle. We need to go back there, to get the antidote for Dana." Hunt had no expectation that Donnelley would show the least compassion, but he had to try. Somehow he had to get back to that antidote. He prayed against all logic that it was still there. It was all that mattered.

And the backpack.

If someone found that and somehow managed to open the canister…

Donnelley chuckled, blowing a cloud of rank fumes into Hunt's face. "That was your doing, heh? All of this nonsense? And you blew it. Tried to be a hero. Look what it got you."

"Donnelley, if we don't retrieve that antidote she'll die! If we don't get the backpack…"

"People die every day. And your wife's a whore."

Hunt made as to turn and attack, but Donnelley gave him a sharp shove, nearly causing him to tumble. "You're handcuffed. I'm armed. Don't be stupid."

They walked another block, Hunt silent, steadying himself, wishing he could pop a couple of Oxycontin. His stomach was tightening, he was sweating, even his joints ached. With all that had happened, he hadn't had a dose in several hours. Blinking, inhaling deeply, Hunt forced himself to remain focused.

He couldn't go after the antidote—not at this instant—but perhaps he could learn something from Donnelley, or, at the very least, distract him. "So, I had the worst seat in the house," said Hunt. "Care to share with me? How did you convince the police to release me into your custody?"

Donnelley clucked his tongue. "The uniformed pukes? Just doing as they were told. My people, top of the ladder. The little ants had no choice, heh?"

There was a momentary shuffle, the sound of quickened footfall, and then, "Ah, yes. And neither, it seems, do you have a choice, Mr. Donnelley. Please, if you will, turn left at this intersection and proceed toward the green Altima."

Thorpe?

Hunt turned to see the Brit walking closely behind Donnelley, his right arm jabbed toward the terrorist's left side. Obviously, he held a gun. "What are you doing here?" asked Hunt through a stifled chuckle. Thorpe was one of Hunt's least favorite people, but he'd suddenly become useful.

They turned at the intersection, crossing in front of a honking taxi cab.

"Yes, well, that will take a bit of explaining. Forgive me if I delay in favor of a more opportune moment." They continued through the intersection and then another third of a block before Thorpe grabbed Donnelley's arm, turning him toward a forest green vehicle. "Mr. Donnelley, stop here. Good. Now, place your hands on the hood of the car."

Donnelley complied, placing his hands palm down on the Altima. It was a big city, but they weren't on a major thoroughfare, the nearest pedestrians were several buildings distant, no car stopped, all likely assumed Thorpe to be an officer of the law as he frisked Donnelley, retrieving two weapons as well as the keys to the handcuffs.

"Who are you?" asked Donnelley as he spit his diminishing Camel onto the pavement.

"A man with many regrets. Please remove the handcuffs from Mr. Huntington." Thorpe handed him the keys.

For a moment it seemed Donnelley might toss them into the street, but he thought better of it and grudgingly did as Thorpe instructed.

"I'm still waiting for an explanation," said Hunt as Donnelley undid the cuffs.

"Of course, well, yes, in good time and all that. Best we be in motion. Kindly handcuff Mr. Donnelley and seat him in the rear. I'd prefer that you drive as I'm a bit sore actually."

Thorpe was limping. He tried not to make it obvious, but Hunt had picked up on this immediately. With each step, the man suppressed a wince. Hunt wasn't sure if Donnelley had been quite so observant, Thorpe had remained mostly behind the terrorist, but it was clear the Brit had sustained some sort of injury, most likely to his right leg.

As Hunt slid into the driver seat, Thorpe handed him his Browning. "This is yours, I assume. Donnelley was apparently keeping it warm for you."

Thorpe sat in the back beside Donnelley and directed Hunt on where to drive. "I've called ahead and rented a suite," said Thorpe by way of explanation. "Our business is such that we'll need a bit of privacy and I certainly wouldn't be comfortable utilizing Mr. Donnelley's lodgings."

"First, the museum," said Hunt. "Dana's been infected with plague. I dropped the antidote."

"Yes, well, you always were a bit of a simian." Thorpe reached into his left jacket pocket and then tossed a rumpled brown paper bag onto the front seat beside Hunt. "This is what you're looking for, I suppose. As to the toxic backpack, it's in the hands of authorities."

Hunt grinned. The uptight little snob did occasionally come in handy. Obviously, he'd been nearby when Hunt had been taken into custody. Hunt would have preferred that it be virtually anyone else, but at this point he couldn't be picky. Nodding a thank you to Thorpe, Hunt reached into his pocket, retrieving three Oxycontin, popped them dry, and then turned the ignition key.

*****

As with Donnelley's condominium, the hotel was of an older sort, but clean and elegant, a notch or two up from the terrorist's digs, and with a similar lakefront view. It was the type of place, Hunt supposed, Thorpe would frequent. There was a large elegant living area with genuine art, not prints, on the walls, a kitchenette, fully-stocked bar, and two bedrooms. Hunt sincerely hoped

Thorpe's intention was not that they would spend the night. He needed to locate Dana, give her the antidote. Her life depended on it and as far as Hunt was concerned this was all a waste of valuable time. He was restless. His legs twitched. He needed to be on the move—to do something.

Donnelley was seated, hands still cuffed behind his back, on a plush black leather couch; Thorpe sat at the bar on a stool, sipping a clear golden cognac, and Hunt paced the room. "Okay, Thorpe, we're here. Dana needs this medication, so whatever it is, get to it."

Thorpe sipped his cognac. "Unless I've misunderstood the situation, you have lost track of our dear Dana. Is that correct?"

"Her last known location was a clinic in Las Vegas. She was taken from there by unknowns and may have only hours left. I can't waste any more time sitting around."

"My point exactly," said Thorpe. "I've acquired information on the men behind the recent terrorist attacks. Mr. Donnelley, I'm sure, has information as well. You, I understand, have a contact within Homeland Security. Perhaps if we pool our knowledge, we might determine where Dana has been taken, thus making the best use of our time."

He was right, of course. Damn him!

"Okay, Thorpe. Got it. My Homeland contact seems to have dropped off the grid, though. Don't know if she's still an option."

"Bedford?" It was Donnelley this time. "Bedford is your contact."

Hunt turned to face the terrorist. This was the second time he'd mentioned Bedford's name. "Yeah. How'd you know that?"

A chuckle and a cluck of the tongue. "Heh. Way I see it, everyone knows more than you." He glanced at Thorpe. "That about right, prissy pants?" When Thorpe didn't respond, Donnelley grinned. "My phone's in my breast pocket. Bedford's number, on speed dial. She'll answer. If she thinks it's me calling."

Hunt marched to Donnelley, reached into his inner jacket pocket, felt about, and pulled free the phone, giving the terrorist a sharp shove as he did so. He was tired of feeling one step behind and Donnelley's condescending smirk was going to win him a trip to the hospital before the day was through. Finding Bedford's name, Hunt tapped the send button and listened as the phone rang.

It didn't ring long.

"Kelvin? I'll assume you're clear of the police. They accepted your credentials?"

"Bedford. Marc Huntington here."

A pause. "Marcus? Where are you?"

"Chicago. Care to tell me why a terrorist has you on speed dial?"

Thorpe eyed Hunt. "Speaker phone, if you'd be so kind."

"Hang on, Bedford. I'm putting you on speaker." Hunt nodded, changing the setting and then setting the phone on a glass-topped coffee table.

"Alright, Bedford. Spill your guts."

Bedford responded tentatively. "Who all is in the room?"

"Myself, Donnelley, and a thief named Thorpe."

"Jonathan Thorpe?"

"Yes. That would be me," said Thorpe. "Though, I'm afraid I know nothing of you."

"Let's not worry about detailed introductions," said Hunt, rubbing his shoulder. Bone and muscle pains were becoming persistent. "Bedford, what's your connection to Donnelley?"

"I work for her," said the terrorist.

"Bedford?"

A sigh. "Remember when I told you we'd infiltrated the organization?"

Hunt looked at Donnelley and then back to the phone lying innocently on the glass tabletop. His stomach went hollow. "Donnelley's your inside man?"

"He was our inside man. Until he went rogue. We've been trying to catch up with him ever since."

"Catch up with him? What you've been doing is trying to cover his tracks— trying to cover your own butt before anyone found out that the man who released a dangerous bio-toxin on U.S. soil was operating under your direction."

"It's more complicated than that."

"You covered for him with the police—just an hour ago. Why didn't you tell them to release me and hold Donnelley? He could be in custody right now."

"Marcus, you are truly intelligent. I've seen evidence of this. But, you can also be simplistic. Think about it. Which of the two of you was more likely to implicate me and those I'm in league with—you or Kelvin?"

Hunt understood instantly. He had a single purpose, to save Dana. He wasn't concerned with keeping secrets, protecting careers, keeping the machinery moving behind the scenes. He would have mentioned Bedford, Donnelley, Bedford's White Eagle group, anything that would get him closer to Dana. Donnelley, on the other hand, benefitted from stealth. The best possible outcome for him was that he be allowed to walk out of that police station and vanish into the sunset.

"Okay. I get it. Now, where's Dana?"

"Her location is presently unknown. We had her under our care, but she's eluded us."

Hunt nodded. So it was Bedford who had been responsible for Dana's disappearance. What the woman failed to mention was that in taking Dana into her "care" she and her White Eagle vigilantes had murdered Jerry Byers and his staff. Obviously, secrecy was much more important than human life. "She eluded you?" asked Hunt. "Last time I saw her she could barely stand."

"Tell that to the two men she killed during her escape."

Killed? Until the Colorado clinic incident, Hunt had never seen Dana use lethal force; he hadn't even been sure she was capable of it. Now, she'd done so yet again. Had she been attacked? Clearly, she must have been. He couldn't imagine that the incident had been unprovoked. Dana wasn't a loose cannon. Bedford was obviously not telling the entire story.

"Where, may I ask was she being held prior to this spectacular getaway?" asked Thorpe.

"I'm not at liberty to…"

"And I'm not at liberty to take evasive answers," shot Hunt. "A straight answer, Bedford. Show me at least that much respect or I take everything I know straight to the media."

Bedford was silent.

"Virginia," said Donnelley, after a moment. "Heh, Bedford? Your safe house? Safe estate really. Big place. Well equipped."

"That's enough, Kelvin," warned Bedford.

"Is it? We'll see."

"Kelvin," said Bedford. "I get the feeling you're yanking my leg out a joint. Would you like to tell me what you're up to?"

Donnelley smiled, clucked his tongue. "Just reminding you. How much I know. How much trouble I can be for you, heh? Think about it. You don't want me as your fall guy. I don't fall well. I don't fall quietly."

"Where in Virginia?" asked Hunt, not caring about Bedford and Donnelley's power plays.

There was a muffled curse before the Homeland Security agent answered. "I'm going to be honest with you, Marcus. She's highly contagious. Essentially, she's a walking bio-weapon. A code red search is already underway. Our intent is to take her alive, but I can't make any promises."

"Bedford, if you do anything to harm her, I'll…"

"What, Marcus? What will you do? Engage my entire strike force? Take just a moment, sit back, breathe, and think about who you're dealing with. The U.S. government. That little mishap you had in Iraq, you'd be amazed the damning evidence that can appear overnight. You would truly be amazed at the charges and allegations that could appear just right out of the blue. Every bit of it documented. Every bit of it damaging."

"And all of it lies."

"I'm sure that would be your position."

"Yes, well, enough of that," said Thorpe, holding up his smart phone as if to display. "While the three of you have been nipping and scrapping, I've already begun booking a flight to Virginia. But, seeing as we still have some time before departure, I'd like to take advantage of this opportunity to pool our information. It might behoove us to have a clue as to just what in the bloody hell is going on here—hmm?"

Thorpe's comment was met with blank stares.

"Very well," he said after a moment. "I'll begin. My involvement in this fiasco started while I was imprisoned in Turkey. A certain Tina Collins offered me freedom in exchange for my services—performing a pair of highly difficult thefts, to be precise."

"The Dallas lab and the CDC," said Hunt. "You stole the plague that Donnelley used to infect Dana."

Thorpe dropped his gaze, avoiding Hunt's intense stare. Good. The man should be ashamed. "Well… Yes. That is quite unfortunate. Circumstances, whatnot. Poor decision, really."

"Your involvement actually began several months earlier," said Bedford. "In Brazil, with the Amazon skull. The bacteria activated when that fossil was exposed to air and sunlight has been coupled with the plague. That bacteria is what these people are trying to spread."

"Dear God."

"Wait a sec," said Hunt. "You're telling me that Dana is not only infected with plague, but with that Brazilian virus too?"

"Bacteria. And yes, I'm afraid so. The plague is merely the carrier."

Hunt stepped away from the center of the room, making his way to the patio door overlooking the vast blue expanse of Lake Michigan. He'd seen the effect of that bacterium. He'd watched Andy Lindell's skin literally drip from his frame like some victim of a nuclear storm; he'd seen Daniel Cook's skin pop and bubble as the man screamed for a relief that would never come. "And this antidote, the one I've been chasing?"

"Well, that's the good news," said Bedford. "To the best of our knowledge it's designed to cure the combined bio-toxin. Both the plague and the Brazilian microbes."

"To the best of your knowledge?"

"Marcus, you've got to understand, we haven't put our hands on the substance. We've had no chance to test it."

"Even though Donnelley was your man and he had it on his person?"

"These people we're dealing with, they're volatile. Kelvin was… restrained from giving us aid." It sounded as if the words strangled Bedford's throat.

"So the antidote may be useless?"

"That's a possibility. Or it might be the cure we're hoping that it is. But, we won't know until we have it."

"You're not getting it. Dana is."

"At the cost of how many others? Marcus, are you willing to let dozens, maybe hundreds or thousands die so that you can give our only dose to your wife?"

Hunt slammed his palm against the wall and then turned, pacing the room. "So, all of this, the whole thing, me tracking Donnelley across the country, it was nonsense? You never intended for Dana to get the antidote."

"That's unfair, Marcus. I have no wish that Dana die. Our goal is to mass produce the antidote for Dana's benefit as well as for others."

"But, she doesn't have the time for you to do that. She was given a far more concentrated dose than the other passengers. She's got to be in the latter stages of the disease."

Bedford's voice was tiny. "I know how difficult it is to risk losing someone you love."

Hunt wanted to scream, to lash out, to hit someone. He reached into his pocket, felt the narrow pill bottle there, and then withdrew his empty hand. Not now. Later. But not now. "Who are these people?" he nearly bellowed. "What insane madmen combine two crazy deadly germs together and spread them across the world? Who are we dealing with here?"

"I can't tell you that, Marcus."

"Damn you, Bedford!"

"Children of the gods," said Donnelley with a smug grin.

"Kelvin!" shot Bedford, her voice distorting through the tiny speaker. Obviously this was information she didn't want made public.

Donnelley clucked his tongue. "Relax your panties, Bedford. Just playing with you. These dip-wads don't know anything."

"Yes, well, this dip-wad has already learned quite a bit," said Thorpe. "I've been doing some research—caused quite a stir, really, may have even gotten one of my contacts killed. Donnelley is correct. The group is called children of the gods. As near as I can tell, it's led by two half-brothers, Linus and Joshua Tull."

"You have names?" said Bedford, her voice tinged with fear and admiration. "Even with our resources, we hadn't acquired upper level identities. I'm fairly certain even Kelvin was kept in the dark where names were concerned."

"I've obtained these two names only," said Thorpe after a sip of cognac. "The apparent death of my friend, Degare Laurent, and the bullet recently lodged in my right buttock by Linus Tull's man seem to bear out my conclusions. Laurent was instrumental. His final email spelled out quite the tale."

Hunt stepped to within three feet of Thorpe. "What have you learned?" The whole thing was spinning out of control. It seemed things were a lot bigger than he'd initially thought. And in his mind that had been huge.

"In truth, not near as much as I'd like," said Thorpe. "The organization, movement, whatever it is you'd like to call it, it's astounding the way they've buried themselves. The gist of it is this. This family, these Tulls, and quite a few various relations, both clear and dubious, believe themselves to be the descendents of ancient gods."

"That's insane."

"Yes, well, indeed, but if you study human history you'll find that the insane have frequently risen to significant power and prestige, and have often caused quite a ruckus on the world stage."

Hunt couldn't argue with this, and so nodded for Thorpe to continue.

"These people," said Thorpe, "claim to be either the direct or descended offspring of unions between ancient gods and human females. Most of the gods are not well known. Names such as Pereh, Athtart, Nergal, Chemosh, Shax. The best known name I've encountered is Baal."

"So, what's their goal? World domination? I'm not sure if I should be calling James Bond or Indiana Jones."

"It is," offered Bedford, now reentering the conversation with a tentative tone. Bedford wasn't a fan of the open exchange of information. "World domination, I mean. But, not in the traditional sense. These men don't want the restraints or visibility inherent to public office. They're goal is to manipulate world events from behind the scenes, to place people in power with whom they have influence, either direct or indirect."

"There's evidence to indicate they were instrumental in Hitler's rise," offered Thorpe.

"And Napoleon's downfall," added Bedford.

"There are dozens of such examples," said Thorpe. "They've been active at some level, it seems, for at least three hundred years."

Hunt waved them off. "Okay. Got it. Really bad powerful people. And the purpose of these recent terrorist attacks?"

"To unsettle the status quo," said Bedford. "They've maneuvered many of their pawns into positions where, under the right circumstances—say a general upheaval and lessening of confidence in current administrations—they could attain a global influence of staggering breadth."

Hunt ran his palms across his scalp and turned again toward the window. "So, how does a guy like Donnelley fit into all of this? He's a common thug."

"Children of the gods recruited him because of his anger at the government. His brother had been killed. He sought retribution."

"Yeah, yeah, I know his sob story. But, what was their angle in using him? He was a thief. What did they do, recruit him, groom him, place him in charge of a cell? They had to know he was volatile."

"Donnelley already sought to damage the government. He'd made contact with the Revolutionary Patriots of America with the hope of avenging his brother. They were a small, ineffective group. But, they shared his anger and distrust of the government. And yes, Marcus, children of the gods did know he was volatile and that's exactly what they wanted. Someone crazy enough to think that spreading a bio-toxin made sense. He was manipulated and used."

"Except," said Hunt. "He had his own agenda. He was happy to release the toxin on the train, but he kept a canister to use on the man he saw as responsible for his brother's death, putting potentially thousands of additional lives at risk here in Chicago."

"True."

Hunt turned to face the phone, pointing his finger at it as if he was confronting Bedford face-to-face. "And this is the kind of person you brought in as your inside man? He infected Dana for his own amusement. He brutally beat her. This is the kind of man you work with?"

"We knew of the organization, but he was the first one, the only one for quite a while, that we were ever able to both identify and turn. Earlier, we'd identified another potential, a CIA operative named Collins. You encountered her in The Amazon, Marcus. She betrayed us. Despite the risks, Kelvin was our best option."

"Despite the risks? You knowingly let him get on that train. You knew he'd infect all those passengers?"

"We couldn't let children of the gods know that Donnelley was ours."

"Yours? You're actually claiming him? Don't you see what he's capable of? Don't you see what he's done to Dana!"

"I know exactly what he's done to Dana," shot Bedford. "He's beat her. He's infected her. He's raped her. Don't you think I carry that burden? Do you think I do what I do without regret? If I had any choice at all, I'd have him hung. But things are beyond my control."

Hunt stood in silence. Bedford's statement hanging in the suddenly still air. "Raped her." It all made sense. Of course he'd raped her. He'd claimed all along that he'd "had" her. He continuously referred to Dana as his whore. And Dana. Her rage, the distance Hunt had felt from her, her evasiveness. God, how hadn't he seen it? How hadn't he recognized it for what it was?

Calmly, he turned, met Donnelley's gaze, held it even as the rapist struggled to maintain his cocky smirk.

Hunt withdrew his Browning.

"Huntington, you might want to rethink…"

"Shut up, Thorpe."

Somewhere in the distance, Bedford was calling Hunt's name, but she was a non-entity. All that mattered was he, and Donnelley… and Dana.

Hunt stepped forward and then kneeled on the plush carpet, only inches before the handcuffed fiend. He shoved the barrel of the Browning into Donnelley's crotch hard enough to cause the man to wince. "Your balls are mine, Donnelley. Maybe not now, not as long as you might prove useful in finding Dana. But, as soon as you stop giving me what I need, they come off, and I feed them to the stinking Coho out in that big old lake. You understand what I'm saying, scumbag?"

Donnelley said nothing, but he got it. Hunt could see it in his deep set eyes, in the subtle twitch of his smallish mouth, even in the roll of his shoulders. Donnelley knew. Oh, he wasn't beaten. He wasn't cowed. Hunt was sure that in the monster's mind he still thought he'd find the upper hand. But, he knew that Hunt was serious, that a line had been crossed, and that the only resolution would lie in the blood of one man or the other.

"Um, excuse me," said Thorpe. "I don't mean to be a bore, but there is another issue."

Neither Hunt nor Donnelley responded.

"I said there's more."

"Thorpe, I've got other things on my mind right now."

"Yes, well, as do I. As much as it irritates you, I still love Dana as well, and truly, I'd just as soon castrate that animal here and now, but there's more."

Hunt pressed the weapon further into Donnelley's crotch, eliciting a strangled gurgle. But Donnelley refused to grant Hunt the satisfaction of a scream. "What is it?" asked Hunt as he rose to face Thorpe.

"A pending attack on Washington."

Hunt gazed at the man. "Children of the gods?"

"Yes."

"When?"

"Imminent. I know the event. It's late this evening."

"Details?"

"Sketchy. Definitely, the bio-strains are involved. It seems there's an additional spin as well. I've yet to learn more."

"Fine. Deal with it. I'm taking that flight you booked to Virginia and giving Dana the antidote."

"No you will not." It was Bedford. Hunt had almost forgotten that she was still connected.

"You're in no position to give me orders, Bedford. Especially considering that you could have prevented most of this."

"Well, no. I suppose I can't order you, Marcus. But, I can sure as hell manipulate you."

"Yeah? How so?"

"I know Dana's last known location. I already have a team tracking her."

"And?"

"You don't. You have absolutely no idea where to start looking."

Hunt remained silent.

"Here's the deal. Children of the gods are preparing a major play. We've known that, but the details have been sketchy. Thanks to Jonathan, we apparently now have a time and a location. I want you to intervene."

"You're Homeland Security. That's your job."

"Marcus, think. Yes. I work for Homeland Security. But, that agency—as well as most others inside the beltway—has been infiltrated by children of the gods cronies. People bribed, or blackmailed, or offered positions of power. Maybe even some nutty enough to believe in this group and its goals. They're like roaches. Most of the time we can't see them, but we know they're hiding within the walls just waiting to scurry out. That's why I've been forced to operate outside traditional channels. That's why I need someone like you. Any official movement on my part and… I'd be found floating face down in the Potomac. These people are very well connected."

"Fine. Send Thorpe."

"That wouldn't work."

"Why?"

Thorpe rose, approaching the table. "I'm known to them. Joshua Tull already has it in his mind to kill me. It seems he didn't much like my curious nature. In truth, he's already made several attempts. As much as it grates me to admit, I would not be an effective choice."

"Here's how it is, Marcus," said Bedford. "You and Donnelley will disrupt children of the gods while Thorpe tracks Dana to give her the antidote."

The woman had to be mad.

"Not happening, Bedford."

"And what choice do you have? You don't know Dana's last known location. By the time you find her she'd be dead."

"Donnelley knows the location." Hunt glared at the man, who offered a cluck of the tongue and a haughty grin.

"He knows only that the safe house is in Virginia. He has no clue as to the actual location."

Donnelley's smile broadened.

Hunt stood silent. The noose was tightening.

"Here's how it will be, Marcus. Assuming that we haven't already located Dana, I will reveal what I know of her location to Jonathan upon his arrival. He will be allowed to deliver the antidote directly to your wife and tend to her in your absence. As for you, children of the gods don't know that Kelvin has been compromised. As well, it's unlikely they know anything of you or your involvement. I've done my best to keep our movements—yours and mine—below the radar. You and Kelvin will infiltrate their event and prevent them from bringing our government to its knees."

Chapter 37

Washington DC

Joshua Tull stared at Marion Dietz from the doorway as she flitted about the subjects, her bony fingers making this adjustment and that on the various pieces of medical equipment. She had not heard him enter the room. She was like that, both highly focused on her tasks while distracted, even oblivious, when it came to all else. Well, except for her honey liqueur. That, she focused on quite well—but not so much so as to derail her ambition. The woman was quite ambitious, but her peculiarities and foibles had sidetracked a promising career. Joshua had given her a chance to redeem herself, such as it was.

And thus his presence now. Marion Dietz sometimes needed a motivational jolt, a reason to forget or even to momentarily abandon her conscience and greater worries.

A pity, perhaps, that Dietz had such difficulties with the navigation of life. The woman, gangly and gaunt, socially stunted and addictive in temperament, had a brilliant mind. Though he'd used her mercilessly for his own ends, he had not been without pity. Unattractive as she was, he'd even made to satisfy her womanly needs, hoping that perhaps a bit of excitement and release would free her spirit. Even this was selfish, he supposed. The spirit needed freeing in order to better perform the task which he had ordered. But, should the woman benefit from the experience beyond that, he would feel some small measure of joy as well.

Useless to contemplate. She had rejected the advance. For the better, really. Dietz was nearly grotesque: tall, perhaps five nine or ten, rolled shoulders, thinning blond/gray hair, cut short, only just slightly over the ears, no breasts to speak of, narrow lips, hollow cheeks, and breath that could make the eyes water. Joshua should be sainted simply for having made the offer.

But, there'd been no risk, really. He'd known she would refuse. Maybe that was it. Maybe, if he was true to himself, he'd admit that it had just been a game. A little tease to perk her ire. He knew what she thought of him. That he knew nothing of science but thrived on the occult, that he was cruel, evasive, a criminal by any standards. Well, let her think what she would. She had known his intentions nearly from the beginning. Strange, how the possession of knowledge does not often prompt a person to act on—or to even believe—what they know to be true. And so Dietz stood, her Barenjager clutched in her quivering hand, most likely marveling that somehow, even as he'd brought the subjects to this capital city, she had never in her heart believed that Joshua would truly do it, unleash the pathogen on a potentially global basis.

Of course he'd do it. Was there ever really any choice in the matter? Events push a person as surely as a hurricane drives the waves. One could adjust a rudder only so much, compensate only to a degree. But once a life course is set, once the hurricane blows, it is a thing of jealous majesty and refuses to release its grasp. And so here they were, Joshua driven by the gale-like force of both heritage and life choices and Dietz believing she'd handed her soul to a devil. And, oh, but this devil would never give it back.

Dietz shook her head and then sipped from the cold metal flask, her narrow bone-like fingers clutching it tightly as a drowning victim might grasp a ring buoy. Joshua simultaneously brought his buttermilk to his lips in a silent toast to the day. So different. So similar. "It is significance," said Joshua. "That... is why you agreed to this, s...significance. One final chance to... prove that you are something more than a second rate also-ran?"

Dietz, turned, quickly shoving her flask into her right lab coat pocket. "Mr. Tull. I didn't hear you come in."

Joshua smiled. "I do believe you say that every... time you see me."

Dietz stared at him, her washed-out eyes wide, perhaps fearful.

"You do possesses a certain... brilliance," said Joshua, now stepping further into the room, a rented conference space, now peopled by the twelve subjects. "There is plenty of evidence to your achievement—or near achievement." Joshua sipped from his tumbler as he strolled about, glancing at each of the subjects. "Oh... I know p...plenty about you. Your early days, your youth, your university days at the top of your... class." He paused, turned to her and winked. "I also know what... came later: the failures, the difficulties, but I still rec...ognized your... inner genius. In truth, even Martin would have to acknowledge this." Dietz looked shocked at the mention of her younger sibling. Surely she hadn't known the extent of Joshua's knowledge. "Yes, I... know about Martin: jealous, spoiled, con...condemning. Fifty-seven years old now, number one in sales for this company or... that for nearly as many years as he's been... shaving. What does that matter, Dietz? D...oes anyone even care who sold how much to whom? Three ex-wives, four estranged ch...ildren, now a coke-sniffing live-in girlfriend—and he's considered the successful one. You do not give yourself fair credit."

Dietz attempted a weak smile, obviously wondering where he was going with this.

Joshua angled his head. "You desire a sip of Barenjager. Proceed."

Dietz gazed at him.

Joshua nodded toward her pocket. "It is no... secret. There need be none be...tween us." At least none that you're aware of.

Cautiously, she withdrew the narrow flask and unscrewed the silver colored plastic cap, bringing the liqueur to her wide narrow lips, all the while eyeing Joshua as if he was a snake, prepared to strike. Of course, he'd already struck, and was in the process of doing so yet again. Dietz was simply too preoccupied to acknowledge the obvious.

"The subjects," said Joshua. "I'm told they are in... the final stages of gestation. That the malignant... strain nearly bubbles through the pores as it seeks the freedom to... infect." Joshua paused before adding, "Frightening. Miraculous. Deadly. Wouldn't you a...gree?"

Dietz shrugged a nervous shrug, her tongue, a square-knot behind chapped and pale lips.

Tull moved to beside the scientist. She seemed to shrink back at his proximity. All the better, he supposed. Fear was a wonderful motivator. "T...welve beds," he said. "Twelve remarkable human beings, alive, or... nearly so, for centuries—and to what end, you ask? To be used as a spectacle? To strike fear? Yes. I say. Yes. Fear. Beautiful f...ear. The motivator of all... civilization. Fear of starvation drove our ancestors to... cultivate the growing... fields. Fear of... attack prompted the production of advanced... weaponry, which spawned te...chnology used in the civilian sector to enrich our... daily lives."

Dietz turned to him, flask still clutched between narrow fingers. "But, isn't the fear enough? Is it really necessary to spread that horrific pathogen among the populace?"

Joshua grinned. Curious. Perhaps the woman had a spine after all. "Do not worry about your... legacy, Marion. The world will surely recognize the scientific wonder of it all. A... bacterium both deadly and enlivening. The curative properties could... change the face of medicine, ex...tend life expectancies far beyond what is currently considered... plausible."

Dietz shook her head. "They will see only the disease."

Joshua shrugged. "This is an... unimaginable biological marvel. Consider this. The scientific community ooed and ahed in 2009 when a... living 120,000 year-old bac...teria was found buried in a Greenland glacier. A decade earlier microbiologists made a splash by reviving over one thousand types of bacteria dating as far back... as 135 million years. But, Dietz, you took their achievements and moved... them into the realm of practical medical advancement, potentially utilizing ancient bacteria to preserve and then... possibly revitalize human subjects. Surely, the world would recognize the brilliance of any mind capable of... not only identifying and isolating, but... manipulating this Amazon strain, unleashing the regenerative sequences. Certainly there would be fear—and condemnation. But, wouldn't there... also be admiration, even praise?"

Could they—the infected populace, even other research scientists—understand her genius? Perhaps. At least the woman needed to believe that they would. The manipulation of enzymes, the delicate work at a nuclear level, the activation of the spores? Blemished reputation or no, professional difficulties be damned, there were only a handful of individuals on the entire globe with the expertise to even attempt what Dietz had actually achieved. Joshua needed her fully on board for this final task. "Marion," he said, in a tone gentle and soothing. "Martin might even... be impressed. And Alex Waxman, your former superior at the institute. This... is your opportunity. Your... time."

"Small minded and dull. All of them," agreed Dietz with a vicious smile. She took another sip of courage from the flask. "The disease," she said. "The bacteria, it won't really spread as you suggested, will it?"

"Small minds, Marion. You are bigger than those. You understand... the mathematics of it, the exposure, the rate of... infection and con...tamination. Don't humiliate yourself with questions unworthy... of your mind."

"But it could be contained. That is also a possibility. It's all simply projection really. If the vaccination is made available within the first twenty-four hours, the death count would be substantially reduced."

Joshua bent to whisper in her ear as might a lover. "Marion, are... you hoping that I... will fail?"

Another sip of Barenjager.

"You cannot be thinking these things. Not... now." Joshua placed his palms gently on her shoulders, turning her to face him. "Dearest, Marion, C...an I trust you? Truly... trust you?" Such a fragile creature. Brilliant yet fragile. This really was what she needed. It was only that the social morals of a lifetime constrained her. A common and most irritating dilemma.

She moved to her left, gazing at the nearest subject, draped in a protective plastic tent. An adult male, perhaps thirty years of age by physical appearance. Short, little over five feet tall. Dark skinned. Features that at once seemed Mexican, but Native American as well. Wearing the garb of an Inca warrior: a golden helm, elaborately decorated gold and white battle garment, even shield and spear lay beside the man.

Dietz offered a wry grin. She had objected to the clothing, arguing that the subjects remain in hospital gowns as they had for the past several months. But Joshua had ordered that they once again be garbed in their original clothing, no matter the level of disrepair, immodesty, or odor. Another piece of the spectacle. Another means to illicit fear.

Dietz moved again, now coming to the young Egyptian woman, the one she claimed as her most promising subject.

"Marion?"

Dietz frowned.

"Marion, can I... trust you?"

After several moments, Dietz nodded as Joshua knew she would. He'd provided her the push, that last bit of necessary motivation, the reminder of her brilliance and historic destiny, with perhaps a dash of revenge on her younger and troubling sibling. So simple it was to manipulate the brilliant. She and he were not of a like mind. She had her motivation, he his own. And fear was such a lovely motivator. Even compliments and implications could instill fear. Joshua sipped his buttermilk. The time was at hand, and, if he was to be honest with himself, perhaps there was a bit of fear to his own motivation. So be it. Fear used properly brought strength, and Joshua was very, very strong.

Chapter 38

Virginia

The blood.

Dana couldn't get the blood to come off of her hands.

Those two men, the guards—they were guards weren't they? Of course they were. They were with Bedford, or so it seemed. Or, perhaps not with. More, they likely worked for the woman. They must have worked for her. They were in the facility after all.

Regardless, they had tried to grab her, to touch her.

Touch her!

No. She'd had no choice but to use deadly force. How could she let them touch her? She couldn't.

Their fingers creeping across her flesh.

Their lusty eyes scanning her form as they pressed up against her.

Despite her fatigue, despite her illness, she had acted with speed and efficiency, her hand-to-hand combat training kicking in: a quick chop, a knee, a flip, a jab. One of the men had carried a revolver. Within seconds it had been in Dana's possession.

And then there had been blood.

The men had been incapacitated. There had been no need.

But…

She couldn't think about that. Of course she'd had to do it. If not, they would have… They would have been the same as Donnelley.

But, they were not Donnelley. All men were not like him. Maybe…

Shaking her head as if to rid her mind of these thoughts, Dana stopped, once again wiping her hands with leaves and dirt. The blood. There was still blood. It wouldn't come off of her hands, her face.

She was in one of the many small wooded areas that separated the large and stately homes situated just off of a two lane highway. The facility, mansion— whatever they called the place she had been kept—was perhaps a half mile to her rear. She needed to put some distance behind her. They would be looking for her and she was in no condition for a prolonged chase. Already, she'd administered a second dose of Epinephrine. It had enlivened her some, but not so much so as had the first dose. Likely her underlying symptoms were becoming worse and the medication was not as effective as it had been even an hour ago.

It was nighttime. Dana wasn't sure of the hour, but the sun had disappeared since she'd left the building, and a subtle breeze brought a chill to the late September eve. Most likely, it was sometime after eight pm. Not terribly late, not terribly early. Dana emerged onto the narrow ribbon of a road. It was of the winding sort and it was difficult to see traffic in the distance due to the many bends.

Not that there was any traffic. She'd seen two vehicles pass in the twenty minutes since the road had become visible to her. Dana stepped over a rather large pothole, wandering toward the yellow center line. Which way to go? Certainly she was exposed as she was and couldn't remain on the road, but her only real chance of escape was to find a lift away from that nightmare of a place. The scattered estates were gated, and Dana would likely be denied admittance based on her ramshackle appearance alone.

A wave of coughing overtook her, causing her body to jerk and convulse. There was that annoying buzzing in her brain and her vision clouded.

Why did she persist? At least in the facility she could have died peacefully in a bed.

Sounds.

Rustling. Voices in the distance. Back from where she'd come.

They'd discovered her missing, possibly found the bloodied corpses. Dana looked one way and then the other. No traffic. Nothing. She was exposed, a clear target, and needed to get off of the pavement, but remain near enough to emerge and flag down a passing vehicle.

She still had the revolver.

The next passing motorist would stop for her. She'd make certain of that.

Dana moved to her right, away from the voices. Yet still they seemed closer. She wanted to run, to flee into the night, but even on the relatively even asphalt, she stumbled and stuttered, nearly falling every dozen steps or so.

Her bare right foot came down hard on a sharp stone causing her to yelp. Immediately, the rustling sounds quickened and the voices became urgent. Despite the pain, despite her vertigo and fatigue, Dana pressed forward in a sort of hobbled jog. She was approaching a streetlight now. There were very few of these, apparently only stationed near the sharpest curves.

It illuminated Dana, made her an easy target.

Another sound, a vehicle. A pickup truck rounding the bend.

The voices were closer, shouts now, calls to her. Running footsteps.

She'd been seen.

The pickup was traveling at perhaps forty miles-per-hour when Dana stepped purposely into the center of the road, legs spread in a shooter's stance, the revolver held before her in a two-handed grip, even as the leather satchel hung awkwardly over her left shoulder. The truck veered slightly to Dana's right, obviously attempting to avoid her by crossing into the oncoming lane. Dana simply took two steps right maintaining her bead on the pickup. The tires locked, the big blue Ford skidded sideways. Dana had left the driver no option but to break.

The racing footsteps were closer now. Dana turned, firing two warning shots toward the three approaching figures before climbing into the truck and shouting, "Move!"

Dana's heart clenched and she nearly lost her breath.

The driver was male.

Lean, middle-aged, with spiked brown and gray hair and a diamond stud earring. He looked wide-eyed at the revolver as Dana aimed it at his right temple, her hands quivering and her breath coming in short quick gasps. Glancing in the rearview mirror, he nodded, offering a barely perceptible "Uh-huh," before taking off with the fury of a hell-bound drag racer. Bedford's crew was left hollering and stomping on the dusty road. None chanced a shot at the civilian-driven vehicle.

They road in silence for a minute or so, the man offering nervous glances in Dana's direction, and she maintaining her death grip on the revolver. She had to be a frightful sight: a surgical mask and hospital gown, a long men's overcoat, barefoot, a leather satchel slung over one shoulder, and a weapon in hand.

And, oh yes, blood.

Finally, the man found his voice. "This might be a silly question, but where are we going?"

"Civilization," said Dana just before moving into a coughing fit. "Get me to the nearest commercial district."

"Uh-huh. And are you planning to shoot me?" he asked.

"Not unless you give me a bloody good reason to do so."

Any reason. A leer, a touch, an innuendo. How was it that she'd been willing to climb into this vehicle? Her finger twitched, slipping up and down across the cool, hard trigger. One move. Just a single move. She didn't care that he was driving, that killing him would mean nearly certain death as the truck spun out of control, likely flipping.

He was a man, a lustful foul thing. And she had the gun.

"Alright then," he said after a moment. "Any chance you can put that thing away? I'd rather not take the chance it goes off the next time I hit a pothole or dodge a deer."

Dana kept the quivering gun trained on the man. Already, he was trying to disarm her, to make her vulnerable. She had been vulnerable once. She would never allow herself to be so again.

"You're rather calm considering the circumstances," Her voice was emotionless.

He shrugged. "Uh-huh. I've seen some action. Panama back in the eighties. Anyway, you look more scared than mean. Mind if I ask just what the hell's going on here?"

"It's a rather lengthy tale."

"How about you give me the Twitter version?"

Dana hesitated for a moment. It probably wouldn't hurt that someone else knew of this. "I was the victim of a terrorist attack and have been held captive as part of a cover up. All very cloak and dagger really."

"And the surgical mask?"

"Infected with the bloody Bubonic plague. The mask is meant to prevent my spreading the vile rot."

"Well, that's comforting."

No. Nothing was comforting, not the plague, her pursuers, not sitting alone with a strange man. She closed her eyes, attempting to pull her thoughts together. The blasted buzzing in her head made it so very difficult to concentrate. What next? What was her plan? Where was she to go? When she opened her eyes again, the man was alternating his gaze between the road and Dana.

"Really, ma'am," he said. "I'm not the enemy. Put the gun down. This road's full of potholes and dips. We don't need an accidental shooting here."

Dana glanced behind. There was no sign of another vehicle. Bedford's people had not been able to get to their transportation in time to pursue. That said, they likely had the man's license plate number and had notified local authorities. It was possible they'd even utilize a helicopter in the pursuit.

And the man. Was he eying her breasts? Were they even remotely visible through the loose-fitting gown and the ridiculous overcoat? Still, it seemed his eyes may have traversed her form. She hadn't thought it possible, but she squeezed the gun all the more.

Now, looking forward, Dana saw the lights of civilization ahead. After a sudden spell of deep and racking coughs, she asked, "What are those lights?"

"Uh-huh. Small little town. Unincorporated. Barely a blip on the map."

"Very well. I want you to drive into town and then pull into the nearest alleyway or small road. I'll get out there."

"I'd rather take you to a hospital. There's one just another ten miles up the road."

She gazed at the man, saw the concern—or was it lust?—in his eyes.

"Listen," he added. "If what you told me is true, you need medical attention. You also need to notify the authorities and get this thing taken care of before something really bad happens."

Another coughing fit. "The authorities have been compromised. Medical institutions will be watched. I can't risk any official involvement."

Dana chanced another glance to the rear. There were headlights now, growing in the distance. It was difficult to be certain, but it seemed the vehicle was traveling at a high rate of speed.

"Listen," said Dana. "We're nearly into town. I'll leave you momentarily. For your own safety, drive directly to a public place: a theater, a mall, someplace where there are a lot of people. Park your truck amidst other vehicles. Do not return to it for at least two days. Pull as much money as you can from a teller machine and then refrain from using anything but cash for as long as possible. If you have a family, contact them, tell them where to meet you and then hop on a bus or take a taxi. Leave town. Once you've made contact with your loved ones, throw away your cell phone. It can be used to track you. Make certain your people do the same." Dana glanced behind again. Yes. The headlamps were much closer now. "Very well," she said. "Pull over. Leave me here. Please do not alert the authorities for several hours. At that time, I'd suggest telling the story to the media as opposed to the police."

"Just like a woman," he said with no hint of a smile. "Totally screw up my life without barely giving a thought to it."

"I'm... I apologize. There was little choice, really."

He nodded and seemed to think before saying, "I'll let you off here if you like. But I'm inclined to believe your story. Are you sure you don't want me to take you further? I have my doctor's home number. We went to high school together. Maybe he could help with your plague—unofficially, I mean. Under the radar."

Dana shook her head. "We're being pursued. My adversaries will be upon you in less than five minutes. I cannot risk being caught. Leave me be, vacate your vehicle and disappear. I'm hoping this will all be at an end within a day. Now let me out while you've still the chance to evade our pursuers."

The man nodded and complied. Without another word Dana exited the vehicle and slipped into a narrow alleyway between two red brick storefronts. The Ford rolled away nearly before Dana had closed the door. She was amazed at the relief she felt at being away from the man. She was being irrational, she understood this. But understanding it and gaining control of it were apparently quite different things.

Two minutes later a black Altima sped past at what had to be better than seventy miles-per-hour. She hoped the man in the pick-up had had sense enough to turn off of the main road and follow her instructions. There was no need for another innocent to die.

Remaining in the shadows, Dana made her way slowly through the uneven and stony terrain of the back alleyway. This was a tiny town, and by the looks of it, more than half of the businesses were already closed for the evening. There was very little traffic either motorized or pedestrian. The night was cool, and Dana pulled the ill-fitting coat tight about her. Shivers traversed her form and it seemed her quivering legs might give out at any moment.

Scanning the area, she looked for a small shop of some kind. It didn't really matter the variety, simply something that was still open. Dana had considered a storefront already closed for the evening, but wasn't sure that she could maintain the steady hand necessary for lock picking. It took less than five minutes for her to find the little bookshop. Moving from between buildings, Dana stationed herself beside a large oak that stood sentinel across the road from the shop. After only a couple of minutes, Dana had determined that the proprietor was alone in the building and was busily going about the business of closing shop for the day.

The store owner, a squat African American woman of perhaps forty-five or fifty years old, was just preparing to lock the door when Dana appeared before her, gun in hand. Though she'd seen no customers or employees, still, Dana scanned the three narrow aisles, before finally addressing the woman. "Do not attempt to run or notify the authorities. I've no desire to harm you. Do you understand?"

The woman nodded, but the fearful brown eyes told Dana that she didn't believe her.

What was Dana doing? She'd scared the poor woman nearly to death. Had she lost her mind entirely? This was not who she was. Slowly, with some bit of trepidation, Dana slid the revolver into her right coat pocket. "Is that better?" she asked.

The woman studied her for a moment, hands now on her too-round hips, head cocked, eyes narrow. "Well, that's a stupid question," said the woman with sudden confidence. Likely the woman thought her mad. "What's this about?"

"I'm in a spot of trouble. Rather desperate, really. Please, would you lock the door and dim the lights. I'm pursued. It would be quite dangerous for us both if I was to be seen."

The woman shook her head as if in disgust while exhaling sharply. Looking over her tortoiseshell reading glasses she said, "I've still got a boy at home. He's likely just home from swim practice and busy raiding the refrigerator. My husband's coming to pick me up any time now. He's a big fella. Are we going to have a problem here? Because I'm just not in the mood for any nonsense."

Despite it all, Dana nearly chuckled. She loved the woman's spunk. "Please, the door, the lights. Hurry. There is danger." Dana nearly faltered. What little strength remained barely held her upright.

Snorting like a racehorse, the woman marched past Dana to the door, and, bending with a mighty grunt, jiggled the door four or five times before finally getting the lock to catch. She then flicked the lights to off. "I'll give you about a minute and a half to explain yourself—and that only because my brother Eldridge looks healthier than you and he's been dead six years. After that, I'm calling the police. You understand?"

Nodding, Dana moved to behind the cluttered sales counter and nearly tumbled into the padded vinyl chair before her. "I'm the victim of a terrorist attack. I've been beaten, raped, and infected with a toxin. I've stolen a computer hard drive from those that held me. I mean to search it for pertinent information before making further contact with the authorities. Persons in Homeland Security and other agencies have been compromised. The situation is volatile." Dana began to cough uncontrollably. Fresh blood appeared on the surgical mask she wore. "I'm going to use your computer," she added after the fit.

The woman stood, arms crossed at her ample chest. "If that's all true, give me the gun."

Dana stared at her. What could this woman be thinking? She couldn't relinquish her weapon to a stranger.

"Come on. Turn it over. I'm no threat to you, but I only have your word that you're no threat to me. If you want my help, then put my mind at ease."

Dana blinked. Her vision was blurry, her head nearly ready to explode. She was at her end. Surely the woman could see that. Even if Dana refused, the woman could easily flee and alert authorities before Dana could make the front door. She really had no option but to enlist the woman's aid. Slowly, she withdrew the revolver, ejected each shell, checked the chamber to ensure that it was empty, and handed the weapon to the woman.

"Alright. Better. Now, what is it you intend to do?"

Dana coughed as she pulled the satchel from her shoulder and withdrew the stolen hard drive. "I need to install this onto your computer and then search it for relative information."

"Isn't that a job for the police?"

Dana swayed slightly left. Even sitting, it was difficult to maintain stability. "Compromised," she said. It was becoming an effort even to speak.

The woman strolled to the wall to Dana's right. There was a small black safe. She punched in a code, opened the door, placed the gun within, and shut it. "Everyone? They're all compromised? Forgive me, but that seems absurd."

"Not everyone. But there are enough." *Cough!* "Any official report could raise an alert to those responsible." *Cough!* "Too much risk. Surely those that pursue me will…" *Cough!* "Be scanning transmissions."

The woman nodded. "Sounds like X-Files nonsense to me, but if you say so. Now scoot over. I'm not a techie but I'm not stuck in the twentieth century either. How do I install this thing? We need to get it done before my Ralph shows up and tries to help. Then you'd be in real trouble."

Ten minutes later the hard drive was installed and Dana was scanning the files. Her vision slid in and out of focus, her fingers trembled, she had sporadic fits of retching coughs. Much of the drive was useless information: spread sheets detailing legitimate expenditures, scheduled appointments, and old emails. Dana honed in on the emails. This was likely where she'd find something, perhaps an offhand comment, a slip, someone accidentally referring to something of import. Most were benign, nothing classified, nothing significant. But Dana had an eye for these things and after only a few moments located some messages that were locked and encrypted. Despite her deathly state, her skills as a hacker were phenomenal and it took less than two minutes to crack the codes and find the answer to at least one significant enigma.

Looking up to tell Anne of her find, she found the woman holding her cell phone to her ear.

"Who?" asked Dana, though she already knew the answer to the question.

"Oh, sweetie, I'm sorry but I just had to call the police. It was the only right thing to do."

Dana closed her eyes and let out a slow sigh. Refocusing, she copied the email and then sent it to Hunt's account with hopes that the information would be found useful. Already, she heard sirens approaching, spiraling red lights danced through the window. Dana attempted to stand, but her legs gave out. Slipping to the floor, she had only enough strength to prevent her head from striking the hard vinyl surface before finally she slipped into a semi-conscious stupor.

Chapter 39

Washington D.C.

The flight to D.C. was short but tense. Hunt had used his credentials as a fugitive recovery agent to keep Donnelley in handcuffs, but even so he was forced to remain constantly in the company of the man who had raped, beaten, and infected his wife. Worse yet, he'd had no opportunity to beat the monster into a steaming heap of bloody pulp.

The terrorist remained mostly quiet throughout the flight, only breaking the silence to complain that he was in desperate need of a smoke. Hunt didn't care about the man's addiction and thought a prolonged and agonizing death by cancer brought about by the habit was far too good for him.

Utilizing his laptop computer, Hunt used the flight time to forward the new information gleaned from Bedford, Thorpe, and Donnelley to Corky Meeks at the Pentagon, asking her to research the Tulls, children of the gods, and Bedford. In just over an hour she forwarded photographs of Joshua and Linus Tull, their father (a man who in no way resembled his supposed sons), a cousin, Ymir Tull, and an uncle, Aeron. Aside from the father, each man was cut of the same cloth, tall, brooding, with light red hair, deep set eyes (one blue, one green) under pronounced brows, angular faces, and broad mirthless mouths. The complexions were sallow, the bearings athletic. The family was wealthy, but there was very little evidence as to where the money had come from. In fact, very little could be gleaned concerning the men beyond birth certificates, land purchases, and scant employment and educational records.

Linus had spent time in finance, and yet his holdings were as if invisible, buried beneath layer after layer of sub corporations. Joshua moved in the political arena as an "advisor." But again, nothing concrete could be found. Who did he advise, on what issues? He wasn't a registered lobbyist, nor was he even a member of a political party, yet he floated freely amongst the D.C. elite, apparently tickling their ears with schemes and agendas. The relations, Ymir and Aeron, were similarly reclusive, but Hunt's gut was that they weren't as highly placed in the organization.

The connection with children of the gods seemed, for the Tulls at least, to originate with the uncle, Aeron. No irregularities or deceptions had been found in earlier generations. That said, through her investigation into the Tulls, Corky had stumbled upon other families with frighteningly similar situations, some of these dating back more than a century. Burns, Kraus, Weaver, Humphreys, Strack, Yu, Dubinski, each family shared a common secret. Though, as of yet, Corky had found no political or business connections between the families, she had followed a photographic trail from one family to another and another. Each clan had suddenly produced offspring of the same physical make-up as the Tulls: over six feet tall, red haired, heterochromia, pronounced brows, and male. Corky had found no females within these families fitting these characteristics. As well, none of these men resembled their parents or other ancestors. Yet each was of natural birth; none were adopted. As he refused to believe that these were the children of mythical gods, Hunt's conclusion was that someone connected to the children of the gods organization—cult? It really seemed more a cult—had impregnated women and then influenced the offspring both philosophically and financially from the shadows, indoctrinating them into his grand scheme.

It sounded fanciful, ridiculous.

And frightening.

In some ways he could almost understand it. A wealthy man makes a proposition to a young couple. They would be of little means, possibly struggling to support other children. The man promises that if the wife would only birth a child—or children—by him, that she and her family would be given substantial wealth, their needs would be forever covered. All the couple need do is to keep the secret and to give the biological father, and/or his associates, access to his offspring, that the child be tutored in certain beliefs and attitudes.

Creepy.

As to the cult, children of the gods, they were equally enigmatic. Corky had found references to them going back over three hundred years, or at least to a group or groups known by this or similar names. Was this the same organization or had the Tulls and their ilk piggybacked onto an earlier concept, hijacking it as their own? It seemed a multi-purpose kind of name, one that could be used in a variety of situations.

Corky had found that many of the names of the "gods" given Hunt by Thorpe were actually tied to demons and not deities, but this meant little to Hunt. In his opinion, it was often difficult to distinguish the two. There were apparently ties to better known organizations often cited by conspiracy theorists. Names such as the Illuminati, Ordo Templi Orientis, the Nizari, the Knights of the Golden Circle, the Thule Society, all appeared to have some connection to children of the gods, but those connections were unclear and dubious. Somehow, this group had flown under the radar for decades, maybe even centuries. The information Corky had obtained had taken high level security access as well as the core information needed to start the search. I.e., unless someone knew what to look for and had access to highly classified files, the connections would not be found. One could not Google children of the gods and find information leading to these people.

Hunt stared at the screen and ran a palm across the top of his head.

Did it matter?

Any of it?

All that mattered was Dana. Hunt couldn't believe he'd allowed Bedford to bully him into pursuing these thugs in D.C. while Dana was missing and likely dying. But, Bedford was the only one with Dana's last known whereabouts, and the woman wasn't talking unless she got her way.

Bedford.

Corky was still working on that one. Apparently the woman was as she claimed, an agent of Homeland Security. Before that, she'd been FBI. At first glance she was clean, but Hunt didn't trust that either. Right now he trusted no one.

God, how he wished Dana was here.

Would he ever even see her again?

Hunt closed his eyes and leaned back in the seat. His head was pounding, his muscles ached, and he'd barely slept in days. He popped three pills and kept his eyes marginally open—aware of Donnelley. He failed to see the new email message appear on his screen.

*****

It was evening, cool, breezy, with spats of drizzle. The capital city had a buzz about it. There was always a buzz about it. Those in power, those feeding off of those in power, and even more so, those aspiring to gain power, were always in motion. It was the way of things. Hunt had no use for it.

He pulled the rental car into a slot only a block from their destination. Donnelley stared at Hunt, offering a jackal's grin. "Time for the cuffs to come off. I walk in like this; I can't get you through the door."

"Here's how it plays, Donnelley. I'm a desperate man. Desperate men are volatile. We don't always do what makes sense to anyone else. You try something and I'll take you down. If that means I go down with you, so be it. You've already taken the only person that matters to me."

Donnelley clucked his tongue. "Your whore might live. Heh?"

Hunt leaned forward, his face only inches before Donnelley's. The man's breath bore the stale stench of tobacco. Was that what Dana had breathed as the man raped her? Was that disgusting odor now part of her memory, part of that horrific experience? Would she relive the event every time some idiot lit up near her? "Let's be honest," he said. "Her chances of survival are probably at less than ten percent. And even if she lives, after what you've done to her, both physically and emotionally, she'll never be the same. So, yeah, Donnelley, you've already taken her from me. You wanna chance giving me an excuse to blow your head off? I'm waiting for the opportunity."

Donnelley shrugged, his expression haughty. "Get these cuffs off me, soldier boy."

Hunt slammed his fist into the man's crotch with the force of a juiced up prize fighter, eliciting a sharp exhalation of air and a sound something akin to *gaawcchhh*. "I may still need you to get me close to the Tulls. But, don't you dare think that means I can't make your life miserable." A quick blow to the kidney. "Got that?"

Donnelly was silent, bent over drooling and gasping.

*****

The event was a banquet, black tie affair, invitation only. The vice president was in attendance, as was the Speaker of the House, numerous congresspersons, several foreign dignitaries including three presidents and a prime minister, a smattering of entertainment celebrities, and a gaggle of CEOs, lobbyists, bankers, and all around hot shots from about the globe. Notwithstanding his bandaged nose, Donnelley was dressed almost acceptably: a five hundred dollar Italian jacket, black silk shirt, open at the collar, a pair of gray slacks, and slick black designer shoes. The thug dressed for success.

Hunt had not had the opportunity to change since Wisconsin, and still wore loose-fitting khaki pants bearing multiple Velcro pockets, a black T-shirt shirt partially obscured by an unbuttoned and untucked flannel, and lightweight boots. He was tired and desperate, unshaven, bruised and battered, living on energy drinks, protein bars, and Oxycontin. He hadn't showered in days. But, he wasn't concerned with appearances. His only goal was to forestall this attack.

Ignoring the curious stares of both staff and guests, he marched the still-cuffed Donnelley through the elegant main lobby of the hotel and down the long ornate corridor toward the banquet hall. Naturally, he was met by security well before reaching the chamber. As there was no way a weapon would get past the Secret Service, he'd come unarmed. Approaching the nearest Secret Service agent, he withdrew his credentials, handing them to the stone-faced man.

"Sir, my name is sergeant Marc Huntington U.S. Army, retired, former Delta Force. I'm a registered fugitive recovery agent and have been tasked by a Marjorie Bedford of Homeland Security to prevent a biological attack planned to be unleashed at this event. Due to suspicion of compromise from within various agencies, she was hesitant to move through official channels and so chose to utilize me." Hunt paused, pulling Donnelley forward with a harsh jerk. "This scumbag is a terrorist named Kelvin Donnelley. He's already made two attempts on U.S. targets this week. I've brought him to help in identifying his fellow conspirators. I also wouldn't be opposed to seeing his brain matter splayed across the wall by the end of the evening. You'll need to vet me, I get that. You can do so through Bedford at Homeland as well as through Corina Meeks or Colonial James Lindell, both at the Pentagon. But first, you'll need to detain two guests, Linus and Joshua Tull. They are implicated in the attack and highly dangerous."

The agent studied Hunt and then dropped his gaze to Hunt's credentials. Two things happened at this moment: Donnelley jabbed a knee into Hunt's groin following it with a head butt that sent Hunt stumbling backward, and shrieks and cries of panic erupted from the nearby banquet hall.

Chapter 40

Joshua Tull smiled. How could he not? Dietz, bless the woman, had come through marvelously. He didn't know the science behind it—didn't care really—but she had manipulated the event magnificently. Or perhaps it truly had been the gods, his forbearers, moving in the shadows, influencing Dietz to perform acts which she believed to be of science and were anything but.

It didn't matter. Not really. These were questions for philosophers, theologians, and scientists.

It would be wonderful if he had the faith he'd possessed as a younger man, if he could stand with confidence in the fact that what he believed was true to the very core. It would grant him such peace of spirit if he could be unwavering and unapologetic in his beliefs. But he could not. And it didn't matter. For no one else need ever know of his doubts or misgivings. He had committed to this cause long ago and too many others counted on his strength for him to show even the slightest fissure. And if what he so desperately wanted to believe was indeed false, what then did anything matter, for then what was man but soulless meat? Those about to be sacrificed would eventually perish anyway. And once people were dead, nothing concerned them ever again. What mattered—all that mattered—was that he remained true to those who counted on him. And here, in this, he would not waver.

The incubation period was at an end. The mass of the vile—wonderful! — mucus in each of the subjects was so great that soon it would ooze from every orifice and even the pores. The puss would bubble as if boiling, and once this process began, with each bursting bubble, the contagion would become airborne and be released into the room full of suddenly undignified dignitaries. Tull had been vaccinated, of course, but would feign fear and outrage with the others. He had not felt the need to be personally present for any of the other events, but this one was so very special, the culmination of such effort, he and Linus were committed to ensuring that it go off as planned.

And that mucus.

Was it truly that mundane, or was there, as he'd been taught, so much more?

Had his ancestors—the gods—truly been unjustly imprisoned in a spiritual cell named Tartarus? A place lower than hell. A cell that in the physical realm resided within a fossilized skull. And in activating the substance within that skull, had he truly revived those ancient deities? Would they move through the earthly substance to slay many but also to inhabit the forms of some the infected, possessing them, their superior intellects supplanting that of the mortals?

He might never know.

And, in truth, he both longed for the tale to be both true and false. If the substance proved to be nothing but an aggressive pathogen, then the world would make much more sense. Children of the gods would succeed in unsettling the world's status quo, influence would be gained, and life would continue. If mythical gods truly invaded human forms, Joshua would know that there was something greater in this universe than that which could be seen. Such a wonderful and horrifying thought.

Joshua smiled to himself and sipped at his buttermilk. Too much thinking. Too many contemplations. He gazed about the unsuspecting crowd. The event was near, and truly, the look of sheer amazement, terror, and confusion on these haughty self-important faces would be a sight to behold. For some he felt sorry, he supposed. It was a natural response. A human response. In any event such as this innocents would be sacrificed along with the guilty. But individual lives were tiny things, easily forgotten when one looked at events that shaped the world stage.

Tull's stomach took one last dive. The subjects were being wheeled into the hall. Here it was. Reality. The point of no return.

There were twelve subjects, each on a wheeled table, each garbed as they had been when found in the Amazon cave so many months before. The tables were pushed by loyal adherents dressed as porters. Young men, university students, mostly. Dedicated. Fanatical. Willing to make the ultimate sacrifice. They could have been vaccinated as had Joshua and Linus, but death for a deeply held belief was, in fact, a motivator. These men were more likely to be committed to the end if they knew this was truly the end, that they need not fear capture, interrogation, the humiliation of imprisonment. Like religious zealots of every fold, they believed that paradise awaited them on the other side, some nebulous reward, a carrot dangled. Joshua did not know if there truly was such a place, or of what form it might take if indeed it existed. In truth, he doubted that it did. He wondered if any of these had doubts similar to his own. That perhaps another in this room had had a crisis of belief, yet soldiered on simply because it was expected. What if everyone had misgivings, but, like him, refused to publically acknowledge them? Would then each non-believing person march forward, even unto death, believing that he alone was the sole heretic?

Curious.

Joshua watched the guests now, their expressions, their curiosity. A low murmur swelled about the hall. A few uneasy giggles. No one screamed or panicked—yet. The stunningly preserved bodies were on the evening's program. An anthropologist on staff at the Smithsonian was to present his miraculous find.

But there was no such anthropologist. The bodies alone would offer the evening's thrill.

There was a gurgle from the left. One of the subjects, an Aztec warrior by the look of him, drooled a yellow-green goo. Those at the table nearest him turned at the sound. A burly man, dark mustache, receding hair, in foreign military apparel, muttered something in Spanish. A middle-aged woman at the adjacent table screwed her face in disgust, turning to her husband to comment. There was a tittering from across the room as two nearby subjects produced visible sputum.

The event host, Senator Harold Finn, hurried across the room in a harried waddle, an angered scowl on his jowly features. "Where is Dr. Lo? What is happening here?"

To a person, the faux porters stood silent beside their charges. In their minds they were already on the road to paradise. The unfolding events were nothing more than a difficult passage into the land of a thousand gods.

One of the subjects coughed. Bile dribbled down his cheeks.

A young woman, situated near the front right of the room, screamed. The chatter increased. Italy's heads of state moved toward an exit. Good, good. As planned, many would flee before anyone thought to quarantine the room. And even then, with so many high-level dignitaries present, political pressure would be applied, traditional bio-terror protocols would be skirted. There would be confusion, outrage, demands. Soon the pathogen would be on airliners, gestating within these dignitaries and fanning out across the globe to infect those at the highest levels of numerous governments. Such a small sample, such a rich reward.

Joshua chanced a glance to the rear. Linus stood toward the back of the room, amidst a small circle of Arabs, undoubtedly involved in some dreary economic discussion. Linus displayed a wisp of joy followed by a mask of feigned outrage. He was such the actor, Joshua's half-brother. So very suited for his role.

Already, Secret Service agents rushed forward, weapons drawn, barking into their ever-present com systems. The faithful subjects, posing as porters, remained solemn and calm as the formerly dignified crowd clamored toward the exits even as the confused Secret Service agents attempted to contain the situation.

It was then that Donnelley entered the room, handcuffed, bruised and band-aged. His deep set eyes darted right and then left, finally landing on Joshua. He did not know Joshua by name but did know him by sight. Joshua's stomach tightened. Another complication, perhaps a disastrous one. He couldn't very well kill the man amidst a crowded room, yet somehow Donnelley must be silenced—and quickly, before any connection could be drawn.

How very inconvenient.

Chapter 41

Virginia

While Hunt preferred a direct, no-frills approach, Thorpe prided himself in subtlety. This Bedford with whom Huntington had dealt, he didn't have a good notion about the woman. True, he'd never met her and had had only the duration of the short flight to investigate her, but his fight/flight alarm was screaming a bloody ruckus and he tended to grant the thing great license. As such Thorpe had booked an American Airlines flight under his own name, a United flight under one of his aliases, Simon Townsend, and a Southwest Airlines flight under yet another pseudonym, William Dane.

Thorpe waited till boarding was near complete and then entered the Southwest flight as William Dane, a thirty year-old rocker with shoulder length blond hair, a walrus mustache, low-hanging blue jeans, and a sleeveless T-shirt. Though Thorpe already had documentation for the Dane legend, he'd obtained much of the costume at a Chicago thrift shop while en route to the airport. If he hadn't found the wig, he would have traveled as the more conventional Simon Townsend, a forty year-old textile salesman from Leeds. Fortunately, he'd found all that was needed as he preferred the flexibility of Southwest Airlines. With no assigned seating it was all the more difficult for undesirables to confirm his presence on a given flight.

As the Boeing 717 neared final approach, Thorpe studied his computer screen. He'd hacked into Marc Huntington's email account hoping to discover what Huntington had learned. Currently he read through the slight and incomplete dossier on Bedford sent to Huntington by his pentagon contact.

Marjorie Bedford, aged forty-eight, maiden name Willis.

Hometown: Montoursville Pennsylvania, currently resides in Washington DC.

Graduate of Stanford University, class of '86.

Married George Bedford in 1987.

Joined the FBI in 1988 and transferred to the Department of Homeland Security in 2003.

Two children, George Jr., 24, and Elizabeth, 22.

There was a list of commendations, promotions, reassignments. There were links to files of major cases she'd worked, as well as a smattering of useless drivel.

Thorpe closed the file. There was nothing of use here.

Almost casually, he glanced at the screen listing Huntington's numerous unanswered email messages.

Curious.

Was that a new email from Dana? It hadn't been there when he'd first opened the file.

Thorpe clicked into the message and began to read. It wasn't the solution to every problem, but the information within did clarify something of import. Clever girl. Very clever.

Thorpe's fingers danced across the keyboard. Dana had sent the message within the last fifteen minutes, with luck, she was still near a computer. If only she'd respond with her locale he might be able to eliminate Bedford from the equation.

He stared at the screen for the final thirty minutes of the flight. No response. No additional messages. For whatever reason, Dana was again offline. His only consolation was that he knew that as of less than an hour ago she was still alive.

*****

Once on the ground, Thorpe maintained the William Dane identity and, after retrieving his bag and securing the antidote from within, stationed himself at a table adjacent a magazine shop near the baggage claim area. He opened his laptop and pretended to flit about Facebook. In truth, he was conducting surveillance. He'd identified three likely agents almost immediately, though none was Bedford. He'd hoped to spot her in the first few minutes but the woman was not readily apparent. Surely she was here somewhere, just waiting to pounce on him and to wrest the priceless vile from his possession. But then, where was she? What sort of nonsense had she planned?

To Thorpe's frustration, nearly a half hour went by before he saw her. She wore a white blouse, a blue blazer, navy slacks, and white tennis shoes. She was paunchy, yet maintained a lively step and, though somewhat heavier, looked quite similar to the photos he'd seen in her dossier. She approached one of the earlier identified agents, and, after a short exchange, turned toward a different terminal. Thorpe casually closed his laptop, slipping it into a leather case, sipped off the remainder of his cola, and sauntered after her. No visible rush. No urgency.

Approaching her from the rear he said, "You have her, I assume?"

"Thorpe?"

"Well, yes. I would think that obvious. And, please, do not signal your men. That would not prove advantageous for either of us. Now, again, Dana, you do have her." Thorpe pressed a hard, and quite sharp, plastic dagger to her back, at kidney level, while simultaneously slipping her gun from its holster and into his pants at the base of his spine. The blade had been disguised as part of the plastic shell to his laptop computer carrying case. Quite clever, really.

Bedford smiled and shrugged an aw-shucks shrug. "I guess you caught me there. The woman can barely move. You really didn't think she could evade us for long."

"Of course not. You knew you'd likely have recovered her by the time I arrived, but needed to motivate me to bring the antidote. You chose me over Huntington as I'm the less volatile of the two. Ah, but here's your conundrum. You see, Dana popped off an email, likely just before her capture. It contained information that you would very much like kept from public scrutiny."

Bedford raised her brows.

"I know about George Jr.," said Thorpe. "Kidnapped by the very group you've vowed to oppose. They've forced you to play both sides. Such a terrible dilemma for a mother, violate your life principles or sacrifice your offspring. It's no wonder you've gained weight these past months. Many people eat more when under duress."

The two moved to the relative privacy of a small alcove adjacent the restrooms where Bedford turned, facing Thorpe directly. "How did Dana Huntington come to possess this information? What else is it you know?"

Thorpe grinned. "Yes, well, her source, that she didn't disclose. But I do know that you, who moved beyond the restraints of your official position to form White Eagle, a coalition meant to undermine children of the gods, are now forced to do their bidding while still appearing to work toward their destruction. No wonder your every move seems a contradiction."

"Listen, Mr. Thorpe—Jonathan. We don't know each other, you and I. We're strangers drawn together by events beyond our control."

"Mmm, yes. Your point?"

"By all logic we're on the same side here."

Thorpe shrugged, offering his near-perpetual grin. "Well, of course you would like me to believe that, but my first concern is Dana. You have another agenda—two actually. One directed by your conscience and profession, the other by the people holding your son."

Bedford studied him for a moment, her round face expressionless. "Alright, so maybe we're climbing two different hills. What do you propose to do? You've got to know, if I do anything to anger these people they'll kill my George."

Thorpe gazed at the woman. Her gray eyes were sincere. "Yes, well, you see, I've been researching children of the gods. I've gained information, both from my own sources as well as from Huntington. I've learned a thing or two: a smattering of names, the locations of three of Joshua Tull's properties, information that might help lead you to your son."

Bedford's eyes narrowed, her lips twisted slightly left. "And what is it you want from me, Jonathan? What do you need in return for this information that may or may not help me locate my son?"

"It's simple, really. Lead me to Dana, allow me to administer the antidote, and I'll give you everything I know."

"That sounds wonderful. Except for one thing."

"Yes? And what, may I ask, is that?"

Bedford's move was surprisingly quick for a woman her size. A leg swept across, left to right, as her left arm slashed right to left, her fist connecting with Thorpe's neck as his feet were swept away. He was on the floor, the knife free of his hand, before he'd fully understood the attack. Bedford landed on him, pressing a forearm across his neck and holding her Glock only an inch from his forehead. How had she recovered it from him so swiftly? Already, her three agents were racing toward them, there were shouts and screams, security would join the agents within moments.

"The problem, Jonathan," said Bedford in a breathy whisper, "is that you're under arrest. And, unfortunately, before you have the chance to tell anyone any harebrained stories about me working both sides, well, you're going to try to escape. It'll be a fatal error in judgment. Am I making myself clear?"

Chapter 42

Hunt dropped to the floor in an awkward tumble, Donnelley's strike having caught him entirely off guard. How had he been so inattentive? Already, Donnelley raced in the direction of the banquet hall, the stone-faced Secret service agent with whom Hunt had been speaking, in pursuit. There were shouts and screams coming from the chamber. Several dozen people raced from the room, creating a general chaos. Whatever form the terrorist attack had taken, it was obviously underway.

Willing the cumulous from his brain, Hunt scrambled to his feet and raced toward yet another secret service agent, this one young and lean. "Hey! Hey, you!"

The agent continued forward in a fast trot.

"Stop!" yelled Hunt, now grabbing the man by his shoulder. The agent whirled, drawing his weapon in the process. Hunt ducked, jabbed, pulled, disarming the agent in one instinctive move. "I'm not the enemy," hissed Hunt, as he held the man from behind. "Sergeant Marcus Huntington, U.S. Army retired. I'm here by order of Homeland Security with important information concerning the attack now underway. Listen to me!"

Hunt spun the agent around to face him, Hunt holding the newly-acquired gun on the agent. Before the man could speak, Hunt said. "We are in the midst of a biological attack. You need to lock down this wing immediately—lock down the whole damn building if you need to. Just don't let anyone leave."

The man narrowed his eyes as if unconcerned with the weapon aimed at him. "Listen, I don't know who you are, but..."

"I'm the guy whose here to tell you what you're facing. Sort this out later. Arrest me if you've got to, but make the call. Lock down this place. If that bio-toxin gets out of this building there'll be no stopping its spread. Do you realize how many nations are represented in that room? Do you understand what could happen if infected persons are allowed to hop on their Leer jets and leave the country?"

There were more shouts from up the hall.

Giving the agent a quick shove with the purpose of leaving him off balance, Hunt turned, racing toward the sound of commotion. The agent, already in pursuit and barking into his com link, was only ten paces behind. So be it. The man was now unarmed and Hunt was leading him directly to the source of the attack.

The Tulls, Joshua and Linus, he couldn't let them escape. They had access to the antidote. Likely everyone in the banquet hall had been exposed, dignitaries from all over the world potentially infected. Locking down the facility and securing the antidote were of paramount importance.

Whirling, Hunt again trained the gun on the secret service agent who was now only a few feet behind him. "Did you make the call? Did you order this place locked down?"

To the agent's credit, he didn't show the slightest fear. "I can't do that without authorization. You should know that."

"Then do it!" shouted Hunt. "This strain cannot leave the building." In an effort to show sincerity, Hunt tossed the gun to the man. "We're on the same side. Take your gun. Make the call." Hunt turned toward the large double doorway even as two additional Secret Service agents rushed forward, weapons drawn.

With a nod to the bewildered agent, Hunt stepped into the banquet hall and out of the line of fire.

Chapter 43

Virginia

Thorpe angled his head toward Bedford, "You'd best reconsider your plan, dear lady. Eliminating me will only ensure that your double dealing is made public."

Bedford's eyes narrowed, but still she pinned Thorpe to the hard cool floor.

"The file, the dossier detailing your connection to children of the gods, it's already in Huntington's hands and I've forwarded it to two associates of mine with the instruction that should anything happen to me, the information be made public—media first, authorities second, no real chance to bury it in bureaucracy, hmmm? Now, will you please get off of me so that we may speak like civilized human beings. You are creating quite the scene."

Bedford nodded, but did not yet rise. Turning toward her three agents, each of whom stood weapon trained on Thorpe, she said. "Stand down, gentlemen. The situation is under control." Then to the airport security personnel now approaching, she hollered, "Homeland Security. Stand back. Stand down. Please use your energies on crowd control." A general panic had erupted when people saw that weapons had been drawn. It would likely take a half hour or better to bring the terminal back under control.

Bedford pocketed Thorpe's plastic dagger, holstered her weapon, moved off of Thorpe, and rose, now displaying her credentials. To her nearest man, she said, "Mr. Thorpe will accompany us to the facility. Confiscate his laptop, luggage, phone, and anything else he has on his person. I want everything electronic to travel with me only." Turning to Thorpe, she said. "Your way for now. We'll take a look at your devices, you know the drill, checking into your claims and all of that horse hockey. Then I'll decide what happens with Dana Huntington and the antidote." With a quick glance toward her men, she added in a hushed whisper. "I'm in a pickle, Jonathan. But, I'm not the enemy. You might remember that. I want these people taken down in a way you could never imagine."

"Well, yes, all well and good, but a threat on my life, that does speak of an enemy by most definitions." He met her gaze. "Listen, Joshua Tull and his ilk have made the last few days a bit of a hell. I will gladly help you bring them to ruin. But first, Dana gets the antidote." Thorpe pulled the blond wig off and grinned. "Oh, and just a note. My laptop, my smart phone, everything is encrypted. Any attempts to override the programming will result in an immediate erasure of all memory—including any clues as to your Georgie's locale. So, you see, it might serve you well to treat me with a tad more courtesy."

Chapter 44

Washington DC

Hunt recognized the bodies immediately. These were some of the people he and Dana had discovered in an Amazon cave several months earlier. The group had been in some form of hibernation, their vital signs almost nonexistent. He'd often wondered what had become of them. Lucky Lindell had sent a team to retrieve them only to discover the cave empty. Hunt had never learned of any reappearance. But here they were, or, at least, some of them, only a dozen— including that of Dr. Gregory Milton, a man they'd met and then watched succumb to this strange malady. There had been perhaps five or six times that many in the cave.

The scene was almost too bizarre to be real. On each of the two long walls of the banquet hall, were six rolling metal tables, each holding a hibernating person. A porter stood as if at attention by each form. The porters were young men, late teens to mid-twenties, all Caucasian. Each had a particular glean in the eyes, a fanatic zeal which Hunt had seen before. The eyes of a zealot. These young men were facing the Secret Service agents who rushed into the room, weapons drawn. The porters did not attack, nor did they cower. Quite the contrary. They stared into the drawn weapons with an expectancy known only to the suicidal devoted. In his gut, Hunt knew these men intended to die.

Hunt's guess was that the bodies were being used to spread the bio-toxin. But these had not been contagious when last he'd encountered them. At least not contagious in any airborne fashion. Maybe if he'd had contact with blood or saliva, but he and Dana had both touched these people with no ill effect. But, the pathogen had been modified, hadn't it? The Bubonic plague infused, the strain corrupted.

He couldn't worry about this now. His primary concern was containment and the verification of the antidote. Did Thorpe possess the true cure or was their another variant, one designed to debilitate the more advanced version of the merged pathogen? Somewhere in the back of his mind it occurred to Hunt that he had now been exposed and was likely infected.

Donnelley was to Hunt's forward left, hands still cuffed behind his back as he made his way around banquet tables and through the waves of fleeing dignitaries. He definitely had a goal, but Hunt couldn't determine just what—or who—he was after. Not any of the comatose bodies, they were all to the right of him.

The stone faced agent, the one Hunt had first approached, spotted Hunt and marched toward him while barking orders to the other agents. "Do not let any of those porters leave. Approach each with caution. The intent is to subdue." To Hunt he said, "That man in cuffs?"

"Yeah, Donnelley," said Hunt as both men moved toward the cuffed terrorist who was weaving through the crowd.

"He's connected to this?"

"Yeah. I was hoping he could help me identify his bosses." A group of six Middle Eastern dignitaries pushed past the men, causing Hunt to lose sight of Donnelley. His muscles and bones ached to the core, and even this minimal contact caused pain and distraction. He recognized the symptom—withdrawal from the Oxycontin—but he couldn't risk a dose. He needed a clear mind, quick reflexes. He'd deal with his personal hell later.

The agent met Hunt's gaze directly. "Well, he's heading toward someone specific. You might get your wish. Listen, I'm going to trust you for now, but you're not leaving until you're thoroughly vetted. Got that?"

"I wouldn't expect it any other way." Hunt continued forward, still attempting to reacquire Donnelley.

The agent nodded and then turned toward the young agent moving up behind Hunt, weapon drawn on him. "Stand down, Daniels."

"Sir, this man disarmed me and I've received no authorization on him."

The stone faced agent offered a hint of a grin. "Apparently, he disarmed you and then returned your weapon. My understanding is he has valuable information." To Hunt he said. "The nature of the threat? And hurry. This thing is unraveling before our eyes." Marching forward, the agent maneuvered around another group. It seemed he might still have eyes on Donnelley.

Hunt nodded as he fell in step directly behind the man. "Biological. Airborne. Highly contagious. The attack is connected to the recent terrorist events overseas. This building needs to be quarantined immediately. We cannot let this bug get out."

Nodding, the agent clicked his con. "Keller here. We've got a potential biological threat. Lock this place down immediately. Do not—I repeat—do not let any person civilian or otherwise leave this building under any circumstances. That includes our own personnel. Is that clear?" A pause. "Good. Notify local authorities. Order a barricade. We'll need additional personnel and will begin with the National Guard outside of the hotel. Have the DC police block off a two block perimeter, no one in or out."

Secret Service agents were now moving about the room, making their ways toward the terrorist porters. It seemed at first the porters were surrendering peacefully, three were already in handcuffs when one of them, a young man, blond, perhaps twenty years old, whipped his head about and bit the agent who had been cuffing him in the neck. As the agent pulled away with a startled shout of pain, two other agents opened fire on the young man who smiled greedily as the first round sent him to his final reward.

Another shout followed by gunfire. Each of the formerly docile porters were now charging agents, biting, head-butting, anything to draw fire. The handful of guests still in the room screamed and scattered, some diving to the floor, scampering under tables, others racing toward the doorways, crouched and fearful.

Death by agent, thought Hunt. They'd rather die a martyr's death than sit rotting in a cell or even in a hospital room waiting for the bio-toxin to eat them away.

And then he was there, Donnelley. With the crowd scattering, Hunt had a clear view of the man. He was racing toward a tall red-haired man, obviously one of the Tulls.

"Donnelley!" shouted Hunt as he bound toward the terrorist. But even as he set his eyes on the man who'd raped his wife he knew his true target should be Tull. Tull was the mastermind. Tull knew about the antidote, whether the vile in Thorpe's possession would cure both strains or only the plague. Tull was key.

Chapter 45

Donnelley slammed into an old woman knocking her to the floor, twirled, and reacquired his gaze on the tall red-haired man. He was a Tull. Of that he was certain. But not the one he needed. Not the one who had recruited him. He'd never known the names. Hadn't cared really—hadn't even concerned himself with the group's agenda. Not so long as it gave him the tools he'd needed to damage the fraudulent government and the man, Calhoun. The man responsible for Colm's death.

The other Tull, the younger one, the one he'd known, had been here when first he'd entered the room. Where was he now? The place was a madhouse. He must have fled with the crowd. Maybe the other one, though. Maybe the other Tull knew of him, of his place in the scheme. Maybe he could help him slip away from that soldier boy Huntington. Donnelley could threaten to expose him if he didn't cooperate. He now knew enough to seriously damage their movement.

The Tull saw him.

There was recognition in his strange eyes. Maybe even fear.

Good. The man should fear him. Donnelley deserved to be feared.

Just as Donnelley made to intercept the man, he was struck from behind and tumbled gracelessly to the wood-planked floor. It was one of the Secret Service agents. The one Huntington had first approached in the hallway. He now pressed Donnelly hard against the floor, a gun held to the back of his head.

"Do not move!" barked the agent.

Angling his head to the left, Donnelley saw Huntington race toward the Tull. Leverage. Donnelley was already thinking of leverage. Likely they had no solid evidence on Tull. He could provide that in exchange for immunity.

The agent frisked him with his left hand while keeping him pinned with a knee and subdued with the gun.

The entire encounter lasted no more than fifteen seconds, for just as the agent again prepared to speak, a gunshot cracked from somewhere off to the left, momentarily distracting the man.

Donnelley rolled, head butting the Secret Service man in the throat. Scrambling to his feet, he stepped backward, grabbing a wooden chair from his rear with his still-cuffed hands, and whirled around slamming a leg of the chair into the startled agent's jaw. The agent tumbled backward as Donnelley fled.

Chapter 46

Marion Dietz was drunk.

We'll, maybe not drunk. Just… insulated.

She certainly wasn't jolly. She wasn't celebrating Joshua's success. She was just…

Insulated.

But, not enough so. Not enough to truly put her mind at ease. Not enough to detour the rumblings in her bowels or the slithering guilt in her head. Was she really party to this thing? Had she truly participated in the potential deaths of thousands?

And for what?

Recognition? Respect?

Had she really been so foolish as to think she would gain respect through such a heinous act? Was she truly so pathetic?

A swig of honey liqueur.

Not strong enough. The stuff was not near strong enough.

And what of her subjects? Her patients. They were her patients, weren't they? These magnificent people, some hibernating for centuries. The knowledge that could be gained from them, the medical advancements made, the good to mankind. That she'd allowed them to be used as mere tools in the hands of a fanatic…

She took another swig.

There was a sound.

A door opening.

Approaching footsteps.

Dietz was in a narrow hallway toward the back of the hotel. It was less than two minutes from the banquet hall and was the location from which she had staged the dozen slumbering souls who would spread the modified plague throughout the globe.

Another door opened and then closed. A figure appeared before her. Tall. Pale. A pronounced brow.

Joshua.

"Oh, Dietz!" he said as if only then remembering her. "Sipping the Barenja-ger, I see. What... a surprise."

He marched past on his way to a stairway at the end of the corridor.

"Joshua!" she said, calling after him.

He continued for perhaps three paces, marching quickly, urgency in his step, and Dietz thought it unlikely he would respond. But then he paused, and turned. "What is it, Dietz?"

"You wanted me. Just this week. You wanted to seduce me."

He studied her for a moment, those peculiar eyes delving into her soul. She felt naked and ashamed. She was not attractive. She knew this. Yet, he had pursued her.

"No, Marion. I sought only to en...liven you to the task at hand, perhaps to offer... you a momentary comfort. Come. You'd best remain with me. Your knowledge is t...too great for me to allow you to... fall into the hands of the officials."

Dietz stepped forward, nearly mesmerized by the charismatic figure before her.

Such a fool.

Such a terrible fool she was.

Draining her flask, she moved toward him, slowly at first, unsure of what to do. They descended the narrow concrete stairs, Tull first, Dietz perhaps five steps behind. Coming to the landing, Tull stepped forward, opening a pale metal door, moving through while holding it open for Dietz to follow. Dietz then clasped the door, taking one step through, and then, as Tull turned to look forward, she reversed her movement and fled up the cold and lonely concrete steps.

Chapter 47

Hunt ran toward Tull as the stone-faced agent, Keller, tackled Donnelley, slamming him into the high-gloss oak floor and jabbing a knee into his back as he immediately frisked him for weapons with one hand while holding a gun to his head with the other.

Tull was before him, distracted by Donnelley he didn't notice Hunt until he was practically upon him. It was Linus, the older of the brothers. Tull was potentially armed, and so Hunt had no choice but to attack and subdue. Questioning could wait until the situation was secured.

Linus was in his upper sixties, yet still he wriggled out of Hunt's initial assault with the skill of a trained fighter, negating Hunt's hold with an agile twirl and pull. Hunt had been distracted by Donnelley, careless, stupid. What was wrong with him?

The pistol appeared in Tull's hand almost magically and Hunt was forced to pivot and feint to avoid the first shot which whizzed only inches to the left of his head.

Hunt grabbed Tull's arm, twisted, jerked. There were two sharp cracks, one the arm, the other the weapon.

The unintended round entered at the base of the jaw and exited at the crown of the head in a bloody splay of bone and tissue. The body jerked once, violent and abrupt, and then collapsed limp to the floor.

Linus Tull would give no information.

Damn!

Scanning the room, Hunt first noticed Agent Keller, just regaining his focus after apparently being struck by a wooden chair. Donnelley was nowhere to be seen. The terrorist porters were all either subdued or dead. Certainly, they would be questioned, but Hunt doubted any possessed useful knowledge. Joshua Tull was his only lead. He alone would have the answers concerning the antidote.

Offering Keller a hand up, Hunt said, "Donnelley?"

A shake of the head. "Fled. How the hell did that man get a gun in here?"

Hunt shrugged. "Your security force. Not mine."

There was a muffled cry from behind, and Hunt turned to see a young woman, no older than thirty, drop to her knees, her skin blistering and popping. Hunt knew the symptoms intimately. The Amazon strain. Hideous and uncompromising. Strange. No one else had become symptomatic so quickly. In Brazil, yes, with the original unmodified pathogen, but not this group, nor those on the train. Perhaps the lab modified version had been designed to slow obvious symptoms until the pathogen had had opportunity to spread, but this woman's system had reacted differently. Hunt couldn't know for sure. He was no scientist. In any event, the woman's disease reminded him of just what it was they faced and of how critical it was to contain this thing.

It was then that Hunt noticed another woman. Tall, gangly, thinning gray/blond hair, and a hollow vacant stare. It seemed she'd just entered the hall, weeping, her gate unsteady; she wore a white lab coat. Approaching one of the comatose forms she bent, caressing the comatose man, straightening the hair, speaking to him as one might a lover.

And then she put her lips to those of the corpse-like form and inhaled deeply.

Suicide.

Pointing toward the woman so that Keller knew his intent, Hunt moved forward. "Hey! Hey, you. Excuse me."

The woman turned, her pale gray eyes focusing on Hunt, a mannish hand wiping bile from her lips. She appeared to be in her early sixties.

"You're involved with this," said Hunt as he and Keller stepped to before her.

The woman stared at Hunt and then, after a moment, nodded with a peculiar smile creasing her narrow lips.

Hunt pointed at the comatose man beside her. "These people. I was there. I found them in the Amazon. They were in hibernation but not contagious. What's been done to them?"

"They are my patients," said the woman, her voice hesitant and confused. "I was made to modify the bacteria."

"Yeah? How so?" Hunt's instinct had been right. This woman could have the answers concerning the cure.

The woman chuckled. "That, young man, is complicated and likely far over your head. But yes, the contagion is now airborne. My wonderful subjects acting as mere incubators, human breeding tanks and a rather dramatic means of spreading the pathogen. Does that disturb you as much as it does me?"

Disturb. Good word. It seemed to describe the woman to a T. "Ma'am, it's clear you've got a lot on your mind, but I need to ask you a few questions."

The woman smiled, broad and skeletal, displaying large and yellowed teeth.

"I was present for the U.S. attack," said Hunt. "I was on the train. My wife was infected, but not with the airborne version. It was administered by aerosol, a more concentrated dose."

"That's unfortunate," offered the woman.

"We've acquired an antidote from the terrorist, Kelvin Donnelley. Is that the right antidote or do we need a variant?"

The woman stared silently at Hunt, that skeletal grin seemingly glued on her face, one hand cupped in the other and cradled to her breast.

"Ma'am, really. I need your help."

"Joshua."

"Pardon?"

"Joshua would know which strain was used where."

"Joshua Tull. Where is he?"

The woman nodded, pointing toward an employee service entrance. "Through there. Third door on your left. Follow the hallway to the stairwell. Go down."

Hunt moved toward the exit, Keller, at his heals, and barking for an agent to take the woman into custody.

Chapter 48

Virginia

Dana was conscious, but only just so. She recognized the room, the plastic tent, the sparsely furnished space she'd occupied only hours before. Attempting to readjust, she found herself encumbered, Her left wrist handcuffed to the bedrail.

Bloody hell! They'd captured her again.

Dana closed her eyes and then reopened them slowly, attempting to bring her vision fully into focus. It was several moments before she realized she was not alone. There were two forms, one male, one female, just within the doorway.

The woman was that Homeland wanker Bedford and the male…

"Jonathan?"

"In the flesh, my dear. So good to see those lovely violet eyes of yours. Feeling better, I hope?"

She'd almost not recognized him. Ratty blue jeans, flannel shirt, unshaven. A disguise, certainly. Nothing Jonathan would wear even on a day lounging about the condo.

"No," she said. "Not better. Perfectly horrid. Why are you here? Where's Hunt?"

"Yes, well, as to your health, certainly you'll soon feel a change for the good. The antidote, the cure, I've acquired it for you. It's been administered."

Dana nodded. Good news that, at least. "And Hunt?"

"Oh, off chasing villains, saving the world, I'm sure."

Jonathan could be such a twit. Clearly he was trying to cast Hunt in a negative light. Still, where was he? Why wasn't he here? Wasn't it Hunt that should be at her bedside?

"Bedford."

"Yes, Dana." The woman stepped forward. "And don't ask to be uncuffed. I trust you about as much as a hound dog in heat."

"Where is Hunt? What is the current situation?"

Bedford hesitated and then nodded a barely perceptible nod. "Pretty much what Jonathan said. Marcus is in D.C. attempting to prevent a terrorist attack. I will add that it was he that secured the antidote and that his first choice was to be here himself. I'm not sure Jonathan would have told you that last nugget."

"Yes, well," shrugged Jonathan. "Be that as it may, the antidote is in your system, you should be on the mend."

Bedford's phone buzzed. She answered and listened. And then, depressing the disconnect button, said, "I'm needed. Jonathan, you'll accompany me. I'm afraid I can't trust you alone with Dana."

Jonathan nodded and moved toward Dana. "Ah, yes. Mustn't trust Jonathan. I'm a thief, after all." Slipping his hand under the plastic tent, he clasped her right hand tightly in a show of affection. After the two had left the room, Dana opened her hand; in her palm was a small key. Dana was certain it would fit the handcuff. Yes. Jonathan certainly was a thief.

Chapter 49

Washington D.C.

There were agents guarding the service door leading into the dark alley at the back of the hotel. Yellow security tape encircled the building. Teams were in the process of securing doorways and windows with thick sheets of plastic. A quarantine zone. Joshua Tull should have anticipated as much. And certainly he'd known of the possibility; he'd simply hoped that he could have escaped before the biological element to the attack became known.

That the lockdown was already in effect troubled him. He truly hadn't expected the Neanderthal-like Secret Service to perceive the nature of the attack so quickly. He hoped the majority of the dignitaries had managed to evacuate before the sequester, otherwise the effectiveness of the event—at least from a terror aspect—would be greatly diminished. As to the spiritual component—in the unlikely event that one even existed—the imprisoned gods would still have been freed from their long captivity to manipulate and control persons of influence. "Long live the thousand gods," he muttered in near contempt.

"Sir, I'm sorry, but you'll need to remain within the building. A quarantine has been put in effect." The man wore a full hazmat suit.

"Well, all the more reason for me to leave," said Tull continuing forward into the alleyway, and pulling his jacket tightly about him in an effort to combat the cool night air.

"Sir, once again, you are not permitted to leave." The man adjusted his weapon, a rifle, not aiming it a Tull, but making sure that his point was obvious. Bathed in the wavering illumination of a streetlight, he looked like a space alien with an Uzi. Peculiar image.

"Do you have any idea who I am?" asked Tull, affecting the air of an uptight dignitary in the hopes that the agent would believe him to be just that and allow him pass.

"The Vice President has been detained. Whoever you are, I'm certain you don't outrank him. Now, if you will please reenter the building, I would prefer to avoid the use of force."

There was a sharp pop from Tull's rear and then a deep rich flower of blood appeared on the agent's chest. Tull turned to see Donnelley, gripping a handgun, broken cuffs still hanging from both wrists. Tull had come across Donnelley in the back hallway and cut his binds with an ax he'd found mounted adjacent a fire extinguisher. He'd instructed the man to find an alternate route, insisting that in no way should they be seen together. In retrospect, he'd been overly compassionate. The prudent thing would have been to kill the terrorist outright. The very fact that he was present jeopardized the movement's secrecy.

Another shot. This one aimed at Donnelley. Tull could hear several sets of running footsteps. The idiot Donnelley had drawn the attention of the entire guard.

Tull looked right and then left, seeking an escape route. He was no longer the focal point. Donnelley owned that honor.

Donnelley fired three more rounds.

There was an exchange of fire.

Tull scampered behind a garbage bin as rounds flew in each direction. Perhaps Donnelley would serve one more purpose, a distraction.

There was a sudden light. The door behind Donnelley had been opened. A figure dove and rolled, coming up behind the terrorist and bringing him down in one swift move.

Chapter 50

Virginia

Dana surprised Bedford with a hypodermic needle to the neck. After freeing herself of the handcuff she'd disabled the guard just beyond her doorway by using the cuffs as a garrote. Coughing and hacking, she'd still managed to traverse the fourth floor corridor, locating some handy drug vials in a cabinet along the way. Her head spun and her legs were the consistency of gelatin, but she managed to stumble and shuffle all the way to the lower level.

To Dana's delight, Jonathan had been clever, steering Bedford away from her three compatriots in order to have a private conversation in what appeared to be a den. Dark paneled walls, book cases lining the entire eastern side, a large stone fireplace with a moose head mounted above. The woman had her back to Dana as she sat on an L-shaped couch facing Jonathan who leaded forward, elbows on knees, as he expounded on some nonsense or another from a throne-like recliner. All that was needed was for Dana to suppress any coughing fits until she could drug the woman.

Somehow she managed just that.

"About time you found your way down here," said Jonathan as he helped to lower the now-unconscious Bedford to a prone position on the multicolor sofa. "I was running low on tales of cunning and daring do. Not quite sure I could have distracted her much longer."

Dana attempted a grin. "I find it doubtful that you were at a lack for words, especially if you were bragging about your escapades."

Jonathan knelt, digging through Bedford's jacket pockets and removing a set of keys and then relieving her of her handgun. "In truth we were discussing information I'd obtained on children of the gods. Her son is held hostage. They've forced her to act as a double agent."

"Children of the gods?"

Jonathan grinned his perpetual grin. "Ah. Right. You've been out of the loop. More on that later. Suffice it to say, they are not our friends. Shall we go while the opportunity presents itself?"

Dana nodded as a new wave of quivering skittered about her form. For a moment it seemed she might pass out.

"Are you alright?" asked Jonathan, his eyes narrow with concern.

"Dandy," nodded Dana as Jonathan grabbed her at the biceps, steadying her. "We'd best be going. A bit weak, it seems."

Jonathan had already determined their escape route, which was just as well, for even though he supported her as they walked, she barely managed to remain upright. Dana lost consciousness just as Jonathan helped her into the passenger side seat of Bedford's vehicle.

Chapter 51

Hunt raced through a long employees-only corridor toward the back of the hotel. Keller was beside him, barking into his com-link, weapon held at the ready. Hunt felt naked without a gun, but there was no way Keller trusted him at that level. Hunt was amazed that the agent had given him the leeway he had and assumed it was because his claims of an attack had bared out almost immediately.

"Up ahead. You see that?" said Hunt, pointing to an open door on the left.

"Is that a foot?" asked Keller, his voice low and secretive. Tull could be hiding behind that door for all they knew.

"Looks like it," agreed Hunt, his tone equally soft.

The men moved quickly forward. "Domingo," said Keller as they came to the unconscious form. It was one of his men, apparently bludgeoned and dragged partially through a doorway. Likely the assailant meant to better hide the man, but had heard Hunt and Keller coming and so left the job half done.

"I'm guessing Tull continued this way," said Hunt pointing further down the corridor. "He's probably not far ahead of us if he left your man exposed." Hunt stepped over the prone man and into the small darkened storage room. It was sparsely furnished, with no closets or alcoves. "Clear," he said crossing back into the hallway.

Keller nodded. "He's armed now. Domingo's weapon is missing."

"Bleeding from the head," said Hunt.

Keller nodded, already removing his jacket to use as a compress on the wound. "I've got to tend to my man."

"Do that. But I can't let Tull get away."

Keller hesitated.

"I'll be a good boy," said Hunt. "Scout's honor. I'll be home for dinner."

Keller nodded, already calling for backup.

Hunt proceeded to the end of the hallway and down a narrow concrete staircase. He could hear gunfire from beyond the doorway at the bottom of the stairs. There was a six-by-six window in the metal door. The glass had been shattered, likely as a result of gunfire. Cautiously, Hunt peaked through the jagged opening. The view was dark and the angle imperfect, but Hunt could see enough to understand the situation.

It was Donnelley, not Tull. Interesting. Somehow he'd freed himself of the cuffs. The terrorist had a semiautomatic handgun and was taking shots at agents in hazmat suits. Donnelley would likely take lives before going down himself.

Hunt acted on instinct, his training and combat experience kicking in as he opened the door, dove, rolled, and came up behind the startled Donnelley knocking him to the asphalt in one fluid motion.

Three shots passed above his head.

"Hold your fire!" hollered Hunt, even as he pressed against Donnelley, pinning him to the asphalt. "Hold your fire! I'm a friendly!"

Snatching the weapon from Donnelley, he jammed the butt twice against the terrorist's temple, dazing him, but not causing him to lose consciousness. Almost immediately, two hazmat-clad agents were before him, weapons drawn. Slowly setting the weapon aside, Hunt said, "Sergeant Marc Huntington. Delta Force. Retired. Here by direct order of Marjorie Bedford, Homeland Security. Call Keller. He'll vouch for me. Another man may have come through here. Tall, red hair. He's responsible for this attack and must be detained. Have you seen him?"

Keeping their guns trained on Hunt, one man radioed Keller to verify his claim while the other stepped forward, cautiously retrieving the discarded weapon.

"Have you seen the other man?" asked Hunt again as he pressed the dazed Donnelley to the ground.

"There was a man. Just a minute ago. Before this lunatic opened fire."

"Where is he now?"

Even through the hazmat suit, Hunt could see the man's unease. "I don't know. All hell broke loose. He disappeared."

"Find him! He's one of the leaders behind the recent wave of terrorist attacks. His name is Joshua Tull. Put out an A.P.B. Get all of your men on it. Don't let him get away!"

"Already on it," said the agent who'd radioed Keller. "The boss verifies your story, Huntington, but he said you're not to leave the premises. You're under quarantine and he still has some questions for you."

Nodding, Hunt returned his attention to Donnelley, smacking him across the face. "You still conscious?"

The man blinked, angling his head left and spitting blood onto the cool gray ground.

"Did you talk with Tull? Did you learn anything more about the antidote?" The question was almost ridiculous. Hunt knew this. So little time had elapsed. Whatever conversation the two terrorists might have had had not concerned Dana's welfare.

Donnelley smiled. One of his front teeth was broken. "The whore's going to die."

There was broken glass scattered about the ground, likely from the blown out window in the door. Spying a long triangular shard, Hunt snatched it, then pressing it against the terrorist's neck. "The antidote you gave me, will it cure Dana?"

Donnelley clucked his tongue. "Don't know. Kinda sucks don't it?"

Hunt pressed the glass further into Donnelley's flesh, producing a trickle of blood. "Is there another antidote? Does Tull have the finalized form?"

Still Donnelley smiled. "Got no answers for you, soldier boy. I think you'd better go home. Screw your whore. One last time. Before she turns cold and stiff."

Hunt glared into Donnelley's deep-set eyes looking for any hint of compassion or humanity. Finding none he said, "Remember Chicago? Remember what I said I'd do to you when this was over?"

Before Donnelley could respond, Hunt withdrew the glass from the terrorist's neck, scooted to his left, and jabbed the dagger-like glass into Donnelley's crotch with the pent up aggression of a cornered beast. Twisting, pressing, rending. Donnelley's eyes went wide, a strangled gurgle spilled from his lips escalating into a falsetto wail. Still Hunt pressed and twisted, now slicing further south and then left. There was the thick moist sound of rending flesh.

"M…mercy!" The single word was nearly imperceptible amongst the garbled babble of agony.

Mercy? The man had the gall to beg for mercy?

Hunt pressed and tore.

Donnelley convulsed and screeched. Inhuman chirps and cries.

Hunt dug deeper, deeper.

Donnelley flopped and grabbed, curling into a fetal ball.

Deeper still. Slice. Tear. Rend. Ruin.

Finally, confident that the beast could never again defile a woman, Hunt rose, leaving the bloody shard protruding from the shrieking terrorist's groin as he twisted and flopped.

Hunt turned to face the stunned hazmat-clad agents. "Go ahead. Arrest me. Just know that this man exposed hundreds of Americans to a deadly bio-toxin and more importantly, he raped my wife."

Neither man moved to apprehend him and so Hunt turned to reenter the building. Chances were he'd face charges. Chances were he could care less.

*****

The scene was now reduced to organized chaos. There were agents racing about, people barking into com-links, giving and receiving orders. Some few people were being treated for minor wounds. There had been one civilian struck in the leg by gunfire. She would live. Another babbled unintelligibly, her arms flaying, her head tilted at a bizarre angle, she spit and drooled. Unsettling. Creepy. But none of Hunt's concern. Pausing, Hunt sought to stave a wave of vertigo. He felt unsteady. Maybe the exertion, he thought, or lack of sleep, or… Nothing.

Hunt continued forward, finding Keller with a group of three agents. "Any word on Tull?" he asked.

Keller shook his head. "Not yet. My men say he slipped away in the confusion. We've widened our parameter. I'm confident we'll find him."

Hunt nodded. He was confident of no such thing.

"Are you alright?" asked Keller. "You seem a little disoriented."

Hunt blinked, willing himself to focus. He hadn't realized that his cloudy brain was so obvious. "Fine. Just tired and concerned."

Keller offered a dubious gaze before pointing at Hunt's hand. "You're bleeding."

"Yeah. Guess I must have found a piece of sharp glass somewhere. Nothing a couple of stitches won't cure."

Keller nodded and undid his tie, offering it to Hunt as a bandage. Hunt didn't know if Keller had been informed of his attack on Donnelley. If so, the agent remained silent on the issue.

"Listen," said Hunt as he wrapped the tie tightly around his palm. He hadn't realized just how badly the thing was bleeding. "That woman I talked with earlier, the scientist. I need to ask her a couple of questions."

Keller nodded. "I'll allow that, so long as you share any relevant information."

"You can stand right beside me for all I care. I just need access to the woman."

"Agreed. Her name is Dr. Marion Dietz. Apparently, she's the biologist that engineered the strain."

"I had that feeling."

They found Dietz handcuffed and under guard in a small conference room adjacent the hall now used as a holding room for persons of interest. The general guest population had been moved to another hall on the next floor up where they would be tested for infection.

"Dr. Dietz," said Hunt as he approached the woman. She sat atop a long table, head lowered, eyes half open. Judging by her odor and general disposition, it was clear that she was inebriated. Hunt prayed that between the two of them they could keep it enough together to help Dana. "My name's Marc Huntington. We spoke earlier."

Dietz raised her head to meet Hunt's gaze. "I recall."

"I know you regret much of what you've done. I saw you inhale the disease directly from one of your patients. You told me you were disturbed by this event. There might be a chance for you to make some of this right."

Dietz remained silent, her washed out eyes nearly glazed over, her face drawn in a tight grimace.

"You're almost definitely infected," added Hunt.

"I don't care to be cured."

"Your decision. But there are a lot of people, my wife included, who would like to be restored to health. I know there's an antidote. No one works with militarized toxins without keeping a cure handy in case of accidents." Hunt paused, squinted, refocused. "I also know there might be variants based on the different strains of the pathogen. Where do I find these? How can we know which will cure what?"

Dietz tilted her head ever so slightly. "I would assume Joshua has those at his disposal. There would also be samples in my Switzerland lab."

Switzerland? There was no chance the right cure could be located and brought to the U.S. in time to save Dana. "Anyplace else? Were any of these brought to America?"

Dietz tilted slightly left, and then right. "Perhaps Joshua has a supply. I was not privy."

"Damn."

"But the antidote does reside one other place."

Hunt's heart skipped. "Where?"

Dietz raised her cuffed hands and tapped her forehead. "Right here, Mr. Huntington. It's all right here. Allow me access to the bacteria and you'll have your cure."

Epilogue

Hunt led Dana into their fourteenth floor condominium located via connecting hallway to the MGM Grand on the Las Vegas Strip. It was Dana's homecoming. Dietz's antidote had been administered in time, though Dana's recovery had been tenuous. Even now, she was weak with very little energy, some loss of coordination, and a recurring cough. Somehow Hunt had tested clean. He must have one heck of an immune system.

In all, twenty-seven people had been infected, thirteen of them foreign nationals. One had been the Prime Minister of his country. Only one had perished. All but three had been released to their homes. Of the remaining three, only one was still in critical condition. Not bad, considering that had that strain left the hotel the potential death toll worldwide could have been in the tens—even hundreds—of thousands. On the downside, Joshua Tull was still at large and children of the gods had gone completely off grid. Hunt was too cynical to believe they were gone for good.

"Oh, my," said Dana as they crossed the threshold.

"Yeah," smiled Hunt. "I thought you might like some flowers."

"Some flowers" was a bit of an understatement. In truth, the place was covered floor to ceiling in flora. Numerous species, dozens of color variations were spread about the spacious living room. Even the ridiculously large HD TV screen featured shots of flora. There were flowers on the granite countertops, on the balcony, in the stone-faced fireplace. The residence was hay fever heaven. Hunt wanted Dana's homecoming to be something special.

"They're beautiful," said Dana, a tear at the corner of her eye.

But not a tear of joy. Hunt knew Dana well enough to know the difference.

"Honey, what's wrong?"

Dana moved unsteadily into the living area and nearly collapsed onto the soft leather couch. Hunt followed, his gut turning. Dana had been distant since the attack, quiet, reclusive. Lowering himself to beside her, he repeated his question. "Dana, you can talk to me. What's wrong?"

She looked to the opposite wall, perhaps studying the numerous bouquets, more likely, avoiding Hunt's gaze. "So much has happened."

Hunt wasn't sure what to say and so remained silent. It was probably better for her to say whatever it was she needed to say with as little interruption as possible.

"I'm changed, darling. Everything that's happened, I'm changed." She turned to face him. It seemed she might have considered taking his hand in hers, but then thought better of it. "I can never go back. Not to the person I was before. That woman is gone."

Hunt fiddled with an Oxycontin in his pocket, repressing the urge to pop it dry. "You've been through a horrible ordeal, hon. But you're getting through it. You're on the backend of this thing."

Dana shook her head, her eyes moist and her face drawn. "No, Marc. I'm not."

"Okay, then we'll work through it. I'll help you. We'll do it together."

"Hunt, you're proving to me exactly what I've feared."

Hunt squeezed the Oxycontin, nearly breaking it. "What do you mean?"

"You're a man. You feel the need to fix things. You think that if you just put your mind to something you can make it better."

Hunt stared at her, saying nothing.

"But, that's not always the case. I'm broken, Marc. Me! I'm broken. There is no we. It's not something we can fix. It's all within me. There's nothing you can do."

Hunt shook his head. "I'm sorry, honey. I know I can be an idiot, but I still don't get just what it is you're trying to say. I took care of Donnelly. He'll never attack another woman."

Dana shook her head, obviously frustrated. "I killed people, Hunt. Several. Some, not entirely deserving."

"No charges have been filed. You were under duress, the pathogen was found to have a psychotic element to it. It wasn't your fault."

"Bloody hell! I'm not talking about charges. I'm talking about me. What's happening inside of me. I've killed people. That's something I'll live with forever, regardless of what any court or physician says. I killed people, and I was infected with a bloody bubonic nightmare, and I was raped. All of that! All of that including the bleeding rape and where were you when I needed you the most? You were off traipsing about the country, chasing villains."

"I was trying to find the antidote—trying to save your life."

"Someone else could have done that. I needed you with me."

Hunt shook his head, stood to pace, decided better of it, and reseated himself. "But, you told me to leave. You said you couldn't have me close. You needed space."

"My God, Hunt, you are so entirely male."

"Huh?"

"You really don't understand, do you? Just because a woman says she wants you to leave does not mean she wants you to leave."

"Oh. Well, now I understand perfectly."

"Don't be sarcastic."

"Okay. Fine. Sorry. I was trying to do what you wanted—what you needed."

He reached out for her hand, but she withdrew it, instead, crossing her arms at the chest. They sat silently for several moments, Hunt's mind racing as he tried to figure out how to help the woman he loved. When finally Dana spoke, he wished to God that they'd remained in the lingering hell of awkward silence. "I know you mean well, darling. I know your intentions are true. But I can't handle it, a relationship, that is. I'm simply not emotionally up to the task. The rape... you have no idea. Even the thought of a man's touch. And the killing, I just can't..." she trailed off into tears.

"Dana, sweetie. I'm sure we can..."

"No, Hunt. There is no more we. I've got to come to terms with this on my own, to reclaim my own inner strength without distraction. Darling, I'm so sorry, but I need you to leave. Find a place of your own. Not nearby. Someplace far away from me. Today. Now. Please, just go."

Hunt stared at her for several moments, simply studying her face. Eventually he rose. Silent. Numb. He moved across the room, picking up a crushed velvet pouch from a bookshelf and then placing it on the narrow coffee table before Dana. "The Stonemeier Diamond," he said. "The thing that first led us to Donnelley. He had it on his person when I frisked him in Chicago. Keep it. The reward will cover the mortgage with money to spare for several months." With that, he turned and marched into the bedroom to pack.

www.ingramcontent.com/pod-product-compliance
Lightning Source LLC
Chambersburg PA
CBHW021313250626
47155CB00002B/507